He retrieved his mobile phone from his pocket, but Claudia assumed there was no reception through the heavy elevator walls as he turned and reached for the emergency telephone.

"This is Dr. Patrick Spencer. I'm in Terrace Park Towers, Wilshire Boulevard, not far from Highland. We're somewhere between the fourth floor and street level and the elevator's come to a halt. I have a female resident with me. Approximately thirty-four weeks pregnant." He paused. "No, no, there's no immediate medical emergency, but I want a crew to get us out stat. And it would be wise to send an ambulance. The patient may need to head to the hospital for a routine obstetric examination."

With that he hung up and turned his full attention back to Claudia.

"We'll be out of here before you know it," he said and very gently wiped the wisps of hair from her brow, now covered in tiny beads of perspiration. "They're on their way."

"Yes, they are... I'm afraid."

"There's nothing to fear. Just stay calm and the crew will have us out of here very quickly. And there'll be an ambulance on hand if we need one."

"It's not the crew I'm talking about...it's the babies. I'm afraid my twins are on their way... This isn't Braxton Hicks, Patrick. I'm in labor."

A Hero for the Twins

SUSANNE HAMPTON
&
LILIAN DARCY

Previously published as *Twin Surprise for the Single Doc*
and *Caring For His Babies*

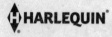

ISBN-13: 978-1-335-45438-6

A Hero for the Twins

Copyright © 2022 by Harlequin Enterprises ULC

Twin Surprise for the Single Doc
First published in 2016. This edition published in 2022.
Copyright © 2016 by Susanne Panagaris

Caring For His Babies
First published in 2004. This edition published in 2022.
Copyright © 2004 by Melissa Benyon

Recycling programs
for this product may
not exist in your area.

For questions and comments about the quality of this book, please contact us at CustomerService@Harlequin.com.

Harlequin Enterprises ULC
22 Adelaide St. West, 41st Floor
Toronto, Ontario M5H 4E3, Canada
www.Harlequin.com

Printed in U.S.A.

CONTENTS

TWIN SURPRISE FOR THE SINGLE DOC   7
Susanne Hampton

CARING FOR HIS BABIES   195
Lilian Darcy

Married to the man she met at eighteen, **Susanne Hampton** is the mother of two adult daughters, Orianthi and Tina. She has enjoyed a varied career path but finally found her way to her favorite role of all: Harlequin Medical Romance author. Susanne has always read romance novels and says, "I love a happy-ever-after, so writing for Harlequin is a dream come true."

Books by Susanne Hampton

Harlequin Medical Romance

Christmas Miracles in Maternity
White Christmas for the Single Mom
The Monticello Baby Miracles
Twin Surprise for the Single Doc
Midwives On-Call
Midwife's Baby Bump

Unlocking the Doctor's Heart
Back in Her Husband's Arms
Falling for Dr. December
A Baby to Bind Them
A Mommy to Make Christmas
The Doctor's Cinderella
Mending the Single Dad's Heart

Visit the Author Profile page at Harlequin.com for more titles.

Twin Surprise for the Single Doc

SUSANNE HAMPTON

To everyone who thought they had closed their hearts to love...only to be proved wrong by a love stronger than the heartache they had survived.

And to Alli and Gilda and all of my amazing friends who constantly provide inspiration for my books.

Chapter 1

'Congratulations, Claudia. You're having twins!'

Claudia Monticello's deep brown eyes, inherited from her Italian father, widened like dollhouse-sized plates against her alabaster skin, a present from her Irish mother. In a rush of panic and disbelief, her gaze darted from the gel-covered bump of her stomach to the grainy black-and-white images on the screen, then to the *pleased as punch* radiologist's face before finally looking up to the ceiling to where she imagined heaven might be. Not that she thought her parents would be smiling down at her after what she had done.

Suddenly the room became very hot and she struggled a little to breathe. The clammy fingers of one hand reached for the sides of the examination table to steady herself. *Two babies*. Her mouth had dropped open slightly, but her lips had not curved to anything close to a smile. In denial, she shook her head from side to side and nervously chewed on the nails of the other hand. There had to be a mistake. The radiologist, still smiling at the screen and apparently unaware of the panic blanketing her patient, gently moved the hand piece over Claudia's stomach to capture additional images.

She must have zoomed in too quickly, Claudia mused.

Double imaged.

Misread the data.

Be new at her job.

But Claudia knew without doubt, as she slowly and purposefully focused on the screen, there was no mistake. There were two tiny babies with two distinct heartbeats. The radiologist was using her finger to point to them. Her excitement was palpable. A reaction juxtaposed to Claudia's. At twenty-nine years of age, Claudia Monticello was anything but excited to be the single mother of twins. For many reasons… The first was her living five thousand miles from home…and the second was the fact her children would never meet their father.

Twenty weeks had passed since Claudia discovered she was to be the mother of two and, as she dropped her chin and looked down at her ample midsection while waiting for the elevator, she was pleased to see they were healthy-sized babies. Her waist was somewhere hidden underneath her forty-five-inch circumference and she hadn't seen her ankles for weeks. Her mood was one of anticipation as she waited for the doors to open on her floor. Her final obstetric visit was imminent and she was thinking about little else than her flight home to London the next day. It couldn't come quickly enough for her. She couldn't wait to farewell Los Angeles.

And turn her back on the disappointment and heartache the city had brought.

Or, more correctly, that she had invited into her life.

The day was warm and she was wearing a sleeveless floral maternity dress, one of three she'd picked up on the sale rack in Macy's when she rapidly outgrew all her other clothes, flat white sandals and her oversized camel-coloured handbag that she took everywhere. Her deep chocolate curls were short and framed her pretty face, but her eyes were filled with sadness. She pictured her suitcases, packed and waiting just inside the door of her apartment. She was finally leaving the place she had called home for almost a year. The fully furnished apartment was in a prime high-rise gated community on Wilshire Boulevard and in demand. The home would have new tenants within days. It had only been temporary, like so much in that town, and she wondered who would be sleeping in the king-sized bed later that week and what the future held for them. She hoped for their sake they hadn't rushed into something they would live to regret.

The way she had.

Patrick Spencer waited inside the elevator for the doors to open. It had only managed to travel down one floor and was already stopping. A sigh escaped from his lips. He prayed it wouldn't stop on every floor on the way to street level. His patience was already tested. He was having another one of those days. A day when he felt frustrated with life and struggled with a cocktail of resentment mixed with equal parts of doubt and disappointment and a dash of boredom with his new reality. Not that his reality was devoid of life's luxuries, but it was missing the passion he'd once felt. It was another day when he felt cheated out of what he had planned and wanted for his future, even though he was the one who'd walked away from everything. A day when he almost didn't give a damn. And whenever he had those days he always put on his sunglasses and tried to block out the world in which he lived. He had been cornered into this new life. That was how he saw it.

If things had not gone so terribly wrong, he would be living in London instead of calling Los Angeles home.

With melancholy colouring her mood, Claudia paid little attention to the tall, darkly dressed figure when she stepped into the elevator. But she noticed the affected way he was wearing wraparound sunglasses with his suit. It was more of the same pretentious LA behaviour.

Sunglasses inside an elevator? In Claudia's sadly tainted opinion, all men were hiding something; perhaps this one was nursing a hangover. She rolled her eyes, confident in the fact he couldn't see anything from behind the dark lenses and even more sure he wouldn't be looking in her direction anyway. Probably obsessed with his own thoughts and problems. Just like so many in this town. A town full of actors, many with an inflated sense of self-worth and a complete lack of morals. Perhaps this man filled that same bill, she surmised.

She felt sick to her stomach even thinking about the man who had wooed her with lies and then walked out of her life as shamelessly as he had walked into it.

She patted her stomach protectively and, not caring a damn what he thought, she whispered, 'You may have been a surprise, boys, but I love you both to the moon and back already.' Then she silently added, *And I will make sure you don't run away from your responsibilities...or wear sunglasses in a lift!*

'They're very lucky little boys.' Patrick said it matter-of-factly. It surprised even him that he had made a comment but hearing the woman speak so genuinely to her unborn children in an accent once so familiar struck a chord with him. In a town so devoid of anything genuine, Patrick felt compelled to comment.

Claudia thought for a fleeting moment his words had been delivered with genuine sentiment. But her body stiffened as she reminded herself there was little or no sentiment in that town. Maternal hormones, she assumed, had temporarily dressed her vision with rose-coloured glasses. His English accent, for some reason, made her drop her guard just a little. Against her better judgement, she looked over to see the man remove his sunglasses. His lips were curved slightly. Not to a full smile, not even a half smile, but she could see his teeth just a little. They were almost perfect but not veneer flawless.

He was tall, six foot one or two, she guessed, as she was five foot nine in bare feet or the flat shoes she was wearing that day. He was broad-shouldered and, she imagined from the way his shirt fell, buff, but he wasn't overly tanned. His hair was short and light brown in colour and it was matched with a light covering of stubble on his face. His grooming was impeccable but, aside from the stubble, quite conservative. While his looks, she conceded, were worthy of a billboard, his styling was more professional than the usual LA playboy slash actor type. Or, in his case, an English ex-pat playing the LA field.

'I'm sorry?' she finally said after her assessment. She was hoping he would shrug his shoulders, put his sunglasses back on and return to thoughts of himself or his most recent conquest.

But he didn't.

'I said that your babies are very fortunate that you care for them so much even before they enter the world. I hope they make you proud.'

Patrick had not said anything like that in twelve years. They were words he used to say every day as a matter of routine, but never so routine that they were not sincere. But something about this woman and the palpable love he could see in her eyes and hear in her voice made it impossible not to make comment. She appeared different from the women he knew.

And a very long way from the women he bedded. She was cute and beautiful, not unlike a china doll. His women were not fragile like that.

And her love for her unborn children was special. It was something Patrick very much appreciated.

Claudia felt her stance stiffen again and her expression become quite strained. His accent was cultured and, with her own English upbringing and resultant class-consciousness, she suspected he had more than likely experienced a privileged boarding school education. His clothes were high end designer. She knew he must have an ulterior motive. All men did. There were a handful of people she had met in the year since she'd left London to make Hollywood her home who had shown a level of genuine kindness but she doubted this man would join those ranks. In fact, she doubted that any man would ever again join that group. Her desired demeanour was defensive and with little effort she reached it. No man was going to get within a mile of her or, more particularly, her children with any line. She had told herself that she had finished with men and all of their agendas. And she decided to prove it to herself.

Her first step would be keeping this man, albeit a very attractive man, at arm's length. Perhaps even offside.

'You really should refrain from eavesdropping; it's rude,' she said before turning her attention back to the blank gunmetal doors. *There—it was done!* She had stood up for herself and it brought her a sense of empowerment.

It had been a long time coming and she conceded her ire was directed towards the wrong man but she had finally felt strong enough to say something. And it felt good. As if she was claiming her power back.

But the elevator didn't feel good or seem to have any power. It seemed to be slowing and, for want of a better word in her head, since she didn't particularly like confined spaces, it seemed to be *struggling* in its descent. She wished it would pick up speed and get her out of the awkward situation. Deep down inside, she knew her response had been overly dramatic and cutting but she was still proud she had found the strength to do it.

There were only another fifteen floors and she hoped the elevator would reach the ground before he handed her a business card and she discovered the reason he'd struck up the conversation. Insurance, investment or even real estate. There had to be something behind the smile. Since she was so heavily pregnant, she felt very confident it was not going to segue into a pick-up line.

With her chin lifted slightly, she felt the colour rising in her cheeks; she played with her small pearl earrings the way she always did when she was nervous.

Patrick considered her in silence for a moment as he watched her fidget with the small pearl studs. He had made an uncharacteristic effort to acknowledge her pregnancy and he was taken back at her disparaging remark. He hadn't expected it as she had appeared at first glance to be very sweet. Her pretty face was framed with dark curls and he thought she had an innocence about her. He hadn't foreseen her reaction and to his mind he definitely did not deserve the harsh retort. He wasn't going to take it on the chin.

Without making eye contact as he stared at the same gunmetal door, he decided to answer her abrupt reply with one equally insensitive. 'I think you're the rude one here. You enter a lift, or should I say elevator, due to our location, with only one other person, that being me, and begin a conversation with your unborn children, for which I did not judge you to be mad, but in fact complimented you, and then you remark that I'm rude for making a comment.'

Claudia was surprised by his formal and acerbic rebuttal. His response had been articulate and he had not raised his voice but she wasn't in the mood to eat humble pie. Men, or rather one man, had just let her down very badly and she wasn't going to break her promise to herself. They were all the same if they were given the opportunity. And she had no intention of ever giving a man such an opportunity with her again.

With her eyes facing straight ahead at their shared focal point, she was about to reply when she was stopped by a twinge in her stomach. Her body stiffened with the pain and she hunched a little, almost protectively.

She knew it couldn't be a contraction. It was too early. One hand instinctively reached for her babies and her stomach suddenly felt hard to her touch. She was grateful the stranger was looking away as she leant a little on the elevator wall. She told herself it must be the Braxton Hicks contractions that her obstetrician had mentioned but it seemed to be quite intense and more than a little painful.

It passed quite quickly and finally, after catching her breath, she replied, 'I think it was obvious I was having a private conversation. And clearly you *are* judging me, by implying that I'm mad. That's hardly a nice thing to say to someone you don't know.'

'You're right,' he responded and turned to face her. 'I concede it was less than polite but you have to agree that you most definitely left your manners back up on the thirty-fourth floor.' He looked away as he finished his tersely delivered response and checked for mobile phone reception.

By his abrupt tone and the fact he had noticed which floor she lived on, Claudia looked out of the corner of her eyes at him and wondered for a moment if he was a lawyer. Lawyers always paid attention to details that the general public ignored. Of course, she thought, she would have the slowest ride to the ground with an over-bearing man with a legal background. She dropped her chin a little but not to admire her middle; instead she looked tentatively across the elevator to where the man stood. He was wearing highly polished shoes. Slightly raising her chin, she noted his perfectly pressed char-coal-grey slacks and finally, with her head turned a little more in his direction as she gave in to her curi-osity, she saw his crisp white shirt and jacket. She had thought initially that he was wearing a suit but on closer, but not too obvious, inspection, she could see flecked threads in the weave. And then there was his expensive Swiss watch. Not forgetting the fact he was already in the elevator when she'd entered, which meant he either lived, or had a client, on the only floor above her. The penthouse on the thirty-fifth floor.

Suddenly she felt another twinge. She wanted to get out of the lift and get to her obstetric appointment im-mediately. She didn't want to be dragged into a con-versation.

'I apologise—I'm sorry,' she returned sharply and without emotion as she once again faced the elevator doors. She rubbed the hollow of her back that was be-ginning to ache. The niggling pain was spreading and becoming increasingly uncomfortable. She just wanted the short time in the relatively tiny space to be unevent-ful, so she took the easy option and hoped the conver-sation would end there.

But it didn't.

'Frankly, I think I'm a little past caring for your less than genuine apology.'

'I beg your pardon?' Claudia knew the handsome stranger had called the situation correctly; she just didn't want to admit it.

'I think you're just giving me lip service,' he continued. 'Forget I said anything nice at all. To be honest, I'm sorry I did, so let's just go back to an awkward silence that comes with sharing an elevator with a stranger and hope the thing picks up speed for both of our sakes.'

Claudia felt a little tug at her heart. The stranger really had been trying to make pleasant conversation and compliment her in the process and she had shot him down.

'Gosh, I did sound awfully rude, didn't I?' she asked, as much to herself as him. Wishing she had not been as dismissive and had put some meaning behind the words, she offered a more contrite apology. 'I really am sorry. I do mean it.'

'Perhaps.'

Her eyes met his and she could see they were not warm and forgiving but neither were they icy. They were sad. They were filled with a look close to disappointment and she felt her heart sink a little further. She had never been quite so rude to a stranger before. Heaven knew what day he had endured and she had behaved abominably.

Circumstance had made her distrust the male population. She had not even thought how her behaviour would affect the handsome stranger sharing the slowest elevator on the west coast of North America, until he'd pointed it out. But she was surprised by his reaction. She assumed most men would have shrugged it off but he seemed genuinely disappointed, almost as if he was directing the disappointment inward for some reason.

With a humble and heartfelt expression she replied, 'I really do apologise. I'm very sorry and there's really no excuse for my behaviour.' Taking a deep breath, she outstretched her hand like an olive branch. 'I'm Claudia Monticello, slightly hormonal mother-to-be and having a very bad day. I could add that I'm perhaps a little stressed right now as I'm flying back to the UK tomorrow and I have so much still to do. I have to see my obstetrician and finish packing. There's so many things I have to remember…' And so much she wanted to forget. But she had no intention of telling the handsome stranger that.

'Well, perhaps you do have a reason to be a little on edge,' he said, looking into her eyes, almost piercing her soul. 'Apology accepted. Patrick Spencer, doctor, not eavesdropper.'

Claudia smiled. She had picked the wrong profession too. As she kept staring into his eyes, she noticed they were a deep blue with flecks of grey. Like storm clouds swirling over the deepest part of the ocean. She felt herself wondering why he hid such stunning eyes behind dark sunglasses. They were too captivating a shade to be hidden. She shook herself. His eye colour was not something she needed to busy her mind with at that time. Nothing about him was her concern, she told herself as she noticed there was only a short trip of eight floors until they reached street level and she would never see the man again.

But it did feel strangely reassuring to be in the elevator with a man with a medical background after the fleeting contraction she'd experienced. She knew they were commonplace nearing the latter part of pregnancy and it appeared to have been a once-off but his nearness made her feel a little safer.

No, *very* safe and she didn't know why.

Out of a sense of awkwardness in the silence that were now sharing, she glanced up again to check how many floors they had travelled. The elevator had not picked up any speed. She was glad they weren't in the Burj Khalifa in Dubai or the boys would be ready for pre-school at the rate they were travelling.

With her mind brought to travel, Claudia was excited to be heading home. Once her obstetrician signed her flight clearance she would be on her way back to London. Her contract with the television studio had finally ended, leaving her free to return home. Instinctively, she patted the recent ultrasound scans tucked safely in her bag. She had no swelling in her legs and her blood pressure had been fine at the last visit. Her pregnancy had been uneventful until the twinge, something which was at complete odds with her disastrous personal life. But she was grateful she had something positive upon which to focus.

As they passed the fourth floor and the elevator seemed to almost pause, suddenly she felt another more intense contraction. Claudia tried to smile through it but suspected it was closer to a grimace. Braxton Hicks contractions were a lot different to what she had expected. She had been told that a woman could experience up to four in an hour but she hadn't thought they would be so close together.

Patrick eyed her with concern but, just as he opened

his mouth, the stalling elevator came to a jarring halt. Claudia grabbed the railing to steady herself and they both looked up to see the floor light flickering and waited for the doors to open. But they didn't. Instead the lift dropped what she imagined to be another floor and stopped. Patrick had already taken two purposeful steps towards Claudia and she felt his strong arms wrap around her to prevent her from falling. His touch should have worried her but instead a wave of relief washed over her. She was not alone.

'Let's get you on the floor. It will be safer.' Hastily he pulled off his jacket and dropped it to the elevator floor before gently lowering Claudia onto it.

'Your jacket—it will be ruined.'

'At this moment, a ruined jacket is not my concern. You are,' he said matter-of-factly but with an unmistakable warmth in his voice and one Claudia didn't believe she truly deserved after her behaviour. 'When are the babies due?'

'The twins aren't due for another six and a half weeks and I'm fine, really I am,' she insisted as she tried to sit gently and not move and crease the jacket underneath her. 'I'm flying out tomorrow with the doctor's approval; it's the last possible day that the airline will allow me to travel.'

'You're cutting it fine with the whole long haul at almost thirty-four weeks,' he replied with his brows knitted. He added, 'You seemed to be in pain a moment ago.' It was a question he framed as a statement. He didn't want to appear overbearing but he was concerned. He was also doubtful whether she should be travelling at such a late stage of pregnancy. Even with a clean bill of health, it seemed risky for her to take a long haul flight so close to delivering.

'Yes, just one of these Braxton Hicks contractions.'

'You're sure?' His frown had not lifted as he spoke.

This time it was a question and she sensed genuine concern. It heightened hers.

'Absolutely,' she said, followed by a nod. It wasn't the truth. The truth was that she had never been quite so scared in her life but she had to push that reality from her mind and remain positive. The worst-case scenario was too overwhelmingly frightening to consider without collapsing into a heap. She had been holding everything together tenuously for so many months her nerves were threadbare.

'If you say so,' he told her, doubt about her response evident in his tone. 'Just stay seated till we reach the ground.' He retrieved his mobile phone from his trouser pocket, but Claudia assumed there was no reception through the heavy elevator walls as he turned and reached for the emergency telephone.

He didn't take his eyes away from Claudia, even when the standard response finished and he cut in. 'This is Dr Patrick Spencer, I'm in Terrace Park Towers, Wilshire Boulevard, not far from Highland. We're somewhere between the fourth floor and street level and the elevator's come to a halt. I have a female resident with me. Approximately thirty-four weeks pregnant.' He paused. 'No, no, there's no immediate medical emergency. I have the resident seated and there's no obvious physical injuries but I want a crew to get us out stat. And after the jolt it would be wise to send an ambulance. The patient may need to head to the hospital for a routine obstetric examination.'

With that he hung up and turned his full attention back to Claudia.

Her resolve to remain calm had deserted her, despite attempts to tell herself she was overreacting. She wasn't overreacting. Her eyes darted to the steel doors, willing them to open, and then back to Patrick, unsure what she was willing him to do.

'We'll be out of here before you know it,' he said and very gently wiped the wisps of hair from her brow, now covered in tiny beads of perspiration. 'They're on their way.'

'Yes, they are… I'm afraid.'

'There's nothing to fear. Just stay calm and the crew will have us out of here very quickly. And there'll be an ambulance on hand if we need one.'

'It's not the crew I'm talking about…it's the babies. I'm afraid my twins are on their way… This isn't Braxton Hicks, Patrick. I'm in labour.'

Chapter 2

Claudia's water broke only moments later, confirming she was very much in labour and going to deliver her babies in an elevator unless a miracle happened. As she wriggled uncomfortably on the hard elevator floor with only Patrick's now soaking wet jacket beneath her, she stared at nowhere in particular and prayed with all of her might that it was a bad dream. One from which she would wake to find herself giving birth in a pretty delivery room in a London hospital surrounded by smiling nurses...nurses just like her sister, Harriet. She always allayed Claudia's medical concerns with sensible and thoughtful answers delivered in a calm manner, just like the way their mother had always spoken to them.

How she wished more than anything that Harriet was with her. She would know what to do. She always did...

but, as Claudia looked at her surroundings from her new vantage point on the floor, she knew it was pointless to wish for her sister to be there. Or for a birthing suite. She would have neither. Harriet was in Argentina to do something selfless and wonderful and she was paying for her own irresponsible behaviour by being trapped in a Los Angeles elevator in the first stage of labour.

Giving birth to the babies of a man who didn't give a damn.

With the help of another she didn't know.

The next painful wave of contractions broke through her thoughts. Labour had not come on slowly or gently. And there was no point worrying about dust soiling Patrick's jacket; the piece of clothing was now past being saved.

The jacket was of no concern to Patrick, who was kneeling beside Claudia. At that moment he would give a dozen of his finest jackets to make this woman he barely knew comfortable if only he could. But he had nothing close to a dozen of anything to make what lay ahead easier. The situation was dire. There was no way around that fact but Patrick intended to do everything to ensure Claudia remained calm and focused. All the while he fought his own battle with a past that was rushing back at him. Fine perspiration began lining his brow but he had to push through. He heard Claudia's heavy breathing turn to panting and knew he couldn't give in to his thoughts. Not for even a minute. He had to stay with Claudia.

For the time being at least.

'There's no cell reception but if I can get through on

the elevator phone, who can I call? Your husband, boyfriend…your family?'

Claudia shook her head, a little embarrassed by the answer even before she delivered it. Harriet was on and off the communication grid for almost two days while she travelled and even if she could contact her it would be unfair to worry her. And she knew there was no point reaching out to the babies' father. He wouldn't care.

'No, there's no one to call.'

Patrick's eyes met hers in silence. He was surprised and saddened to hear her answer. While she clearly had her defences up initially, Patrick had not suspected for even a moment that a woman like Claudia would be alone in the world.

Unexpectedly, he felt himself being pulled towards her. He was never pulled towards anyone. Not any more. Not for years. He had locked away the need to feel anything. To need anyone…or to be needed. But suddenly a tenuous and unforeseen bond was forming. And he suspected it was not due just to the confines of the elevator.

Claudia wriggled some more and looked down at the jacket. 'I'm so sorry…'

'Claudia—' he cut in as he looked intently into her eyes, not shifting his gaze for even a moment, not allowing himself to betray, to any degree, the very real risks that he knew lay ahead '—you're in labour and you think I'm worried about a jacket.'

'But it's ruined.'

'The only thing I care about now is finding something clean for the babies. Do you have anything in your bag? Anything I can wrap them in?'

Claudia shook her head. While her bag was the fashionably oversized style, it held very little, other than her wallet, apartment keys, her phone, a thin, flimsy scarf, a small cosmetic purse and a bottle of water. And her ultrasound films.

Patrick couldn't wait any longer. There would be two babies arriving and they needed to have something clean to rest upon while he tended to their mother. He was not going to put them on the floor of the elevator. Without hesitating, he began to unbutton his white linen shirt and, slipping it from his very toned and lightly tanned body, he spread it out.

Claudia knew she was staring. She was helpless to pull her gaze away. The man about to deliver her babies had stripped bare to the waist. It was overwhelming and almost too much for her to process. The whole situation was quickly morphing from a bad dream into a nightmare. She was about to give birth to the sons of a man who didn't love her and they would be delivered by a half-naked stranger in a broken elevator. Tears began welling in her eyes as the waves of another contraction came. This one was more powerful than the last and she struggled to hide the level of pain.

Patrick reached for her hand. 'I want you to squeeze my hand when the contractions happen.'

'I'll be fine,' she told him as the contraction passed and she felt uncomfortable getting any closer to the semi-naked stranger than she already was. His arms looked lean but powerful. And she could smell the light tones of his musky cologne.

'I know you'll be fine but if you squeeze my hand each time you have a contraction I'll know how close together they are.'

'I think you will be able to tell without me squeezing your hand.'

Patrick nodded. 'Have it your way, but my hand is here if you need it.'

Still feeling wary, Claudia eyed him suspiciously, wondering who this man was, this man who was so willing to come to her aid. Only a few minutes before, they had exchanged less than friendly words. Now the man she had initially assumed to be a lawyer hiding a hangover behind dark glasses was in fact a doctor literally on bended knees helping her.

'The contractions seem to be evenly spaced at the moment,' he said, breaking through her thoughts.

'But they're awfully close and awfully painful. Does that mean the babies will be here soon?'

'It could but it's impossible to tell.' Patrick hoped that it would be a prolonged labour. Prolonged enough to allow the technical team to open the elevator doors and bring in help.

'Do you think there's any chance they will get us out before my babies arrive?'

'They're doing their best.'

Ten minutes passed with no news from outside and two more contractions. Claudia caught her breath and leant back against the cold walls of the elevator. It was soothing on her now clammy skin. The air was starting to warm up, and she imagined it would be stifling in a short time if the doors were not opened soon. But they would be. She had to hold on to the belief that any minute paramedics would burst through the steel barriers and transport her to hospital.

Patrick stretched his long legs out in front of him and rested against the adjacent cool wall. 'So which London hospital had you planned on having the boys?' he asked as he looked up at the ceiling for no particular reason. All sense of reason had left the elevator when Claudia began labour.

'I thought the Wright Street Women's and Children's Hospital. I checked in online a few months back and it has a lovely birthing centre with floral wallpaper and midwives and everything my babies and I would need. I've booked an appointment with a midwife there next week.'

'Well, you won't be needing that appointment. Not for this delivery anyway, but perhaps you could book in for your next baby.'

'I'm not sure there will be a next,' she replied quickly with raised eyebrows, still not forgetting the pain of the contraction that had barely passed.

'Perhaps you will change your mind and have more but these children will definitely be born in LA. With any luck, the paramedics will have us out soon and they'll be born at the Mercy Hospital.'

Claudia felt her pulse race a little. 'What if that doesn't happen?'

Patrick turned to her and took her hand in his. Suddenly the sensation of her warm skin on his made him feel something more than he had felt in many years. It made him feel close to being alive. He swallowed and pushed away the feeling. That sort of intimacy had no place in his life. For the last decade, whenever he felt a woman's body against his, there was nothing more than mutual pleasure. It didn't mean anything to either of them. They served a purpose to each other and walked away. Feeling anything more was not worth the risk.

He couldn't get attached to a woman he didn't know who was about to give birth to the children of another man. The idea was ridiculous.

'Let's not go there, Claudia. The medical team will be here soon.'

'But they may not...' she argued.

'Then we'll bring two healthy boys into the world on our own.' He said it instinctively but as the words escaped his mouth he prayed it would not come to that.

Claudia took another deep breath. There was a chance they weren't going to be rescued. And she had to prepare herself for the imminent wave of the next contraction and then worse. She closed her eyes.

Patrick studied her. 'Now don't go closing your beautiful eyes on me,' he told her. 'I need you to listen to me and work with me. You will get through this but you have to stay strong. You have your children to think of.'

Slowly she forced her lids open and found herself looking into the warmest eyes she had ever seen. Her stomach did a little somersault and it wasn't a contraction.

'That's better,' he told her with a smile filled with so much warmth she thought her heart would melt. Everything he was making her feel was unexpected. And the feelings seemed so real. Was it just the intense situation they were facing or was there something about the man that was very different from anyone she had ever met?

She wasn't sure.

But his nearness was affecting her. She doubted he was trying to affect—he just was.

'What about you—do you have any children? Did your family move here to LA too?' She rattled off successive questions, trying to deflect the blush she suddenly feared he had brought to her cheeks. She could see there was no wedding band on his hand but, as she knew first-hand, the lack of a ring on a man's finger did not bring any certainty there was no wife. It was out of character for her to be so direct but nothing about the situation was normal.

'No, I'm not married, Claudia, and the rest of my family...well, they're back in the UK...' Patrick's words trailed off. He wasn't about to tell Claudia about his life, his past or his loss. After twelve years it was still raw at times but now focusing on Claudia removed his desire to give any consideration to his own pain. He had to be in the moment for the woman who needed him. He couldn't think about what had happened all those years ago or the price he still paid every day.

He had to let something go.

And that had to be the past—for the time being. But he knew that it would come back to him. It always did.

'Do you want children one day? I guess if you've done this before, bringing them into the world would make you want a brood or run the other way,' she cut in again. As she felt the warmth in her face subside she was slightly relieved on that front but the need for the banter continued. Any distraction would do.

He felt a muscle in his jaw twitch. She was unwittingly making it very hard to stay in the moment. 'No,' he said, not wanting to go into any detail. The answer was not that he didn't like children; in fact it ran far deeper than that. Children meant family and he never planned on being part of a family again. The pain still lingered, twelve years after he had been forced to walk away from his own.

'So am I right—you don't want to take your job home?'

'You're full of questions, aren't you?'

Claudia didn't answer. She felt the next contraction building and as it rolled in she couldn't say anything. She dropped her head to her chest and took in shallow breaths.

Without prompting, Patrick's hands gently massaged her back. Instinctively, he knew what was happening and he kept up the physical therapy until it passed. And then a few moments longer.

She felt his hands linger, then shook herself back to reality. He was a doctor doing his job. Nothing more.

'Why did you move to LA?' she piped up, then bit her lip as she realised it was none of her business and she had no clue what had driven her to ask him such personal questions. She felt as if the pain had taken over her mind. She was acting like a different person, someone who suddenly wanted to know everything about Patrick. Perhaps it was to distract herself. Perhaps not. But she knew the moment the words fell from her mouth that she had overstepped the boundaries of polite conversation. 'Please forget I asked. Blame it on the stress. I really am exhibiting the worst manners today. I've asked the most improper questions and ruined your jacket...'

'Forgiven for both.' Patrick hesitated. 'I guess I'm just a private person, Claudia. I'm happy to answer any medical questions, anything at all, but I'd prefer to leave the rest alone. Suffice to say, my family and I didn't see eye to eye about something that happened and this opportunity came up. So I left London and headed here.'

'Oh, I'm sorry.' Claudia suddenly felt even more embarrassed that she had asked but she also felt a little sad for him. She barely knew the man but, with the way he was taking care of her, she suddenly felt that she wanted to be on *his side* in a situation she knew nothing about.

Patrick knew it sounded as if they had parted ways on something insignificant. He thought it was best to leave it at that. There was no need to mention that he'd made the opportunity to allow him to move to the US. It was something he'd had to do to help everyone with their grief. To not be there, reminding them every day of what had happened.

It was not the time or place to tell a woman he had just met that his sister had died.

And he had taken the blame for her death.

An unspoken agreement not to revisit the conversation about his family was made in the awkward silence by both of them.

'I'll need to examine you in a few minutes and assess whether you have begun to dilate and, if you have, if the first baby is visible,' he told her as he pulled himself from the past back to where he belonged.

Suddenly the elevator lights began to flicker. Claudia bit her lip nervously. She felt her chin begin to quiver but was powerless to stop it. All questions disappeared. She didn't want anything from Patrick other than reassurance that her babies would survive.

Patrick drew a deep breath but managed to keep his body language in check. If they lost the lights, then he could not convince himself there would be a good outcome but he would never let Claudia know that. He even refused to admit it to himself.

'I need to do the exam while we still have some lights to work with; if we lose them it will be challenging as I'll have to work by feel alone. But, whatever happens, I'm here for you and your babies, Claudia, and together we'll all get throughout this,' Patrick told her with a firmness and urgency that did not disguise the seriousness of the situation, but he also managed to make her feel secure in the knowledge that he was with her all the way. He filled his lungs with the warm air that surrounded them, determined he would do his damnedest to make his prayers a reality.

She nodded her consent as the contraction began to subside, along with her uncontrollable need to push.

'Breathe slowly and deeply,' he said while he stroked her arm and waited for the contraction to pass before he began his examination. Twins made the birth so much more complicated, along with his lack of equipment and the risk of losing the lights.

'Have you delivered many babies?'

'Yes, I've delivered many babies, Claudia, but never in an elevator and not for…'

The elevator phone rang and stopped Patrick from explaining how long it had been since his last delivery. Instinctively, he answered the phone. 'Yes?'

'This is the utilities manager. We're working to have you out as soon as possible but it may be another twenty minutes to half an hour. Our only rostered technician is across town. How's the young woman?'

'She's in labour.'

'Hell… Okay, that's gonna be brutal on her.' The

man's knee-jerk reaction was loud. 'I'll put the tech to get here ASAP or get an off-duty one over there stat. We've already got an ambulance en route.'

'That would be advisable,' Patrick responded in an even tone, not wanting to add to Claudia's building distress. 'I'm about to assess her progress but you need to ensure there are two ambulances waiting when your technician gets us out. We're dealing with the birth of two premature infants so ensure the paramedics are despatched with humidicribs and you have an obstetrician standing by with a birthing kit including cord clamps and Syntocinon.' Then he lowered his voice and added, 'And instruct them to bring plasma. There's always the slight risk of a postpartum haemorrhage.' With that he hung up the phone to let the team outside do their best to get medical help to them as soon as possible.

He immediately turned his attention back to Claudia, who lay against the elevator wall with small beads of perspiration building on her brow and the very palpable fear of what lay ahead written on her face.

'I don't want my babies to die.'

'Claudia, you need to listen to me,' he began with gentleness in his voice along with a reassuring firmness. 'We *are* going to get through this. Your babies will be fine but you need to help me.'

Claudia couldn't look at him. She couldn't lift her gaze from her stomach and the babies inside of her. Fear surged through her veins. It was real. They weren't getting out of the elevator. No one was coming to rescue them. No one was going to take her to the hospital. The harsh reality hit her. Her babies would be born inside the metal walls that surrounded them.

And they might not survive.

'I am going to have to cut your underwear free. I don't want to try and lift you and remove it.'

Claudia felt her heart race and her mind spin. She was losing control and the fear was not just physical. Deep inside, she knew the odds were stacked against her and her boys but she appreciated that Patrick hadn't voiced that. The man with the sunglasses wasn't anything close to what she'd thought. He was about to bring her sons into the world.

And she suddenly had no choice but to trust him.

Her hand ran across her mouth and tugged at her lips nervously. 'Fine, just do it,' she managed to say as she steeled herself for what was about to happen to her, her boys and Patrick as the urge to push and the pain began to overtake her senses once again.

Patrick ripped off the gloves that had handled the elevator telephone, covered his hands in antibacterial solution and slipped on another pair of gloves. Carefully using sterile scissors, he gently cut her underwear from her and checked the progress of her labour.

'You are fully dilated and your first son's head is visible,' he told her. 'Labour is moving fast and you're doing great. Just keeping breathing slowly…'

His words were cut short by the cry she gave with the next painful contraction. More painful than the previous one.

'I can't do this. I can't.'

'Yes, you can.'

'Should I be as scared to death as I am right now?'

'No,' he said, leaning in towards her. 'Just remem-

ber, Claudia, you're not alone. We'll get through this together. You and I will bring your babies into the world.'

He prayed, as every word slipped from his now dry
mouth, that he could do what he promised. He had the
expertise, he reminded himself. But he also knew that
was not always enough. There were some situations
that no skills could fight.

Steeling himself, he knew he was prepared to fight
for Claudia and her boys.

She closed her eyes and swallowed.

'I need you to try and get onto your hands and
knees…'

'Why?' Her eyes opened wide. 'I thought you have
babies lying on your back. Is there something wrong?'
Panic showed on her face as she stared into Patrick's
eyes, searching for reassurance but frightened of what
he might tell her.

'It will be easier on you and your babies if you're on
all fours,' he told her. 'It opens up the birth canal and,
even though it may seem uncomfortable, believe me,
it will be far better than being on your back. Just try it.
Here, I'll help you.'

He reached for her and she felt the warmth and
strength in his hold as his hands guided her into the
position he needed to best deliver the babies. He made
sure her hands and knees were still resting on the damp
jacket, not the bare floor.

'I'd like to put a cool compress on you. It's getting
warm in here but I'm running out of clothing to give
you.'

Even in pain, Claudia smiled at his remark. It was
true. He had given his jacket and his shirt. 'There's a

clean scarf in my bag but it's very small. You could wet that.'

Patrick reached for her large tan leather bag and dragged it unceremoniously across the metal flooring. He emptied the contents onto the floor, found the small patterned scarf and then noticed the films.

'Are those films for your obstetrician?'

She turned her head slightly. 'Yes, he was going to check them and then sign the papers to allow me to fly home to London.'

He pushed the envelope to the side and took her bottle of water and sparingly dampened the scarf. Gently lifting the sweat-dampened curls on the nape of her neck, he rested the tiny compress on her hot skin. There was nothing he could do about whatever showed on the films now. They wouldn't change anything in the confines of the elevator. He had no idea what the next few minutes would hold but he would be beside her and do whatever he could to keep Claudia and her babies alive.

Feeling his hand on her skin felt so calming and reassuring and Claudia wondered if it was the touch of his skin against hers as much as the makeshift compress. But neither gave relief when the next powerful contraction came and she cried out with the pain.

Her cries tugged at Patrick's heart. He hated the fact there was nothing he could do. But he needed to focus on delivering both babies or risk losing them all. He wouldn't let that happen.

Suddenly the first baby began to enter the world. A mass of thick black hair curled like a halo around his perfect tiny face.

'Just push slowly and think about your breathing,'

he instructed her. 'We need that to control the baby's arrival. We don't want to rush him. You can tear your skin and I want to avoid that.'

The urge to give a giant push was overwhelming but Claudia knew she had to let her breathing slow the pace. She thought of Patrick's handsome face and tried to follow his instructions. There were a few more contractions and finally Claudia's first baby was born into Patrick's waiting hands. He let out a tiny cry as Patrick quickly cleared his mouth of mucous and quickly checked his vital signs.

The baby was small but not so small as to put him in immediate danger by not having access to a humidicrib. Patrick had feared he might have been tinier considering the gestational age and the fact he was a twin. He clamped the cord with a sterile surgical tie before he laid him on the shirt. The baby had endured a harsh entry into the world and the shirt was a far cry from a soft landing but, until his brother was born, there was little Patrick could do for the new arrival. He could not put the child to Claudia's breast as she needed to remain on all fours until the second baby was delivered.

Another contraction began and the second baby was quickly on its way. Patrick hoped that he would not be faced with a foot. That would mean a breech birth and complications he did not want to contemplate.

That next painful contraction came and Claudia cried out loudly but managed with each following breath to push her second baby head first into the world. And once again into Patrick's arms, where the baby took his first breath and cried for the first time. Patrick checked the second baby's vital signs and again was relieved that the delivery had no complications. It had progressed far better than Patrick had imagined.

With beads of perspiration now covering her entire body, Claudia looked over at her two sons and felt a love greater than she'd thought possible.

And a closeness to the man who had delivered them. He was like her knight in shining armour. And she would be indebted to him forever.

Quite apart from being an amazing doctor, Patrick was a wonderful man.

Through the fog of her emotionally drained state, Claudia suddenly suspected her feelings for Patrick ran deeper than simply gratitude for saving them all.

Patrick remained quiet. There were still two afterbirths and Claudia to consider. Despite the peaceful and contented look she wore, he knew they were not out of the woods yet.

Gently he placed the second baby next to his tiny brother and wrapped the shirt around them both before he carefully helped Claudia from her knees onto her back again. He grabbed her leather bag and made a makeshift pillow for her head. Claudia was past caring about the bag or her own comfort as she watched her tiny sons lying so close to her.

Patrick reached for them. 'I'm going torest the babies on you while we wait for the afterbirth.'

While the delivery had been relatively straightforward, Patrick was aware that Claudia's double birth put her at increased risk of haemorrhage. Gently he placed the two tiny boys into their mother's arms and he watched as her beautiful face lit up further as she cradled them. Her beauty seemed to be magnified with the boys now securely with her and, with her genes, they would no doubt be very handsome young men.

Within minutes, part of the placenta was delivered but as Patrick examined it he was concerned that it was not intact. Claudia would require a curette in hospital if the remaining placenta wasn't expelled. But, that aside and despite the surroundings, Claudia had delivered two seemingly healthy boys. Patrick took a deep breath and filled his lungs as he looked at Claudia with a sense of pride for the strength shown by a woman he barely knew.

Then he noticed her face had become a little pale.

'I sort of feel a little cold now,' she said softly, as her body began to shiver. 'It feels odd; I was so hot before. There's no pain but...'

Patrick noticed her eyes were becoming glassy and she was losing her grip on the boys. There was something very wrong. Quickly he scooped them from her weakening hold and placed them together beside her, still wrapped in his shirt. He felt for her pulse. It was becoming fainter. He looked down to see blood pouring from Claudia and pooling on the jacket underneath her.

It was his worst nightmare—a postpartum haemorrhage.

Claudia had fifty percent more blood in her body because of the pregnancy, which would help, but, with the amount of blood she had already lost on the floor, it would still only buy them a small amount of time. He needed to encourage her uterus to contract, shutting off the open blood vessels. Immediately he began to massage her belly through to her uterus but after a minute he could see there was no difference. She was barely lucid and he needed to administer a synthetic form of the hormone that would naturally assist, but that was on the other side of the closed elevator doors with the paramedics. It wasn't something he carried in his medical bag. Not now anyway. Once he would have had everything he now needed to save Claudia—but that was a lifetime ago.

'Claudia—' he ceased the massage momentarily and patted her hand '—I need you to try to feed one of the boys. It will help to stimulate a hormone that will lessen the bleeding. Do you understand?'

'Uh-huh,' she muttered while trying to keep her eyes from closing. 'I feel so light-headed.'

'That's the blood loss. I'm going to do everything I can to stop it until help arrives, but again we need to work together. You'll be on your way to hospital very soon.'

He reached down and gently unwrapped the babies and, picking up the larger of the twins, he lifted Claudia's tank top and bra and placed him onto her breast. Instinctively the baby latched onto his mother and began to suckle while Patrick continued the massaging.

'Do you have any names for the boys?' he asked, trying to keep Claudia focused as he dealt with the medical emergency that was unfolding before his eyes.

She tried to think but the names weren't there. They were special names and they should have spilled out without any effort but she was befuddled, which wasn't her. 'I think…' She paused momentarily as the names she had chosen now seemed strangely out of reach. She blinked to bring herself back on track. 'Thomas…and Luca…after each of their great-grandpas.'

'I think they are strong names for two little fighters. Is this baby Thomas or Luca?'

Claudia smiled down at her son, still attached to her breast but not really sucking successfully. 'Thomas… but I think he's tired already and a bit too small.'

'I think you're right on both counts.'

'I'm feeling quite dizzy again.' She paused as she felt herself wavering and her vision was starting to blur. Fear was mounting again inside her. 'Am I going to die?'

'No, you're going to pull through and raise your two sons until they are grown men.'

Claudia felt weaker by the minute. She knew there was something very serious happening, even though she couldn't see the blood. 'If I don't make it…'

'You will,' he argued as he reached for Thomas, who was unable to suckle, and placed him safely on the floor beside his brother, Luca.

She closed her eyes for a moment. She felt too weak to fight. 'You need to contact my sister, Harriet. Her details are in my phone. She needs to be there for my boys if I can't be.'

'Claudia, listen to me. You're going to make it, but I'm going to have to do something very uncomfortable for you.'

'What?' she asked in a worried whisper.

'I'm going to compress your uterus with my hands. It will further slow the bleeding.'

She nodded but she felt as if she was close to drifting off to sleep. 'If you have to, then do it.'

'Try to stay awake,' he pleaded with her as he attempted to manually compress the uterus with the firm pressure of his hands.

Minutes passed but still the blood was flowing over his hands to the floor beneath her. Claudia needed to be in a hospital and she needed to be there now. This was something more serious than the usual postpartum blood loss.

She was dangerously close to losing consciousness as he gently removed his hands. The manual pressure could not stop the bleeding. Claudia needed surgical intervention if she was to survive. He reached for the films and ripped open the envelope. The films scattered on the floor but, as he grabbed the report, his worst fears were confirmed. Claudia's placenta had invaded the walls of her uterus. Every part of his body shuddered. It was déjà vu. The prognosis was identical to what he had faced all those years ago. There was no way her obstetrician would have allowed her to board a plane with the condition. Claudia would have delivered her sons in America, whether it had been this day or another.

With a heavy heart, he dropped his gloves and the report to the floor and pulled a barely conscious Claudia into his arms, where he held her while he stroked the faces of the little boys lying on the floor beside them. If help didn't arrive within a few minutes he would lose Claudia.

And her two tiny babies would never know their beautiful, brave mother.

Chapter 3

As Claudia's body suddenly fell limp in Patrick's arms, he heard the doors open behind him and instantly felt a firm grip on his bare shoulder.

'We've got it from here,' the deep voice said.

Patrick turned his head to see a full medical team rushing towards them. He had never been happier in his life than he was at that moment and, with adrenaline surging through his veins, he immediately began firing instructions at lightning speed. The miracle Claudia needed had arrived at the moment he had run out of options.

'We're dealing with a postpartum haemorrhage—she needs Syntocinon immediately and a catheter inserted so that the uterus has a better chance of contracting with an empty bladder. If she doesn't stabilise she'll be looking at a transfusion. Forget cross-matching as there may not be time; just start plasma now and have O negative waiting in OR.'

Patrick moved away as the medical team stepped in to begin the treatment he had ordered. Immediately they inserted an IV line, began a plasma transfusion then administered some pain relief and Syntocinon in an attempt to stop Claudia's bleeding while another two paramedics collected the baby boys and left the elevator with them securely inside portable humidicribs.

'Any idea why she's still bleeding?' the attending doctor asked.

'Placenta accreta,' Patrick said as he reached for the films lying on the floor. He kept his voice low so he would not alarm Claudia. 'I checked the report on the ultrasound films. Only a very small amount of the placenta was delivered and the rest is still firmly entrenched in the uterus wall. If the report is correct, she may be looking at a surgery but a complete hysterectomy should be the surgeon's last option. I doubt she's more than late twenties, if that, so she might like to keep her womb.'

'I'm sure they'll proceed conservatively if they can.'

Patrick nodded. He had no idea what the future would hold for Claudia and he wanted her to have every choice possible. 'The boys appear fine but they'll need a thorough examination with the paediatrician,' Patrick continued, not taking his eyes from Claudia. 'One is a little smaller than the other but let's hope there's no underlying issues with their premature arrival.'

'You did a remarkable job, all things considered,' the paramedics told Patrick as they watched the barely conscious Claudia being lifted onto the gurney and then securely but gently strapped in.

Keeping his attention on Claudia, who was beginning to show signs of being lucid, the doctor added, 'And you, young lady, are very lucky this man was sharing the elevator. It would not have been this outcome without him, that's for certain. You and your boys all owe your lives to him.'

Claudia smiled a meek smile and held out her hand in an effort to show her gratitude. Patrick cupped it gently in his own strong hands and smiled back at her then he turned to the attending doctor. 'I'll be travelling side-saddle to the hospital if there's room.'

'There's definitely room.'

For a little over three hours, Patrick divided his time between pacing the corridors outside Recovery and visiting the Neonatal Intensive Care Unit to check on Luca and Thomas. They had given him a consulting coat to cover his bare chest upon arrival at the hospital. Claudia's dark-haired boys, one with sparkling blue eyes and the other with deep brown like their mother, were doing very well and he felt a deep and very unexpected bond with them. A bond that he hadn't felt towards anyone, let alone tiny people, for more years than he cared to remember.

But these boys were special, perhaps because he'd delivered them in a crisis, or perhaps because their mother was clearly a very special woman. Perhaps it was both but, whatever was driving him to stay, he knew the three of them were bringing out protective feelings in him. A sense that he was needed and almost as if he belonged there. He should have felt unnerved and wanted to run but he didn't. That need to protect himself from being hurt was overridden by the need to protect Claudia, Thomas and Luca.

Both boys weighed a little over four pounds, which was a relief. They were still in their humidicribs and being monitored closely but both had passed all the paediatrician's initial tests and were being gavage fed by the neonatal nurses when Patrick left the nursery and headed back to check on their mother. Her surgery had taken far longer than he had anticipated. He had for a moment contemplated scrubbing in to assist when they'd arrived in Emergency and were rushed around to the OR but he'd immediately thought better of it. A reality check reminded him that his last obstetric surgery had ended his career.

Patrick wanted her to be spared the additional stress and long-term repercussions of the hysterectomy if possible and voiced that again upon arrival. The surgical resident had reassured Patrick that Dr Sally Benton was well respected in the field of gynaecological surgery and that Claudia would be in expert hands. Patrick hoped that the option to give birth again one day in the pretty delivery room with floral wallpaper, midwives and pain relief was not taken away. But, three hours later, he knew the reality of her surgery taking so long meant she had probably undergone a hysterectomy. And she would have to give up on that dream.

'I'm Sally Benton.' She pulled her surgical cap free and outstretched her hand.

'Patrick Spencer,' he responded as he met her handshake. He looked at the woman before him. She was tall and thin, her short black hair with smatterings of grey framed her pretty face and he suspected she was in her early fifties.

'Dr Spencer, I assume.'

'Yes.'

'I wanted to personally thank you for the medical intervention you provided in the elevator. Miss Monticello is in Recovery now and she certainly wouldn't be if you hadn't done such an amazing job delivering her sons and keeping her alive. If you hadn't been with her today, there would most definitely have been a question mark over their survival.'

Patrick drew a deep breath and chose to ignore the compliment. 'Was it conservative surgery?'

'No, unfortunately, Miss Monticello underwent a full hysterectomy to stop the haemorrhaging. She retained her ovaries but her uterus has been removed,' Dr Benton continued as she took a seat in the corridor and indicated Patrick to do the same. 'The attending doctor briefed me on your diagnosis of suspected placenta accreta, but the depth of invasion was not first but second grade. I was faced with placenta increta as the chorionic villi had invaded the muscular layer of the uterine wall so I had no option but to remove her womb. She was lucky that it had not spread through the uterine wall to other organs such as the bladder. Let's just say I'm glad I didn't have to deal with that; as you would know, even in this day and age, there's still a six to seven per cent mortality rate for that, due to the complications.'

Patrick knew the statistics for death only too well.

'Thank you, Dr Benton.'

'Don't thank me. As I said before, you did the hard

work keeping her alive. And she has two wonderful little boys. Perhaps the loss of her womb will not be a complete tragedy.'

Patrick nodded. He wondered how Claudia would react to the need for a hysterectomy.

'And how are her sons doing?' the surgeon enquired.

'Very well,' Patrick said with a sense of pride that surprised him. 'They're handsome young men and a good weight for their gestational age.'

'Great. Now that's out of the way and we've spoken about our mutual patients, I have a personal question for you,' Dr Benton continued. 'How do you know Miss Monticello?'

'We were just sharing the elevator.'

Her expression revealed her surprise. 'Well, that's serendipity for you. I don't think she could have asked for a better travelling companion. Where do you practice obstetrics?' Then, without waiting for an answer, she added, 'Am I right in assuming, with your accent, and because I haven't heard of you around LA, that your practice is out of state or perhaps abroad?'

Patrick hesitated. He didn't want to talk about himself but he knew the doctor sitting beside him had every right to enquire. 'No, I practice here in LA but I'm not in OBGYN.'

'Really?' Her brow wrinkled as she considered his response. 'What's your field then?'

'I'm a board certified cosmetic surgeon.'

Once again, she didn't hide her surprise. 'I'd never have picked that,' she said with a grin on her somewhat tired face as she stood up and again offered a handshake. 'Well, Dr Spencer, if you ever get tired of your current field, you should consider obstetrics. There's a shortage of experts in the field and you're very skilled. Your intervention was nothing short of amazing in the conditions you were forced to work in. As I said, Miss Monticello owes her life to you. She will be in her room in another two hours or so. She lost a lot of blood, as you know, so we'll be monitoring her in Recovery for a little longer than we normally would. But I'm sure she'd be pleased to see you.'

Patrick met her handshake and she smiled before she left him alone.

Patrick spent the next two hours with Luca and Thomas. He had called his practice and rearranged his schedule. While the boys were being monitored closely he still didn't want to leave. Not yet anyway. Thomas was in a humidicrib and Luca required additional oxygen to be provided through an oxy-hood so he was in an open bed warmer. The neonatologist felt certain that would only be a temporary measure as both appeared to be healthy and a satisfactory weight for their gestational age. Patrick was aware they had some basic milestones to achieve, both in weight and development, before they would be released; he doubted it would be more than three or four weeks before they would be allowed to leave hospital with their mother.

He went downstairs to the florist and picked the largest floral bouquet they had and two brown bears with blue bows. Claudia had told him she had no one she could reach out to and he knew how that felt only too well. He tried not to think of what he had lost when he'd walked away from his family.

Only now at least Claudia did have two little people to call her family. Still, he knew her room would be devoid of anything to brighten her day and lift her spirits and, after the day she had endured, she deserved a room filled with flowers. And something to remind her of the boys when she was resting and not able to be with them in the neonatal nursery. And when she had to face the reality of the hysterectomy she had undergone without her consent.

The nurse at the station arranged for the flowers to be placed near her bed.

Waiting outside the room twenty minutes later, he couldn't contain, nor fully understand, the smile that spread across his face and the warmth that surged through his body when he saw her hospital bed being wheeled down the corridor towards him. She was still pale but not as drained as when he had last seen her, and she hadn't noticed him. In the pit of his stomach he still remembered her limp body collapsing against his and he'd thought the boys had lost their mother.

Patiently he remained outside as she was settled into her room but, as the nurses exited, he tapped on the door that was ajar.

'Are you up to a visitor?'

'Patrick?'

'How did you guess?' he asked as he quietly entered her room. 'Perhaps it's the British accent—there are not a lot of us around these parts so I guess it's a giveaway.'

'In this city, it's a dead giveaway.' It was more than just his accent, but Claudia couldn't tell Patrick that it was also his reassuring tone that told her exactly who was at her door. It was the same strong voice that had kept her going when she'd wanted to give up. It was the voice of the man who had saved her and her sons.

'May I come in?'

'Of course,' she said, ushering him in with the arm that wasn't connected to the IV providing pain relief after her surgery. 'What are you still doing here?'

'Keeping an eye on…your handsome young sons.'

'They are gorgeous, aren't they? The nurses wheeled me on the bed into the nursery to see them a few minutes ago on the way back from Recovery. They were sleeping but they told me they're both doing very well.' She paused and nervously chewed on the inside of her cheek to keep her emotions under control. 'Thanks to you.'

Patrick moved closer to her in the softly lit room. 'Not because of me; you did the hard work, Claudia. I just assisted.'

'Maybe the hard work, but you did the skilled work. Without you,' she began, then her chin quivered as she struggled again to keep her tears at bay, 'they could have…well, they might not have made it if you weren't there with me.'

He reached for her hand. It was instinctive and something he had not been driven to do in a very long time. 'Not a chance. They're as strong as their mother.'

Claudia looked down at his hand covering hers. After the trauma of the preceding hours, it made her feel secure. But she couldn't get used to that feeling of being safe. Not with anyone, no matter how kind. She knew that she and Patrick were bonded by what they had been through and it was a normal reaction to the traumatic experience they'd shared. But now, in the safety of the hospital, she had to accept it was nothing more. Although he had proven her initial assumption of him very wrong, she couldn't afford to get swept away by some romantic notion there was more to it. As if he'd appeared like her white knight, saved her and would steal her away to his castle. That wasn't the real world.

Knowing she needed to create some distance between them, she slipped her hand free and haphazardly ran her fingers through her messy curls that had been swept up in a surgical cap for hours.

The move was not lost on Patrick and he graciously accepted her subtle rebuff. He had overstepped the mark. And he never overstepped the mark with a woman. Perhaps it was because she looked so lost and vulnerable that he wanted to make her feel less alone, but clearly she was not looking to be saved again. And he needed to step away. He was grateful she'd reminded him subtly that he wasn't looking to become attached to anyone.

That time in his life had passed. Being alone was what he did best. *What had he been thinking?*

'So…how are you feeling?' he asked in a doctor-patient tone. 'Your body has been through a lot today, quite apart from bringing Thomas and Luca into the world.'

'You mean the…hysterectomy?'

He nodded then waited in silence to hear Claudia's response to the emergency life-changing surgery. She was a resilient woman but he knew this would certainly test any woman and he would not be surprised if she struggled to come to terms with it.

She dropped her gaze for a moment then, lifting her

chin and her eyes almost in defiance at what the universe had dealt her, she nodded. 'I'll be okay. I'm alive and I have my sons. It would be stupid to mourn what I can't change and perhaps it would be selfish to ask for more than what I was given today. My life and the lives of my children is miracle enough.'

Patrick was already in awe of the strength that she had shown in the elevator but her reaction to the news almost brought him to his knees with respect for her courage and acceptance of what she couldn't change. She was a truly remarkable woman.

Her fingers nervously played with the woven blanket for a minute before she looked back at Patrick. 'When I think of how terribly wrong everything could have gone today, losing my womb is a small price to pay.'

While Claudia looked like a porcelain doll, Patrick had learned over the few hours since their lives collided that she was made of far tougher material. Still, it puzzled him that she was alone in the world. Had she pushed people from it? Or had they abandoned her? Had being alone made her that strong? He couldn't imagine anyone walking away from such an amazing woman.

Then he realised none of his questions mattered. She had been his unofficial patient for a few hours. Nothing more.

'That huge arrangement of flowers is stunning. I'm guessing it's from you,' she added as she looked around the room and spied the huge bouquet on a shelf near her. It was getting dark outside and she could see the lights of the Los Angeles skyline. But the flowers were more spectacular than any view.

Patrick nodded and tried to look at her with the doctor-patient filter but it was becoming a struggle with each passing moment. It had been an intense first meeting in the elevator but there was more pulling him to her than the fact he had delivered her babies under such conditions. They were not in the confines of that small space any more and she no longer needed his help but still he wanted to be there for the stunning brunette still dressed in a shapeless white surgical gown.

And he was confused as hell. He had unexpectedly become a passenger on a roller coaster of his own emotions. Before, he had always been the driver. He needed to gain control. Quickly. He needed to make it less personal.

'Have you noticed how drab the walls in these rooms are? I needed to brighten your room somehow. I thought flowers would do the trick.'

'The rooms are not that bad, young man,' a stern voice replied from the doorway. 'My name's Vanda, and it would do you well not to complain. I'll be tending to your wife tonight and, for your interest...'

'Oh...we're not married,' came their reply in unison.

There was a moment's uncomfortable silence as the three of them looked at each other in silence.

'Sorry if I presumed your marital status; it's just habit at my age,' the nurse, who Patrick imagined to be in her early fifties, with short auburn hair and twinkling blue eyes, said. She crossed the room, manoeuvring around Patrick to get access to her patient. 'I have two grandchildren and their parents aren't married either. *Haven't got time*, they say. Well, as long as they're happy, I'm happy.'

'No, we're not together,' Claudia began before the

nurse wrapped the blood pressure monitor around her arm. 'He's my...' She paused, not knowing how to describe Patrick. *What was their relationship?* she wondered. They weren't friends, but nor were they connected as patient and doctor in a formal sense. Their relationship really couldn't be defined...not easily at least...except, perhaps, for *intense* and *sudden*.

'I'm her emergency elevator obstetrician...not the father of her babies.'

As Patrick said the words, he wondered, against his better judgement, who was the father of her children. What sort of man was he? And why wasn't he rushing to Claudia's side? Patrick knew that if he was the father, no matter how forcefully the mother of his children tried to push him away, he would stand fast to the spot.

But he wasn't the father of Claudia's children or anyone's children. And he never would be.

'Oh, of course, you're the young woman who delivered in the elevator this afternoon,' Vanda answered. She confirmed that Claudia's vitals were stable, then unwrapped the arm wrap and packed it away before she turned back to Patrick. 'And you must be the doctor who was in the right place today and brought this young lady's twins into the world.'

Patrick nodded. His mind was still filled with questions about Thomas and Luca's father but he needed to block them out. It wasn't his business. Claudia was alive. And now he could walk away as he should, knowing they were safe.

'Well, I'll compliment you on your skill in the baby-delivering field, which was on the six o'clock news, if you didn't already know. But you'd still do well not to criticise the rooms.' With a tilt of her head that signalled she meant business, then a wink that left them both wondering if she was serious or joking, Vanda left the room and Patrick and Claudia found themselves staring at each other, both confused by her demeanour and a little surprised at her announcement of their prime-time notoriety.

'We were on the six o'clock news?' The inflection at the end turned Claudia's statement into a question.

'Apparently—let's hope they didn't manage to find out your identity so you're not bothered by reporters.'

'I hope not,' she said, slumping back into the pillows and nervously fidgeting with her pearl earrings. Her parents had given them to her for her sixteenth birthday, while Harriet had been given a pearl necklace.

'I'll let the nurses' station and the main admissions know you don't want any interviews or fuss made of you or the boys. I'll head them off at the pass.'

Claudia looked at Patrick and thought once again he was her knight in shining armour… Or, with his modern good looks, perhaps he could be riding in on his stallion, tipping his Stetson and saving her. She hadn't even needed to ask. He just kept rescuing her. But she had to stop him doing it. She needed to save herself and her boys. Patrick wouldn't be there for them going forward. It would only be the three of them until they got back to London and Harriet returned.

'Don't worry,' Claudia replied. 'I'll let Vanda know to tell them I'm not interested in speaking to anyone. You've already done too much. Honestly, I appreciate more than anything all that you have done but you don't have to do any more. I can take it from here.'

Patrick agreed with her. He had done all that was needed and now she would be taken care of in hospital. She would leave for the UK once she and her children got clearance so there was no point in forging any sort of relationship. Romantic or otherwise.

'Here's my number,' he said, putting his business card on the tray where Claudia's water jug was placed. 'If you need anything, call me. Otherwise, I wish you and Thomas and Luca a safe trip home to London in a few weeks.' He fought the desire to kiss her forehead and stroke the soft curls away from her face. With a deep and unexpected sense of regret that he would never see Claudia again, he turned heavily on his feet and headed to the door, pausing for the briefest moment to look at the beautiful woman who had captured more than his attention that day.

Claudia wasn't sure what was suddenly stirring in the pit of her stomach and surging through her veins, making her heart beat faster, but she knew she was torn about watching him walk away. The day had been so intense but something inside of her wasn't ready to let that happen.

She knew she had to be crazy but she had to call after him.

'Please…wait,' she said then, taking a deep heart-felt breath, she continued, 'I didn't mean to seem rude or ungrateful in any way. I just mean I've put you out and I know you're a doctor and you probably have patients and…'

'Claudia—' he turned back and stopped her speech '—it's fine, really; you're right. I'm sure you can take it from here. I'm glad that you and the boys are well and through the ordeal that was today. I couldn't ask for more and I just want all the very best for the future for all of you.'

Patrick smiled at Claudia before he left but he knew in his heart her first instincts to push him away were right. There was more to the way he felt about this woman than a simple doctor-patient relationship so he had to keep his distance.

The only relationships he had were one-night stands with no strings attached and no feelings involved. And he doubted with Claudia it would be anything like that. She was already stirring feelings he didn't want to have.

It had to be just the intense experience they had shared, he reminded himself. He needed to walk away and let her *take it from here*.

Chapter 4

'So what exactly are you saying is the issue with Miss Monticello's international health insurance?' Vanda demanded of the caller on the other end of the telephone. She was frowning and her cheeks were becoming flushed.

Patrick's ears tuned in to the conversation and, against his better judgement, he slowed his steps. Her serious tone caused him some concern, as did her expression as he neared the desk. The exchange of words confirmed it. He couldn't walk away and pretend he hadn't heard there was a problem. Something was driving him to want to protect the woman who he knew he should stay away from. A woman who had given him no information about herself, other than the fact she was returning to London with no explanation of why.

Questions were starting to mount in his tired mind. Was the father of her children in London, waiting for her? Or was he no longer in her life? He felt sure Claudia would have asked to call her husband or boyfriend, if she had one, even if he was away on business or fighting for his country. But she'd told him there was no one. Patrick knew he had no right to ask anything about her life that she had not willingly surrendered. Wanting to know more, let alone feeling the way he did about a woman he had known less than twelve hours, was ridiculous.

It had to stop. He knew he wanted to protect Claudia but he had to be realistic about his feelings. She was alone and he felt sorry for her. That had to be the driving force of his desire to protect her. Perhaps coupled with the desire to see her and her children safely out of hospital. He didn't want to think that there could be setbacks with any of them.

He needed to know they were safe then his job was done.

How could it be anything more than that?

'Uh-huh…okay… All right, I'll will let her know in the morning that someone from Finance will have to come and see her and make arrangements. I know she told the nurse in Recovery she was worried about the bills but we don't want her to stress. Perhaps she can extend the policy.'

Patrick looked as Vanda's expression fell further and her brow furrowed at what she was hearing. 'Oh, I see, so the twins can't be covered… Well, that's a bit of a mess but I'm sure the hospital will work something out and she'll have to pay the debt over a period of time.

Yes, I appreciate it's an international policy and there are restrictions but in my ward there are no restrictions to her care.' She paused for a moment, drumming her fingers on the desk. 'No, I do hear what you're saying but please listen to my concerns.'

She continued listening with anxiety showing clearly on her face while the other staff bustled around her with the change of shift and handover. Patrick kept his focus on the conversation. She was being very polite but firm with the caller, despite her expression and the colour in her cheeks. He doubted she was the type to lose too many battles, but he couldn't help but notice she was struggling to hold her ground.

'I'd rather not. No, let it wait until the morning. Miss Monticello needs her rest and if she's stressing about hospital bills it won't help her sleep and, after what she has been through today, sleep is what she needs,' she said firmly then paused. 'I will be moving her to a ward tomorrow but tonight she's in a private room that was available. No, she doesn't have any next of kin in California or anywhere in the United States on her admission forms. She has a sister, and she appears to be her only living family, but she resides in the UK.'

With that, Patrick learnt a little more about the mystery that was Claudia's life. She had no one else in the world to call family other than her sister. Then why didn't she call her? he wondered.

'Yes, I do understand the seriousness of the situation but we will handle it in the morning. I'm back on at six,' Vanda said. She was becoming short. 'No, absolutely no. I won't budge on it. My patient comes first so please do not send anyone up now because I won't allow them in to her room.'

Patrick paused for a moment, wanting to offer assistance, but then thought better of taking over the situation. He made a mental note to have his lawyer contact the hospital administration the next day and sort through the insurance issues. After bringing the boys into the world, he wasn't about to stand by and let their mother be stressed after the fact. He tried to tell himself it was his gift to Thomas and Luca. But he knew it was not the boys alone that he was thinking about.

'I'm hanging up now,' Vanda continued sternly. 'We'll continue this conversation in the morning. There are far more practical problems to solve, like sourcing some fresh pyjamas for my patient. She'll remain in a hospital gown tonight but she has no nightdress or toiletries, not even a toothbrush, poor thing, so I can't sit around chatting to you; I'll have to go and sort out something before I finish my shift or she'll look like Orphan Annie in the morning.'

Patrick continued walking and made his way outside to the cab rank and, as he did, he sent a text to his receptionist. He needed her to run an errand for him.

Claudia woke after an uncomfortable and restless sleep and wanted desperately to see her babies. The uncomfortable part of her night was due to post-operative constraints but the restlessness, she suspected, was a combination of anxiety for her sons and then a strange feeling of emptiness, knowing that she would never see Patrick again. She knew it was absurd to even have any sort of reaction to not seeing Patrick, let alone this feeling in the pit of her stomach. Less than twenty-four hours before, she hadn't known him and now she thought she would miss him. It was as if by meeting him she'd found a piece of the puzzle she hadn't known she had been looking for.

As she lay in bed thinking about the facts she realised how silly she was being. Fact one, she told herself, you are a single mother of twins so your life is already full. Fact two, you are a month away from being an illegal overstay in the US so you need to get back to the UK as soon as possible. Fact three, you don't trust men and never will again. Fact four, you know very little about the handsome man who delivered your babies except that he doesn't seem to want children and you have two of the most adorable children ever born. He was just checking you were all right when he visited last night, as any doctor would, she reminded herself. And he walked away. Said goodbye and good luck. That is as final and impersonal as it gets.

'Besides, it's ridiculous', she mumbled out loud. 'To even think you could miss someone you barely know.'

Her practical side forced her to push any thoughts of Patrick from her mind and blame the funny feeling in her stomach on her internal stitches or her reaction to the general anaesthetic. It had to be one or both making her stomach feel uneasy, she decided, as she pushed the nurse call button. She wanted to see Thomas and Luca as soon as possible. She wanted to hold them in her arms, if she was allowed. If not, she wanted to reach inside their humidicribs and stroke their soft warm skin and tell them that they were safe and she was there for them forever.

That they would never be apart. That she would protect them from life's harms in any way she could.

Just the way Patrick had protected them all the day before.

Her eyes were suddenly drawn across the room to the flowers. The beautiful blooms did just as Patrick wanted in brightening the borderline drab hospital room and she felt her mouth curving a little. The walls of her room were a light beige colour and the blinds a deeper shade of the same with the floor a mottled light grey. The night before she had not paid too much attention to the flowers other than thinking there was a pretty pop of colour in the room. In the morning light she could see cheerful yellow and white gerberas, a white daisy spray and blue chrysanthemums in a lovely white-blue vase, with a checked blue and white ribbon giving a pretty finishing touch. And the two small brown bears with blue bow ties. It was so thoughtful of him to have them in her room when she arrived. But then it seemed that everything he did was so considerate.

But why? she wondered. What was motivating him to be so kind to a stranger? He had already done more than could have been expected of anyone. Blinking furiously, she looked away from the floral arrangement. She had to put Patrick out of her mind. She couldn't allow herself to think of him that way. She had learnt her lesson the hard way not to trust anyone, not even herself.

The nurse, who introduced herself as Alli, arrived and unhooked the IV line. 'I'll leave the cannula in, but I'll tape it down,' Alli told her as she thoroughly flushed the tube and placed strong clear tape across Claudia's wrist where the small cannula had been placed. She was one of the youngest nurses on the ward and, Claudia would quickly come to learn, one of the cheekiest. 'Just in case you want IV pain relief during the day or tonight. Believe me, if they offer drugs, take them.'

Slowly, Alli helped her out of bed and assisted her to take small steps into the bathroom. Keeping the dressings dry, the nurse bathed Claudia while she sat on the shower chair.

'Do you have a clean nightdress?' she asked as she towel-dried her patient.

Claudia shook her head. She had no one to collect anything from her apartment and she only had oversized T-shirts, nothing really suitable for hospital. She had packed a suitcase for her trip home and only left out a pair of comfortable leggings, sweater and coat with flat boots for the flight. The other small boxes of her belongings would have been collected and already be on their way with the shipping company back to London. She had planned on shopping for pretty nightdresses for her hospital stay when she returned to London.

While she had made a few acquaintances in Los Angeles, after she'd found out the truth about her relationship with Stone and then about her pregnancy, the obvious questions that would raise had made her keep everyone at arm's length. She didn't want to make friends and then have to hide the truth from them, so she'd chosen to be alone.

'Looks like you'll be in a stylish hospital gown again today,' Alli replied as she left to retrieve another gown. Moments later, she reappeared and helped Claudia to dress. 'At least it will be clean.'

'Thank you.'

'Since they have that revealing back opening, I'm going to give you a second one to wear the other way. Like a coat to complement your stunning runway ensemble.'

Claudia smiled. Although normally she did care how she was dressed and paid particular attention to her grooming, that morning she wouldn't have cared if the nurse had dressed her in a giant brown paper bag. She just wanted to get downstairs to the neonatal nursery.

'Not before you eat, Miss Monticello,' Vanda said, walking into her room and spying Claudia in the wheelchair, ready to go downstairs. 'You'll be no good to your sons without both rest and nutrition.'

'But I want to know they're all right,' Claudia argued as she sat upright. The anticipation was building and she wanted nothing more than to be with her little boys.

Vanda picked up the breakfast tray and put it on the bed near her impatient patient, handing Claudia a small plate with some buttered wholemeal toast. Standing directly in front of Claudia and not taking her eyes from her, she said firmly, 'Thomas and Luca are doing very well. I had a call from the resident paediatrician in the neo-natal ICU about an hour ago. They're expecting you but I won't let you visit unless you've had some toast and juice. I'm quite serious, Claudia. Your body suffered a huge shock yesterday and you need to take things slowly and not forget to eat and rest, just as your little boys are doing. I'm Italian and, by the sound of your surname, so are you, so you'll know that Italians take their food very seriously. You will not get away with skipping meals with one of your countrywomen on duty. Food first, before you head anywhere.'

Just then there was a knock at the door and another young nurse brought in a delivery box with the insignia of an exclusive store on Rodeo Drive; it was about a foot long and just as wide and tall. Vanda reached out and took the box.

'Well, what's this then? It's addressed to you. Have you been shopping online overnight, Miss Monticello?'

As Claudia took a bite of her toast, she shook her head. 'Are you sure it's for me? I couldn't afford to shop there in a mad fit.'

'Well, it definitely has your name on it, so someone's been shopping for you. I'll pop it on the bed and you can check it later.'

'P'raps it's a present from a handsome stranger because you were on TV last night,' Alli added before she left the room to continue her rounds.

'Oh, gosh, I hope not,' Claudia said as she put down the toast, as her already fragile appetite completely disappeared. 'I'm hoping no one knows my name or Thomas and Luca's.'

'With the proximity of the apartment complex and the fuss made on the evening news, viewers would probably assume you'd be here but neither your name nor your sons' were released and we've told the main admissions desk to refuse any media requests. It's our usual protocol,' Vanda replied. Then, spying the still uneaten toast on Claudia's plate, she continued, 'Would you like me to help you open the box and put you out of your misery?'

Claudia nodded as she tentatively sipped her orange juice.

'All right, here's the deal. I'll get some scissors from

the nurses' station while you finish your breakfast but I won't open the box until you've had both pieces of toast and either your juice or a cup of tea.'

Claudia nodded begrudgingly.

Vanda stayed true to her word and when she returned with the oversized scissors she waited until Claudia had eaten and finished her juice before cutting through the packaging tape on the box. She opened it and handed it to Claudia.

Claudia lifted the tissue carefully. 'Oh, goodness, they're beautiful,' she exclaimed as she pulled the stunning jade-green silk pyjamas from the box.

'Very nice. Whoever arranged for those to be sent has great taste. Hold on a minute; now it makes sense…' Vanda paused for a moment, a strange look on her face.

'What is it? Do you know who sent this to me?'

'No idea, actually, but I had a conversation in handover this morning about a call one of the young nurses took from that store after I finished my shift last night. Apparently they had a phone order and wanted to check if they could deliver to a patient in our ward. They didn't say who and of course we would not have given your details even if they had asked.'

'How curious,' Claudia replied as she reached inside to find there was more. A short nightdress and a long one in varied tones of apricot and a matching floral wrap that picked up the colour palette of all of the other items and added some black trim for dramatic effect. There were also some jade satin slippers wrapped in more tissue at the bottom of the box, along with a toiletries bag. She unzipped the bag and it was filled with everything she would need.

'Was there a card?' Claudia asked, peering inside the box and then closing the lid and carefully checking the packaging. She couldn't see any sender other than the store—it had been a telephone order.

'No, it appears to be anonymous. As you said, very *curious* indeed,' Vanda replied.

Claudia put everything back into the box. 'I can't accept an anonymous gift.'

'I would—they look like silk and they're a whole lot better than your current outfit,' Alli argued as she stepped back into the room to collect the breakfast tray with a huge smile. 'I'll be back in ten minutes to take you to Neonatal Intensive Care so it gives you time to slip into one of those stunning pieces if you like.'

Claudia looked down at the shapeless white gown and came close to agreeing for a split second but then bit her lip and shook her head. 'No. I can't.'

Vanda took the box and put it on the bed again. 'You don't have to accept it; however, you are in need of everything that's in that box, so—' she paused to put her words together '—what if you accept the gift on the condition that you will repay your generous benefactor when you've been discharged from the hospital? I'm sure you can track them down through the store.'

'I don't feel comfortable with the idea and I'm not sure I could afford to anyway.'

'Do you feel comfortable with the idea of staying in your present outfit for a few days? You'll get a fresh one each day, of course, but still the same white number with the lovely back opening! Do you have anyone who could go shopping for you?'

Claudia nodded. 'No, there's no one I can call.'

'I thought as much. You'll be in the nursery a lot over the coming days and the pyjamas and gown would be most helpful. I did manage to find you some toothpaste and a toothbrush and a few other bits and pieces but they are pretty basic and I'm sure whatever has been sent to you would be a whole lot nicer.'

Claudia once again bit her lip as she tried to put everything into perspective. 'I know I need them, particularly the toiletries, but do you really think I will be able to find out who sent the gift and repay them?'

'All I can say is that we'll do our best.'

'I *will* find them and I *will* send them a cheque for the entire amount as soon as I can. I mean it.'

Vanda left the room and Claudia slowly and carefully changed without contorting too much. The softness of the pyjama fabric felt glorious on her skin. Feather-light and cool to wear. Her body felt as if it had done battle the day before and this was a little bit of pampering.

Claudia sat down again to rest. She wanted so much to see her sons. She couldn't wait to hold them and tell them how much she loved them. Alli had not arrived so she decided to call Harriet and give her the good news about Thomas and Luca. Her sister had no idea of what had transpired over the last twenty-four hours or that she was now the aunt of two wonderful little boys. It was eight o'clock in the morning and, knowing that Argentina was five hours ahead of LA, Claudia felt confident she wouldn't wake her sister.

Harriet answered the phone after only two rings.

'Hi, sis, how are you? I miss you so much and I have *soooo* much to tell you.' Her voice then dropped to a loud whisper. 'Oh, I'm so confused. My boring, predictable as mud life has turned completely topsy-turvy. I met this man, as close to Adonis as you would find, well, the Argentinian version of the Greek God anyway...I don't know if there is an Argentinian version, to be honest, but he is so ridiculously handsome as well as intelligent and we, well, sort of had a thing, just one night, actually, back in the UK, and I never thought I'd see him again. But now I'm here in his country. He looks even better under the Buenos Aires sun than he did in London—and he was already an eleven out of ten...'

Claudia was surprised to hear Harriet sound so nervous and clearly smitten by this man but, ecstatic as she was to hear that her sister had a love interest, she was aware that Alli would return to take her to the nursery so she blurted out her news. 'I had the babies, Harriet. You're an aunty!'

'What?'

'I had my babies.'

'So early, Clau? Are you and the babies okay?' She stopped in her tracks.

'Yes, I'm fine and Thomas and Luca are so handsome.'

'Thomas and Luca! You named them after both grandfathers?'

'I hope you don't mind that I took both names in one fell swoop. I didn't leave you a grandfather for when you have children.'

Harriet laughed. 'Phuh—me? No, I don't think I'll be having children anytime soon. I'm happy you used Nonno's and Papa's names. I still can't believe you had twins! So tell me about my nephews—are they happy and healthy little boys considering they were early?'

'They're doing well, particularly since they were born in a lift.'

'In a lift?'

'Yes, a lift, or maybe I should say an elevator since I'm here in LA.'

'LA? I'm confused. I thought you were heading back to London to have the babies?'

'I was but my water broke in the elevator and Patrick helped me to give birth. Actually, Patrick saved my life because I haemorrhaged and passed out and then paramedics rescued us all and I had an emergency hysterectomy.'

'How can you tell me you're okay with all of that going on? I need to get there now.' Harriet began pacing nervously.

'No, Harriet.' Claudia's voice was firm. As much as she wanted more than anything to have her sister with her, she refused to pull her away from the first adventure of her life. She was proud that her twin was finally jumping into something with both feet. Maybe they weren't so different after all, or maybe they were switching roles. For a while, at least. 'You can't do anything. For once you need to stick with your plans and stop trying to rescue your big sister. I'm fine, the surgery went well and I have two adorable little boys. We'll be heading home to London as soon as they're strong enough and you can meet them.'

'I need to hop on a plane and get to LA now.'

'Harriet, please listen to me. The orphanage needs you more than me. I'm well taken care of. Everything's fine here. I have a place to live until I leave for London.' Claudia had to lie or she would risk her sister doing what she always did—stepping in to save the day. Claudia had no idea where she would live. Her apartment was gone, she assumed her suitcase would have been taken down to the concierge's office, but she had barely any savings to her name and only a changeable ticket back to London. She would have to work things out quickly, but not at Harriet's expense. Her sister had finally found her dream job and perhaps even her dream man and Claudia was not taking either away from her.

'Is the ex keeping his distance? Does he know about the birth?'

'Yes, he's keeping his distance and no, he doesn't know I've had his sons. He wouldn't care. His lawyer told me he didn't want to be updated about the pregnancy. So I thought I would keep the news to myself. It would hardly have had him skipping with joy.' Claudia paused. 'His wife still has no idea that the boys or I even exist. Just as I had no idea she existed when I fell for his lines. It's amazing how he hid his marriage so well. I must be the most stupid woman in the world.'

'You're not stupid in any way,' Harriet countered softly. 'Just way too trusting for your own good. But you're better off without him, Clau.'

'I know,' she said then, thinking back to the tiny little boys waiting for her in the nursery, she smiled. 'But I have the most wonderful sons so my regrets about my relationship with that man are tempered. He gave me the greatest gifts, Thomas and Luca…and permission to *not* have him in my life. The papers arrived from his lawyer last week. He doesn't want his name on the birth certificates and waived any parental rights.'

'That's so cold!'

'He offered me a trust fund for the boys but I told him to keep his money.'

'Will you be all right without an income?'

'I'll be fine once I get back home in a few weeks. My life will be perfect…'

'I worry about you being alone.'

'I'm won't ever be alone. I have Thomas and Luca, and I'll always have you.'

'That's the truth,' Harriet agreed.

There was also someone else who had momentarily stepped into her life. Claudia was determined that in the future, when he would be just a memory, she would tell her sons as they grew up about the man who'd brought them into the world and also saved their mother's life. Even though they might never meet Patrick, they would always know about him. And how very special he was.

'I'd better say goodbye, though, as the nurse will be back to wheel me down to the nursery any minute.'

'Okay, but you call me if you need me. I can be on a plane and there with you in a few hours. I love you, sis,' Harriet told her.

'Love you too, Harriet,' Claudia replied then hung up before she had a chance to answer her sister's final question.

'Wait, who's Patrick…?'

Chapter 5

'Miss Monticello, I'm Dr Wilson, the neonatologist here at Los Angeles Mercy Hospital. I need to speak with you in private for a moment.' The doctor leant down and held out his hand and Claudia tentatively met his handshake. She had only just arrived in Neonatal ICU and had not yet seen her sons. She had no idea why he wanted to speak with her but she felt her heart pick up speed as his tone seemed quite serious. She hadn't considered there could possibly be any bad news after yesterday. The boys both seemed perfect despite what they had all been through.

What had changed?

'Please call me Claudia,' she replied as she began to nervously play with her freshly scrubbed hands and continued observing the doctor suspiciously. She tried to contain her emotions and wait for the doctor to speak but questions driven by mounting fear came rushing out. 'Are my babies going to be all right? Is there something wrong? I thought everything was fine yesterday.' She wanted to jump from her wheelchair and find them. Her eyes darted around but she could not see the boys as their humidicribs were blocked by a tall beige partition.

'Claudia, they are both doing very well, all things considered,' he returned, clearly trying to calm her down.

'What do you mean—all things *considered*?'

'I mean their delivery in an elevator and the simple fact they are six weeks early. I was going to come to your room but the charge nurse said you were on your way down here so I thought I'd wait. You can see your boys the moment we've finished speaking. I didn't want you to be anxious in the elevator.' The neonatologist, in his late fifties, had a warm smile; his hair, which was grey around the temples, and his deep brown eyes reminded Claudia of her father. Although the doctor's very contained demeanour was not like her father's passionate, gregarious Italian personality. He was controlled and that was reassuring to Claudia but she was still scared.

'Tell me, is there something wrong?' Her eyes widened as she spoke. While he had said nothing dire nor even hinted at it, Claudia had a sense of foreboding but she was trying very hard not to fall to pieces.

'There's been a small setback with Luca and I would like to talk to you about his treatment.'

Claudia's chin began to quiver with the words coming so calmly from the neonatologist's mouth. She had just been wheeled from the scrub room where Alli had helped her to put on a disposable gown over her pyjamas and suddenly she was being ushered into a small consulting room. She had been so excited to see her boys. She hadn't thought for a moment she would hear bad news. She'd had enough, she felt sure, to last a lifetime.

'I can take Claudia from here if you'd like,' he told Alli and reached for the handles of the wheelchair. 'I'll call the nurses' station when she's ready to go back to her room,'

'Certainly Dr Wilson; I'll come back whenever Claudia's ready,' Alli said gently and reassuringly patted Claudia's shoulder. 'You'll be fine, honey. Just breathe slowly and stay calm.'

Dr Wilson wheeled Claudia into the small office and sat opposite her. His expression was stern.

'How serious is it? I need to know.' Claudia felt her stomach tie in knots and it was nothing to do with her surgery.

'Luca had a few breathing problems yesterday and that is why he was in the open bed warmer so that we could provide oxygen through an oxy-hood, or head box as we often call it. It's a small perspex box that allows babies to breathe more easily, but Luca didn't improve overnight. In fact he seemed to be struggling so I suspected a condition called PDA. It's short for a longer medical term, and I can give you more information later. I ordered an echocardiogram an hour ago to confirm my diagnosis…'

'What's an echocardiogram? Did it hurt him?' Despite her resolve to remain in control, tears began to well in her eyes but the questions kept coming. 'Where is Luca?'

'Luca is fine at the moment, Claudia,' the doctor continued in a firm but calm tone. 'The echocardiogram didn't hurt because it's much like an X-ray. Luca and Thomas are over there, where they both were yesterday.' He motioned with his hand in the direction her sons. 'The humidicrib with Thomas is beside Luca's open bed warmer and they have one nurse looking after them both. The setback at this time, Miss Monticello... I'm sorry... Claudia,' he corrected himself, 'has been confirmed by the echocardiogram and, while it's not serious and more than likely just due to his premature arrival, we need to keep an eye on Luca and you need to be aware of his condition.'

'Will Thomas develop the condition too?'

'No. There's no sign of PDA with Thomas. We're just monitoring Luca around this issue.'

'And what exactly is the problem, Dr Wilson?'

'He has an opening between two major blood vessels leading from his heart.'

'Oh, my God, no.' Claudia's hands instinctively covered her mouth. She didn't want to cry but the news brought her to the brink.

It was all too much. She'd thought bringing her babies into the world under such harsh conditions was terrifying but this was so much worse. She felt so helpless.

'Claudia, I know you must be very scared by what I'm telling you but that is why I asked you in here to talk,' the doctor continued in a very soothing tone. 'All parents have that initial reaction—it's perfectly normal—but you need to understand a little more about

Luca's problem and the treatment options. The opening between the blood vessels I'm discussing is a normal part of a baby's circulatory system *before birth* but it normally closes shortly after birth. While a baby is in the mother's womb, only a small amount of his or her blood needs to go to the lungs. This is because the baby gets oxygen from the mother's bloodstream.'

'So why did Luca's not close?'

'It is probably due purely to his prematurity. You see, after birth, the baby is no longer connected to the mother's bloodstream and the baby's blood needs to go to his or her own lungs to get oxygen. When a baby is born on or around their due date the baby begins to breathe on his or her own and the pulmonary artery opens to allow blood into the lungs, and the other opening closes. But in premature infants it is not uncommon for it to remain open and a small PDA often doesn't cause problems.'

'Does Luca have a small PDA or a big one?'

'We don't know yet but if it's small then he may never need treatment.'

'But if it isn't small, what then?'

'A large PDA left untreated can allow poorly oxygenated blood to travel in the wrong direction, weakening the heart muscle and causing heart problems.'

Claudia's world just became a little darker and her own heart sank. 'Will he need surgery?' She felt increasingly powerless to do anything as she waited on tenterhooks for the answer.

'Not at this stage. His treatment for the time being will involve monitoring and medication.'

Her mind was spinning and her body reeling from the news about her baby boy. She felt so overwhelmed and unsure of where to turn. Then she realised there was nowhere to turn. She only had herself. And her little boys only had their mother. She drew a deep restorative breath and faced the doctor. She had to be strong for the three of them.

'What sort of medication?' she asked, shaking her head.

Before the doctor could respond, there was a knock at the door.

She looked over her shoulder to see Patrick standing in the doorway with the same expression she remembered from the day before. The expression that told her she would get through whatever lay ahead when she had no idea how. Her brow was lined in confusion and a single tear of relief trickled down her cheek. Quickly she wiped it away with the back of her hand.

'Claudia, I came as soon as I could,' he began as he stepped inside the room. And closer to her.

'But I didn't call.'

'No, I asked the hospital to keep me posted about the boys as I was listed as the doctor who delivered them. It was professional courtesy for them to keep me updated. I called late last night and asked to be informed if there were any problems with either Thomas or Luca. I knew, with their premature births, there may be issues and I wanted to be here for them.'

What Patrick wanted to say was he wasn't just there for Thomas and Luca. He wanted to be there for her. But he couldn't bring himself to say it. He felt certain she wouldn't want to hear it and he didn't want to say it and believe it. Having feelings for someone—wanting to be a part of Claudia and the boy's lives—was so foreign to him.

He had collapsed onto his bed after a long hot shower the previous night. After returning from the hospital, he had tried to put Claudia out of his mind. He'd hoped as the steaming water engulfed his body he would come to his senses. But he didn't. Her gorgeous face, her feisty nature and her strength in the face of pain that would have crippled the strongest of men, kept pulling his thoughts back to her. And then there was her instant love for her boys. All of it made it impossible for Patrick to push her image away. He couldn't erase her from his thoughts. He had spent hours trying but failed and gave in to what he knew he wanted to do. Against his better judgement, he wanted to be there for them all if they needed him.

Claudia felt relieved to have Patrick so close but so torn at needing him. She was confused. She said nothing as she looked at him. There was nothing in her head that would have made any sense if she'd tried to speak.

Patrick turned his attention to the doctor. 'Dr Wilson, I'm Patrick Spencer. We spoke on the phone earlier.'

The doctor stood and extended his hand to greet Patrick and, in doing so, broke the tension between Claudia and Patrick.

'Nice to meet you in person. Please call me Geoffrey. And I must commend you in person for your medical intervention in the elevator. You wouldn't want to do all your deliveries that way, I'm sure.'

'No, an elevator delivery is not something I would've willingly opted for,' he responded with a lightness to his voice. He met the other doctor's handshake but gave away nothing more. Patrick's current medical specialty bore no relevance in the neonatal nursery. He had been honest with the obstetric surgeon when asked directly the day before, but offering up information not requested was pointless. His former medical knowledge was still very much intact, even if his career with babies was long gone.

Claudia watched the men's conversational banter with a blank expression on her face. Her emotions were a roller coaster but she still had questions about her boys that were clear-cut. Even if anything to do with her own heart and head was not close to straightforward.

'You mention drugs, Dr Wilson. What drugs are you talking about for Luca? Do they have any side effects?'

The doctor immediately returned his focus to Claudia. 'Ibuprofen will be the drug that will be given to Luca. It's an anti-inflammatory that could help to block the hormone-like chemicals in Luca's body that are keeping the PDA open. Ibuprofen could very simply allow it to close in a very short space of time.'

'Is this condition common?' Her voice was steadier and she felt as if her co-pilot had returned and was standing beside her. Still hugely confused by her own feelings, she was slowly digesting the idea that together they would navigate a problem that only moments ago she'd found overwhelming.

'It occurs in about eight in every thousand premature births but most correct themselves in a very short time frame and some in only a few hours.'

'So Luca will be all right?' she asked with her eyes still searching for reassurance, moving from Patrick to Dr Wilson and back again.

'I am fairly sure that over the next day or so the condition will correct itself,' Dr Wilson offered. 'But you still needed to be informed. I don't like to hide anything.' Claudia felt reassured to hear those words. She didn't want anything to be hidden from her ever again.

'And you agree, Patrick?'

He nodded. 'I do.'

Patrick's eyes met hers. The level of vulnerability in Claudia's eyes made him want to pull her into his arms and comfort her but he couldn't. He was providing medical advice. He had to behave as a medical practitioner and refrain from doing what he wanted to do as a man.

'I don't think we should cross a bridge that hasn't presented itself,' he volunteered from his professional viewpoint. 'Luca has a high chance of avoiding any invasive treatment so let's not overthink the situation.'

'Then I won't worry any more.'

Patrick sensed from the doctor's curious expression that he was trying to read the relationship playing out before him; he opened his mouth to speak but Patrick cut in quickly. 'Have you visited with Thomas and Luca today, Claudia?'

'No.'

'Then, Dr Wilson, now Claudia is fully versed with Luca's condition, may I wheel her over to see her babies?'

'Certainly,' the older doctor replied before he could ask anything else. Together they left the small room, with Dr Wilson showing the way and Patrick pushing Claudia's wheelchair. Patrick glanced down to see Claudia still fidgeting with her fingers and suddenly felt very protective. She lifted her face and smiled at him and a warm feeling rushed through his body.

It was as if he was where he needed to be and where he belonged and he hadn't felt that way in a very long time.

He pulled Claudia's wheelchair between the humidicrib and the open bed and then sat down beside her. The neonatologist tended to some new arrivals to the nursery and left them with the neonatal nurse.

'They both look almost red, and I can see their veins…I didn't notice it yesterday.'

'You didn't notice because you were so happy to see them alive and you were lucky to be alive yourself. I don't think you were up to focusing on the details.'

'But is it normal?'

'Yes, premature babies appear to be red as well as much smaller than you had imagined. You can see all the blood vessels through their skin because there hasn't been sufficient time to develop any fat underneath.'

'There are so many wires attached to them. Will I be able to hold them?' Claudia asked as the desire to have them both in her arms was stronger than any need she had ever felt before.

The nurse approached and shook her head. 'Not yet, but you can certainly stroke them both and that is important. They need to feel their mother's touch. While Thomas and Luca aren't the smallest babies in here, we still need to allow them to remain in temperatures stable enough to keep them both warm without needing to be wrapped up in blankets.'

'It also decreases the risk of an infection,' Patrick added as his eyes panned from one baby to the other.

'The humidity in the crib is controlled to help maintain the baby's hydration and prevent water loss. And Luca on his open bed is wearing a cap to help limit the heat loss.'

Claudia gently stroked Luca's tiny arm and prayed that Patrick was right and the problem with his heart would pass in time.

'Patrick,' she began, 'I know you said not to cross a bridge that isn't in front of me, but I can't put blinkers on and pretend there's no chance of something serious. I need to ask just one question and I want you to be completely honest with me.'

Patrick had a million questions for Claudia but he knew she might not stay in town long enough for all of them to be answered. He accepted the simple reality that whatever time they shared in the next few days might be all they would ever have.

Their lives had collided and they had both shared the most precious and intense experience. But it was not the real world and it would all end soon enough. And one burning question in particular still resonated in the back of his mind. *Where was the man who should be by Claudia's side?*

He pushed that thought away and took a deep breath. 'Certainly—what's your question?'

Claudia looked over at Thomas inside his glass humidicrib and then back to tiny Luca. The question erred on the side of the worst-case scenario, which she didn't want to think about. But she needed to know and, if she had to, she wanted to hear the worst from Patrick. 'Can they guarantee the ibuprofen will work?'

Patrick paused, wishing he could tell her there was a

written in stone guarantee but there was no such guarantee. 'No, to be honest, the medications aren't one hundred percent effective and if Luca's condition is severe or causing complications surgery might be needed, but that is not something you have to consider now. Luca's doctor seems very hopeful that the drugs will work.'

'But if they don't?'

'Claudia,' he said, taking her hands in his instinctively and, against his better judgement, he looked at the tears welling in her eyes. She wasn't looking at him any more. She was lovingly watching her tiny son but he noticed she didn't flinch or pull away and left her hands in his. He hated admitting it but there were undeniable sparks as her skin touched his. She was lighting a fire inside him where he'd thought there were only cold embers incapable of feeling any warmth ever again. 'Like I told you before, let's not worry about something over which we have no control. If surgery is needed we'll deal with it then but now is about remaining positive and optimistic about your boys and getting yourself well too.'

Claudia turned her gaze back to Patrick and then to his hands protectively holding hers. Who was this man who kept saving her? she wondered. Should she let him get close to her? He appeared to be so upfront and honest and caring but she still needed to protect her herself from further disappointment. He'd only come into her life twenty-four hours before and she really knew very little about him. There were so many unasked questions. Maybe he wasn't hiding anything but he wasn't overly forthcoming either and that worried her.

She had been promised a life by the boys' father that

was just a lie. How could she be sure that Patrick was any different?

She felt herself wanting to believe in him and everything he was saying and she was feeling, but she was scared. Was it just because of what they'd shared the day before that made her feel that she could trust him? Or was it more than that? Perhaps she felt indebted to him for saving her life and her babies. She knew she had never felt about a man the way she did at that moment.

It was as if she had known him for years.

Her head was spinning. Why could she imagine herself wrapped in the comfort of Patrick's strong arms, her body pressed against the warmth of his…and his lips reaching for hers…? She shook herself back to reality. She was in no place to be having those thoughts.

It wasn't right…but it was happening. And, try as she might, she couldn't pretend it wasn't.

She had feelings she didn't understand for a man she really didn't know.

It didn't make any sense, she thought, as she slipped her hands free.

She had to channel thoughts of Harriet: what her sister would do and how she would think. She would certainly be more realistic and practical. That was how she had to behave. It had to be about her sons from now on. There was barely enough of her left emotionally to give both sons the love and undivided attention they deserved. She had to consider them in every decision she made. She needed to keep it simple, despite the way she felt herself drawn to the handsome Englishman. To her knight in shining armour.

Perhaps they could be friends.

She threw away that idea as quickly as it had arrived. The electricity she felt surge through her body when Patrick was near made *friends* untenable. She just had to manage her feelings for the short time he was around and behave as the unofficial patient of a very handsome, charismatic doctor would. However difficult that would be.

'Is there something else on your mind?'

'No, my mind's still reeling from the news about Luca. You'll think I'm absurd if I keep asking questions…'

'Claudia, never apologise for asking questions. These are your babies and you have every right to have each and every question answered honestly and to ask it again and again if need be.'

Claudia drew breath and with a tremble in her voice continued, 'Why is only Luca affected?' As she spoke, she looked at Thomas and wondered if she had been told everything. Or if there was more she should know.

Patrick wanted so much to hold her close and comfort her. She was frightened and there was nothing as a professional he could do other than provide standard advice, albeit in an empathetic manner. For some inexplicable reason, he wanted to offer so much more but he couldn't. He had to veto the feelings that were stirring in him. And before he swept her into his arms and kissed her more passionately than he had ever kissed a woman before.

It wasn't going to be easy but he couldn't allow romantic thoughts to invade his mind and his heart. With his arms folded across his chest, he answered her. 'Dr Wilson isn't worried because Thomas doesn't have the condition now, so he can't ever have it. The opening between two major blood vessels leading from his heart closed naturally after birth. You need to understand that Thomas and Luca are fraternal twins so they are quite different developmentally in a number of ways. While they're twins, they're essentially just like any siblings so not all of their developmental conditions are going to be shared. Fortunately, this is one of them.'

Claudia was relieved to hear everything that Patrick was explaining and his calm bedside manner was alleviating her concerns. 'I have a non-identical twin sister,' she offered, as he watched her appear to relax a little. 'Harriet. She's the complete opposite of me. She's my rock. She's a nurse, quiet and sensible, always thinking about other people. We've been there for each other since our parents died nine years ago.'

'I'm sorry you lost your parents while you were still young.' Patrick had been an adult when he'd found himself alone so he could understand the overwhelming sadness that must have been Claudia's world when she lost her parents.

'It was just before our twentieth birthday, so we weren't that young, but we had been very protected, growing up in what was essentially a close-knit household. We grew up quickly. Harriet more so than me.'

'You're obviously close to her. Was there a reason that you didn't call her from the elevator yesterday?'

'She was on her way to Argentina. I wasn't sure if she was still in transit and I didn't want to worry her. I mean, there wasn't anything else she could have done except worry.'

'I suppose you're right. Have you spoken to her yet?'

he asked as he sat back in his chair a little and glanced over at Thomas and Luca, both still sleeping soundly. 'Does she know she's an aunt?'

'Oh, yes, I just called before the nurse brought me down here.'

A smile crossed Claudia's face. It was the first full smile that he had witnessed. And it made her even more beautiful, if that was possible.

'Of course,' she continued, unaware of the effect she was having on Patrick. 'And, in typical Harriet style, she wanted to rush here to be with me. Drop her life to rescue her big sister. I was born first so I'm older by three minutes but she always behaves like the older, far wiser sister.'

Patrick smiled. 'So she's on her way here then?'

'Absolutely not,' she said with an expression that told him she thought he should have known better. 'I wouldn't allow her to. She's working in an orphanage and I'm not going to have her alter her plans. I'll see her at home when she finishes her work over there in a few months.'

'So you lived together back in London?' he asked and then curiosity got the better of him. 'Were you on holiday here or a work exchange of sorts?'

Claudia went a little quiet and Patrick wondered if he had asked too many questions. Perhaps he'd been too intrusive.

'You know what, forget I asked. It's none of my business. I'm here to help answer any questions you have about your boys, not interview you.'

She paused before she spoke although she hadn't intended on opening up about the details of her past.

Looking at Patrick, she couldn't help but feel they had known each other for a long time. She had felt that way from the moment he'd taken off his sunglasses in the elevator and she had looked into his grey-blue eyes.

'My sister and I still share our family home. I came over here for work. I won an internship with a weekly drama series on a major network. It was a huge opportunity and I took it. Again, I jumped in with both feet like I always do,' she announced as she gently ran her finger over her tiny son's shoulder.

'I don't think jumping in is a bad idea. You experience all that life has to offer that way.'

'And some,' she muttered under her breath and felt a shiver of regret run down her body. 'Anyway, my contract is over so, as soon as the boys are strong enough, we will all head back to London. That's where I want to raise them,' she added, turning to look Patrick squarely in the eyes. 'And my leaving is something the boys' father does not object to… In fact, he is quite…' She stopped. There was no need for Patrick to know any more. 'Let's just say my leaving is not causing him any grief.'

'Well, then, we need to get them strong enough to travel.'

Patrick stayed with Claudia for another twenty minutes, then excused himself as he needed to get to his practice. He had an afternoon roster of new patients and a few post-operative.

'I'll leave you with your boys, but if you like I can call again over the next few days to check up on all of you.'

'I'd like that,' she said instinctively but the moment

the words passed over her lips she knew she shouldn't have given him that answer. It was opening them both up to the inevitable.

She now had a date with a potentially sad farewell looming on the horizon.

Claudia had spent two days sitting beside Thomas and Luca, praying for them to reach the next tiny milestone and, despite the rush of hormones after the birth, she was feeling better emotionally but physically exhausted. She had stroked both boys between their gavage feeds and she chatted with the nurses and doctors. The doctor had reassured her that Luca's condition was already showing improvement and he believed that within days they might be able to stop the ibuprofen.

She had also received a call from Harriet. Her sister wanted an update on her nephews but she seemed distracted. She hadn't been disinterested at all but there seemed to be something on her mind. Claudia put it down to the tireless work she must be undertaking at the orphanage. She had nothing but admiration for her sister and could hardly wait for Thomas and Luca to meet her.

After she hung up, she suddenly felt tired and a little sore as they had ceased the IV pain relief and she was just having four hourly tablets. She decided after dinner to stay in her room and have an early night and get up early to spend the next day down in the nursery. To her surprise and relief, she had been able to stay in her private room.

She had missed seeing Patrick the previous evening and during the day and wondered if she would ever see him again. Perhaps he had done his heroic act and then disappeared into the night, she thought. Her eyes drifted to the night lights of Los Angeles that she could see from her bed and she wondered where he was. Was he thinking about her and the boys?

While he had every right to be enjoying dinner or drinks with another woman, a crazy part of her felt jealous. Was he dining at an elegant Beverley Hills restaurant or somewhere swank in downtown LA? Was his stunning date enjoying his company, laughing at his anecdotes or just mesmerised by his stunning eyes?

Was the thought of the woman who had ruined his jacket and shirt the furthest thing from his mind?

Hesitant to overstretch, she gently moved her body to the edge of the bed so she could put her teacup back on the bedside cabinet. Then she eased back into a comfortable position and plumped up her pillow before she nestled under the covers. Thinking about Patrick and actually spending any time caring what he was doing at that time of the evening was ridiculous, she berated herself. And having flashbacks to the moment he'd removed his shirt in the elevator was borderline torturous since she knew they would never have a future together.

She looked up at the ceiling, wishing suddenly that her parents were alive to meet their grandsons. They would stroke their tiny cheeks and kiss them from morning to night and the boys would have loved their grandparents. If only they'd had the chance to meet them.

And how would her parents have reacted to Patrick? They would most certainly thank him for bringing Thomas and Luca into the world. Her father would shake his hand and then pull him into his strong embrace with a hearty laugh. Her mother would be a little more reserved but still tell him how grateful she was for what he had done in saving their precious grandchildren.

She felt a tear slip from her eye and onto the pillow.

Her heart ached for what she had lost, now more than ever.

Chapter 6

Patrick stood outside the door of Claudia's hospital room, trying to resist the temptation to knock. He wondered why he had returned. He had tried to stay away and had almost succeeded. But something drove him to see the gorgeous brunette.

Was there a man who still owned Claudia's heart? Despite alarm bells ringing, he knocked on the door. Why was he going against every rule he had followed for over a decade? Never get close to someone, never form a bond or risk his heart, never look for more than one night. His decision to become an island had been born of necessity and it had served him well. But that resolve had never been so tested as it was now. The idea of Claudia, Thomas and Luca featuring in his future was a recurring thought that haunted him.

His rejection of family and his family's rejection of him were combined in fighting his thoughts about Claudia and the boys. And Claudia and the boys were winning.

'I hope it's not too late. The nurse said you were still awake.'

It was a voice that the sensible part of Claudia's brain didn't want to hear but one that made her hopeless heart do a little dance. She wiped her eyes with the back of her hand and tried to pull herself up in the bed as Patrick walked into the room. He was dressed in dark clothing and he cut a ridiculously attractive figure. His trousers were black and he had a charcoal polo top and black leather shoes. His clothing highlighted his sun-kissed brown hair and light tan and the stubble that she imagined would be soft to her touch.

His appearance was intoxicating. He wasn't fighting fair, she thought. How was she supposed to keep her thoughts to doctor-patient when he looked so damn good?

'You shouldn't have come; it's so late and you probably have far more important places to be than here.' Her voice was crisp and it belied how truly happy she was to see him. She didn't want to need him the way she did. She didn't want to repeat the mistake of thinking she knew everything about a man, only to have her heart broken by what he was hiding.

But something about Patrick made her think he wasn't hiding anything.

Was he an exception to the rule?

* * *

Patrick looked into her eyes in the dim light of the room and searched for something.

He didn't find it immediately but he persisted and moved closer to the bed.

He saw her full lips curve into a smile. And her eyes were smiling too. He found what he was looking for. Despite what she was telling him, there was a welcome on her beautiful face. Part of him didn't want to see any warmth there. He normally chose women who weren't looking for the picket fence and happily ever after because he couldn't provide it.

With one look he was reminded of just how different she was and how he didn't want to walk away without knowing more about her.

'I'm sorry I couldn't be here earlier today or last night. I had patients until late and a surgical roster today that finished about an hour ago.' There was more he wasn't saying. He had forced himself to stay away. Tried to push thoughts of her from his mind and pretend that she hadn't crept under his skin.

He had no choice but to give in to his desire to see her.

'You know there's no obligation to come. You're a busy doctor and I suppose there are lots of women having babies.' She fussed with her bedclothes and averted her gaze as she spoke. She didn't want to fall into the warmth of his eyes.

He looked at her for a moment in silence with a curious expression.

'What is it?' she asked, sensing she had said something silly but not understanding why.

'I'm a doctor, Claudia, but I don't spend my days delivering babies.'

She shot him a puzzled look. 'What do you mean— are you a children's doctor, not an obstetrician?'

While he had not articulated his specialty during labour, with the risk of raising her anxiety level, she had obviously not read his business card.

'Do you still have the card I left you in case you needed to reach me?'

'Yes, it's in the cabinet. Why?'

Patrick crossed to the cabinet with long purposeful steps. 'May I?' he asked as he reached for the drawer.

She nodded. There was nothing personal in there.

'Here it is,' he announced, the small white card in his hand. 'You haven't read it, have you?'

Claudia shook her head. 'I had no reason to. I haven't called you.'

She put her hand out and he passed the card to her. Squinting in the soft lighting, she searched the card for his details and read the words aloud.

'Dr Patrick Spencer…cosmetic surgeon?' She collapsed back into her pillow in horror. Her arms instinctively folded across herself in an attempt to feel less vulnerable. There had to be some mistake. 'You're a plastic surgeon? You're not an obstetrician? Why didn't you tell me?'

Patrick shook his head and drew in a deep breath but, before he could begin to answer Claudia's questions, she asked more.

'Then…how did you know what to do—are you even qualified to deliver my babies?' Her voice was a little raised and equally shaky. She felt physically sick that she'd put her life and the lives of her babies in the hands of a cosmetic surgeon.

'I knew what to do because I'm a doctor.'

Claudia frowned. She felt exposed. 'Why didn't you mention that you were a cosmetic surgeon?' she asked, looking directly at him. She was angry that he hadn't told her. His announcement brought reality home. She really knew very little about Patrick and, except for the few words they'd exchanged, which had come mostly from her, he was like any man she could have passed in the street.

Only something inside had made her want to believe that he would not wilfully hurt her. *Had she done it again? Had she trusted someone at face value?*

Patrick rubbed his neck slowly and in silence. 'You need to listen to me for a minute.'

'I'm listening. Go ahead—explain why you never shared your real medical specialty with me when you were cutting free my underwear and examining me!'

Not needing to give his reply any thought because it was the truth, he answered her quickly. 'Because telling you might have sent you into a panic. The situation wasn't desirable, you were understandably anxious and the last thing you needed to hear was the man about to deliver your babies hadn't done so in over a decade. I was confident I could do it as well as anyone but you wouldn't have known that.'

'So you have delivered babies then?'

'Yes, I delivered babies many years ago and, to be honest, in the situation we were in two days ago, any-one sharing that elevator with you would have been sufficiently qualified to help. You could not have done it alone.'

With the bedclothes tucked up firmly around her like a shield, she continued. 'So these babies you delivered, were they during your training then?'

Patrick didn't want to go into too much detail but knew Claudia deserved more of an explanation. The boys were safe now but she needed to know that they had been safe the entire time. 'I was an obstetrician in the UK. I worked in the field for a number of years so that's why you and your boys were, all things considered, in safe hands.'

It made sense and it was logical but it still unsettled her. 'Why didn't you just tell me that?'

'Because it had been almost twelve years and I knew that it still would have heightened your fear. You would have worried that I might not have been competent. I knew I could do it but I couldn't spend my energy reassuring you of the fact.'

Claudia accepted his reasoning and even agreed in part but still…

Was there anything else he hadn't told her? Was there something else she should have known?

She fixed her eyes on him intently and decided to just ask. 'So why did you change profession? Why did you stop delivering babies?'

Patrick lowered his tall frame onto the chair beside her bed. He had never wanted to tell anyone anything about his past as much as he did Claudia at that moment. He wanted to be honest about what had transpired and the future that had been so unfairly taken from him, but he couldn't. It had been locked inside for too many years to bring it up. He had moved on and so had everyone else. He would have no idea even where to start and he was worried where it might end.

So telling Claudia made no sense, he thought. He shook his head. 'I needed a change of scenery and thought I would change my specialty at the same time.'

'So you just upped and moved countries so you could surgically create perfect noses and big...' She paused and looked down towards her breasts.

'Yes, I perform breast augmentations and facial enhancements,' he admitted. He was proud of the work he performed but it had never been his dream. Bringing children into the world had always been what he had wanted to do until he'd had to walk away.

'You said it was over a decade but when exactly did you deliver the last baby before Thomas and Luca?'

Patrick felt his jaw tense. He had made his mind up not to relive that painful time in his life, so made his answer brief. 'Twelve years ago next month and it was back in the UK...'

'Why did you give up?' Claudia interrupted him as she sought to uncover a little more detail. She sensed Patrick was perhaps not telling her the entire story. His story about leaving obstetrics in England to pick up cosmetic surgery in Los Angeles seemed to be missing a piece. What was his motivation for the change? She was curious about the handsome man beside her, whose subtle woody cologne was suddenly penetrating her senses.

'Like I said, time for a sea-change and a challenge.' He felt cornered. It wasn't a lie but it wasn't the entire story either. 'You need to know that I wanted only what was best for you in that elevator. Maybe I should have told you, maybe I was right in not telling you. We'll never know now.'

'I guess we won't.'

'You're an incredibly brave woman; I hope you know that.'

'I had limited choices.' Her mood was still pensive and his compliment didn't sit well. She had been deceived by the father of her children and, while this situation was different, it felt horribly similar. She didn't like the truth being hidden from her, no matter what it was.

'You're an amazingly resilient woman. You made a conscious choice to face adversity head-on,' he replied. In a perfect world he would open up to Claudia and let her into his past. But his world wasn't perfect. In a perfect world he would still be Dr Patrick Spencer, OBGYN in the Harley Street practice he had dreamt of opening. But if compensation for his years of disappointment came in the chance meeting with Claudia, and even if it only lasted a brief time, he felt at peace with that. She had a positivity and strength that he had never witnessed before and he felt in time he would be a better man just being around her.

Not that he would have much time.

Claudia had been let down once; he didn't want to be the second man to let her down. He wouldn't make any promises other than to enjoy the weeks until she left. To be someone she could depend on during those weeks.

A rock for her.

It all sounded so logical in his head but his body had different ideas and it took every ounce of willpower not to kiss her. Not to press his lips against hers and taste the sweetness he knew her mouth would hold.

Claudia Monticello was testing Patrick in a way he had never expected.

Claudia leant back against the pillows and felt her eyes becoming heavy.

Being close to him and reacting the way she did confused her. Looking at the curves of Patrick's handsome face in the soft lighting of her hospital room, she struggled with what she knew she had to do. What she wanted to do was to find any excuse to have him nearer to her. To feel the warmth of his breath on her face, smell the sweet muskiness of his cologne and wait expectantly for his mouth to claim hers.

But what she had to do was to push him away. She had to have learned something from her last disastrous relationship. She couldn't allow herself to develop feelings for Patrick, only to find herself disappointed again. This time she had her boys to consider. Becoming involved on any level with Patrick would be risky for everyone. Not to mention pointless. She was leaving soon anyway.

Patrick watched as Claudia seemed lost in thought. 'I should go.'

'I am a little tired,' she said, agreeing.

'Would you like me to call in to see you tomorrow?' he asked as he stood.

Claudia hesitated before she replied. She was torn. 'I'm not sure that's a good idea, Patrick,' she replied in a low voice.

'I really am sorry that I didn't tell you everything

outright but there was nothing self-serving about what I did, I can assure you of that.'

'It's not that.'

'Then what is it?'

'There's no point to this…to…you and me…' She stumbled over her words, unsure of how to define a relationship she didn't understand. And one that scared her.

'To me visiting you when you have no one else in the country because your only family is the other side of the world?'

'It's not that, it's just that I don't really know you and…'

'We shared a life-changing experience and, quite apart from that, I enjoy your company. It doesn't have to become complicated.' Patrick knew that wasn't entirely true. Just being near her was driving him to want more.

'I'll always be grateful for what you did, saving my boys and myself, but I'll be returning to London soon. And there's no need for you to keep me company when you have your own life.' She paused for a moment to cement the resolve in her mind. To make sure that she was doing the right thing. To remind herself that no good would come from stringing out the inevitable. Nor could she become involved on any level with a man who hid the truth, no matter how seemingly insignificant it might appear or whatever logical reason he could provide. It was a shaky point to hang her argument on, but it was all she had and she would use it.

She had to try to be more sensible like Harriet and less impetuous. And it had to start then and there. There was no time to rethink.

'You should find a nice young woman who lives in

Los Angeles. Remember I have two little boys and you don't want children. You told me as much in the lift.'

'Whoa, slow down,' he said. 'You're thinking way too far ahead.'

Claudia smiled at his response. 'I have to, Patrick. I have my sons to consider.'

'And I would always consider your children. I helped bring them into the world and they are special little men. I couldn't forget about them.' It was the truth. Patrick's feelings for Claudia and her sons had grown very real. And his desire for her was equally real. 'Can you just let this play out and see what might happen?'

'No...' She drew a breath. Whilst it was lovely to know how he felt, it didn't change what she had to do. She needed to look after her boys and forget about romance. It wouldn't be in the cards for her now or anytime in the near future and he was making her feel that it could be. And *should* be.

She had to cut him free and remove any risk of her becoming attached.

'I'm sorry, Patrick, but I think it's for the best if we say goodbye tonight...for good.'

Chapter 7

Patrick walked into his house, feeling more alone than before he'd met Claudia. He dropped his keys by the door and decided to take a shower and try to forget her. Put everything in perspective and move on.

As he lay in his bed, looking up at the ceiling in a room lit only by the moonlight, he wondered why he cared so much.

He didn't want a future. Or a family. She was being sensible and clearly he wasn't. For the first time in more years than he could remember, he had allowed his heart to lead him.

And his desire to kiss the woman whose face would not leave his mind that night.

He had so many questions he'd wanted to ask Claudia but he hadn't. Perhaps that was where he had gone wrong, he thought as he tossed again, throwing the bedclothes free of his body, dressed only in boxer shorts. If he knew more about Claudia he might better understand her need to push him away. She had obviously been hurt by someone.

He ran his fingers through his still damp hair and looked towards the bay window of his bedroom and the full moon suspended in the clear night sky and knew it had to have been Thomas and Luca's father who had broken her heart. She had put on a brave face when she had spoken of him having no interest in his sons but there had to be more to it. Walking away from the boys' father or watching him walk away surely wouldn't have been easy for a woman like Claudia. Her family values seemed so strong.

In that case, the man who'd fathered her children must have made her fearful of getting close to anyone. But why, he wondered, would any man treat a woman that way? It didn't make sense in the way he saw the world. A man should protect a woman, and particularly the mother of his children. He should lay his life down for her and his sons.

That was what Patrick knew in his heart he would do if he had been Thomas and Luca's father.

After a restless night and the acceptance that Claudia wanted to be alone, Patrick knew he had to keep a distance between them. But there was one last thing he intended to do. He would visit Thomas and Luca one final time to say goodbye. Even though they would never remember him, he would never forget them.

And he would always remember their mother too.

* * *

Claudia showered and changed into the silk night-dress and wrap. As the cool softness of the fabric fell against her skin, Claudia wondered who had been so kind yet secretive in gifting them to her. Could it even have been Patrick? She shook the thought from her mind. He couldn't have known she needed a night-dress and he'd had no time to go shopping as he had been spending all of his spare time with her. Running a soft brush through her hair, she looked in the mirror and thought it was definitely the prettiest nightdress she had ever seen, let alone worn.

And, as soon as she could, she would be contacting the store to find a way to repay them.

Claudia was feeling physically stronger by the day but emotionally drained. Insisting a man like Patrick leave her had been a choice she hoped not to regret but one she had an uneasy feeling that she just might. But she wasn't prepared to take the risk that she might be hurt again. Not any more.

The man made her feel butterflies in her stomach whenever he was near. Dropping the brush onto the bedside cabinet, she wondered what on earth had come over her. If she didn't know better, she would think that she had developed a crush on Patrick.

'Thank goodness, he's left your life,' she muttered to herself as she put the brush into her handbag and waited on the bed for her breakfast. She could hear the clang-ing of the metal plate covers as the trays were being delivered in the adjacent rooms.

'Here's yours, sweetie,' the food service worker said, bringing the tray into her room. He was an older man of African-American heritage, and he'd served her dinner the evening before. He'd been quite chatty then too.

'Thank you very much.'

'You're looking happy this morning. Any reason?' he asked, a curious smile on his time-weathered but cheerful face. 'I hope it's contagious 'cos there's some biddies on this floor that don't smile near enough for me. It's like they drink vinegar not tomato juice!' His smile wrinkled the skin around his warm brown eyes.

Claudia laughed at his words. 'I'm just looking forward to seeing my sons in the nursery as soon as I've had breakfast. The head nurse insists I eat before I'm allowed to travel downstairs so I'll eat quickly and get back down there.'

'They are very lucky little boys to have you as their mother,' he said before he left the room.

Claudia felt a lump form in her throat. That was exactly what Patrick had said when they'd met in the elevator. He had given her the same compliment and she had spat back at him something acerbic. She couldn't remember exactly but she knew it had been rude and uncalled for. She felt ashamed. Had she pushed him away unnecessarily? Had she overreacted yet again?

She also felt terribly confused. How could those few words from a friendly old man bring her emotions back to a level of chaos?

What was happening to her? Was Patrick already inside her heart and that was why the words hit home? She took the first bite of her toast and then dropped it on the plate and slumped back in her bed.

Patrick arrived at the hospital a little after eight. The heaviness in the warm morning air set the tone for the day. He had been gutted by Claudia's hasty and unexpected dismissal and had no choice but to accept he wouldn't see her again. But he would see the boys one last time.

The first patient at his private practice was scheduled for nine-thirty so he had plenty of time to visit Thomas and Luca and then head to his surgery near the corner of Rodeo Drive and Santa Monica Boulevard. He had been practicing in the ultra-modern office building for almost seven years and had no need to advertise as the post-operative faces and bodies willing to admit to having been his patients were testament to his skills. As were those people who wanted further freshening up over the years. However, he did set a limit and directed those who he suspected of addiction to cosmetic procedures to a therapist who was better placed to address their issues with body image.

The waiting list for a consultation and surgical procedures was growing but his passion for his work was not. He was dedicated and skilled but not excited. He missed that sense of excitement. The delivery in the elevator had been everything he missed about his former profession…and more.

Patrick strolled into the nursery and spoke with the attending neonatologist about the boys.

'So Luca has improved? How is the closure of PDA progressing?'

'It's looking good.' The doctor nodded as he continued to read Luca's notes on the computer screen. 'I think we'll be able to cease the medication in a day or so.'

Patrick's mouth curved to a smile as he looked at the tiny infant, dressed only in a nappy and pale blue booties that had been kindly knitted by the Mercy Hospital Women's Auxiliary.

'And Thomas? Is he still progressing?'

The doctor nodded again. 'Yes, no major problems with Thomas. There's a few milestones to reach yet, including weight gain for both of them, before they'll be discharged but they're going from strength to strength.'

'Great to hear.'

'I'll leave you to visit with them,' the doctor said and walked away to attend to another tiny patient.

Patrick stood watching over both boys. It had been three days since their birth. Three days since he had met their wonderful mother. He wondered what their future would hold on the other side of the world and knew if things were different that he would ask if he could visit. Travel over to London and spend some time with them—and with Claudia. But that couldn't happen. He would never visit that city again.

He stayed longer than he had planned; being with them was a joy to him that was unexpected but welcome. Finally he stroked their tiny foreheads and turned to leave.

'What are you doing here?'

Patrick's gaze lifted to see Claudia staring at him. He couldn't read her expression.

'I came to say a final goodbye to the boys. You made it clear that you didn't want to see me again so I thought I'd call in and check up on them for one last time and leave. I didn't mean to stay as long as I did. I won't intrude again.'

Claudia looked closely at the man standing next to her sons. He had been watching them the way a father should look at his children. She knew their father would never do that. She had noticed the gentle way Patrick had stroked their little faces. They would never feel that love from the man who had requested she sign a confidentiality form and not mention his *involvement*.

Claudia wasn't sure if she was doing the logical thing but it suddenly felt right. At least it felt right for the next few weeks.

'Please, Patrick, you can sit a while longer if you like.'

Patrick did just that and then did it again every day for the next four days. Just after breakfast and before his day began, he travelled to the Mercy Hospital to sit with the boys and with Claudia. He still knew little about her past but whatever had happened had made her the woman she was and that was all he needed to know. Just being around her made him feel alive.

Could he possibly feel more? Could he take a chance of being a part of their little family? He wasn't convinced he would ever be ready but Claudia had made him want to believe it was possible. He tried to ignore the simple truth that his happiness would be short-lived, with her imminent return passage to London. Instead he enjoyed every moment he spent with her and refused to question the reality of what they shared and for how long it might last.

Claudia needed to stay until Thomas and Luca were discharged and that would give them even more time to get to know each other better. Perhaps if things went well she might extend her stay. He knew he was being hopeful but nothing about their meeting in the first place had been straightforward. Perhaps fate would intervene again.

Patrick smiled as he scrubbed and entered the nursery. Claudia was already with the boys and he couldn't help but let a grin spread wide across his face as he approached the three of them.

'How's my two favourite little men and their mother this morning?'

Claudia looked up at him from where she sat holding Thomas. 'We are all very well, thank you. In fact the doctor said the boys could be released before their due date. They might be ready to go home in four weeks.'

'That's great news,' Patrick said, feeling a little deflated that the three of them would potentially be leaving his life. Although he was thrilled to hear that Thomas and Luca were progressing so well, it also dashed his hopes that something might develop between Claudia and himself. All they had now were the next four weeks. He just had to make the most of every minute.

'I have a small confession,' he said one morning as they took a walk around the hospital gardens for fresh air after visiting Thomas and Luca in the nursery. Claudia was to be released the next day and he doubted they would see much of each other after that.

'What?' she asked, feeling very relaxed in his company and equally not wanting their time together to end.

'I'm very sorry that you gave birth in the lift and all that you and the boys have been through, but I'm not sorry that you shared *my* lift that day.'

Claudia felt her heart flutter but she knew she should fight her desire to make more of it than it was. Patrick lived in LA and she was heading back to London. She had to put their relationship in context. This feeling would not lead to more. No matter what her heart was trying to tell her head.

'I'm exceptionally glad I shared *your* lift,' she said lightly, patting his arm. 'If I'd shared a lift with a pizza delivery boy none of us might have survived…or at the very least the pizza boy would have been scarred for life.'

'Pizza boys do have to deliver under pressure, so that the pizza's still hot. He might have coped.'

'Now you're being silly,' she said.

Claudia turned to see the look in his eyes. His expression was serious. Almost a little brooding.

He took her hand to draw her in. 'I mean it, Claudia. I'm glad I was there. But not just because I could help deliver your sons. I'm very glad I met you.'

Claudia couldn't agree more but she couldn't tell him that. She felt her stomach fill with butterflies at the tone in his voice, the intensity in his eyes and the feeling of his hand against her skin. It was soft and warm and it pierced through all of her defences but she didn't want to give in to how she was feeling. She didn't want to get hurt again. She had to make him believe that she saw nothing between them when in fact she thought she was close to falling hopelessly in love with him.

They arrived back at the entry door to the nursery. They both stepped back as a nurse entered and collided softly with each other. Claudia felt the warmth of Patrick's firm body against hers. A tingling sensation overtook her entire body and it took a few seconds to calm herself. She closed her eyes for a moment, not trusting herself to turn and look up into his eyes so close. As she turned tentatively to face him, his lips hovered only inches from hers and she wanted nothing more than to lean in to him a little longer.

But she couldn't. She had to put a stop to any hint of her feelings. She was leaving the hospital. She had leased an apartment the other side of town and, while it had been wonderful with Patrick visiting every day and demystifying everything medical that was happening with the boys and being there when they'd both been transferred to the nursery on day six, she had to face the rest on her own.

She would be happy if Patrick continued visiting her sons but she needed to stop fantasising about what might be between them. Nothing could become of them because she couldn't stay and explore that possibility. She belonged back in London with her only other family—her sister. She didn't want to be on the other side of the world in this city where—apart from with Patrick—she'd experienced little kindness. Her boys deserved a clean start in life and so did she. While Patrick seemed so very perfect, he was also perfectly settled in LA.

She couldn't tell all of that to Patrick. She would rather he didn't know the sordid story about Stone and hoped he would think of her fondly after she left. She had reminded herself of that every night as she lay alone in her hospital bed, wondering how it would feel with his strong arm around her. Or imagining the softness of his lips against hers when she woke in the middle of the night and all she could think of was him.

She waited until they were alone and Patrick had

taken a seat beside the bed. 'There's something I need to say.'

'I'm all ears,' he told her as he stretched out his long legs and leant back in the chair.

'It's just that I'm leaving the hospital tomorrow so I guess this is the last morning we'll be spending together.'

He sat up, pulling his legs underneath the chair. 'You're leaving the hospital, not the country, Claudia. There's no need to make it sound so final.'

'It is final,' she replied. 'I've leased a place for a month...'

'You've found a place? I could have helped you out,' he said, cutting in, a little surprised that she had found somewhere to live without mentioning it before then. He'd planned on helping her to secure somewhere or even offering a room in his own home. It was far too big for one person and he would have been happy for her to take the guest room. But it was too late.

'I think you've been too gracious in offering help so I did this alone. I found a realtor and he secured a home for me. It's a little bit further out of town but it will be fine for the next few weeks.'

Patrick could sense her need for independence so he backed off.

'I'll more than likely be visiting the boys during the day and you'll be at your practice or operating so we might not bump into each other. That's all. But I'm happy for you to call in and see the boys if you like. They smile whenever you're around.'

'I don't think they recognise me quite yet; I think

it's more likely wind but I'd like to continue to keep an eye on them.'

Claudia laughed. 'That means so much to me.'

'And you mean so much to me.' As soon as he'd said it, he knew it was too soon. But it felt natural and he didn't regret telling her.

'Please, don't. You don't know me. Not really.'

'I'd say, after what we shared, we know each other very well. We survived the most stressful situation. Surely we share a special bond.'

Claudia wished her world was different. But it wasn't.

'You're a good man, Patrick, but we can't be more than friends.'

Patrick reached for her hands and he wasn't deterred when she pulled away this time. He reached further until he had them firmly inside the warmth and protection of his own. 'We can be anything you want us to be while you are here.'

That was just it. It would only be while she was in LA. *Then what?* Claudia felt tears welling in her eyes and she couldn't blame it on hormones. Her heart was breaking just a little.

'I enjoy spending time with you,' he continued. 'There—I said it. I'm not promising anything, any more than you are. We are two expats on the other side of the world who happen to enjoy each other's company. Unless you don't enjoy my company?'

She took a deep breath. 'Of course I enjoy your company. I enjoy your company very much, but…'

'There are no buts from where I'm standing.'

'You're not making this easy.'

'No, I'm not. I think you're amazing and I think that

it would be stupid to say goodbye tonight when you will be in the same city as me for the next four weeks, maybe more.'

'It seems a little pointless…'

'I disagree.' He paused over the words. 'I think we should continue to enjoy each other's company until you have to leave.'

Patrick knew that their relationship, whatever it might be, would have to end. He would never set foot back in the UK for reasons that he couldn't bring himself to share. His family were there and he couldn't see them again. Not after what had happened. In his mind it was better for everyone concerned for him to forget he'd once had a family.

'How are you getting to your new home tomorrow?'

'A cab,' she quickly replied.

'How about I take you? Absolutely no strings attached to my offer,' he continued with even greater speed. 'I'm operating in the afternoon. So I have the morning free to pick you up and settle you in. It's your choice, a smelly cab or chauffeur driven by me?'

Claudia felt her lips curving to a smile. He wasn't giving up. 'Not all LA cabs are smelly.'

'Not all…but why take the chance?'

She shook her head a little with frustration. Why did he have to be so handsome, so charming and so persistent? 'Okay…thank you.' There were a hundred things she could have said and each one would have been closer to how she was feeling but she couldn't allow herself that luxury.

'I'll see you back here in the morning,' he told her as he walked away.

Claudia offered him a smile as she wondered what she had let herself in for. And that thought played on her mind all through the night.

Chapter 8

Patrick arrived mid-morning, just as he had promised. He knocked on her door.

'Anyone here needing a smelly cab?'

'Come in,' she replied, still feeling apprehensive about spending time together away from the hospital. It became a little more frightening to be in the real world with Patrick. 'I'm nearly ready. I spent a bit more time in the nursery with Thomas and Luca as I wasn't sure if I would be back again today until late.'

'No need to rush,' he told her. 'The meter's not running.'

She came out of her tiny bathroom with a few toiletries and, as always, her breath was taken away. He looked gorgeous and she felt sure his smile could melt an iceberg. She dropped the things into her oversized handbag and went back in to brush her hair.

'The address is on the bed,' she called out. 'I wrote it down on a scrap of paper.'

Patrick crossed to the end of the bed and picked up the paper. As soon as he read the address he shook his head. It was not a good part of town. In fact, it was straight out unsafe and, despite his resolve to respect her boundaries, he couldn't let her unknowingly put herself at risk. He decided not to say anything until she had seen it first-hand. It might not be as bad as he suspected. Her independence was akin to stubbornness, and he hoped once she had seen the location she would change her mind. He typed the address into his telephone so he could get the directions. He knew the general direction but it wasn't a part of town he frequented so he would need the GPS to find the street. He waited until she emerged in a pretty sky-blue sundress. It skimmed her knees and against her porcelain skin it looked, in his opinion, stunning.

'You look beautiful, as always.'

'Thank you,' she replied with a smile.

'Shall we go?' he asked as he picked up her bag and headed for the door.

'What about the account?' Claudia asked at Administration.

The young assistant flicked through the paperwork and then checked the computer screen. 'It's all been taken care of.'

'Are you sure?'

'Yes, your insurance company has covered you. Your sons' accounts will not be due until they leave the hospital in a few weeks' time, according to the notes.'

Claudia was relieved to hear that and Patrick was

relieved she didn't ask any more questions about the insurance. His lawyer had contacted the international carrier and worked out an arrangement so that Claudia had no out of pocket expenses. But, with all the uncertainty between them, he didn't want her knowing he had stepped in to help.

They drove along with the top down on his sports car. The fresh air felt good after so long in the hospital air-conditioning. They talked about the boys and a little about Patrick's surgical roster for the afternoon and the time went quickly. As they drew closer to the street, Claudia began nervously chewing the inside of her cheek. The suburb was not what she had expected.

Finally they pulled up outside a run-down semi-detached house. It was worse than Patrick had thought it would be. He suspected a cab driver would have dropped her off without so much as a second thought so he was glad that he had insisted on taking her there. The two foot high wire fence was rusted and missing a gate and the front yard was devoid of any plants or lawn, save for the weeds that had made their way through the broken concrete. He looked over at Claudia and, while he could see her expression had dropped, she said nothing as she released her seat belt.

'You don't have to go in, you know that,' he told her.

'Don't be silly. I've given the realtor a deposit and I'm moving in today. The shell's a little worn, but I'm sure it's probably lovely inside. Besides, I'm not buying the property, I'm only renting it for a month.'

Patrick remained silent but he felt a chill run through him as they walked up the cracked pavement to the faded teal-blue house that looked as if it had not been loved in many years. Perhaps many decades. The wire screen on the security door was torn and would be useless in providing any level of security.

He watched as Claudia took the key she had been given by the realtor and, pulling back the screen door, unlocked the wooden front door and stepped inside. He followed closely, pausing for a moment to look over his shoulder at the neighbouring properties as he did. It was not a good part of town.

The house was quite dark inside for the time of day. Claudia reached for the light switch but nothing happened. They both looked up in the poor light to see the globe was missing from the hallway. An electrical cord was hanging down from the ceiling but there was no light fitting.

'I can get a new one,' she said as she made her way down to the brightest room at the end of the short corridor, which turned out to be the kitchen and was equally well worn. The floor was covered in pale green linoleum and it was almost bare, torn in more than a few places and lifting by the back door. There was a small table and two chairs but the wicker weaving was unravelling on one of the chairs, rendering it useless. The refrigerator motor was rattling and the back window looked out onto a car-wreckers' yard. There were no curtains or blinds and the hotplates on the stove were coated with years of burnt grime.

'It's only for a few weeks until the boys are ready to travel home. It's not as if I'd be bringing them here. It will just be me.'

Patrick remained silent, but he arched one eyebrow

as he followed her into the bathroom. The shower was over a bath stained with rust where the water had been dripping from the tap and running down towards the drain. And the shower curtain was missing. The mirror on the cabinet above the basin was cracked and blackened in places by mildew. There was a small window of smoky glass for privacy but it too was cracked and Patrick suspected that with very little force the window would break completely.

'Let's see the bedroom,' Claudia announced, swallowing hard and trying to sound optimistic as she made her way into the larger of the two bedrooms. There was a double bed but no bedhead and a blue nylon bedspread with a faded floral pattern that couldn't mask the dip in the mattress. A free-standing oak stained wardrobe that had one door slightly ajar stood by the window. The dirty cream-coloured net curtains covering a stained blind sagged where they were missing hooks. Claudia crossed the dark brown shaggy-carpeted floor to close the wardrobe door and discovered that the handle was broken. 'I'll be living out of my suitcase anyway so the door doesn't matter. I'm not about to be picky,' she said.

'Claudia,' Patrick began in a serious tone, 'you can't be considering living here.'

'Of course I am. I backpacked around Europe in my late teens. It'll be an adventure just like that,' she replied as she walked towards the front door, noticing there were holes in the plasterboard that looked as if someone had put their foot through the wall. 'Shall we get my suitcase so I can settle in and you can get back to the hospital? I know you have surgery this afternoon.'

'So you're moving in?'

'Yes.'

'Then I'm moving in too; we'll be house mates. I backpacked around Europe in my late teens too, so I'll share the adventure with you,' he announced. 'Let's go take a peek at my room. I hope it's as nice as yours.'

'You're not living here; that's ridiculous.'

'And you don't think you living here is ridiculous?'

'No, that's different.'

'Not in my opinion. If you move in, then we'll do it together and both risk our lives and general wellbeing!'

Claudia shook her head and narrowed her eyes at him before she walked across the narrow passageway behind Patrick to the darkened room. Reaching for the light switch, Patrick discovered it didn't work so he used the light of his phone to see the room. It was smaller and there was a single bed and what looked like a grey chest of drawers. He walked across to the window and lifted the blind to allow them to see the room properly. It took him three attempts to lift the damaged blind but when he did he could see another short electrical cable hanging down from the ceiling. There was no light fitting and again the globe was missing.

'Looks like we both need light bulbs when we head to the store.' He patted the bed, not daring to think about how many years the faded orange bedspread had gone without washing. It was stained and frayed in places along the hemline. Then he noticed the chest of drawers was actually a filing cabinet and he walked over and pulled open the top drawer. 'Great, I can keep some of my patient files in here to work on in the evenings.'

'Don't be awful. You're teasing me now.'

'Not at all. If it's good enough for you, then it's good enough for me.'

'You're being stupid. You don't need to babysit me.'

'I'm not thinking of babysitting. In this part of town my role would be more bodyguard.'

Claudia put her hands on her hips and shook her head. 'It's not that bad. I used to drive through here on the way to the studio every day. I never saw anything untoward happen.'

'And what time was this exactly?'

'What do you mean?'

'I mean did you drive through this street after dark?'

Claudia thought back. 'Not dark but early evening and early morning.'

'Then you and I will spend one night here together and if everything is fine then we'll discuss it again but I think you'll find that after the sun goes down this isn't a nice place to live. There are gangs in adjacent areas.'

'I have an idea. Why don't I ask a neighbour, or the business out the back? They'll tell me what it's really like.'

Patrick ran his long fingers through his hair in exasperation. Claudia was as stubborn as she was beautiful and intelligent. 'Let's ask, but if you get the answer I expect then I hope you agree we should just leave.'

Claudia didn't agree to anything. She showed no emotion as they walked out of the house and along the sidewalk beside the fence to where they found the owner of the wrecking yard locking up for the day. He was pulling the tall wire fence closed and securing it with a heavy padlock. Claudia picked up speed so he didn't leave before she had a chance to speak with him.

'Excuse me,' she called out. 'I'm wondering if you could tell me a little about the area. I'm thinking about renting the house that backs onto your property.'

Patrick watched as the man's face fell.

'Listen, lady, do you see the two dogs over there?'

'Yes,' Claudia answered, looking at the two heavy-set black guard dogs that were chafing at the bit, waiting for their owner's signal to begin patrolling the yard.

'They're not here for their good looks. There's not enough money in the world to make me live in this neighbourhood.' He tapped his watch with his grubby fingernail. 'Three o'clock every day I'm outta here. I've got some clients that look after the yard, if you know what I mean. I work on their cars and they make sure that my yard and my dogs are still here in the morning.'

'Perhaps the dogs will look after me too. They'll scare away anyone who thought to break into my place.'

'Not a chance unless you want to live in my office. Sorry, miss, but you're on your own if you move into that house. You'd be dead crazy if you did.' He signalled to the dogs before he climbed into his utility and drove away. Immediately the dogs rushed towards the wire fence, gnashing their teeth and making Claudia jump back nervously.

'So do you think you need a second opinion or can we leave now and find you other accommodation? Unless you want to wait and ask a not so friendly gang member his opinion.'

'Okay, I get it. I suppose you may have a point,' she said with a decidedly sheepish look upon her face.

'May have?'

'Fine, the man confirmed your suspicions about the

suburb. And I concede the house is not as nice as the realtor described on the phone. I can't believe he lied to me.'

Patrick didn't comment. There was nothing he needed to add except to ask her to get into his car while he locked up the house.

A few minutes later they were on the freeway and heading towards Beverly Hills. 'I'll only stop at your home long enough to make some calls and secure another short-term rental,' she told him. 'I can make a reservation in a hotel tonight if necessary.'

'Whatever you think is best, but my home is big enough for both of us.'

'Thank you, Patrick, but I won't get too comfortable. I'll be leaving in a few hours.'

It was only ten minutes on Freeway 405 and then three miles on Wilshire Boulevard before Patrick turned into a street lined with towering palms. The sweeping grounds of each of the palatial homes was perfectly manicured, and small gardeners' vans were dotted along the street with men in wide-brimmed hats busily planting and trimming the gardens. They drove a little way to a slight bend in the road and then slowed. Heavy black electric gates slowly opened and Patrick drove the car inside and the gates closed behind them.

He drove the car up the driveway to the front door of the double-storey white stucco mansion he had called home for two years. The property also boasted a tennis court, a heated swimming pool, spa and a four-car garage but Patrick didn't mention any of it. Cosmetic surgery had been kind to him, he admitted, but equally he had worked hard in his new field and had been recognised as one of the best by Hollywood's very particular clientele.

He helped Claudia out of the car and then opened the front door. 'Please go in; I'll get your bag.'

'I won't be staying,' she reminded him. 'Perhaps you should leave my things in the trunk.'

He smiled to himself. He wondered again if she had always been that fiercely independent or had circumstance made her that way? But, whatever the case, he understood she had every right to want to make her own decisions. He just hoped they didn't include another dubious choice of realtor.

'I'll get your belongings in case there's anything you need.'

Claudia spun on her heel to take in the magnificent surroundings. The foyer had a large atrium with a stone water feature. The sound of running water echoed in the large open space. Looking past that to outside, she could see more gently moving water. It was, she assumed, an endless pool and a panorama of the Hollywood Hills formed a backdrop.

'I will let you find your way around. The guest bedroom is on the ground floor, third door on the left, if you'd like to have a shower or a lie down. It might do you good to rest for a while. I can take you back to the hospital to visit the boys this evening.'

'You're being too kind. And too generous. It's unnecessary, honestly.'

'Claudia, it's a big house. I live here all alone and you're most welcome to stay here until you leave. I'd rather you were here than making *friends* in that neighbourhood! And, by the way, never recommend that realtor unless you really dislike someone,' he said with a wink before he closed the door and left her alone.

Claudia was more confused than she had ever been in her life.

The most handsome, kind, considerate man wanted her to live with him. She owed her life to him. And she wanted to be with him more than anything, but she couldn't. He had made it obvious he had feelings, not only by opening his home but also the way he kept reaching for her. But she wasn't ready to take that leap of faith and trust again. He was a kind man and as much as she wished he was the father of her sons, he wasn't. And she couldn't risk them all falling in love with Patrick. What if he walked out one day— the way that the boys' father had done? And turned her life upside down.

She had to be sensible and see the world the way Harriet would. Put a practical filter across her decisions and stop being led by her heart.

Certain and confused in equal amounts, she found her way to the guest bedroom and, kicking off her shoes, she sat on the bed. She suddenly felt a little tired and the bed felt very soft and comfortable so she thought she might just lie down for a moment. She told herself that she wouldn't fall asleep but just close her eyes for a moment, then she would call another realtor and find another short-term lease. And that night she would stay in a hotel.

Patrick came home to a darkened house but in the light from the porch he could see Claudia's suitcase still lying against the wall in the hallway. He turned on the lamp in the living room, unsure if she was at home or had caught a cab to the hospital. Quietly, he walked through his home and found her asleep on the bed. While it was still warm outside, the air-conditioning had kept the house cool and she was wearing a thin sundress so he pulled the throw rug up over her and closed the door. She was exhausted and he had no intention of waking her so he put a call through to the hospital to check on the boys. His call was connected to the neonatal resident.

'Dr Spencer, I've just finished reading the boys' notes for today. I did try to call Miss Monticello but had no luck getting through.'

'It was a big day for Claudia and she's taking a nap now so that's why I've called. I will pass any updates on to her.'

'Thomas is still progressing well, as he did from day one, and Luca's PDA appears to be self-correcting. He'll be having another echocardiogram tomorrow but Dr Wilson is confident no further treatment will be required. So please let Miss Monticello continue to rest. She can come in the morning to see them. Both boys are asleep and will have their gavage feed in another two hours. There's no need for Miss Monticello to be here when the rest would do her more good.'

Patrick thanked the young doctor and hung up the telephone before he ran upstairs to change into shorts and a T-shirt. He would take a dip in the pool later but first he would cook some dinner for the two of them. He knew it was stupid to think there would be anything between them after the next few weeks but she was getting under his skin and he couldn't deny it.

For some inexplicable reason, he didn't want to let the dim future get in the way of a happy few weeks.

Life was short and so he intended to enjoy whatever time he could with her. She challenged him and just being around her made him feel alive. Her accent and her very British mannerisms surprisingly made him think almost fondly of London and even fleetingly of his family. And, in a deep dark corner of his mind, he thought perhaps there was a chance, however slight, that she could change her mind and stay in the US.

Claudia woke to the smell of cooking. Her eyes struggled to focus and for a moment she forgot where she was until suddenly it came back to her. She had lain down for a moment in Patrick's guest room. It was dark but she could feel the light weight of a throw rug over her. She didn't remember pulling it up so assumed Patrick must have returned home and covered her. The curtains were billowing with the cool evening breeze and there was light creeping under the now closed bedroom door.

Suddenly she sat bolt upright. She hadn't called a realtor. She reached for her phone and discovered it was after six, in fact closer to seven.

'Darn, bother, you silly cow,' she said as she rubbed her forehead and silently continued berating herself for falling asleep. Now she would have to find a hotel as soon as she had visited Thomas and Luca. She swung her legs down and felt around for her shoes before she headed in the direction of the light. She would thank Patrick for his hospitality and get a cab to a hotel, check in with her bags and then head straight to the Mercy.

There was no way she could accept his hospitality. Their relationship had already overstepped the boundaries of common sense.

Moments later, Claudia stood in the doorway to the kitchen, watching Patrick stirring something that smelt delicious on the stovetop. Suddenly her heart felt lighter. But her head felt terribly confused. He turned to see her watching him and she felt very self-conscious. A tingling sensation crept up her neck and onto her face and she felt certain the blush had spread across her cheeks.

'Well, hello sleepy-head. Did you have a nice nap?'

His eyes twinkled as he spoke and she tried to ignore her increased heartbeat.

'I did, thank you, but you should've woken me. I slept for far too long. I need to get to a hotel and then see the boys.'

He lowered the heat underneath the pan and turned around to face her. He was wearing a tight white T-shirt and cargo shorts. His toned physique was cutting through both. His feet were tanned and bare on the large terracotta tiles.

'I've checked on Thomas and Luca and they are both doing very well. They were sleeping when I called but,' he said, glancing at the roman numerals of the large wall clock and then back to Claudia, 'they will have been fed again and should be tucked in again for another four hours or so.'

'I should have been there for that feed.' She was angry and disappointed in herself. She was convinced her boys needed her more than she needed sleep.

As if he sensed her self-reproach, he added firmly, 'You can't do everything, Claudia. The rest you had this afternoon was important. In fact, I told the neonatal unit that you wouldn't be back to visit the boys until tomorrow.'

Claudia was taken aback by his announcement and she felt her body tense. 'Why would you say that to them without asking me? Whether I see my sons or not is not your decision to make.'

'Well, in my capacity as a doctor it is. You need to get your own strength back, as I have said to you more than a few times. You'll be no good to your sons if you run yourself into the ground the first day out of hospital.'

'But I want to be with them.'

He shook his head and turned back to the stove. While he admired her strength, he found her stubbornness in ignoring her own wellbeing frustrating.

'I'm all they have in the world.'

There it was again. Her reference to Thomas and Luca having no one but her.

Patrick nodded his understanding of her need to be with them but he wanted to at least get some food into her so she could keep up her strength. 'Then I'll take you there after dinner.'

'There's no need for you to take me. I can do it after I book into a hotel.' Her arms were crossed across her chest and her eyes were narrowed.

'Claudia, I know you have a need for independence above all else, but you have to look after yourself. And since you don't seem to understand the importance of taking care of yourself I'm more than happy to step up to do the job.'

'I'm perfectly capable of looking after myself and my boys on my own. I'll be doing that when I return to

London in a few weeks.' She felt her neck tense with the thought of depending on any man again.

Her words cut through him like a knife. He wasn't sure if that was her intention but, if it was, she had succeeded.

'Point made,' he replied as he returned to the task at hand. Listening to his heart had been something he'd successfully avoided for many years and it appeared, from Claudia's reaction, it was something he needed to continue avoiding.

Disappointment suddenly coloured his mood. The heat was still under the large pan of boiling water so he dropped in the fresh pasta. 'If you want to share dinner before you grab a cab then you're welcome. If not, then I can help you out with your bag when the cab arrives.'

Claudia looked at him as he turned his attention back to preparing dinner and wished they had met under different circumstances. Before she had been so badly hurt and disillusioned. He appeared to be everything she'd once dreamed of finding in a man…but she was no longer looking and she doubted she ever would again.

He turned back to her for a moment. 'I don't want you to feel pressured, Claudia. That was never my intention.' His reply was truthful, his voice gentle and low—almost a whisper. 'I just wanted to help you…but I would never force you to do anything or stay anywhere you didn't want to be.' His voice trailed off.

Claudia wasn't sure how to respond. He had been a gentleman up to then and she doubted that would change…unless she invited him to alter his behaviour towards her. She started to wonder if perhaps she had overreacted. Once again since meeting him, she had been rude.

The first time had been due to her aversion to men and now, looking back, she knew he didn't deserve to be punished for another man's mistake. At the time she couldn't seem to help herself. But this time it was something else driving her to push him away. It wasn't his fault she was starting to have feelings for him. She wished she had Harriet on speed dial to give her logical, solid advice but it would be selfish to pull her sister away from something far more important in Argentina to ask her whether she should stay for dinner, stay the night or stay for a month.

No, she had to do this alone. She had to make a decision not based on another man's behaviour or her own doubts and insecurities. She had to make a decision based on Patrick's behaviour. And that had been nothing other than exceptional.

Just as exceptional as his broad-shouldered silhouette looked while stirring the delicious-smelling pasta sauce.

'If the invitation is still open, then perhaps I'll stay for dinner. But only for dinner.'

Chapter 9

As Claudia hung up her clothes in the walk-in wardrobe she prayed she had made the right decision. This was the second time she had rushed into moving in with a man she barely knew. Her life had changed so completely in the time since she'd arrived in Los Angeles and not much of it had been for the better, except for the arrival of her sons. She longed to return home. To where she felt life was a better fit and to where she felt a sense of family. Her internal compass was directing her back to London.

But she had unexpected mixed emotions about Patrick.

Where did he fit into her life? Would he be a part of it once she left Los Angeles or would he become a memory? A sweet memory, but nothing more.

Claudia had tried to think logically about moving in. They had only known each other a short time, but she and Patrick had a bond that she knew she would never share with another man. He had brought her sons into the world, saved their lives and saved hers as well. He was a brilliant obstetrician and while she wondered why he had not continued in that line of work, it was not her place to question him.

Was the fact he too was of English heritage a deciding factor in her feeling comfortable enough to move in? she wondered. Did he remind her of home? Did that make her feel safe? She prayed it wasn't a false sense of security.

There had been absolutely no pressure from Patrick over dinner; in fact he had even suggested a couple of hotels near the Mercy Hospital for her to stay in that night. His lack of insistence that she stay in his home but his genuine offer made her feel more comfortable to accept his invitation. And to apologise for being rude.

Everything happening in her head, and her fear of accepting Patrick's help, was her problem to deal with and in no way related to him.

'I will pay you exactly what I would be paying at a hotel,' she'd told him as they'd put the dishes into the dishwasher and sat down in the living room.

'The going rate for a hotel around here is just over a dollar a night.'

'Beverly Hills certainly isn't as expensive as it's alluded to be,' she joked. 'In all seriousness, I must insist…'

'Here's my business proposition,' he interrupted as he looked into her eyes, melting her heart a little further.

'Since I arrived in the US I haven't been able to find my favourite English toffee with almonds. It's amazing and nothing comes close. The almonds are toasted and the toffee's covered in dark chocolate. If you manage to find some, we'll call it even. Perhaps even arrange some to be shipped over after you return home. It used to be available at Harrods. There's no deadline, just a promise that one day I'll get my toffee.'

'English toffee in exchange for living in a home this beautiful?' She turned her head and, from her seat on the sofa, she surveyed the beautifully decorated room. It was elegant but simple. It wasn't stark but nor was it cluttered and the colours were warm earthy tones and the lighting softly added a glow to the room.

'You don't like the terms? Too steep?' he asked, staring into her eyes when they came back to meet his gaze. His lips curved to a smile and softly lined the stubble-covered skin on his jaw.

His voice sounded like the warm dark chocolate he was describing as the words flowed from his lips and Claudia involuntarily bit her own. Her heartbeat picked up unexpectedly and she closed her eyes and tried to blink away thoughts she was having about her landlord. He was far too gallant and handsome for his own good and most definitely for her own.

The French windows onto the balcony were open and the warm July breeze felt wonderful after the hospital air-conditioning so she carefully stood up and made her way to the door. Each day the physical scars were healing, but she just wished the emotional scars inflicted by the city would fade as quickly.

At that moment she needed to move away from Patrick, and the feelings she was having, being so close to him. She needed to step outside and clear her head in the balmy night air. She looked over the balustrade to the moonlight on the gently moving water of the pool. It was a perfect evening. The perfect house. The perfect man.

But, in Claudia's mind, she was so far from perfect. And life for her had never been perfect.

Patrick watched Claudia from his vantage point on the sofa. Her feet were bare and her short hair was gleaming in the moonlight. She seemed so at peace with the world at times, but at other times almost tortured. And so vulnerable. He had to control the urge to step behind her, pull her into his arms and tell her that everything would be all right. Protect her from whatever had hurt her or could in the future.

But he had no clue what the future held for her or for him. He barely knew anything about Claudia's past, apart from her losing her father and mother. Where had she gone to school? What had made her take the position in Los Angeles? And why didn't the father of her children want anything to do with them…? But, strangely, nothing about where she came from mattered to him any more. It wasn't her past, her family or her career that made him want to be with her. It was her attitude to life. Her strength. Her independence. Her beauty.

And her love of her children.

The next morning Claudia woke early and dressed in the shorter of the two nightdresses before making her way to the kitchen for breakfast. She thought she would make something to eat for them both and then head in to change before Patrick rose. Cooking breakfast would be her way of repaying his kindness.

But he was already up. And he took her breath away. Standing at the bench with a knife in his hand, he was cutting vegetables and fruit and placing them into a large glass bowl. Nearby was a small high-tech food processor. But her eyes were drawn to his bare chest and his low-slung shorts. Swallowing and trying not to stare at the perfection of his body, she looked out onto the patio, where she could see a gym bench and weights.

'Good morning, Claudia. I hope you slept well. If you need more covers or anything just let me know.'

She coughed to clear her throat. She needed to be polite and meet his gaze but that meant looking at his half-naked body again and worrying about her clothing being a little skimpier than she would normally choose. Ordinarily, that would not be a problem, but Patrick had to remain in the generous landlord category and she had to stay inside those parameters. She couldn't afford to entertain fantasies. She vigorously rubbed her arms as if she was cold. She wasn't. His presence was making her hot and self-conscious.

'Good morning,' she managed, trying to look around the room and avoid the obvious. Gorgeous, jaw-dropping Patrick, with both a body and smile to die for. And, first thing in the morning when most were struggling to open their eyes and look human, he was poster perfect. 'So you've been working out.'

He smiled back. 'Yes, I like to get up early and start the day using the outside gym. There are deck lounges out there so be my guest today and enjoy the stunning weather.'

'Stunning…weather.' She found it difficult to look at him and not have her eyes wander over his body in appreciation.

'I'm making a health blend with kale, carrots and a bunch of fruit. I didn't want to turn it on until you woke up since it sounds like a small lawnmower,' he said with a smile. 'Would you like one—I've prepared enough for both of us.'

'I'd planned on getting up early and cooking for you. You're already done so much for me.'

He shook his head as he crossed to the sink and washed the stickiness of the fruit from his hands then he slipped on a T-shirt that was hanging over the back of the high-backed kitchen chair. 'I'm always up at the crack of dawn in summer and I like a liquid breakfast after a workout. It gives me energy to face the day and I've got a full day of surgery scheduled so this will keep me going. Will you join me?'

Claudia was relieved that he was partly covered and her breathing had slowed accordingly. 'I'd love to, thank you.' She sat on a chair near to the bench where he was working and thought she would steer the conversation towards his work. 'So what surgical procedures are on today? Which starlet is going double D?'

He was dropping the chopped fruit in to be blended but paused to answer her question. Both of his lean hands rested over the top of the machine as he looked at her. 'I have two post-mastectomy reconstructions. A young mother in her early thirties and a slightly older patient who just celebrated her sixtieth birthday.'

Claudia felt so stupid. 'I'm sorry.'

'Don't worry; everyone does it...'

Shaking her head in frustration at herself, she continued. 'Just because everyone thinks the same way doesn't make it right. I was condescending and I made a sweeping generalisation. I'm so stupid for saying that. I should have known there would be more to your practice.'

'Thank you. Most people just shrug and don't apologise so please don't feel bad.' He paused for a moment. 'And, to be honest, I do my fair share of purely cosmetic augmentations. The holy grail of boob jobs, the double Ds and a few Es. Those surgeries allow me to perform the worthwhile ones at a much lower cost.'

'That's wonderful.'

'Well, I have a lovely home. Don't go putting me up on a pedestal.'

Despite what he said, in Claudia's mind he was a true gentleman and already up on a pedestal and she doubted he would fall off anytime soon.

One morning after Patrick had left for work, Claudia thought she would sort out the matter of the generous benefactor before she left for the hospital. She found the delivery docket in her purse and called the Rodeo Drive store. She was determined to repay the stranger's kindness and at the same time ensure she was not in their debt.

'I'm sorry, madam, but I can't divulge the sender's details. As with all of our account holders, they're a highly valued customer. This is an awkward situation and I would truly like to help but store policy won't allow me to do so. However, you are very welcome to exchange anything that you don't like or need in another size.'

'No, I don't need to change anything. It's all perfect.'

'We do pride ourselves on the styling and quality of all of our garments.'

The young woman's delivery was very eloquent and her tone leaning towards pretentious but Claudia knew that came with the location of the store. She bit the inside of her cheek. She wasn't going to accept the gift. She had to repay the sender but she needed to think of a way quickly before the young woman ended the conversation, no doubt politely, but, however it ended, her chance to repay her benefactor would be over.

'I have an idea,' she began in an equally polite tone, hoping to sway the sales assistant to agree to the thought that had popped into her head. 'Could I buy a gift certificate to the same value as the gift sent to me and you could mail that to them? If they have an account then you would have their mailing address. You are not breaking confidentiality because their details have not been given to me and you have just doubled your sales because they will have to visit your store to spend the certificate.'

There was no answer for a moment and Claudia assumed the sales assistant was considering her proposal. 'But they may want to know who sent it.'

Claudia wondered at the slight double standard when it came to account holders and mere mortals.

'That's fine. I don't have any problem if you let the sender know it was from me. In fact, I would be happy for them to know I had repaid the gift.'

The deal was done. Claudia gave her credit card details over the phone but the amount was even more than she had imagined. But, since she wasn't paying rent, she could afford it. There was nothing more she needed to buy for herself. She drew a deep breath at how extravagant the anonymous benefactor had been and would be hand-washing everything, hoping that it lasted for a few years, knowing what it had cost.

Claudia watched her little boys grow day by day, week by week. She was able to hold them and bottle-feed them and on the twentieth day they moved from the neonatal nursery into the general nursery. The warmth and serenity that she experienced every time Claudia held them made her happier than she thought possible and she didn't want them to be out of her arms. As she touched their soft warm skin and looked into their big trusting eyes she knew her life was complete. There was nothing she wouldn't do or give to Thomas and Luca for as long as she lived. Each milestone they reached in weight or developmental markers made her heart sing. She could imagine decorating Christmas trees with them and watching the joy on their faces as they unwrapped their birthday presents.

The boys' little faces filled out a little more every day and she could see subtle differences. Thomas was a little bigger and his mouth a little fuller and his mop of hair was thick and straight, while Luca's hair was curly and he was a leaner baby. Whether that had anything to do with his initial heart problem, she was unsure.

Claudia would arrive first thing in the morning at the Mercy Hospital and leave just after the sun set as the boys had settled into a routine and were ready for sleep.

They had two feeds during the night, one at eleven and another at three in the morning, but the nursing staff insisted she get rest and come in the morning. The first time she was allowed to bathe them one at a time she had tears of joy in her eyes that fell from her cheeks into the tepid water. She was so nervous as she supported their tiny bodies in the water and then gently let the water splash over them before she wrapped them in a soft white towel and held them for the longest time.

When the weather cooled just a little so it wasn't too extreme, Patrick suggested a picnic outside for the four of them. At first Claudia was uncertain but when he walked her downstairs she caught sight of the checked blanket on the ground, complete with picnic basket, she nodded her approval. Together they collected the boys after their feed and took them down to the shady place beside the small pond. The sound of the water trickling over the rocks and running into the pond filled with oversized goldfish was relaxing.

'I think they'll enjoy fishing.'

'And what makes you think that?'

'It's just a feeling I have.'

Patrick didn't want to say that if they were his sons he would teach them about fishing, the way his father had, and they would learn to love it as he did.

Claudia watched him fussing over her sons and she had the feeling that, despite what he said, he would be a wonderful father.

The basket was brimming with wonderful picnic food; there were assorted sandwiches. It truly was a family outing. Whatever family meant, moving forward.

Claudia took photos of the boys with her phone cam-

era every day as they grew. It would be a reminder of
how far they had come and a keepsake for them when
they were older. She decided to have a photo of each
of them framed for Patrick. He had been so wonderful and she wanted him to have a memory of the little
boys he had brought into the world. It saddened her
that soon they would be worlds apart but it was a fact
she had to accept.

She stopped at the drugstore on the way home one
day and had two of the cutest photos printed and bought
two silver-plated frames. And as she walked into his
bedroom that afternoon to place them on the dresser
as a surprise, she felt strangely at home. The room had
a masculine feel to it but it was also warm…and inviting. It was decorated in muted warm tones of grey.
Heavy deep grey drapes framed the window and the
softest pale grey carpet covered the floor. The bed and
bedside cabinets and the dresser were black and there
were three large charcoal drawings on the wall behind
the bed, also framed in black. The bed cover was the
same tone as the drapes. It was a simply decorated room
but stunning. The longer she stayed, the more she felt
at home. She would have preferred that she felt like an
intruder but she didn't.

Placing the frames on his bedside table, she left the
room, her eyes surveying one final time where he slept
every night. She wondered if his bed was as soft as hers
and if he slept on his back or on his side. Did he toss
the covers off or did he sleep peacefully…?

Every few days Patrick would stop at the hospital to
check up on the three of them. And each time he did,

Claudia felt her heart flutter as she watched him tenderly hold one of her sons. She couldn't help but notice that he was completely and utterly consumed by whichever baby he was given. He didn't take his eyes away for even a minute and he spoke to them in great detail as if they understood every word. Claudia had to remind herself that he was not their father. He gave such attention and love to them, it was often difficult for her to remember that simple fact.

Patrick gave her the use of his silver imported SUV to travel to Mercy Hospital. He knew it would help her to feel independent by not asking to be dropped off or catching cabs at all hours. He wanted her to feel the freedom she needed but still feel a sense of belonging. And it worked. She was extremely grateful to him but he did not exploit that gratitude in any way. She initially refused, as he expected she would, but when he pointed out the safety of late night trips back from the hospital she reluctantly agreed. But she insisted on putting in the gas and having it washed each week.

She cooked dinner for him two or three nights a week. And he continued to rise early and make smoothies in the morning. Occasionally Claudia would eat at the hospital so she could stay a little later with Thomas and Luca. And Patrick made Friday night their night together at the hospital. He brought fish and chips from a store owned by an expat from North Yorkshire who had relocated to LA and opened a café on Melrose. The shop was always busy and he would line up for thirty minutes just to place his order. Then Claudia would meet Patrick downstairs in the visitor gardens to eat their fish and chips together. It felt so good for both of them to step outside. They had enjoyed four Friday date nights and they were planning the fifth, the date they both knew would be the last. Claudia would be heading back to London in less than a week and, while she was looking forward to returning home, she realised leaving Patrick would be one of the hardest goodbyes she would ever have to say.

But she had no choice.

As they sat together on the patio at home one evening, Claudia sipped on her iced tea and looked up towards the stars, wondering if her parents approved of the man sitting beside her. She felt certain they would and it made her want to be honest with him about something they had never discussed. She curled her bare feet up under herself and turned to him.

'Is there anything you want to know about me? I mean, I've been living here and you've never pressed me about anything.'

'You have a sister, whom you adore. And she's over working in South America. And you worked in television.'

'What about the big elephant in the room? The one we've walked around since we met.'

'And that would be?'

'The fact you've never asked me anything about Thomas and Luca's father.'

He studied her for a moment. 'It's not my place, Claudia. I've just thought all along, if you want to tell me you will but if you don't then I respect you. You must have your reasons for wanting to keep it private,' Patrick told her honestly. He knew he had no right to ask. After all, he'd kept his past to himself.

Claudia smiled at his reply. It was so refreshing in a town where everyone wanted to know everyone else's business and it somehow made her want to tell him. Many times over the weeks they had spent together she had wanted to open up but hesitated, a little scared that his opinion of her might change if he knew the truth. Then she questioned why it mattered so much what he thought of her.

'I assume it's over between you.'

'Over as soon as he discovered I was having a child.'

'Don't you mean children?'

'No, he never stayed long enough to find out I was having twins. His lawyer informed me early on that he didn't want to have his name on the birth certificate and relinquished all parental rights. He's actually...' She paused as she stumbled over her words.

'There's no need to go there,' he cut in angrily. He was furious any man would behave so poorly and sensed she was feeling torn about discussing the boys' father. 'Unless you're in witness protection and hiding from a mobster, I have no interest in knowing about a man for whom I have no respect.'

Claudia smiled. 'I'm not in witness protection.'

'That's good news then...nothing else matters.'

Claudia nodded in silence. Up until now, she had given too much thought to telling anyone, let alone Patrick, that her sons' father was a married man. *Don't do it now*, said a voice inside her head. She felt confused by her desire for him to know everything about her. 'I thought he was a good man when I met him...'

'Claudia, any man who would leave you alone and pregnant with his children is a low-life bastard. I never want to lay eyes on him. If I did I wouldn't hold back so maybe it's best I don't.' His voice was loud and filled with anger.

Claudia was taken aback. She had not seen that side of Patrick. His emotions had always seemed so moderate but hearing that reminded her of her father. She knew he would have said the same if he was still alive. Suddenly she felt more protected than she had since her parents died.

'I didn't expect that response from you.'

'I don't sit on the fence, Claudia,' he responded. 'I don't tolerate cowards or fools and the man was both.'

Claudia was compelled to confess her part in the ugly situation. She was shaking inside because she was so aware that his opinion about her might change but all of a sudden she knew she wanted to tell him anyway.

'It's more complicated than that,' she began and then paused for a moment. 'The boys' father...he was married.' The words just came tumbling out. Her heart began racing as she saw his jaw tense and his eyes become more intense.

'Married! The guy is a bigger low-life than I thought. How dare he hide that from you and disrespect his wife at the same time?'

'You're assuming I didn't know he had a wife without me saying anything?'

'Claudia, I know that you would never have become involved with a married man if you'd known he had a wife. It's not who you are. It's obvious he kept it from you.'

'He did,' she said with her head bowed a little. Patrick was visibly distraught but Claudia realised with relief that he wasn't disappointed in her. His anger was towards the man who had betrayed her. But she wanted him to know the full story. She had to take the blame for her part.

'I should have asked more questions. I was naive...'

'He was probably a seasoned cheat and wouldn't have told you the truth anyway.'

'Perhaps,' she agreed.

'This town is full of predators. I've *freshened* up a few of them. Actors, producers, agents.'

'He's a producer, quite well known in the soap opera industry. I was working on his show and, as I said, I had absolutely no idea that he was married. He managed to hide it because his wife was away overseas, working on a remote set. She's an actress, much younger than him but not well known, not yet at least. She was apparently heading back to LA about the same time I discovered I was pregnant. He left the apartment we were sharing the day I announced we were to have a baby and I haven't heard from him since. Only his lawyer.'

Patrick ached inside to reach for her but he didn't. He didn't look at her; he stared straight ahead, scared that if he did look into her eyes he would sweep her into his arms and never let her go. It had only been nearly six weeks since they had met on the day the boys had been born but it seemed longer to Patrick. All along he'd suspected she had been hurt and now he knew by whom. The father of her children had been the one who'd inflicted the heartache.

He wanted her more than any woman he had ever met but he needed to wait until she was ready. If that never happened then so be it. But if she did open up and let him know she wanted him then he would make love to her with every fibre of his being and he would hold her in his arms all night long for as many nights as she would give him. He would try to heal every hurt she had every experienced. He would make her whole again, if she would let him.

'He'll pay the price for the rest of his life by not knowing his sons.'

Claudia opened her mouth to respond but couldn't think what to say. He had not questioned her or doubted her for a moment and she wondered how and why such a wonderful man had come into her life. Without thinking too much, she leant in to kiss his cheek but he turned his face at that moment and the softness of his lips met hers. It was an unexpected kiss but neither wanted it to end. She willingly pressed herself against his hard body. She wanted him as much as he wanted her. A welcome vulnerability washed over her as she realised how much she trusted the man she was kissing.

She trusted him more than she'd ever thought possible. And she was falling a little more in love with him by the day.

His hands trailed down the curve of her spine and she could feel his heart racing through the cool fabric of his shirt. Her heart synchronised with the beating of his and their kiss deepened as he explored her mouth. Without warning, he slowly and purposefully stood and reach for her hand to pull her up from the sofa. Once she was on her feet, he swept her up off the ground and into his arms, his mouth possessing hers again. Claudia's hands wrapped around his neck as he carried her into his bedroom, where he slowly removed every piece of her clothing. And then his own.

That night they both opened their lives, their hearts and their bodies to each other.

Chapter 10

The early-morning sun slipped through the gaps in the drapes and filtered onto the bed where they lay entwined in each other's arms. Claudia opened her eyes to see Patrick's handsome face only inches from hers. He was still asleep and she could feel his warm breath on her skin. Gently, she eased herself from his arms and moved to the edge of the bed in search of her clothing. It was his room, not hers, and there was no clothing in reach. Her eyes roamed the room, to find her things scattered all over the floor in a trail that led to the bed.

'Looking for something?'

She turned to see him propped up on his elbow watching her.

'My underwear.'

'I don't think you'll need that today,' he said, a spark in his eye as he pulled her back into his arms.

* * *

An hour later, Claudia woke to the smell of freshly percolated coffee. They had made love again and she had drifted into a deep and wonderful sleep. Patrick appeared in the doorway in denim jeans but no shirt. His face was freshly shaven. His hair was wet and slicked back.

'Why didn't you wake me?'

'Because, my darling, you needed your sleep.' He crossed to the bed and kissed her tenderly. 'You can have a shower and, when you're ready, there's breakfast on the patio.'

'You are spoiling me terribly.'

'I hope so,' he said as he kissed her again and she melted into his arms.

'I should get ready now,' she finally said as she pulled herself away. 'I want to be at the hospital for the boys' feed and bath.'

'Not a problem. We can eat and head over there together—it's still early.'

With that he disappeared and left her alone in the still warm bed with even warmer thoughts of him.

'There's one thing I really want to know,' she said as she traced circles with the tip of her finger on his warm bare chest and looked up lovingly at the man who had captured her heart as they sat together on the patio sofa enjoying the morning sun as they shared breakfast. She had showered quickly and they planned on being at the hospital by ten. 'Why did you really change career?'

'I found something else I enjoy—something that's rewarding and important.'

'I know, and I appreciate that you're not just fixing starlets' noses and breasts. I understand the other wonderful work you do, but you're very good at delivering babies too.'

'You only have your delivery to go on so I think your opinion may be somewhat biased.'

'There's no bias; I'm serious. You stepped in and saved us all. We owe our lives to you, Patrick.'

'You were the perfect patient…'

'Perfect patient?' She laughed and she lay back on the soft oversized outside pillow, staring at the cloudless sky as her thoughts rushed back to the day she'd given birth. It was overwhelmingly frightening sometimes when she thought about that fateful day and other times she felt so blessed and fortunate, as if the stars had aligned to place them both in the elevator. That morning, as she snuggled next to Patrick, she felt as if it must have been serendipity and she was so very lucky. 'I was perfectly horrible to you.'

'Initially, perhaps, but when labour started I think you handled yourself incredibly well. You were braver than any woman I know.'

'I don't know about the brave bit, but I do know that I was flat-out rude and chose the most inconvenient place for you to deliver the boys.'

'You didn't have much say in choosing the venue.'

'That's true…' she began but her words were cut short when his warm, soft lips pressed hard against hers and he didn't let another word escape until he had tasted her sweet mouth for the longest time.

Finally he released her. Her head was spinning, her heart was racing and it took her a moment to catch the breath he had stolen. Her thoughts about everything except the man beside her were muddled. Those thoughts were crystal-clear. She was unashamedly falling in love with him. She knew they had no certain future and they had no past, having known each other for not long over a month, but they had the present. She was falling for Patrick the way she had never fallen for a man in her life and knew she never would again.

'Let's get to the hospital and see your strapping young sons—they may have gained weight overnight and be ready to come home.'

It wouldn't be *come home*—it would be *go home*—to somewhere far away, she thought with a pang of sadness in her heart.

Claudia smiled as Patrick helped her to her feet but his words had cut like a hot blade, piercing her heart and reminding her that home for the boys and her would be London. And Patrick's home was in Los Angeles. Their brief romantic affair would be that.

Just a short, sweet affair.

As they drove to the hospital, Claudia glanced over at Patrick. His slender masculine hands that now held the steering wheel had only a few hours before been stroking her naked skin and bringing her such pleasure that she'd never wanted it to end. His profile in the morning sun was the same handsome face that had woken next to her that morning. And she hoped they would wake together every morning until she left.

But, no matter what the future held for either of them, she wanted to know more about her devilishly good-looking obstetrician. And that meant understanding the decision he had made over a decade before. She wanted to be able to answer any questions her sons might have over the years. And even if they never asked a single question, she still wanted to know all there was to know about Patrick. He was such a wonderful man, but she sensed there was something he was hiding behind the sunglasses resting on his high cheekbones, gently shaded by morning stubble. It still seemed unusual to move to the other side of the world and begin all over again. To study another medical specialty and leave behind his family and friends. To never return home when there were clearly no financial barriers was all very puzzling. And, for an inexplicable reason, she had to know what had driven him away from the country she loved.

'Patrick,' she began softly as they pulled up at traffic lights only two blocks from the Mercy Hospital. 'Can I ask you a question?'

He turned to her with a smile that melted her heart. 'It depends.'

'Depends on what?'

'Will you let me plead the Fifth Amendment if I don't like the question?'

'The Fifth Amendment? But you're not an American citizen!'

'No, I'm British—we both know that,' he replied as he changed gear and took off as the traffic lights turned green. 'But I've been here long enough to feel comfortable using their constitutional loopholes.'

Claudia watched him smile. He was obviously trying to find a way to make light of something about his past he didn't want to discuss and his expression showed her he thought he had won.

'You know what, let's talk tonight.'

'Sounds fine to me,' he said as they drove along in the traffic heading towards the hospital.

Later, as they sat together on the patio in their swim-suits after a late-night swim, Claudia broached the subject again.

'I think you know everything there is to know about me,' she began as she ran her fingers through her wet curls to push them away from her still damp face.

'Where exactly is this going?' he asked as he began to kiss her neck where the water was trickling down from her hair. 'Because I would like to take it back to the bedroom.'

'Me too…in a minute, but first I want to take it back to the question I wanted to ask this morning.'

He stopped kissing her. 'Do we have to go there?'

'But you don't even know the question.'

'Do I really want to know? Let's leave the past where it belongs… I'm doing very nicely without it.'

Claudia sat up and turned to face Patrick. She doubted what he said was accurate. He had left every-thing behind. The reason had to be enormous. 'What is the deal with your family? Did you fall out?'

'I'm definitely pleading the Fifth Amendment. I told you I would this morning. Nothing's changed.'

His smile seemed forced. There was more behind it. She intended to find out exactly what. A man had once hidden a secret from her that not only changed the course of her life but that of her children. She would not and could not accept a man at face value, no mat-ter how handsome that face.

'Patrick, I need to know a little more about you. It's important to me.' She drew a deep and slightly nervous breath. 'My cards are on the table. You know everything, good and bad, and you still want me in your bed, so please give me the same credit.'

Looking into Claudia's deep brown eyes, Patrick felt her searching his face for answers and realised that she wasn't going to let it go. Perhaps she had a right to know. She had opened up to him about her life. Perhaps it was his turn. Maybe if she understood his reasons then she would consider staying in Los Angeles and they could be together. He suddenly had to face the truth that he had more to lose by not opening up.

He could lose Claudia.

'Fine. We are…estranged. There's been no contact with anyone from my past for close to twelve years.'

'That's sad; I couldn't imagine life with Harriet.'

'Well, I suppose that's where you and I differ then,' he said flatly. 'I can live quite nicely without my family.'

Claudia suddenly felt as if the man beside her was not the same person. How could he not want to be with his family? Family meant everything to her. Losing her parents had been a crushing blow and to think he'd just walked away from his confused her.

'Have you tried to sort out your differences?'

'This is a little deeper than simple differences. I've rebuilt my life and don't want to look back or go back. My past and my family are not relevant to me.'

As he said it he knew it wasn't the truth. Every day he thought about his family. Where his mother was, what she might be doing. His nephew would be twelve now and he had not seen him grow up and it saddened him.

But there had been no other option but to walk away and let them live their lives without him.

'It's relevant to me…I mean it was significant enough to make you pack up and leave,' she replied softly. 'I don't want to open old wounds but I do want to understand you better, understand why you won't return to the place you were born.'

He stood and reached for Claudia's hand and helped her to her feet 'Then let's go inside and forget about this conversation. Just accept my past is something I don't want to relive. It will do no good. My family and I have all moved on from each other. End of story.'

Claudia lay in Patrick's arms that night but they didn't make love. Nor did she sleep well. She couldn't. It worried her that there were things in his past he wouldn't share but they were significant enough to make him leave the country he had called home, leave behind his family and never make contact again and even change his profession.

It was all so confusing.

Who was the man lying beside her? Had she made a mammoth mistake in letting him have a piece of her heart?

She climbed from bed early the next morning and had a shower before he woke. She didn't want to pry any further. Clearly he had shut down her attempts and she was not going to push him for answers. But she knew she couldn't continue to see anything between them. Honesty and openness could not be a one-way street. And while he had not promised he would open up to her, in fact he had made no promises at all, she couldn't plan a future with a man who didn't have the same values as her.

What if she and the boys did stay in LA to be a family with him and he walked away from them all and never looked back if it became too difficult? Family was everything to her and she and Harriet had already lost those they loved most. How could he not value family the way she did? To not reach out in so many years, to patch up differences and make amends—it was all incomprehensible to her. Even if she had planned on staying in LA, it wouldn't work between them if he could place such little value on the importance of family and not explain why.

She gathered up her belongings, set them by the front door and sat on the patio and waited for him to wake.

'I'm guessing you can't leave this alone?' he said as he appeared in the doorway, dressed in shorts and a T-shirt. His expression was serious.

'No, I *can* leave it alone; in fact it's what I'm planning to do, but if I do then I have to leave us alone too. I rushed into this,' she said, shaking her head as she looked around the lovely home they had shared for over a month. 'I didn't really know you when I moved in. And I shouldn't have shared your bed for the past two nights. We're too different.'

'We're not different…'

'We're so different,' she argued. 'I would give anything to have my mother in my life. And you haven't spoken to yours in years for a reason you won't explain so I can't begin to understand. I think in time we will find more differences and I can't bring the boys into something that maybe won't last. What if you up and walk away one day and don't look back at the boys and me? My life back in London will last. My family is there. My sister. It's where I belong.'

'You don't think we have any future?'

'Not when you won't share a past that has fundamentally changed everything about who you were.'

Patrick sat down on the chair opposite her and took in a breath that filled his lungs. His long fingers ran through his hair as he looked at the ground. He realised he had no choice but to share his past or risk losing Claudia completely.

'It was almost twelve years ago,' he began without prompting. 'August seventh, to be precise.'

She remained silent but the fact that the date of his story came so easily to mind showed her just how traumatic the memory was for Patrick.

'It was a Thursday night and I took a call to assist with a high risk delivery in the county hospital where I worked in Durham,' he volunteered but the strain in his voice was obvious. 'I was an OBGYN resident and I loved what I did.'

She waited in silence for him to continue, which he did without any prompting.

'It was late, about ten o'clock, when a young woman was rushed into Emergency, presenting at the hospital in the early stages of premature labour.'

'You said you were called in; you weren't on duty then?'

'No, I had the night off. I was at the local pub with some friends from med school. It was a warm summer night; one of them had secured a placement at a hospital in New Zealand and we were giving him a send-off. Anyway, I got the call to head back. The senior obstetric consultant had left for London to speak at an OBGYN conference and couldn't get back until the next morning.'

'But if you were at the local pub you would've been drinking,' she cut in, her frown not masking her concern at the direction of his story.

He shook his head. 'Normally the answer would be yes, and by ten o'clock I would ordinarily have had a pint or two. But that night I'd finished my shift at the hospital with a bit of a headache coming on and, since I had an early start the next morning with a surgical schedule, I thought if I had even one glass of alcohol that I wouldn't pull up well. I stayed on ginger beer all night. I was perfectly fine to take the call—to be honest, I wish I had been drinking and had to refuse but I accepted and headed in to what would essentially be the end of my career in obstetrics.'

Claudia began nibbling on her lower lip. 'I still don't understand. You did nothing wrong; you hadn't been drinking...'

'I hadn't...but, with the tragedy that unfolded, some thought otherwise. That was the only conclusion they could find for what happened in the operating theatre. They couldn't accept that a high risk pregnancy extends to a high risk delivery. Anyway, I scrubbed in and began the Caesarean, but very cautiously as there was a complication, as I mentioned. The placenta was growing outside of the uterus wall and, despite me doing everything textbook and taking precautions along the way, the patient began to haemorrhage. I lifted the baby boy clear of the womb but as there was so much blood

I couldn't see where to begin the repair. The blood loss was too great and, despite the whole team doing everything we could, we lost her on the table. There was nothing I, or anyone, could do. The theatre staff knew I had done everything right and told me as much but the jury were sitting outside in the waiting room and, to be honest, the worst juror was myself. I took the blame before I saw them—they just reinforced my feelings.'

'Why would you do that? You knew it wasn't your fault and the medical team knew it wasn't...'

'For me, overwhelming guilt that I had not been able to save her and, for them, their own grief turned to anger when they were told I had been seen having *drinks* at the local only an hour before. It cemented it in the minds of the family that I had to have been drinking and that was why their little girl died giving birth.'

'Why didn't you fight? Surely there must have been something you could have done? It's so unfair that you did the right thing in returning to the hospital and you tried to save the woman and you had the family blame you on circumstantial evidence.'

'It shattered my world. I was grieving too, and they needed someone to blame for the loss of her life. I decided it was my duty to take that blame.' Patrick paused and stared at Claudia thoughtfully and in silence for a moment. He didn't want to tell her any more. He had omitted the most important fact in the entire tragedy. The one that had changed his life completely. But he had to be honest. She deserved to know the truth.

With a heavy heart, he closed his eyes. 'The young woman who died...was my sister.'

Chapter 11

'Your sister died having her baby?'

He nodded, unable to bring himself to say the words again.

'So it was your own family that blamed you? It's so sad that she died, but why would they do that? I don't understand—families don't do that to each other.'

'It's not their fault. It was complicated,' he said, trying to validate their behaviour. 'No one knew Francine, or Franny, as we always called her growing up, was a high risk so to them her death had to be due to negligence.'

'Surely your brother-in-law knew there were complications?'

'No, he had no idea.' Patrick shook his head. 'I assume she kept her medical condition from us because she didn't want anyone to worry. We had just endured another tragedy a few months before, so she was trying to protect everyone.'

'What sort of tragedy?

'My younger brother, Matthew, died six months before.'

Claudia covered her mouth with her hands as she gasped, 'Oh, no.'

'My father and mother had divorced a long time before; I was young when it happened. My mother raised us. One Saturday my mother went up to Matthew's room to wake him as he had friends waiting downstairs to head to Brighton for the day. She found him in bed, which was unusual since he was an early riser. She patted his legs to wake him, but my brother was unresponsive so she pulled the covers down and found he was bleeding from the nose and mouth. My mother called out for help from his friends and dialled for an ambulance, hoping the paramedics would somehow revive him. They couldn't and he was pronounced dead on arrival at the hospital.' Patrick's jaw was clenched and Claudia could see he was struggling to make eye contact.

Claudia's brow was knitted in confusion. She wondered if it might have been a drug overdose but she said nothing. Asking such a question seemed cruel and unnecessary. The details made no difference. Patrick had tragically lost his younger brother.

'The autopsy report from the coroner's office came back with suspected lung aneurism,' Patrick offered without prompting. 'In simple terms, it's a ruptured artery in the lungs, which meant he drowned in his own blood. It's extremely rare and nothing that could have been predicted. Matthew had been a medical time bomb for a very long time.'

'I'm so sorry.' Claudia couldn't find any other words. Nothing she thought to say seemed to be adequate for the tragedy she had heard. His family had been dealt an overwhelmingly sad time.

'It was the worst time in my mother's life, in all of our lives. My father attended the funeral but after that he kept his distance again. My maternal grandmother was alive, but only barely, as she was living in assisted care; the shock of the broken marriage was difficult but hearing that her grandson had died was what I believe sent her into a depression that she never really recovered from.

'Then Franny discovered she was pregnant. It brought some joy back to our mother and to our family. She was focusing on the new baby on the way and I don't think that Franny wanted to bring her down with worry. She wanted her to hold on to something. The thought of a baby arriving gave us all a light at the end of the tunnel. We knew she was having a boy, that part she shared, and in some way I think the fact another boy would join the family made losing Matthew *almost* bearable for our mother. I'm assuming Franny didn't want our mother to be anxious and, while I understand her wanting to protect her, she should have confided in me. I could have ensured the best antenatal care and would have been prepared, going into surgery.'

'So she never took her husband to any of her obstetric visits?'

'No, Will never attended any of them.'

'Still, whether they knew or not, I can't believe they would blame you.'

'They didn't understand, even when I explained that her medical condition translated into a high risk delivery.'

'But, without any medical knowledge, it still doesn't make sense to throw the blame your way; it all seems unfair and so wrong.'

'Don't forget I'd been seen in the pub; they forgot everything about her condition and focused purely on my supposed drinking.'

'But you hadn't been drinking. Couldn't you have a blood test and prove it?'

'I didn't think to have the test the night she died as, since I hadn't been drinking, it didn't cross my mind to cover myself and the allegations came out the next day from my brother-in-law's family. One of his cousins had seen me at the pub and, despite me telling them otherwise, they didn't believe that I had been completely sober.'

'But couldn't your friends corroborate your story?'

Patrick nodded. 'They tried, but his family was convinced it was just my medico mates covering for me. The whole medical fraternity banding together to protect each other conspiracy theory.'

'And your brother-in-law believed them?'

'He was upset, he was half out of his mind and he got swept up in the witch hunt. There was even footage taken on a mobile phone of another celebration in which I featured in the background. It was all over. You have to remember I lost my sister that day. I couldn't argue in my frame of mind. I was grieving too.'

'What about the rest of your family? Your mother and father?' Claudia frowned in perplexity. It all seemed so wrong.

'My mother was barely functioning and she believed what she was told. My negligence had taken away her beloved daughter.'

'But you had tried to save your sister, with no knowledge of her medical condition…and I know it couldn't bring her daughter back, but she had a grandchild. The grandchild that you had brought into the world.'

Patrick ran his hands through his hair in frustration. 'I was hung, drawn and quartered by the town. There was no coming back from that so I left. It was best for everyone.'

'Are you sure about that?'

'The grief blanketed both families and I guess I just couldn't face the arguing. I made the decision to leave. If either family wanted to look into it further I left the name of her obstetrician, but they never called. They didn't want to look further than me for the cause. It was their choice to direct the blame at me and it was my choice to walk away.'

'It's all so terribly unfair.'

'Yes, but it's done.'

'And your brother-in-law and his son…?'

'Will named the little boy Todd after his father. Todd turned twelve this August. He's a tall boy like his father and doing well at school.'

'So you speak with your brother-in-law then?'

'No, I haven't heard a word from him since I left. A friend from university lives not far from him; their boys go to the same school. He keeps an eye out for them and keeps me up to date. I set up a trust fund to cover his college education. Will gave up work for a period to raise Todd and then found it hard to get back into the workforce so had to start again at entry level. I feel I owed him to take care of Todd.

'So now you can understand why I choose to live over here. It's simpler for everyone.'

Claudia saw everything so differently. 'While I understand your need to leave, and I think what happened to you is almost unforgivable, it's still your family. You can't turn your back on family. Your mother lost her daughter and both sons within months of each other.'

'I'm still here. I didn't die.'

'No, but you left her life. For a mother it would be the same level of grief.'

Patrick leaned back against the chair. 'No, it's not the same. I'm here but she chose not to contact me. Nor did Will.'

'Perhaps your absence cemented their doubts about what happened. You could have gone back anytime over the last twelve years and cleared it up.'

'I'm not about to stir up all that again. I have built a new life here and reconstructive surgery has been good to me.'

'So you gave up obstetrics because you couldn't save your sister.'

'Yes,' he said solemnly and without hesitation. 'I had nightmares about her lying lifeless on the table at my hands…I lost the will and drive to practice.'

'But it wasn't because of anything you did.'

Patrick felt his body tense. 'I couldn't face that sense

of helplessness again. Being unable to save Franny was something I could not relive.'

'But you did...with me. And you saved me. You didn't know I had a serious condition and you saved me from dying.'

'No, the paramedics came in time to save you.'

Her face became even more serious. 'They took over but you had kept me alive.'

Patrick knew the best thing he had done was to walk away from obstetrics and his family. And he knew that Claudia was testing that resolve. 'Fine, I kept you alive but I can't go back to that. I'm content with my work. I live here now and I'll never set foot back in the UK.'

'But your work here, now, it's not your first love.'

'No, but you can't always have everything you want, Claudia, including your first love.'

She couldn't ignore the resolve in Patrick's voice. 'Have you never thought about returning to Durham and facing your accusers and telling the truth?'

Patrick rolled his eyes and did not hide his exasperation. 'There was no evidence. Nothing to support me and everything to support their accusations.'

She shrugged. 'But you walked away from your career...and your life...because of lies.'

Patrick's body went rigid and his voice became harsh. 'I didn't walk away from anything. I left to make it easier for everyone.'

'Why can't you face the past now then? Rebuild your life in London? It was twelve years ago and I'm sure your mother would give anything to hold you in her arms again. You're her only living child.'

'No. I can't and I won't go back. My life there is over. It ended the day I left.'

Gaping at him, Claudia exclaimed, 'That's so dramatic!'

'My sister died, Claudia. They all think I caused her death. *That* is dramatic.'

Claudia frowned at him while she scrutinised his face. His expression was severe. His jaw appeared more pronounced. 'I'm just saying perhaps you could explain it properly. Have your peers explain it again. Franny's obstetrician could sit down with your mother and tell her the truth. It would have been near on impossible for your mother to pick up the telephone and speak with him. But you could facilitate that conversation. Make her see reason. Would that be so hard for you to do?'

'It's too late. They've moved on with their lives.'

'It's never too late. No mother moves on from a child.'

'I'm not so sure.'

'I am. I couldn't imagine a day without Thomas and Luca in my life. I would travel to the end of the earth to be with them and you should do the same for your nephew. You've chosen to give up without a fight.'

'Fighting is overrated.'

'Not in my books. I need a man who will fight for family.'

Patrick stood up and crossed back to the doorway. His face was taut as he knew at that moment exactly how Claudia felt.

Claudia sat staring ahead. Her heart was aching with the reality that had just been spelt out to her. 'It's been a long time and your mother would probably be stronger now. Don't you think you owe it to her to let her know what really happened? I would want to know.'

'Claudia, let it go.'

'You mean let us go?'

He rubbed his clenched jaw. Claudia noticed his eyes suddenly looked tired, almost battle-worn as he spoke. 'The choice is yours.'

Chapter 12

Patrick stirred from a tortured sleep the next morning, knowing that his every reason for waking up was gone. Claudia had left. She had grabbed her belongings and caught a cab. She'd told him where she would be staying if he changed his mind and wanted to talk but he left the slip of paper by the bed. He had no intention of calling. She was right—she deserved to be with Harriet. Family was important to her. He had learned to get along on his own for a long time. He missed his mother and his brother-in-law and wished with all of his heart some days that he could be there to watch his nephew grow up. But he couldn't. The wounds had healed on the outside and he didn't want to rip them open by travelling home.

It was better to let her rebuild her life back in the UK. She would settle in quickly and no doubt move on.

She would forget about what they'd shared in time and someone else would take his place.

But he wasn't sure he would ever move on.

Claudia had brought more joy and happiness into his life than he had dreamt possible. She was everything he could wish for in a woman and more. And he had let her walk away.

He had never felt so empty and it filled him with regret to walk away from Claudia but there was no other choice. What she expected from him was impossible. How could he face his family again? Where would he start? Would the blame still be there? The desolation in his mother's eyes—so empty, so blank, so lost and hurt by him that he could never go back. He just couldn't. It was better to leave the past behind.

When he'd discovered she had left that morning he had tried to push what they had shared from his mind but, waking on the second day, it became a reality. And he could no longer ignore the way he felt. A cloud had moved over his world and it was suddenly a much darker place, devoid of everything he had come to love.

Glancing around the room, his eyes came to rest on the bedside table, where the framed photos of Thomas and Luca were resting. It was the first time she had reached out to him and let him into her world. He now knew how difficult that had been for her but she had fought her doubts and insecurities, and waded through the hurt, to let him know that he meant something to her and the boys.

Next to the photographs was the note she had left— and her pearl earrings.

A rush of memories assailed his mind.

The day they'd met in the elevator. How beautiful he'd thought Claudia was and how he'd quickly discovered her looks were matched with her feisty spirit. She was a strong woman on the outside but inside she was filled with love. That day he had witnessed the level of that love for her sons and, weeks later, experienced first-hand her capacity for love when she'd shared his bed.

And he had let her leave.

Perhaps she was right. He had taken the easier option. But that suited him. He had adjusted to the values in the city. At least that was what he would have to tell himself. He climbed from bed and headed for the shower. He had the day off and no idea how to spend it. Claudia was gone and he couldn't visit Thomas and Luca. He had to become accustomed to life without them and that wouldn't happen if he tried to reach out to them even one last time.

After a quick shower, he dressed in a polo shirt and jeans and, looking for something to occupy his mind, he decided to head to his practice. His hair was still wet and he was unshaven but he knew he wouldn't be seeing anyone at that hour. There had to be some paperwork to finish, reports to finalise and mail to check. Anything to stop him rethinking the decision he had made.

As he entered the garage he looked at the SUV that Claudia had been driving and made a mental note to call a dealership and trade it in. He didn't want to be reminded of what he had lost every time he saw the car that he now considered to be hers.

There was little traffic that early in the morning and he was at work in less than ten minutes. The cleaner was leaving as he pulled into the undercover car park;

they acknowledged each other with a wave before the young man climbed into his van and left. Patrick took the stairwell to his first floor office. It was empty and quiet. So quiet that his own thoughts were almost deafening. He wished the cleaner had stayed so the sound of the vacuum could drown out the doubts that were pounding inside his head.

He rifled through the papers on his desk and then noticed the pile of mail that his receptionist had sorted and put aside as not urgent. He hadn't looked at it for a few weeks but he trusted Anita would have brought anything important to his attention.

He read them one by one but nothing brought even a hint of enthusiasm to him. There was an invitation to attend a benefit for the Screen Actors Guild at the Beverly Wilshire; an invitation to drive a new luxury sedan that had arrived at a dealership in Santa Monica; a bi-monthly magazine from the Cosmetic Surgeons of America and numerous professional association offers and advertisements. It was all as he'd expected.

Then he spied a gift certificate from an expensive women's store on Rodeo Drive; it was only three doors down from his practice. He picked up the beautifully presented certificate and noticed it was for a sizeable amount. He wondered if they had made a mistake sending it to him, then he froze. This was the same store where his receptionist had ordered some pyjamas and toiletries for Claudia all those weeks ago. But why would they be sending him a gift certificate? It was far too generous to be a thank you in return for his business. He turned it over and found a note on the back.

Dear Dr Spencer
Miss Monticello insisted that she repay the kind-
ness of the 'anonymous' customer. We did not re-
veal your details; however, she insisted that she
provide a certificate of equal value to you. We
hope a lovely lady in your life can enjoy shopping
in our store in the near future.
Warmest regards
Camille and staff

He closed his eyes and dropped his head back to look up at the ceiling. He knew he had to be the most stupid man in the world. She still had no idea that he had sent the parcel. She'd just wanted to repay a stranger. She could have just walked away but she had so much pride and honesty she had found a way to return what she didn't feel in her heart was hers. In a city of people who were only too willing to take, Claudia wanted only to give. And he knew she would have struggled to have covered the cost. She had so little money but she still did the right thing. She never let her values slip or chose the easy way out.

She'd fought so hard to bring her boys into the world. She never gave up on who or what she loved, no matter what obstacles she faced.

Claudia was an amazing, wonderful woman and he had just let her go.

She had dropped her walls, despite all the disappointment she had endured; she had let him into her life and her heart, and how had he repaid her? He had been as cruel as the father of her children. Perhaps even worse, he berated himself, because he knew what Claudia had been through. And she had allowed him to become a part of her babies' lives.

His head was upright as he stared at the door. His jaw flicked with mounting fury. At himself and the lies that had changed his life. He drew breath and filled his lungs, and suddenly felt adrenaline rush through his body.

He wouldn't let it happen again. Walking away from a life with Claudia, Thomas and Luca was not what he wanted to do. Not now, not ever. He wasn't sure he deserved them but he knew he wanted to fight to have them in his life. The thought of the boys' birth certificates having no father listed made him want even more to be the father figure in their lives. To guide them and to love them. If Claudia would let him, he would willingly take on that role. Forever.

He knew that meant reconciling with his family, no matter how difficult that might be. Perhaps time had healed some wounds, perhaps not. But Patrick wasn't about to base his future on assumptions. He would visit and see first-hand. And if they didn't want him back, then he would accept it but he wouldn't run away. He wanted a life back in London with Claudia…if she would have him.

He threw down the certificate and raced from the office. He had to prove to Claudia that he would fight for her and her boys and their future. He would do whatever it took. It was time to take a stand.

There was just one thing he had to do before he left to find her—he had a flight to book to London.

Claudia had packed her suitcase and left it by the door for the concierge to collect as she made her way to the hotel lobby to check out. Her tears had finally dried. She told herself firmly that Patrick Spencer would be the last man she would waste precious tears on. She would concentrate on raising her sons and forget about any other love. Her boys would be enough to fill her life and she knew they would never let her down. And, more importantly, she would never let them down. She would be there for them and give them everything they needed, growing up. And she hoped one day as grown men each would find their true love and she would be happy for them.

With a sigh for what might have been, she approached the reception desk.

'Good morning, Miss Monticello, are you checking out today?'

The young woman was dressed in a corporate charcoal suit, tortoiseshell glasses and a pleasant but predictable smile. Her hair was pulled back in a sleek chignon.

'Yes, I am. Can you please add a bottle of lemonade I took from the minibar to my credit card along with the room charges? I was staying in Room 303.'

The receptionist checked the computer screen and handed over the account.

Claudia passed over her credit card then tucked her hair behind her ear as she stood waiting for the card to be processed. She felt for her pearl earring, the way she always did when she was nervous. But it wasn't there. Her hand switched to the other ear. That one was missing too. She hadn't even thought about them for two days. Her head had been filled with thoughts so much more demanding of her time than her jewellery. She suddenly remembered she had left them on the bedside table. Patrick's bedside table.

'Are you looking for these?'

Claudia spun around to find a dishevelled Patrick standing behind her, her earrings in his outstretched hand.

'I would like to speak with Miss Monticello in private,' Patrick told the young woman at the desk, now looking at both of them. 'Do you have a room available?'

'The business centre has some private meeting rooms,' the receptionist told them, adjusting her glasses. 'You're more than welcome to use one of those.'

'Thank you,' Patrick replied, glancing around the lobby and spying the business centre.

'There's no need to thank her; we won't be using the room,' Claudia retorted, shaking her head in defiance. 'There's nothing I need or want to say to you, Patrick. I'm leaving today. We're over.'

'There's so much I want to say to you and I'd like to say it in private.'

With a look of discomfort Claudia felt certain was due to the potential for a situation to play out in her lobby, the receptionist interrupted. 'As I said, you're both more than welcome to use any of the meeting rooms and at this hour they're all free.'

Patrick led the way and crossed the lobby foyer with long purposeful strides and waited by the door of the business centre for Claudia's response. In silence she begrudgingly walked up to him. With each step across the large Mexican-inspired tiled floor of the lobby, the ache in her heart made her more resolute in her decision to end this meeting as soon as possible and never see Patrick again. She was angry and hurt in equal proportions that he had made her so vulnerable. She would hear him out then leave before she weakened and let her heart tell her what to do. She couldn't live her life with a man who had such different values to her own.

He softly closed the door behind them. 'I've got so much to say to you, Claudia, and it begins with an apology.'

'There's no point. I don't want an apology.'

'But you deserve one. I should never have let you walk out of my life and I apologise for that. I've been the biggest fool and you were right. I need to fight for what's important. That's you *and* my family. Claudia, I don't want to lose you and I'll do whatever it takes for us to be together, if you'll let me.'

'What do you mean *if I'll let you*?' she demanded. 'What are you telling me?'

'I want a life with you and your sons.'

'I can't stay here in LA; I told you that.'

'I know that and I wouldn't want you to stay here,' he said, taking her hands in his. 'I want to come home with you. I want to go back to London and do what you made me realise I should have done years ago. I want to set things right with my family. At least try to anyway.'

Claudia didn't pull her hands free as her expression turned from confusion to something closer to joy. 'Are you really serious about that?'

'I've never been more serious.'

'But why now? What's changed in two days?'

'I had time to think. Time to miss you and realise

it's something I should have done a long time ago. Because I don't want to lose you or the boys.'

'And when are you planning on doing this?' Her voice did not betray the happiness she felt building inside. She did not dare to allow herself to believe he wanted a life with her, only to be disappointed again.

'As soon as I can sell the practice, I will move home to the UK permanently. You're right, my first love has always been obstetrics. And I can do it. I can honour my sister's life and her bravery by bringing more children into the world, not trying to forget what happened.'

'You really want to go back to what you had before?'

'It won't be exactly what I had before. So much has changed, but I will deal with everything if I have you in my life.'

'This is a huge commitment to change everything about the life you lead. It's a big adjustment.'

'And it's one I need to make.'

'Then I will see you when you arrive,' she said, hoping with all of her heart that it wasn't an empty promise. She had become a realist and knew it might take time to sell the practice. In that time he might change his mind.

'You will see me sooner than that. I'll be travelling with you in about four hours' time,' he told her as he looked at his watch. 'You'll need help with the boys on the long haul flight...and to settle into your home.'

'You're travelling from LAX to Heathrow with me tonight?'

He pulled the airline ticket from his back trouser pocket. 'If you'll let me.'

Claudia smiled in return and immediately felt herself being pulled into Patrick's strong embrace and his lips pressed tenderly against hers. He pulled back for a moment to look lovingly into her eyes.

'I love you, Claudia Monticello, more than I ever have or ever will love anyone and more than I thought possible. You've given me the reason and strength to fight for what I want. Don't doubt, even for a moment, that you're my reason for waking up every day because that is what you've become. I don't want to live without you and if you'll marry me you will make me the happiest man in the world.'

Tears of happiness welled in her eyes as she nodded. 'Of course I'll marry you, Dr Spencer.'

Epilogue

'Daddy!' cried Thomas and Luca in unison as they ran to greet Patrick.

Thomas was a little taller than Luca but they both had mops of thick black hair and smiles as wide as their chubby, and slightly ruddy, little faces.

'How was your first day at school?' he asked as he scooped both of the boys into his strong grip, resting one child on each hip as they wrapped their little arms around him. 'Did you enjoy it?'

'I like it home with Mummy and you better,' said Luca and he nestled his head onto Patrick's broad shoulder.

'Me too, Daddy,' Thomas agreed. 'But there's a turtle in the classroom so it'th not too bad.'

'Yeth, I like the turtle very much.' Luca lifted his

head from Patrick's shoulder and chimed in. 'I think I might ask Father Christmas for one.'

'And Mummy got some of your favourite toffee from the lolly shop today too,' Thomas exclaimed. 'The special one with the yummy chocolate all over it.'

Just then, Claudia walked down the hallway of the beautiful Knightsbridge townhouse they had called home for almost five years and a smile spread over Patrick's face. She looked as stunning as she had the day they married and he loved the thoughtful things she did, like buying his favourite chocolate-covered almond toffee and kissing him every day, the same way she had done the very first time. He placed the boys both down on their feet again and ruffled their hair with his hands before they ran off to play outside.

'And how was your day, darling?' she asked as she threw her arms around Patrick's neck and kissed him.

'Not too bad, but it just became much, much better,' he told her as he kissed her tenderly and pulled her closer to him.

Claudia held her body against his, relishing the warmth of his embrace. Every morning she woke in his arms and fell a little more in love with the man who had made her believe in love again.

'Did you deliver any gorgeous babies today?'

'Two, actually,' he replied with a proud grin. 'And I'm inducing one of my IVF patients tomorrow morning. She's overdue, so she's been admitted to hospital this afternoon. The whole family is on standby and very excited.'

'Well, my day was wonderful too. Harriet and Matteo have finished renovations on their kitchen and want us over for an early dinner on Saturday. Matteo built a sandpit for the twins so the four of them can get messy together.'

'Sounds great. Matteo's quite the handyman. Perhaps he can help me to build one for the boys.'

'Oh, and Will called and he's coming over on Sunday with Todd and your mother for a roast. Todd's looking at universities for the year after next and wants your advice. His heart's set on studying medicine like his uncle. Thinks he wants to specialise in OBGYN.'

'Well, I'll do my best to talk him out of that.'

'You'll do no such thing. Where would I be today if you hadn't studied obstetrics?' she argued playfully. 'Just tell him to always have his medical bag handy when travelling in elevators and be prepared for anything if there's a pregnant woman in there with him.'

'Even falling in love.'

'Yes, even falling in love,' Claudia replied as she looked lovingly at her husband.

He pulled her close to him and kissed her again. 'Did I ever tell you that I am the luckiest man in the world and that I couldn't possibly love you any more than I do now?'

'You haven't told me today, Dr Spencer,' she said, running her fingers lightly down his chest. 'But you have mentioned it once or twice over the years.'

'Once or twice?' He laughed as his hands slipped down her spine and rested on the curve of her bottom. 'Well, just so you know how much, I will show you, Mrs Spencer. Once the sun has set and our boys are in bed, of course.'

She kissed him again and, hand in hand, they walked down the hall, both hoping the sun would set early that night.

And every night for the rest of their lives.

* * * * *

Lilian Darcy has written over eighty books for Harlequin. She has received four nominations for the Romance Writers of America's prestigious RITA® Award, as well as a Reviewer's Choice Award from *RT Book Reviews* for Best Silhouette Special Edition 2008. Lilian loves to write emotional, life-affirming stories with complex and believable characters.

Books by Lilian Darcy

Harlequin Medical Romance

Pregnant with His Child
A Mother for His Child
A Nurse in Crisis
A Proposal Worth Waiting For
Long-Lost Son: Brand-New Family
The Honourable Midwife
The Midwife's Courage

Visit the Author Profile page at
Harlequin.com for more titles.

Caring For
His Babies

LILIAN DARCY

Chapter 1

The phone line between Sydney and Riyadh was far clearer than Keelan had expected it to be, and there weren't the few seconds of delay he sometimes experienced with international calls. He'd had more difficult connections when talking to his cousin two suburbs away.

'Tell me about the babies,' said Jessica Russell, at the other end of the line.

It was four o'clock in the afternoon in Riyadh, but her voice sounded slightly husky as if she'd only just woken. Maybe she was working nights and sleeping days. Whatever her hours, she would be on a plane two days from now, heading home to Australia to meet her tiny new patients and Keelan himself.

'Well, Tavie's a lot better off than Tam at this stage...' Keelan began inadequately.

Keeping the cordless phone against his ear, he paced to the window of his study and looked out into the night. The harbour-scape appeared the same as always—a wide stripe of glittering black water, dancing with blue and red neon reflected from the city on the opposite shore and framed by a huge Moreton Bay fig tree on the right and his neighbour's house on the left.

So much else had changed, however, in just ten days.

'That's why I...we...need you on board so soon,' he continued.

Why had he changed the pronoun to 'we'? he had time to wonder, as he paused for breath. His various cousins, uncles and aunts applauded what he was doing, but had all declared, not without cause, that they had too much going on in their own lives to get involved on a practical level.

His mother had shown more enthusiasm and desire to help. She'd visited the hospital on the weekend, but she lived almost four hours away, north of Newcastle, and technically she was no relation at all to the twins. He wasn't going to foist on her the grandchildren of the woman who'd broken up her marriage twenty-three years ago.

Dad should have stepped forward perhaps, but he seemed frankly terrified—quite paralysed—and ready to run a mile from any involvement. Was it grief, or regret, or the fact that the babies were so fragile and small?

'All going well,' Keelan finished, dragging his focus

back to more practical concerns. 'The girl—Tavie—should be discharged next week.'

In a more perfect world the little girl twin would have been discharged into her mother's care, but Brooke—Keelan's half-sister—was dead and...

He revised his thought.

In a more perfect world, twenty-two-year-old Brooke would never have become pregnant in the first place, through one of her many unsuitable affairs, and even if she had, she would have sought the right prenatal care, the twins might not have been born so prematurely and Brooke would certainly have realised that the post-partum bleeding she'd experienced after her discharge from the hospital had been way heavier than it should have been.

Too many ifs.

Too much drama, in too short a time.

The babies were ten days old, having been born at just over twenty-eight weeks gestation, and the little boy, Tam, was clinging to life by a thread. Brooke had collapsed in a café a week ago, but emergency treatment had come too late and she'd bled out in the ambulance on the way to the same hospital, North Sydney, where she'd given birth. The Hunter clan had survived the funeral—and the publicity—with its usual dignity and repressed emotion.

Keelan's ex-stepmother, Louise—Brooke's mother—had fallen apart in private afterwards, however. She was still heavily medicated, apparently, back home in Melbourne with her new husband, Phillip.

He'd told Keelan categorically, 'We can't take them. It just wouldn't work. Especially if they turn out to be delicate or damaged. I'm too old, and Louise isn't very strong emotionally. Especially now, of course. Some other arrangement will have to be made.'

Keelan had known, at that moment, that there was really only one option. Discounting the babies' father, since he'd disappeared from Brooke's life months ago, and they didn't even know his last name, Keelan was the babies' closest blood relative of an appropriate age for fatherhood. He was a paediatrician at North Sydney Hospital, and knew exactly the kinds of problems that the babies might face now and in the future.

So he'd adopt them himself.

It wouldn't be an ideal solution but, as he'd just concluded, this wasn't a perfect world. He felt uncomfortable about how much the babies' new nurse needed to know about all of this. With four generations of highly successful Hunter lawyers, doctors, politicians and financiers preceding him, Keelan valued privacy and discretion. He wondered uneasily just which boundaries he'd be able to keep in place during the coming months.

'So I'll mainly be settling in until that happens?' Jessica Russell asked over the phone. 'Until she's ready to come home?'

'Spending as much time with both of them at the hospital, I would hope,' he answered firmly. 'I'll be pushing for the earliest discharge that's safely possible, given your experience with preemies, so I'll want you liaising closely with the nurses in the unit and getting familiar with each baby's condition and needs. Settling in can happen in your own time.'

She gave a wry laugh. 'Is there going to be much of

that? My own time, I mean. The twins themselves will call the shots on my hours.'

This comment reassured Keelan, yet served to confirm that he hadn't quite trusted her before, and probably still didn't. Wouldn't for a while, if he had any sense. This would be merely a job for her. She could never have the same investment in the twins' well-being as he did.

He'd intended to go through an agency here in Sydney, get someone local. He liked to make his own judgements about people. But a medical colleague in Adelaide had recommended Ms Russell, and when he had gone to a Sydney nursing agency, her name, by coincidence, had come up again.

'She registered with us quite recently, and has first-class credentials and references. I'd jump at her, if I were you. I imagine she'll be looking for a permanent hospital position before too long.'

Jessica had been working in a high-level neonatal unit in Saudi Arabia, but she'd had enough of it after two years and was about to come home. She would be ready to start exactly when Keelan wanted her—that was, immediately.

Keelan was wary of the coincidence rather than reassured by it. He didn't go in for 'signs'. But he couldn't ignore Ms Russell's level of experience when it was coupled with a recommendation from someone he trusted.

'Why's she been in Saudi, though?' he'd asked his colleague, Lukas Cheah, phoning the man for a second time in search of more details. 'It can be a dangerous part of the world for Westerners.'

'Not sure. A bit of a wanderer?'

'A risk-taker?'

'Not necessarily. Saving for a mortgage? Some nurses manage to build a nice bank balance over there. From what my wife has said—' Jane Cheah was also an NICU nurse, Keelan knew '—I don't think she has much family to fall back on.'

Keelan, in contrast, had far too much family. He felt the pressure sometimes. At other times he felt pride.

'Sounds as if you're not worried about working long, erratic hours,' he said to Ms Russell.

'Well, no, since it's obviously a requirement and, I assume, the reason for the… uh…generous salary you've offered. Anyway,' she added quickly, 'I've done it before.'

She sounded uncomfortable about discussing money. Keelan was, too. Probably for different reasons. The Hunter family had a fair bit of it, but he liked to be as discreet about that fact as possible. He went back to the subject of the twins' health and medical status instead.

'Let me give you more details about what you'll be dealing with. They were born somewhere between twenty-eight and twenty-nine weeks. The girl—Tavie—is significantly heavier and stronger.'

'What was her birth weight?'

'She was 1220 grams. Tam was just under a kilo—990 grams—but we'll get to him later. I'll try and go through this systematically. Tavie is still on oxygen.'

'CPAP?'

'She started on a respirator, but yes, she's up to CPAP now.'

Of course Ms Russell knew the abbreviation—continuous positive airway pressure, delivering oxygen via a tube taped to the baby's face. It was good not to have to explain.

'She's also on light therapy for jaundice as of two days ago,' he continued. 'She had a heart murmur indicative of PDA—' again, it reassured him to use the abbreviation for the common preemie heart problem, patent ductus arteriosus, knowing she'd understand it '—but that's resolved on it's own, fortunately.'

'Sometimes those can re-open.'

'It'll be monitored, of course.'

'Gut problems? As and Bs?'

'Her gut is good, but she's still having recurrent apnoea and bradycardia episodes, yes. With you on board, she can be discharged with oxygen and monitors, if that's still necessary, and I expect it will be.'

'Yes.'

'We want to see her get back up to her birth weight and show some steady gain before her discharge in any case.'

'She's on tube feeds?'

'Yes.'

'And the boy—Tam—isn't so good, you said?'

He couldn't hold back a sigh. 'No, unfortunately. His heart problems are more serious. We…uh…realistically…don't know if he'll make it.'

'Sometimes they don't.' It wasn't an unsympathetic line. She'd just seen it before, that was all, and knew there wasn't a lot to say.

'We heard a heart murmur when he was a couple of days old,' he continued, keeping to facts, not feelings. 'An echocardiogram showed two ventricular septal defects—VSDs.' It was one of the most common congenital heart defects, more prevalent in boys and more prevalent in twins than single births.

'Serious ones? Can they tell?'

'We're still hoping they may close over on their own, but so far they haven't. Four days ago his oxygen levels began dropping. They did another scan and found a third VSD, large, around 7 millimetres. He also showed coarctation of the aorta.'

'He wouldn't be strong enough for surgery yet,' she guessed. 'Although that thinned aorta must be a concern for you.'

'Definitely, but yes, before surgery we need to grow him and stabilise him, steer him past a few other risks.'

'Infection, gut problems, jaundice,' she murmured. 'Is he on bili lights, like his sister?'

'Yes.'

'I love bili lights—something we can do for them that doesn't cause them pain.'

'I know what you mean.'

'And they've lost their mother, too... Rough way to come into this world.' The husky note in her voice had deepened. 'I hope someone's told you what a heroic thing you're doing, Dr Hunter, taking them on.'

'There was no choice,' he answered shortly, wondering if he should have saved the story on their circumstances until he'd met the twins' nurse face to face.

She'd rubbed him up the wrong way with her statement, well intentioned though it had clearly been. He didn't want editorial commentary from an employee. A compliment like the one she'd just given him implied that she had the right to criticise as well, and she didn't.

She was just a paid carer, chosen for her expertise not for her opinions and feelings.

Except…

Premature babies needed love. It was a medically established fact that fragile infants did better when they had periods of warm, peaceful body contact. Tavie and Tam needed Jessica Russell to care about them.

Keelan wasn't married or seriously involved with any woman right now. There was no other female under his roof to fill a maternal role, and yet he didn't want Ms Russell to get too close, or too indispensable, because eventually, inevitably, she would leave. What would that do to the babies, a few months down the track, if they'd become deeply attached to her?

Lord, this wasn't going to be easy!

Jessie put down the phone after Keelan Hunter's call and squinted out into the glare of the desert's afternoon light. Her eyes ached for the relief of Sydney's lush, almost tropical foliage. Two more days. It would be fun to try a new city, a place she'd only ever seen during a couple of brief holidays. And it might be refreshing to get back to some private nursing for a while, she told herself.

A feeling of restlessness tugged at her heart, dragging her spirits down. She'd been so *good*, so sensible these past two years. She'd lived so frugally, sending as much of her wages back to the investment fund in Australia as she possibly could.

With both her parents remarried, living on opposite sides of the continent, absorbed in their new families, and not particularly keen to be reminded of the miserable marriage they'd endured as their punishment for having conceived her out of wedlock when they'd both been far too young, she'd responded in the most practical way to her realisation that she was essentially alone in the world—she'd saved money.

And then the investment fund had gone bust and she'd lost it all.

If there was a lesson to be learned somewhere in this development, she hadn't yet worked out what it was. The fun-loving, live-for-the-moment grasshopper in the Aesop fable had had it right after all? The serious, hard-working ant should have its legs pulled off for setting such a bad example to impressionable nurses?

Hmm.

She did know one thing, though.

She was homesick. Gut-wrenchingly, tearfully, desperately homesick.

Bit sad that she didn't really have a home to go to. Not Adelaide. Too long since she'd first left, and the in-between experiment of a year she'd spent back there after the stints with Médecins Sans Frontières in Liberia and Sierra Leone, and before the rather crazy time in London, hadn't been enough to re-establish her roots. Jane Cheah was the only friend she missed from that time.

So she was trying Sydney, and a live-in position that offered the dangerous promise of being able to pretend she had a home. From the impression Dr Hunter had given her over the phone, she didn't think he'd do much to foster this illusion, and that was probably for the best. There were many things she liked about a footloose life, perhaps the most important being that you knew exactly where you stood.

She tried to form a picture of Dr Hunter in her mind, based on the way his voice had sounded and the things she knew about him, but couldn't do it. Even his attitude to the babies had been hard to read. She'd just have to wait.

Two days. The long flight. Then Keelan Hunter himself would meet her at the airport and take her…home?

No.

Not home. Not really. Just the next waystation.

Her stomach churned.

Ms Russell looked like what she was—a seasoned Australian traveller returning home after a long absence. Keelan had her name held up on a large piece of card, and when she saw it she steered straight towards it through the crowded terminal, looking tired, relieved, a little dishevelled and wary.

He could match her on three out of those four attributes. Tired because he'd been up half the night at the hospital, relieved because he hadn't been one hundred per cent convinced that she would actually be on the plane, and he was definitely wary.

He would try not to let it show, but the wariness would probably last for weeks. Until he worked out how this was going to operate. Until he knew if Tam would live, and how long both babies might need in-home professional care.

'Hello.' She put down two distinctly battered suitcases and held out her hand. 'Dr Hunter?'

'Yes.' He thought about inviting her to call him Keelan, but held back and said instead, 'How was your flight? This is all your luggage?'

'I've got used to travelling light.' She took it on trust that he remembered the details of her résumé, with its references to periods spent in two different clinics in the developing world, in contrast to the high-level neo-natal experience he'd employed her for.

'You need some new suitcases,' he told her.

'And travelling cheap.' She grinned, inviting her to meet him halfway, which he did, because she'd taken him by surprise.

She had an infectious smile, careless and open like a boy's. It went with the liberal splash of freckles across her nose and the red-brown hair, bushy after the flight. Her eyes were a startling blue, and seemed to light up like the flash of sun on water, making the smile dazzling as well as infectious. She was thirty-two, he knew, but she looked younger.

'Fair enough,' he said, and nudged her gently aside so he could grab the pair of shabby handles.

The things weighed a ton, belying her statement about travelling light. Couldn't be clothes. She was wearing a long, modest skirt and long-sleeved top, with a wide white scarf around her neck that she would have used to cover her head in Saudi, and in that part of the world he doubted she would have needed much more than a few repetitions on the same theme. No thick coats or evening clothes or sports gear.

'I'm sorry,' she said. 'Too many books in there. I tended to hoard them in Riyadh, because they were hard to get.'

'Didn't you have someone equally desperate to pass them on to?'

'I passed on all the ones I could bear to part with.' Then she apologised again and finished, 'I hope your car's not far.'

'It's fine. And there's an empty bookcase in the room I've set aside for you.'

She frowned for a moment as if picturing this unfamiliar idea—that she might unpack her books and put them on shelves—then said, 'Something we didn't sort out before—how long are you expecting this arrangement to continue? I mean, once the babies reach, say, one month corrected age, four months since birth, they're hopefully not going to need the level of specialised care I can provide. And a full-time, in-home nurse is…' She stopped.

'Expensive,' he finished for her. 'Look, that's not an issue.'

Another beat of silence. 'No, OK.'

Keelan could almost feel the mental backstep she took as she considered what he'd just revealed. Well, it was pointless to pretend that he struggled for money. The income from his investments competed, to a healthy extent, with his salary as a hospital-based paediatrician, and he'd benefited from an inheritance as well. She'd see all the evidence of his established lifestyle soon enough.

'I'll keep you as long as I feel it's in the twins' best interests,' he said. 'You're right. That'll probably be around four months, from a medical perspective.' In other areas, it was more complex, but he didn't want to thrash this through with her now, when they'd only just met. She might not last a week, if they weren't happy with each other. 'Do you need to know? Do you have a future commitment elsewhere?'

'No, no commitments. Just wondering.'

'Whether it's worth unpacking the books?'

'Something like that.'

A silence fell, slightly awkward. He guessed she was sorting and arranging her first impressions, the way he was, and the way she might, or might not, sort and arrange this forty-kilogram load of books in her new room.

On the whole, he'd had no surprises so far, either pleasant or otherwise—unless you counted that smile, which was dazzling. Great for Tavie and Tam, when they got to the smiling stage. Or Tavie, anyway. He wasn't letting himself count on little Tam yet.

His gut whipped like a snake suddenly, and his eyes stung. He hadn't wanted these babies in his life, and now, already, he didn't want to lose them. He didn't want to be defeated on this.

If he was going to step in, do the right thing, the thing no one else was prepared or equipped to do—even though everyone agreed that the babies must be kept within the Hunter clan—he absolutely did not want to fail in any part of it.

This, at heart, was why he'd chosen an experienced neonatal nurse as their initial carer, instead of a nanny with a mere first-aid certificate. The babies had to live, and they had to thrive. That was all he needed from Jessica Russell. Her competence, her diligence, her professional care. For around four months.

'Can I take you up to the hospital as soon as you've unpacked?' he said.

'Make that unpacked and had a shower, and you have a deal,' she answered at once.

'I'm sorry. Maybe you need to sleep as well.'

'If I let myself do that, I probably wouldn't wake again for the full eight hours, and then I wouldn't sleep tonight.'

'Right.' He had a fleeting image of her wandering around his house at one in the morning, and didn't like it.

'The shower will do. And I'll unpack later, on condition that you show me where the coffee is.'

She tried her smile on him again, but this time he didn't respond. He'd got caught up in the implications contained in her mention of coffee.

The two of them would be sharing a fridge and a coffee-maker, living under the same roof.

His house was idiotically large for one adult. He'd inherited it from his grandfather seven years ago, when he'd been twenty-eight. He'd kept it and renovated it, but he'd been married back then, so there had been two people to make use of the space, with the vague prospect of children in the future. The marriage hadn't lasted, however, and Tanya had gone back to New Zealand after the divorce.

He loved the house too much to think of selling it, which meant that now there was plenty of room for an adoptive father, a pair of newborn twins and their nurse. He felt uncomfortable about it all the same. Babies weren't good at boundaries. Some adults weren't either.

'Of course,' he told Jessica quickly. 'I'll give you a tour of the kitchen. I don't eat at home very much, so we shouldn't get in each other's way there.'

'I'll certainly try not to get in yours!'

'Put whatever you want in the fridge and pantry. You have your own bathroom and sitting room. Anyway, you'll see it soon enough.'

They cleared the airport a few minutes later, drove up Southern Cross Drive past bevies of Sunday golfers enjoying the spring sunshine, then swooped down into the traffic tunnels that now ran beneath the city and the harbour. There weren't many cars about, and they turned into his driveway in the North Shore suburb of Cremorne within fifteen minutes of leaving the airport.

They hadn't talked at all during the journey, because Ms Russell had thoughtfully closed her eyes and pretended to be asleep. Keelan appreciated the gesture. When she shifted in the passenger seat, arching her spine, getting herself comfortable, his skin prickled and stood on end, like that of a tomcat confronting a back-yard rival. She seemed to impinge on his space somehow, and he didn't like it.

He brought her luggage upstairs for her. Since she followed in his wake, he couldn't see from her face and manner what she thought of the house. She'd hardly be able to complain, however. It was a prime piece of real estate, with harbour views, privacy, a large garden and spacious interior.

He'd had the place professionally decorated in a clean, warm yet unfussy style—lots of pale yellow, creamy white and sage green, with accents here and there in rust and teal. There were leather couches, botanical prints, the odd well-placed antique or original painting that he'd acquired from the family. It felt like home to him.

'There's a living room, dining room, study, breakfast room and kitchen downstairs,' he told her, keeping it clipped and brief. 'A terrace opens off the breakfast room and leads into the garden. Oh, and there's a powder room and laundry, too.'

'I'll need the laundry, I'm sure, as soon as Tavie comes home!'

'Up here, there's my master suite, and everything else is essentially yours. Babies' room here, next to your bedroom.'

They both stood in the doorway and looked at it, Ms Russell poised just in front of the arm he rested against the doorframe.

'Looks as if you have some shopping still to do,' she said.

The room contained a couch, a rocking chair and a chest of drawers, and there was still plenty of space, but he hadn't had a chance to fill it yet. In a spirit of superstition that he privately mocked in himself but couldn't shake, he wouldn't buy Tam a cot until after his heart surgery. Well after it.

'I'll get you to buy what we need,' he answered. 'I've made a list. But if there's anything I've forgotten, you have *carte blanche*. Clothes, toys. I've noted all the obvious stuff, I think.'

'Do you want to use disposables or cloth?'

'Your choice.'

'Both, probably. Cloth is better for preventing rashes.

Disposables are easier to change when they're still all wired and tubed.'

'I wish there was a connecting door between your room and this one. I thought about getting one put in, but there just hasn't been time.'

'Of course there hasn't,' she murmured. 'Can't imagine…'

He moved on down the corridor, seeking to escape her empathy. 'Next comes the bathroom, and then the room you can use as a sitting room. It opens onto a balcony, and there's a TV. Towels, sheets… I have a part-time cleaner…housekeeper, really…and she's set everything up for you. I can increase her hours once Tavie comes home, if you need extra help.'

'Thanks,' Jessie said.

She stood in the middle of her new bedroom, feeling a little awkward, while Dr Hunter put down her embarrassing suitcases. She glimpsed his palms, and they looked reddened and creased by the inadequate, scruffy handles. Really, next time she took off to some distant corner of the globe, she needed to invest in new luggage.

'Let me get you that coffee while you have your shower,' he said. 'Come down to the kitchen when you're ready.'

She nodded. 'I won't be long.'

'No, take your time. I have a couple of calls to make.'

About her, possibly. To announce that she'd safely arrived, thus keeping the twin project on track.

She had the impression, after the flurry of phone calls and e-mails that had passed between the two of them, and between herself and the nursing agency, that the twins were a family obligation which had been delegated to him, and that he would have to report on any developments to certain relatives.

Sad.

Difficult.

Not surprising, though, maybe.

The nursing agency had told Jessie something about Keelan Hunter's very well-established family background, and on first impression he fitted it to a T. With his impressive height went an instinctive confidence and arrogance of bearing. With his brown eyes—not a dark brown, but intense, all the same—went a sharpness of perception that came from looking at the world from a more exalted perspective than most people enjoyed.

And with his strong body, honed from a childhood spent rowing and playing rugby at some top-flight Sydney private boys' school, went expensive casual clothes and a conservative haircut that should have looked anything but sexy.

Hang on.

Sexy?

Well, yes.

This was a dispassionate observation, not a declaration of interest, though, she told herself hastily. He had a well-shaped head and a smooth, tanned neck, and the way his dark hair was cut definitely…surprisingly… qualified as sexy. She'd never be interested in a man like Keelan Hunter on that level, however.

She wasn't that much of a fool, and she knew how to learn from past mistakes. She knew exactly what chasms of difference in outlook and history would yawn between them, and he'd been formal and cool enough to make his own desire for distance quite clear. She could protect herself with the same kind of shield.

In the shower, she felt a rush of almost painful pleasure at being back in Australia. All the little things, the tiny, familiar details told her, You're safe. This *is* home. The sound of the Sunday morning lawnmowers over the distant hum of traffic, the spring scents in the air—eucalyptus and frangipani—the way the taps worked and the fragrance of a familiar brand of soap.

She found clean clothes to dress in—a knee-length summer blue skirt and matching short-sleeved, figure-hugging top that she hadn't worn for two years—pulled a comb through her knotted hair and blasted it with a hairdryer until the bits that framed her face were dry. Then she pulled it up and back into a ponytail, slipped on some flat-heeled black leather sandals and followed that fabulous smell of coffee that wafted up the stairs.

'Much better now!'

Keelan turned. 'Yes, I can see that.' His tone dampened the comment down to the level of understatement, and he managed to hide the fact that he hadn't realised until she'd spoken that she'd arrived in the kitchen. The espresso pot still hissed on the stove and had masked the sound of her shoes on the hardwood floor of the hall.

She flashed her grin at him, and he grinned reluctantly back, then turned to pour the coffee into the two blue and white mugs he'd set on the blue-black granite benchtop in an attempt to hide the discomfort he still couldn't shake.

She was actually very pretty. He hadn't noticed it at the airport, or while showing her to her room. Now the realisation didn't please him. His ex-stepmother, Louise, had been his father's secretary. He didn't trust the illusions generated when a man and his female employee spent too much time in each other's company.

With Ms Russell's hair straight and damp and pulled back from her face, he could see—reluctantly—what lovely bone structure she had. Beautiful skin, too, despite the freckles. The shower had left her face clean and rosy, framed by the shiny silk of hair whose escaping strands contained a dozen different shades of copper and mink and gold.

And her figure was a knock-out, now that the disguising contours of the loose top and long skirt had gone. She had long legs, a rounded and very feminine backside, a long, slender torso and breasts that would comfortably fill a man's hands. Without being too tight or showing very much skin at all, her top and skirt advertised these assets quite plainly. They advertised the grace in her movements, too.

The blue of the new outfit was reflected in her eyes and reminded him again of sunlight on the sea, and he felt as if someone had flung open a window on a breezy day and let in the smell of salt water and the sound of gulls. His breath caught for a moment, and he shoved aside a surge of sensual awareness that he didn't remotely want.

'Milk?' he said.

'Yes, please, a big slurp of it, and please don't tell me it's that UHT stuff!' Her frankness should have been awkward, lacking in class, but somehow it wasn't.

'No, it's fresh,' he answered.

She was fresh.

'And look,' he went on quickly. 'I'll leave cash in the top drawer, here, for grocery shopping. Buy anything you want, a different brand of coffee. As I said, I eat on the run mostly, but that needn't stop you from cooking, or filling the freezer with microwave dinners, whatever.'

'Thanks.' Another smile. 'I expect Tavie and Tam will limit me to the microwave option.'

'Hmm. I'll leave the menus for the best local take-away places in the drawer as well, shall I?'

They sat in the breakfast room and he offered her a section of the Sunday newspaper, as well as some sweet biscuits he'd found to go with the coffee. She accepted both, which meant they could eat and drink and read and not have to talk to each other. A sense of peace descended over the room and over his spirits, and though he knew it would be temporary, it lightened his outlook a little.

Jessica Russell seemed to be the kind of woman who didn't need to chat constantly, thank goodness. Maybe there was a chance they'd eventually be comfortable with each other after all.

When he looked at his watch, on reaching the paper's sports section, he discovered they'd been sitting here for nearly half an hour. Ms Russell's eyes looked glazed, as if she could easily have slept despite the coffee.

Where were his wits this morning? He'd intended to be at the hospital by now.

'We should go,' he said, standing up with the effort of a much older man as he felt the weight of his new circumstances crush down on him again.

Chapter 2

'The babies have unusual names,' Jessie said. 'Did you pick them, Dr Hunter? Or…'

She trailed off. Having intended her comment as small talk, she found she'd quickly trespassed into difficult territory. This man had lost his half-sister less than two weeks ago. Jessie couldn't pretend that Brooke Hunter had never existed, but she didn't want to cause her new employer any unnecessary pain.

He frowned, and as they approached the automatic glass doors that led into the main building at North Sydney Hospital, she could see that his reflection showed tense shoulders and a tight mouth.

'Brooke picked them,' he said, his tone clipped and short. There was a stiff silence, and for a moment Jessie thought he wasn't going to say anything more, but then he added in a different voice, much more slowly, 'She was sitting in a café, poring over a baby name book when the full-on haemorrhaging began, and those were the names we found on a sheet of paper folded inside the book. If she was still here, I'd have thought they were… I don't know…too odd and too frivolous, or something.'

'You think so?' Jessie murmured.

'I've been—' He broke off, and muttered something that she didn't catch. 'Hell, pretty critical of my sister, over the years. But as things are, the names seem important somehow. A gift from her. I like them now. I'd never think of changing them.'

'Mmm,' she said, ambushed by a degree of emotion she hadn't been prepared for.

She'd learned a lot about Keelan Hunter in the space of that short, palpably reluctant speech. He'd loved his half-sister, but he hadn't been close to her and held regrets about it now. And he cared a lot more about the twins than he knew. More, probably, than he wanted to care, especially given Tam's fragile state.

It was good to get more of a sense of this man and what made him tick, but that could be dangerous as well. Sometimes, in this sort of situation, you could get way too understanding, and way too involved.

The hospital swallowed them up and engulfed her in warring impressions of familiarity and newness. She'd been in this type of large metropolitan teaching hospital many times before. She'd crossed similar sprawling parking areas, signposted for visitors or reserved for staff.

She'd seen sunsets and sunrises reflected off similar tiered rows of windows in the multi-storey main building, and had imagined Nightingale-like ghosts flitting around similar original colonial buildings. These buildings still existed at many older Australian hospitals, now typically used for things like clinics and support groups. She'd also become lost in a similar maze of extensions and connecting walkways in the past.

Every hospital smelled different, however, and no two hospitals were set out the same way. Dr Hunter led the way to a lift and pressed the button for level seven, which would be easy enough to remember when she came here on her own. He'd already given her the use of his second car, a late-model Japanese sedan, and she had its keys and the keys to his house in her bag. She got the impression he didn't want to have to drive her around, beyond this first trip to see the babies, and that was fair enough.

'Have you had a report on them this morning?' she asked, thinking he might have phoned the unit before picking her up at the airport.

'I was called out to another patient during the night, and spent some time with them after that,' he said. 'Pretty quiet, at that hour. Tam's on a diuretic and prostaglandins, and that treatment is managing his heart condition for the moment. He's being monitored for NEC and IVH. So far so good. I don't think we're out of the woods on those yet, though.'

'Particularly the gut problems.'

Necrotising enterocolitis, in other words. NEC was a jaunty little abbreviation, or you could refer vaguely to 'gut problems' as Jessie just had, but there was nothing fun about the irreversible death of sections of a preemie's bowel.

Dr Hunter, however, focused on what she hadn't talked about—the good news on intraventricular haemorrhage.

'Yes,' he said. 'Statistically, if Tam was going to have a brain bleed it should have happened by now, and even over the past few years they've got better at preventing those. Here we are. Let's take a look at them. I didn't bring the camera today, but I took some pictures a few days ago, and I'm hoping you'll use it sometimes. Louise—Brooke's mother—doesn't want to see photos yet but I hope she may be ready for that in time.'

'Just tell me how the camera works, and of course I'll take some.'

'It's easy. Point and click variety. I'm not expecting artistic shots, and mine certainly haven't been.'

He greeted a couple of nurses on his way in, and Jessie saw that here was another area in which relationships and feelings hadn't quite settled, yet, into their appropriate slots. Keelan Hunter wasn't fully a doctor in this unit, and not exactly a parent either. No one knew quite what he was, at this stage, least of all himself.

One nurse had a vial of blood in her hand, and another was racing for the phone, so Jessie wasn't introduced to anyone yet. The nurses' greetings were polite and respectful—warm even—yet remained formal. No one used his first name.

Something about his bearing didn't invite that, perhaps. He stood out here, taller than the nurses, more upright and contained than a couple of the harried-looking junior doctors moving about the unit. His stride seemed longer than theirs, and his shoulders squarer and stronger.

It was a big place. With techniques in keeping preterm infants alive and healthy improving all the time, NICUs in most major hospitals were a growth area— crowded, like this one was, expensive to maintain, busy and bright and noisy, with different staff constantly coming and going, despite the best efforts of the dedicated doctors, nurses and technicians to give their fragile charges the peace and quiet they really needed.

The two babies weren't together. Even though some studies had shown that twins did better when placed in the same incubator, there were arguments against this practice. In Tavie's and Tam's case, too, the little girl's comparative health and strength classed her as a level one. Tam was with the sickest babies in the unit, at the opposite end—level three.

They reached Tam first. He lay in an incubator, which counted as a 'graduation' of sorts. He would have started out in a radiant warmer, which gave better access to staff when a baby was very unstable and needed constant treatments and tests. Even now, he had equipment and monitors all around him.

He had a cardiorespiratory monitor attached to sensors on his chest and limbs, with alarms set to signal an unsafe change in blood pressure, heart rate, temperature or respiration. He had a pulse oximeter clipped to his foot, measuring the level of oxygen saturation in his blood by shining a light through his skin.

Amazing machine, Jessie always thought. By detecting the fine shadings of colour between red oxygenated blood and blue de-oxygenated blood, the machine could provide an accurate measurement of the blood oxygen level, expressed as a percentage. You wanted to see that percentage up in the high nineties, which Tam's was.

Poor little guy. Little sweetheart.

'Here he is,' Dr Hunter said, his voice hardly more than a growl. He didn't touch the top of the incubator. Some babies found even this stressful, and their nurses had to learn to avoid casually placing charts or pencils there, while going about their work.

Or was her new employer's lack of contact with Tam more a statement about his own distance than his awareness of the baby's needs?

'Hi, Tam,' Jessie whispered.

She was accustomed to babies like this. Most people weren't. Their dry, reddish skin, their spindly limbs, the dark vestiges of downy hair on their shoulders and backs as well as their hat-covered heads, the sheer *smallness* of them. The tip of an adult finger would fill Tam's whole fist when he grasped at it.

'He is jaundiced, isn't he, poor love,' she added.

With the yellow tinge of jaundice on his skin and the blue of the 'bili' lights above him, he looked as if he'd been stained with some strange dye, and his little nappy, a startling white in contrast, was hardly bigger than a folded envelope.

It would get weighed every time he was changed, as a method of calculating his output of urine. You wanted the right amount of fluid going in, and the right amount coming out, and with preemies you measured it all obsessively.

'Have you been able to hold him yet?' she asked.

'No, not yet,' Dr Hunter said. 'Hospital policy is to wait until he hits the kilogram mark.'

Jessie wasn't surprised, although the arbitrary nature of the cut-off point bothered her. Some babies responded very well to being held at nine hundred grams. Others couldn't take it at twelve hundred. Weight was only one way to measure a baby's fitness for certain things. In this case, though...

Tam was still being fed via total parenteral nutrition—intravenous feeding, mainly through a line into his navel. On the plus side, this avoided the digestive problems that could occur if a delicate preemie wasn't yet ready to have its little stomach filled. The down side was that it increased the risk of infection via the entry sites of the different lines, and made a preemie even more difficult to hold—so much equipment in the way.

And a baby like this would tire very easily, too, even through something as simple as being lifted from his incubator into someone's waiting arms. In Tam's case, the no-holding-yet policy was probably the right approach.

'I touch him, though, when he can handle it,' Dr Hunter added. He looked at the baby with narrowed eyes, an expert's judgement and a powerful aura of human will. If he could have pushed a two-ton rock up a hill to increase Tam's chance of survival, he would have done it, Jessie suspected, whether he cared to call this 'love' or not.

Again, she found herself understanding Keelan Hunter's feelings more than she wanted to.

'Is he showing a lot of stress?' She kept her voice low.

Research on the youngest preemies in recent years showed that they could get dangerously stressed through over-stimulation. Their nervous systems were too fragile and immature. They couldn't listen and look at the same time without tiring themselves. When they were being touched, they didn't want to be talked to. NICU nurses and caring parents learned to read the baby's state.

'He has a couple of great nurses, who try to minimise it as much as possible,' Dr Hunter said. 'They're aware of the situation and looking forward to having you on board. Here's Stephanie now. I'll introduce you.'

He stepped away, and only then did Jessie realise how close the two of them had been standing. A draught of cool air eddied around her bare arm, contrasting with the body heat he'd given off. Thinking back, she wondered if she'd been the one to move closer, without realising it, drawn by some indefinable quality to him that she didn't have a name for yet. The force of will she'd just seen in him, perhaps.

He wasn't as urbane and as civilised as she'd somehow expected, with his classy background. He wasn't as tame or as bland. There was something almost… what…primi-tive about him. Primitive? That couldn't be the word. Something, though, that left her feeling strangely edgy and stirred up inside.

Just tired, probably.

'Stephanie, here's Jessica Russell, to see the babies,' he said. 'She's just off the plane this morning, so it's only a quick visit today.'

'Welcome to our unit, Jessica,' said the neat, athletic-looking woman. Vincent. Stephanie Vincent. She had some threads of grey in her dark hair and a twinkling, brown-eyed smile.

'Call me Jessie,' she answered at once, realising that

she hadn't mentioned the usual shortening of her name to Dr Hunter.

It seemed fairly obvious that he wanted to maintain a more formal relationship. Wise, probably. She wasn't sure if it would be possible in the long run, however, when they'd be caring for two babies together.

'He's looking good, isn't he?' the NICU nurse said. 'Kidneys keeping up, nice steady colour. He's not awake very much. That heart's tiring him out.'

Efficiently, she noted Tam's hourly observations on a chart, checked that the fluid in his lines was flowing as it should, and made some notes about his state. Jessie watched her, aware of the baby's reluctant yet determined adoptive father still standing beside her, as rigid and solid as a tree trunk.

A warm tree trunk. Somehow, they'd moved closer to each other again, and she could feel his heat.

'Well, let's go and see Tavie,' he said after a moment, before she was quite ready to move on. She took a last look at the little boy, wishing she was officially his nurse, wondering if she should let herself feel anything like his mother.

Tam lay on his back, with his head to the side and his eyes closed. His little face looked so still, but then he twitched and grimaced and stiffened his limbs, and she knew he couldn't be very comfortable. Jessie had seen parents weeping in frustration at having to watch their babies like this, and had sometimes cried herself.

You just wanted to hold them against you, take out all those awful lines, pull the sensors away. It was so hard to accept that the lines and sensors were ultimately keeping the baby alive.

A few minutes later, on the other side of the unit, Tavie looked a lot better, but she was still tiny—the smallest of the level one babies.

'Wednesday, we think, for her discharge, if you're comfortable with that,' Dr Hunter said to Jessie. 'She'll be done with the bili lights by then.'

'How's her weight?' she asked.

'Oh, big milestone when I weighed her this morning,' put in her nurse, Barb McDaniel, who hovered nearby. She looked to be in her late forties, with rounded hips, hair tinted a pretty mid-brown shade and that aura of experience and competence that no one could fake. 'She's hit her birthweight, 1220 grams.'

'Fantastic,' Dr Hunter said. 'That's great.'

And he actually smiled.

He blinked at the same time, twice, as if his honey-brown eyes felt gritty, but his mouth curved and his straight white teeth rested for a moment against his full lower lip, and Barb shot him a curious glance that softened into approval. Clearly, she'd been concerned about how he was handling all this, how involved he was, whether he'd eventually crack.

'Could one of us hold her?' Jessie asked.

'Do you have time, Dr Hunter?' Barb turned to him, tentative and respectful.

But he deferred at once to Jessie. 'Best if you do it, I think. The two of you need to get used to each other as soon as you can.'

'I'd love to,' she answered, and it came out sounding more like a rebuke at her employer's distance than she'd meant it to.

If he noticed, he didn't comment, and his expression

didn't change. Jessie tried to forget about him standing there, and focused on the baby instead.

Funny.

In the past, so many times, she'd been the one carefully passing the tiny, swaddled bundle to an eager, tearful parent for that first precious hug. She'd been the one to make sure that feed lines and medication lines and oxygen lines and monitor lines were still firmly taped in place, yet as much out of the way as possible.

She'd been the one to give murmured instructions. Watch for this. Be careful of that. And then she'd been the one to stand back and get choked up herself at the softening in a mother's face, the total focus, the gentle hand movements.

Now I'm on the opposite side of the fence, her thoughts ran, skittish and woolly from fatigue, and from her awareness of Keelan Hunter keeping his distance—and judging this first moment of interaction, probably, behind the mask of his classically handsome face. But I'm not her mother… She's a little darling… How is this going to feel?

Warmth. That was the first sensation.

Tavie was a nugget of feather-light warmth in her arms, like a kitten asleep on her chest. She had that cheesy, salty-sweet newborn smell, and breath so light that Jessie couldn't even feel it. She had her nasal cannula in place, though, giving her oxygen, and her breathing alarm wasn't going off, so she definitely was breathing, despite the lack of evidence.

And then, as Jessie settled into complete stillness, she felt the evidence after all—the tiny, rhythmic movement of Tavie's chest expanding and contracting against her own, so faint that Jessie had to stop breathing herself in order to feel it.

She's going to live, the thoughts ran once more. Whatever it takes, whatever I have to do for her. She's going to thrive, and get strong and smiley and bright and curious, and Keelan Hunter will love her more than he can imagine. Way more than he wants to.

She didn't talk out loud, just let Tavie get used to the feeling of being held. The baby was in a drowsy state, but her little hand moved and tightened in its primitive grasp reflex, and Barb McDaniel warned, 'Watch her oxygen tube, she's going to grab it any minute.'

'Sorry, baby,' Jessie murmured, and carefully lifted it over the baby's head to her other shoulder.

'Might leave the two of you for a few minutes,' Barb said.

'I have a phone call to make,' Dr Hunter came in at once.

He would, wouldn't he? He'd have a repertoire of easy outs, ready for the times when he didn't want to get too close. Jessie thought she might be glad of this fact, too.

'I'll hear if her breathing alarm goes off, but it shouldn't,' Barb continued. 'She's usually pretty good when she's being held.'

'You've been holding her?' Jessie asked. Dr Hunter had already moved towards the door.

'Since last week. Hard to fit it into the routine some days. With these little ones who don't seem to have a mum or dad, I never know if we're doing it for the baby or for us.'

'Both,' Jessie said.

She knew which babies the other nurse was talking about. A disproportionate percentage of premature and low birth-weight babies were born to very young or drug-addicted mothers, who often had trouble bonding with such tiny, fragile infants. A distracted, nervous or uncomfortable visit once every couple of weeks didn't impress NICU nurses, who did their best to compensate.

Apparently the NICU nurses here had judged Dr Hunter in the same way, and found him wanting. For some reason, Jessie felt a strong need to leap to his defence, even though she'd seen his barriers and his boundaries for herself.

'Can you imagine how it must be to suddenly find yourself in his position, though?' she said, her throat suddenly tight. 'I think a lot of people would hold back.'

'Hang on,' Barb said. 'No, I didn't mean him. He's been in here as much as he can, from the day they were born, even when that poor, silly mum of theirs was still in the picture. No, I meant… Even with him around—I wish he was married!—they still don't have a mother.'

'They have me.'

The nurse shot her a quizzical sidelong glance. 'Planning to stick around? How long?'

'As long as he pays me,' Jessie answered, because she had to remember that this was a job, probably lasting around four months, not a labour of love with an accidental salary conveniently attached. She'd blurred that boundary once before, and still bore the emotional scars.

'So there you go,' Barb said gently, and Jessie knew she was right.

It would be a fine line to tread.

* * *

Was Ms Russell asleep?

When Keelan returned from phoning a colleague about one of his patients in the paediatric unit upstairs, she still had the baby snuggled against her chest. Tavie's eyes were closed, and so were Ms Russell's. He watched them for a moment, bathed once more in the out-of-body sensation that had become frighteningly common since Brooke's death.

Was this really happening?

Or had he been thrown back in time to the rotations he'd done in various neonatal units during his training? In what sense was that tiny baby *his*? And what bond should he hope for between the twins and their new nurse?

She'd opened her eyes. The nurse, not Tavie. She'd caught him studying her. Had no doubt seen his narrowed eyes and tight mouth.

'Just do your utmost to make her thrive,' he said abruptly. Almost angrily. 'That's all I want. If you need to leave, to move on, give me fair warning. I have no choice but to depend on you. Don't leave me in the lurch.'

She shook her head slowly, her chin raised. She had encountered angry doctors before, and there was a strength to her, radiating like fire. She wasn't the type to be easily cowed. 'Not planning to,' she said. 'I want them to thrive, too. As much as you do.'

Their eyes met, held as if mesmerised, and exchanged a silent promise.

We have two human lives in our hands. We'll work for them, and we'll love them, no matter how hard it is and how much it might hurt, because that's what they need and what they deserve.

'Barb?' he said, finding it hard to break the moment of contact and look away. His throat had constricted, and his whole body seemed flooded with heat.

The older nurse looked up from another patient's chart. These level one 'growers and feeders' didn't need one-to-one care, and she had two more babies to look after today. 'Ready to put her back?' she said.

'Enough for today. Ms Russell—'

'Please, call me Jessie,' his new employee cut in, sounding as if the issue was important.

'Jessie,' he corrected obediently. OK, yes, he had come to his senses about it now. Artificial boundaries wouldn't mean much, if the real ones weren't in place. How hard would it be to keep those? He finished his sentence. 'Jessie needs to get some rest.'

'Bub's looking pretty tired too, aren't you, sweetheart?' Barb cooed softly, and started shifting lines and moving the drip stand so she could lift Tavie back into her incubator.

They took another quick look at Tam on their way out. Oxygen saturation at ninety-four per cent. Heart rate at 150. No mottling, pallor or cynosis in his skin. Keelan searched for something cheery and upbeat to say—about the baby, his appearance, his stats—but a kind of weariness descended over him and he just couldn't do it. Jessica—Jessie—didn't say anything either.

On their way home, he realised that he was hungry, and that he should offer her a chance at lunch, too. It was already noon. When he asked, she admitted she'd been thinking about a meal. He knew of a deli-cum-sandwich shop nearby, open on Sundays, and found a parking place right in front of it.

'We'll pick up some cheese and meat, and some tubs of salad,' he said. 'Want to choose a couple?'

She picked out a Greek salad, and something with artichoke and avocado in it, and he chose a couple more salads, and bought two cottage loaves as well. She might get hungry in the night. She looked like the sort of woman who had an energetic appetite. Her slender arms and legs had a strength to them, despite their grace, which showed she kept herself fit.

He should have thought to stock his kitchen a little better, in anticipation of her needs. Tethered to the house by Tavie as soon as the baby came home—three days from now, if everything continued as they hoped—and committed to visiting Tam whenever she could, she wouldn't have much opportunity for shopping.

He set the various offerings out on the kitchen bench and they served themselves directly from the plastic tubs, then ate together, once again, in his breakfast room. He made himself ask her what she'd thought of the unit at North Sydney, and whether discharge for Tavie on Wednesday seemed too soon.

'I'd be nervous about it,' she answered, 'if I was on staff there, and handing her over to a mum with no medical training. She'll still be under three pounds, and not out of the woods for various complications. But as long as we have the oxygen and breathing alarm here, and if she has no setbacks between now and Wednesday, I think it's a good idea. I'll be able to establish a routine, give her some peace and quiet.'

'That's what I thought, and one of the reasons I opted for someone with your level of skill and training.'

The other reason was Tam.

He didn't want to ask her specifically what she'd thought about Tam. She had too much experience. She would have seen too many babies like him who hadn't made it.

Keelan didn't linger over the meal.

'I'm going sailing with my cousin this afternoon,' he told her. 'Won't be back until fairly late, probably. As I've said, make yourself at home, sit in the garden, use the car, whatever you want. There's a street directory in it, so you can't get lost if you go out.'

'Right now, I'm contemplating the chance that I might get lost between here and my bedroom,' she answered, and that dazzle appeared on her face, that gorgeous smile, radiating out from her sleepy eyes.

'If I come home and find you asleep on the couch, I'll put a blanket over you,' he said. It sounded too personal, almost flirtatious, and Keelan felt his jaw tighten.

She looked like a child about to fall asleep in her plate, her body crumpled and soft, her elbow propped on the table and her hand cradling one pink cheek. Tendrils of slippery clean hair had begun to escape from her ponytail at the front, like a halo in the midday light. She probably even smelled sleepy—warm and sweetly scented from her shower a couple of hours ago.

Keelan felt an idiotic urge to scoop her in his arms, deposit her on the nearest bed and spend a long time tucking her in.

Crushing it, he stood up. She couldn't possibly be as vulnerable as she looked right now. Better remember that. Keep the boundaries in place. An anchorless wanderer like Jessica Russell couldn't possibly be his type, even if *he* was the type who took his staff to bed whenever the opportunity arose.

And he wasn't.

He took his plate to the kitchen and put it in the dishwasher, then changed into his sailing clothes and got out of the house as quickly as he could.

Jessie heroically managed to stay awake until four.

She cleared up the lunch supplies. She phoned her mother in Brisbane and her father in Perth, and got a hearty 'Oh, you're back!' from both of them, followed by a token enquiry about her well-being and a litany of detail on their own news.

In both houses, there was a background of noise from her half-siblings. Mum had eight-year-old Ryan and six-year-old Lucy, while Dad's new three were even younger, just five, three and six months.

Her parents had been seventeen and nineteen, respectively, at the time of her own birth thirty-two years ago. She'd had a messy upbringing, getting handed over to anyone who'd been willing to babysit, encouraged to be as independent as possible from an early age. By eight, she'd had her own key and had come home from school alone to perform a required list of chores—breakfast dishes, laundry, vacuuming.

And she'd apparently been a difficult child—colicky as a baby, stubborn and grumpy as a toddler, fat and giggly in primary school, lacking in confidence in her teens.

Mum and Dad both seemed to be enjoying marriage

and parenthood a lot more this time around. When incidents involving spills and fights disrupted both calls, she wasn't sorry to put down the phone.

She went for an exploring walk around the steep, crooked streets that led down to the harbour at Cremorne Point. Back at the house, she drank a glass of iced water while sitting in a jarrah-wood garden chair reading one of Keelan Hunter's suspense thrillers.

She desperately wanted to lie down on that sun-warmed stretch of lush green grass beyond the shady reach of the Moreton Bay fig, but didn't let herself, and when her eyes closed over her book and the sloping back of the garden chair began to feel as soft and comfortable as a down-stuffed pillow, she knew she had to go inside.

She would probably be keeping erratic hours in the coming months, in any case. Best get her rest when she could.

When she awoke again, after hours of deep sleep, the house was dark and silent, and the clock radio beside her new bed read 11:05 p.m. She knew it was pointless to try and get back to sleep, and she felt starving. Was Dr Hunter asleep, or still out? Dressing quietly to be on the safe side, she crept past his room and, through the partially open door, saw his long bulk in a king-size bed.

She kept going, a little rocked by the reality of sleeping just metres away from a near-stranger—her employer, too. Did he have a girlfriend? She hadn't seen any obvious evidence of anything serious and long term. A bathroom cabinet full of make-up, for example, or pantyhose hung up to dry. What would happen if he brought a woman home? How discreet would they be, with Jessie in the house?

Still, a girlfriend would be better than no girlfriend. Safer, somehow.

As she tiptoed down the stairs, she heard him move and mutter something in his sleep that sounded like 'fluids'.

In the kitchen, she made herself a substantial snack of cheese and tomato on toasted cottage loaf, as well as tea, then considered the seven remaining hours until dawn. There was one place where other people would be awake at this time of night. The hospital. More specifically, the NICU.

She couldn't think of any good reason not to go up there again. There was a slight chance that the noise of the car reversing up the driveway might awaken Dr Hunter, but he was a doctor after all, accustomed to grabbing onto sleep and keeping it.

Different staff were rostered in the unit at this hour, and she received some questioning looks on her arrival, but was able to present her passport for identification and they found her name in Tam's notes.

'Too jet-lagged to sleep. I'm just going to sit with him,' she told Helen Barry. 'Get to know him.'

'Touch him?' Helen yawned behind her fist, and apologised. 'Sorry, my kids didn't let me sleep today. You might even be able to hold him.'

'But Dr Hunter says hospital policy means I can't do that till he hits a thousand grams.'

Helen looked at her for a moment, her brown eyes steady.

'Yeah, but the really serious hospital policy enforcers aren't around at this hour, are they?' she said very softly.

'Are you including Dr Hunter himself in that statement?' Jessie couldn't help asking. She didn't want to defy her employer's wishes. She also wondered, as she had wondered that morning, how he was viewed here at North Sydney.

'Dr Hunter's good,' the other nurse answered cautiously. 'I don't know him that well. But I get the impression he judges each case on its merits, and that's what you need to do with preemies, isn't it? You can't tell by their stats which ones are going to do well and which aren't. This little guy...'

'Not telling us much yet?'

'See what you think. Have a look at him for a while, keep an eye on his sats and his heart, then we'll think about it,' Helen decided.

Jessie nodded and pulled a chair close to the incubator. In one corner of this part of the unit, a doctor and nurse worked over a very fragile newborn, creating more noise and requiring more light than she would have liked for Tam. Helen had draped a flannel sheet over the top of the incubator, but that didn't provide the baby with much of a shield.

His respirator did some of the work of breathing for him, but it was important to turn the settings down as low as possible to encourage him to get ready to breathe on his own. As she watched, he stirred, grimaced and twitched in his sleep, looking fussy and uncomfortable. His skin drained of colour and his saturation immediately dropped several points, while his heartbeat slowed.

Jessie took in a hiss of breath, waiting instinctively for the alarm, which should kick in if his heart got any slower. Helen heard the sound she'd made and looked at the monitors, but the figures hovered just within the right range.

The other baby's heart alarm went off and the activity from the doctor and nurse got even more frantic. What were they doing? Putting a central venous catheter into an uncooperative vein, by the looks of it, and administering urgent meds. Tam opened his eyes, flailed his arms and tried to cry, but the respirator tube down his throat wouldn't let him.

'Can we mask his incubator with something better?' Jessie asked Helen.

'Always seems it's the noise that bothers him, that's the problem. I've tried a thicker blanket, but he still does this whenever there's a crisis close by. Poor love.'

The other baby, a little girl named Corinne, with a pink teddy in her incubator, continued to give her staff a hard time. Her breathing alarm went off, but at least they had the central line taped in place now. The nurse hooked up a tiny bag of fluid and calibrated its flow rate carefully.

At one point, the doctor—undoubtedly a neonatal resident on call—flung the pink teddy on the floor with a hissing curse, and Tam's limbs went stiff and his eyes panicky. His levels on the monitor were bouncing around, and his own breathing alarm went off. Helen changed the settings on his respirator slightly and frowned at the blood-pressure reading.

She looked across at the resident and opened her mouth as if to summon him to look at Tam, but then she frowned, shook her head and said nothing.

Finally, the doctor left the girl baby alone, while the nurse quietly noted her hourly observations.

'OK, let's see what happens with him now…' Helen said, her voice more breath than sound.

They watched Tam and his monitors. Gradually, his limbs curled up and went still. The oxygen figure climbed back up and so did the heart. Jessie looked at his blood-pressure reading and agreed with Helen's silent, frowning assessment. It was a little higher than she would have liked. She wondered if there was any plan to put him on medication to lower it, as a way of lessening the workload on the heart.

After half an hour of peace, she asked the other nurse, 'Could I put a hand in there?'

Helen nodded. 'Let's try it. We won't have you hold him tonight, though, after all the fuss.'

'No, it'd be too much, wouldn't it?' Jessie agreed.

She went to the nearest sink and washed and dried her hands carefully, then sat in front of the incubator and carefully reached her right hand in through one of the cuffed ports, making her movements calm and unhurried. Tam remained peacefully asleep.

She didn't touch or stroke him lightly, but cupped her hand around his curled up legs and tiny, padded bottom and kept it there firmly, the way the muscles of his mother's uterine wall should still be doing. She didn't chafe or massage, just held her hand quite still.

She knew how to do this, but it felt different with this baby, and she had an illogical, emotional wish that Dr Hunter could be here to share the moment. Looking at the monitors, she saw a nice, high oxygen saturation and a good heart rate, both of which stayed steady. His colour was far better now, too, an even-toned pink.

His jaundice seemed less evident than it had been fifteen hours ago.

The baby liked what she was doing.

Jessie liked it, too.

She responded at once to the sensation of precious life held beneath her hand, and to the miracle of technology, which could chart those small fluctuations in a heart's power to beat and two lungs' power to breathe so that someone who cared could read this tiny baby's well-being the way a healthy baby's parents could read its cry or its smile.

Emotion overwhelmed her, more powerfully than it had done with Tavie earlier today. It might have been sensible to keep reminding herself that this one could still die, that she'd be protecting her own feelings by staying uninvolved, but she just couldn't do it.

She wanted life for Tam so badly—and health, happiness, a sense of belonging and love—that she had no choice but to invest her own heart.

Chapter 3

Jessie spent much of Monday and Tuesday shopping.

Dr Hunter had told her that she was free to spend whatever she thought necessary, and he'd set up accounts at two different baby shops and an upmarket department store. At first she was tentative about it, comparing prices, telling herself that the cheaper cot was almost as good as the gorgeous one that cost nearly twice as much.

But then he called her from North Sydney's paediatric unit, reaching her on the mobile phone he'd given her, and asked a few searching questions about where she was up to. He then told her categorically, 'If in doubt, go for the top of the line. Don't compromise. I don't care what you have to spend. Please, don't get the cheap cot. I—I really don't want that.'

Family money, she knew.

Something else, too, which she understood just as well—an irrational, unacknowledged fear that if they cut corners and bought the cheap cot for Tavie, Tam might not survive. Interesting that a man like Keelan Hunter should be emotional enough about these babies to submit to that sort of superstition, that sort of irrational bargaining with God. He was complex.

After their phone conversation, she went a bit giddy. She'd never shopped like this in her life. There were such gorgeous things for little girl babies! Stretchy little sleepsuits in pink and lemon and mauve, little tops and pants with lace edges at the cuffs and sleeves, appliquéd dresses and soft cloth bootees. Even the practical purchases, like a change table, a baby bath and a nappy bin, were fun to make.

It just seemed a pity to Jessie, at times, that she was doing it all on her own. This was really a task for two people in love, who were thrilled to be parents.

The next day, Tavie left Barb McDaniel's care and came home, with her fixed oxygen tank, her portable oxygen tank, her tank regulator, CPAP cannula, pulse oximeter, nasogastric feed tube, infant weighing scale, apnoea and heart alarms. The hospital kept the baby's medical charts and notes, but Jessie had already set up a similar system to keep track of Tavie's progress, pick up any warning signs and provide an overview for Tavie's father whenever he wanted it.

On discharge, the tiny girl weighed a fraction over her birthweight, and although Dr Hunter had taken the day off, and they'd both tried to make the transition as smooth and unfussed as possible, it must have tired

Tavie out. With jet-lag still mucking her body clock around, Jessie felt like a limp rag herself by the time Tavie was set up in her new nursery.

Dr Hunter had been shopping, too. A space heater for the baby's room and a thermometer to keep track of the air temperature. Enough pantry and refrigerator supplies, it seemed, to feed a large family for nearly a month.

'Because I realised you wouldn't get the opportunity,' he told Jessie stiffly, as they stood in the kitchen together, just before lunch. 'I'm sorry, I'm thinking some of this through as I go along.'

'It's fine. You didn't have a lot of time to make plans. Neither of us has.'

'Thanks for being flexible.'

'It's one of the things I'm good at.'

They smiled cautiously at each other, and their eyes met and held just a little bit too long. Not for the first time. It had happened in the hospital on Sunday, too, and yesterday afternoon when the cot and change table had arrived, and they'd set them up in the baby nursery together.

Now Jessie looked quickly away. The spacious kitchen seemed too small suddenly, and she had to fight to get her perspective and her priorities back in place.

Tavie. Tam. Putting money aside. Making some decisions about her long-term future when she wasn't needed here any more. What was the best way for a woman to go in search of a home?

Tavie was asleep upstairs, and Jessie had a baby monitor clipped to the pocket of her skirt, feeding her a constant stream of little sounds—a high-pitched baby snuffle, birds outside the window, some rattly noises as Tavie kicked. She focused on the sounds instead of on Keelan Hunter's brown eyes.

'I'm going to bring you dinner every night, too,' he continued, after a pause in which he seemed to be listening to the baby monitor noises, too. 'Until we see how you're managing.'

'I thought you didn't eat at home, Dr Hunter,' she blurted out.

'I'm making an exception for a week or two. And I'm not saying I'll cook at home.' He grinned suddenly, unexpectedly, and again something shifted uncomfortably inside her. His smile was much more open and uncomplicated than it should have been. 'It'll come in plastic containers, still steaming,' he finished.

'Well…thanks.'

'Please, let's stick to first names, by the way. You suggested it the other day, and you were right. So it's Keelan, please. It's not that hard to say.'

'Keelan,' she echoed, and liked the feel of it in her mouth. 'You're probably right about the meals. I—' *Bipbipbipbipbipbip*…

'Heart alarm,' Keelan said, and bolted for the stairs, just as Tavie's breathing alarm began to sound as well. Jessie followed right behind him.

They didn't know what had happened. Something going on in her little stomach maybe. Keelan got to her first and touched her shoulder, and she began breathing again right away. Jessie switched off the alarms and watched the monitor. The heart rate bounced back up too high, and then the baby lost most of her stomach contents in a puddle on the sheet beside her head.

She seemed distressed the whole afternoon. They cleaned up the bed, changed a nappy and slowed the flow rate through the feed tube, so that her twenty mils went in over forty minutes instead of twenty. They checked her monitors and her meds obsessively—she was still on an infant antacid and a couple of other things—then they cleaned the bed again, because she'd lost another feed.

Which was ungrateful of her, because neither of the adults had found an opportunity for lunch.

Through all of this she cried, or slept an exhausted sleep during which she twitched and grimaced and forgot to breathe, setting off her breathing alarm three times.

'Let's try and kangaroo her on your chest,' Keelan finally decided. 'Maybe she'll keep her feed down better if she's more upright, and the body contact should soothe her. We're making classic first-day-home-from-the-hospital mistakes, I think, fussing over her and making her more distressed.'

'I think you're right.'

'Can you change into a top that buttons down the front?'

Jessie almost shot him a panicky look. OK, the accepted 'kangaroo' technique involved having carer and baby in skin-to-skin contact, but...

No, be reasonable, she told herself. As if he'll care. As if he'll even *notice*.

She nodded and went to her room, where she found one of the conservative, long-sleeved blouses she'd worn in Saudi Arabia. Lapping its roomy front panels across her breasts and stomach, she didn't bother with the buttons, since they'd have to be unfastened again anyway. Her pale blue bra was pretty and lacy but decent as far as such garments went. And her breasts weren't that exciting in their dimensions, although she'd had a few compliments in her time.

'Sit down, and I'll give her to you,' Keelan said. 'Ready?'

He unsnapped the fastenings on Tavie's tiny suit, managing her various tubes and sensor lines adeptly. Settling a little deeper into the rocking chair, Jessie parted her blouse and Keelan laid the baby against her chest. His fingers brushed her stomach, just below her breasts, but they didn't linger. In fact, he moved away a little too soon.

'Careful,' she blurted out, and hugged the baby too tightly.

Tavie squirmed for a moment, but she seemed to find the firm contact soothing. Jessie relaxed, loosened her hold a fraction, steadied her own breathing and felt Tavie's delicious warmth mingling with her own. Keelan tucked a cot-size quilt around them both, anchoring it in place between Jessie's back and the back of the chair.

'Comfortable?' he asked a moment later, watching them from several paces away now, his amber eyes narrowed beneath a frown.

'I could do with a pillow behind my back.'

He brought the one from her own bed and slid it in behind her, while she arched the base of her spine. She felt his hand come to rest on her quilt-covered shoulder for a moment, and then the wash of his breath against her bare neck, where the blouse was open and the quilt didn't reach. Her body tingled from head to toe and she felt that magnetism again, that strange, primal pull he'd begun to exert on her senses, beyond her power to control.

She closed her eyes, willing it away, fully aware of how disastrous it could be.

'She seems happier,' Keelan concluded. From the sound of his voice, he'd retreated as far as the doorway. 'I'm going to head up to the hospital in a minute, if that's all right. I have a four-year-old patient going in for heart surgery tomorrow, and Keith Bedford, his surgeon, wanted me to take a final look at him today.'

'That's fine,' Jessie said. She didn't want to mention that she was hungry. The sooner he left, the better.

She held Tavie on her chest for two hours after Keelan had gone, and it felt precious and right. Like this, it seemed as if she could almost feel the baby growing. Tavie's latest feed stayed down and neither of her alarms went off. She slept, and Jessie did, too, in a light doze that still had her able to respond to Tavie's movements.

She didn't open her eyes until she heard the rumbling hum of the garage door, just as the September light was fading from the sky.

Keelan came up the stairs a minute later and appeared as a shadowy figure in the doorway. 'How's it going?' he said softly. 'She looks peaceful.'

'She has been, the whole time,' Jessie whispered back, without moving. 'It's been… absolutely precious, really. Just delightful.' A little bit scary, this sense of warm delight like a pool of liquid inside her. She'd never sat like this with a baby before, in a home rather than in a primitive clinic or a high-tech hospital unit.

Was it her fault that she'd failed to bond with her

much younger half-siblings? she suddenly wondered. Could she have spent this sort of time with them as babies, if she'd pushed?

Thinking back, all she could remember was Dad's wife, Natalie, snatching her babies back after a scant minute in anyone else's arms, and hovering so suspiciously over any attempt to read to them or take them out to the back-yard sandpit that Jessie had soon given up.

Mum, meanwhile, had brought her second brood up on bottle feeds propped on pillows and long periods alone in their cots. 'Don't go in there, Jessie. I'll be furious if you wake him up when he's taken so long to settle.' And a couple of years later, 'Don't get him all excited like that, Jessie. He'll be unbearable after you've gone, and I'll never get him down for his nap.'

But perhaps she'd been too sensitive about it, and too easily put off. She could have tried harder.

'You must be starving,' Keelan said, breaking in on her self-critical train of thought.

'Um, yes, there is that,' she conceded, and he laughed.

He had a surprisingly attractive laugh, so much warmer and more open than she would have expected. Every time she heard it—which wasn't often enough—she felt as if she'd been let in on a delicious secret that he'd shared with no one else. It made her curious, in an illogical and too emotional way, about what other such secrets he might have.

'You should have got me to make you a cheese sandwich before I left,' he said.

'I was hardly going to do such a thing!'

He left a beat of silence before he answered, 'No, I

suppose not.' Then he added, 'But I've got dinner down-stairs now, so if we can get her back in her cot and hook up another feed…'

'Let me do the feed, and I'll check her nappy, too.'

'Do you want to pass her to me?'

'No, I can manage, but if you could check that her lines are in the right place…'

By shifting her own weight, Jessie tipped the rock-ing chair forward enough to stand easily, without jolt-ing the baby. Keelan twitched various tubes and sensor lines out of the way.

Jessie leaned over and laid Tavie in her cot, brush-ing the baby with the open front panels of her blouse. The tops of her breasts felt cool and heavy above the edges of her bra. Straightening, she did up the blouse, glad that she had her back to Keelan. It was her own awareness that troubled her, however, not any potential signals coming from him.

'Come and eat as soon as you can, then,' he said. 'I'll set it out. How about we forget the formal approach and have it on the coffee-table, in front of the TV? We can pull out some videos, find a movie neither of us has seen.'

'Sounds good!'

Tavie didn't seem to need a change. Jessie swaddled her as tightly as her tubes and sensors would allow, then held her breath. Monitors looked fine. Face looked peaceful. Room was warm, but not too hot and dry. She'd hear those alarms again through the audio moni-tor if they went off.

She went downstairs to greet the delectable smell of Italian food, and found Keelan with a stemmed glass and an open bottle of white wine in his hand. 'Could you use some of this?' he said.

'Not to sound like a lush, but could I ever!'

'Me, too, actually. Not to sound like a lush,' he parroted on a drawl. 'It's been…quite a day.'

He'd bought a salad, garlic bread and minestrone soup, as well as fettucine with a creamy salmon and caviar sauce, and a big slice of spinach and mushroom lasagne, and it was all set out on the table in front of wide, brightly coloured Italian ceramic plates and cream cloth napkins.

Jessie felt giddy with hunger, and surrendered any awkwardness about sitting down to another meal with Keelan, after he'd been so careful to stress that their personal lives wouldn't intersect very much. She would eat, then retreat to her own sitting room. She doubted very much that he'd try to hold her here until the end of the movie.

He put it on straight away, as soon as he found one in his cabinet that she said she hadn't seen. It was an American romantic comedy, fun but forgettable, and with it burbling away in front of them, the wine and food slipped down very easily.

Tavie's alarms stayed quiet. Jessie forgot that she hadn't planned to watch the whole movie. The end credits began to roll just as she was wondering how that last piece of garlic bread would taste now that it had grown cold, if she washed it down with the three inches of wine still left in her glass.

Three inches? Had she drunk less than half a glass?

No, Keelan must have topped it up. Possibly more than once. He had the bottle in his hand again now, and she grabbed the stemmed piece of crystal beneath the hovering green glass rim to pull it away before he could waste another drop.

'It's fine,' she blurted. 'I'm fine with this.'

Both of them moved clumsily. The bottle connected with the glass and it tipped and spilled, splashing Jessie's hand and Keelan's knee. They spoke in unison.

'Sorry, I shouldn't have—'

'I'm sorry. That was—'

'No, it's all right,' Jessie said. 'My fault.'

While her hand still dripped with wine, she grabbed a paper napkin and pressed it onto his knee, imagining the unsightly stain that might be left on what were undoubtedly expensive trousers. The napkin soaked through, so she took another one and put it on top, curving her palm over the knob of bone and solid muscle beneath the fabric.

Keelan's knee, warm and hard. Her hand, moving like a frightened bird. Several layers of paper and a layer of cloth separated his skin from hers, but the contact still mesmerised and magnetised her.

This was the first time they had really touched.

She looked up, past his long, solid thigh and angled torso to his face, where she saw the same electric prickle of alarm that he must be able to read on her own features. His eyes gleamed darkly, and his lips had parted. She could see the tip of his tongue held between his teeth. She pulled away from his knee too fast, and the wine on the back of her hand splashed several more drops onto his thigh.

'Hey,' he said. 'Let's deal with this properly.'

For a second, she thought he meant the attraction. It

frightened her, the way they could both see so clearly what was going on, reading each other's body language like a newly revealed and fascinating code. She didn't want it, but she didn't know how to rein it in.

But no, he wasn't talking about that.

To her relief.

Spelling it out could only make it worse. More real, somehow. And it was clear that he didn't want it either.

He took a napkin and dropped it onto her hand. 'There. Soak it up, then go and wash, before...' He stopped. 'It'll be sticky.'

'I'm really sorry.'

'And stop apologising. It's as much my fault as yours.'

He could equally have been talking about the spill, or about what they felt.

She jumped to her feet, feeling giddy and awkward, and had time to see a flash of relief in his eyes and a dropping of tension from his shoulders. Her whole body crawled with awareness.

In the kitchen, with the taps running, she couldn't hear what he was doing, but when she turned to dry her hands, she found that he'd brought in a pile of containers and the plates from their meal.

'I'll stack it here,' he said tersely. 'Mrs Sagovic can deal with it in the morning.'

'Oh, she comes Thursdays?'

'Sorry, didn't I tell you?' He paused in the doorway, at a safe distance of several metres. 'And I'm going to talk to her tomorrow about coming Mondays and Tuesdays as well from now on. She's very willing to help with Tavie's care as the baby gets stronger, and she'll handle the laundry for you.'

'See how I manage, first.'

'No,' he told her decisively. 'I don't want you to get exhausted. Without her help, it'll be very difficult for you to get to the hospital to see Tam, and that's too important to let slide.'

He seemed angry—trying to hide it, obviously, but not totally succeeding. Jessie had the impression that he was reminded at every turn about details in this new life of his that he didn't like, and that one of those details was her.

'Let me check the baby now,' she murmured.

'Yes,' he answered at once. 'I'll finish down here. Goodnight,' he added, just in case she hadn't picked up on the fact that she'd been ordered upstairs.

'Goodnight, Keelan,' she echoed in the same firm, distant tone.

Tavie slept peacefully in her cot in the warm nursery.

'I'm going to enjoy interpreting your signals more than your dad's,' she told the baby softly.

Moving carefully, she checked temperature, heart rate and oxygen level, and noted the readings down in the chart she'd started, adding her observations on Tavie's colour and state as well. The familiar task settled her fluttery stomach and cooled her down inside, and she didn't see anything to be concerned about in her tiny charge.

Preparing another feed and setting its flow rate through Tavie's nasogastric tube, she considered a nappy change, but decided to wait until the baby woke up.

Tomorrow, she would try a bottle feed—just a small

one, so that Tavie could practise. Her sucking reflex had been weak at the hospital, and she'd tired very quickly when she'd tried to feed, but she would get stronger every day. They didn't want to keep her on tube feeds for longer than necessary.

Next week or the week after, all going well, they'd try some spells without oxygen and maybe even a trip outside, a little push in her pram on a sunny afternoon. Only a few weeks after that, Tavie should begin to smile…

In the middle of the night, at around 2:00 a.m., the smiling, feeding and breathing milestones seemed a long way off.

Jessie dragged herself out of a deep sleep in response to the piping of the heart alarm and reached Tavie's darkened room just after Keelan. He hadn't put on a robe, and wore dark silk pyjama pants and a white T-shirt that looked warm and rumpled from his bed, just the way Jessie felt. She wore pyjamas, too—a women's fashion lingerie version of classic male blue-striped flannel, with navy piping and a drawstring waist.

They eyed each other, and Jessie searched for some clever, downplaying, soufflé-weight comment.

Love the PJs.

Must get some slippers.

Is it cold in here, or are you just pleased to see me?

Um, no. Not that.

Not anything. She couldn't come up with a word.

'What's wrong, princess?' she said instead, to the baby. Her voice came out creaky. 'Jumping the gun on your next feed?'

Help me out, Tavie. Play chaperone for us. OK, yes, fill your nappy. That'll do, for a distraction.

The baby was apparently locked in a titanic battle with her digestion. She screwed up her face, then opened her eyes wide and forgot to breathe. Her oxygen alarm went off, and Keelan reset it while Jessie tapped Tavie's feet to encourage her to breathe properly again.

'Nothing serious, I don't think,' Keelan said. He blinked the sleep out of his eyes.

'No, she's just being a preemie.'

'Can you handle the rest?' He hid a yawn behind his fist.

The nightlight plugged into the wall socket etched a gold sheen onto his skin, highlighting the fine, dark hairs on his bare forearms. Again, Jessie was slammed with an awareness of just how male he was. She'd never met a man before who had drawn her with quite this instinctive, sensual power, particularly when she didn't want it at all.

'It's fine,' she answered. 'She's still not happy, though. I'd…um…close your door.'

'It was closed,' he drawled. 'And I think her cry is louder than the alarm.' He didn't leave, however. He hovered, frowning and square-jawed, clearly unable to let go.

'I'll close this one as well,' Jessie offered.

Her steps towards it had the effect of chasing him out, and he muttered over his shoulder, 'Thanks. I've got a couple of tough patients at the moment, and some decisions to make tomorrow. A case conference I'm not looking forward to.'

'Sleep, then.'

But he'd already disappeared into his dark bedroom and didn't reply.

Jessie set up the next feed, took some routine observations, changed a full nappy and discovered skin which had begun to look a little inflamed. Debating on the best approach to head off a serious case of nappy rash, she patted the area gently with a pad of cotton wool dipped in clean, lukewarm water.

Apparently she hadn't been gentle enough. Tavie shrieked, Jessie winced and Keelan appeared in the doorway again, just seconds later. He looked as if he'd once more been dragged from sleep.

'Problem?'

'Her bottom's looking a bit sore. I hate waking her to change her, but I'll have to if her skin's this sensitive. I'm going to try a cloth nappy this time. Sorry, sweetheart, I'm sorry.'

'You're using something, though? A barrier cream? An antifungal ointment?'

She shook her head, and began, 'I don't think—'

But he cut her off. 'Surely. Wasn't she prescribed something at the hospital? Isn't it obvious that this would happen?' His tension shrieked at Jessie far louder than the baby.

'No, it's not obvious,' she answered, calm but sure of herself. Doctors often extrapolated a simple problem to its worst-case scenario. She could understand Keelan doing so, but she would resist his attitude all the same. 'Some babies never get nappy rash, and others do worse if they're slathered with creams and ointments.'

She turned to Tavie again and started folding the soft

piece of gauze cloth in place, ready for pinning. Keelan stood and watched her.

Still angry.

She could sense it.

'I'll keep a close eye on this,' she promised, with her back to him. 'I won't put her in plastic pants. In fact, I didn't even buy any. I bought these open weave nappy covers—which I'm not going to use tonight either. Just the gauze will be fine. If there's any sign that it's thrush, or something else that needs medicinal treatment, I won't let it slip, Keelan, I really won't.'

'Hmm.'

He was still watching her. With her back to him again, she completed the change and wrapped Tavie up, checked her oxygen and her heart and her skin colour. The baby seemed ready to settle, and the feed was going in as it should.

Now, if the baby's dad would just go back to bed...

She turned.

Nope. Still there.

'What is it about me that you don't trust?' It came out before she could stop it. 'This shouldn't be so complicated and so difficult for both of us, should it? Don't we feel the same about most things?'

'What things?' he asked, and it seemed like a dangerous question when he was standing so close, looking at her like this, in his night attire.

'That it's important to keep our own personal space. That I'm just here to do a job, even if it's a pretty intense and emotional one. That the needs of the babies come first. That neither of us is really prepared for everything this situation might entail, because no one ever is. No parent ever is.'

'I don't feel like a parent yet. I don't feel remotely like a parent.' He pressed his fingers into his tired eyes, suddenly. 'I feel…numb half the time.'

'That's OK, isn't it?'

He ignored her. 'Like a doctor, the rest. Wanting to win against death, not out of love but because that's what doctors do. We win against death. How is it going to be for these babies if I can't care for them? Love them? Really fit them into my life? What's wrong with me?'

'Nothing's wrong.' She stepped forward, flooded with an intense need to reassure him, to tell him that she understood and that he was expecting too much of himself too quickly.

She even reached out a hand, not thinking about the magnetism between them but about giving him support and human warmth. He did have the capacity to love them. She was sure of it, having read some of his reactions more clearly than he could read them himself. Her fingers made contact with his cheek and jaw, and the magnetism was instantly there, but he flinched away at once, shook his head and stepped back.

Jessie felt as if she'd been burned.

Or as if she'd burned him.

'My marriage broke down several years ago,' he said, speaking quickly. 'One of those relationships that only works when it's fresh and new and sunny, and can't withstand any of the pressures of day-to-day reality.'

'There are quite a few of those around,' Jessie murmured. She didn't know quite where this was going.

'Yes, too many! Tanya was the one who got bored first. She went back to New Zealand straight away—she was a doctor, well situated in her career, we had no children, we could make a very clean break. I hardly ever think about her. Only now I'm suddenly regretting that she, no, *we*—I'm not going to let myself off the hook—that both of us didn't try harder, so that she'd be here now. On paper we had everything going for us, everything in common. Similar careers, similar backgrounds and priorities and goals—which was, I always assumed, why my father's marriage to Brooke's mother failed, because they didn't share those things.'

'What are you saying, Keelan?'

He shook his head. 'I don't know. Just retracing my route, wondering where I went off track.'

'I don't think you should conclude that you did. I'm not sure you should conclude anything at all at this point.'

'In my life?'

'At this hour of the night!'

He said nothing for a moment, then sighed through a tight jaw. 'You're right. I shouldn't have said any of that,' he told her.

'Well, that's not what I meant,' she murmured, although perhaps it should have been. If he hadn't spilled his tortured feelings, she would never have reached out like that, earning not only another moment of hot, reluctant awareness but also his swift rebuff.

'Look, let's agree that in future we'll have a system to this,' he said. 'We'll prearrange which nights I'll go to Tavie and which nights it'll be you. There's no sense in both of us having every night disrupted.'

'There's no need for you to get up in the night at all. It's my job.'

'No, it's a parent's job as well.'

Hearing the distancing way he'd worded the sentence, Jessie ached for him, but he'd just denied her any right to involve herself in his feelings and his struggles, so she said nothing.

'Given my responsibilities at the hospital,' he went on, 'I'm not pushing for a fifty-fifty arrangement, but I'll do two nights a week.'

'That would be good.'

'Let me know if you have a preference for any night in particular.'

'It's up to you. You have on-call nights at the hospital to consider, too. I'm flexible.'

He nodded. 'OK, I'll let you know. For now, let's both get some sleep.'

Keelan's pager sounded at 4:00 a.m., and the readout on the illuminated panel showed the extension number of the neonatal unit.

Full, instant wakefulness broadsided him like an unexpected wave and he felt nauseous as he flung the covers aside and shot out of bed onto his feet. He was dressed within a minute, knowing that the unit wouldn't have paged him at this hour unless it was urgent.

He didn't page them back. If it was bad news—and in relation to Tam, he couldn't imagine any other kind—he didn't want to hear it over the phone, when he'd feel even more powerless than he felt already.

Across the corridor, Jessie had both her own door and Tavie's shut tight. She must have the one-way baby audio monitor switched on, so that she'd hear the baby or her alarms through that and give Keelan himself a better chance of staying asleep.

Now he attempted to show her the same consideration, creeping down the stairs with his shoes in his hand, while a cold draught from the open window on the landing chilled his neck. He scribbled a note to her, to leave on the front hall table in case he wasn't back by morning, then let himself out of the house.

They'd had a difficult night, beginning with that deceptively pleasant interlude over dinner and the video. He wished they hadn't spilled that wine—and he didn't give a damn about the stain on his trousers. Her hand on his knee had been the big problem.

Driving down the street, damming back a need to floor the accelerator pedal, he realised he'd always considered his father to have a vein of weakness in him, because of the whole disaster over Louise.

Keelan's former stepmother had carried a torch for Dawson Hunter for a good two years before their professional boss-secretary relationship had progressed to an affair. Couldn't Dad have seen it coming, exercised some self-restraint and sacked the woman before things got out of hand?

It wasn't as if their eventual marriage had been a success, as he'd told Jessie tonight. It had lasted for eight years, long enough to produce Brooke, whom Louise had always spoiled while claiming, 'She's far too strong for me. I can't understand her, or manage her.'

And then the infatuation had worn off, for both parties. Dad found Louise endlessly irritating, while she was constantly getting hurt over some imagined insult or slight, often involving Keelan's rather strong-minded mother, whom Louise seemed to fear.

In his late teens by this time, and living on campus at Sydney University, Keelan stayed out of the whole thing as much as possible, with a young man's smug confidence that he'd never get his own life into the same mess as his father's.

Now, sixteen years later, he found himself divorced from a fellow doctor, not interested in any of the women he'd met socially over the past couple of years and in danger of developing the same kind of raging, unsuitable, *unworkable* attraction that had ultimately set his father adrift from family life and left his mother on her own.

If it *was* a vein of weakness, then he feared that he might share it—feared it to the extent that he'd gone too far the other way tonight. He'd got angry, he'd questioned Jessie's judgement, he'd launched into an unburdening of his inner feelings that was quite inappropriate, then he'd flinched away from her touch as if her fingers could cast magic, hypnotic spells.

He needed to get back on a straight course. He knew that. He'd gone to sleep on a very firm resolution about it. But now something was going on with Tam, and his whole body felt stiff and cold with terror.

Turning into the doctors' parking area beside the hospital, he found himself making the kind of classic bargains with the universe that ill people and their loved ones made all the time.

If Tam is OK, I'll do everything I can to get close to Dad again.

If Tam is OK, I'll tell Jessie she's free to resign, no questions asked. Before something else happens.

If Tam is OK, I won't ask for anything more.

The lift was waiting for him, and he jabbed the button hard, as if that might make the doors close faster. The fluorescent lighting of the corridor on the seventh floor seemed garish and harsh as it always did at this hour. He couldn't hear any commotion coming from the unit, which gave him an absurd and totally illogical rush of reassurance.

Seconds later, his spirits crashed again when night nurse Andrea Stanton met him in front of the nurses' station and told him, 'We didn't want to wait until morning before calling you in, in case—'

'No, I'm glad you didn't.'

'Look, he's not in good shape, Dr Hunter. His heart is failing, he's showing evidence of a major candida infection, and Dr Nguyen has concerns about his kidneys. He's here now, and he wants to talk to you about options.'

'Let me look at the baby first.'

She nodded, her face betraying the helpless empathy she'd given to desperate parents so many times before. 'Of course,' she said. 'Of course, Dr Hunter.'

Chapter 4

'The heart is having a tougher time than we had hoped, I'm afraid, Keelan,' neonatologist Dr Daniel Nguyen said.

Keelan knew the other doctor quite well. They were around the same age, and they'd shared patients in the past. Sometimes a chronically ill baby graduated directly from the neonatal unit to the paediatric ward upstairs. In such cases, the prognosis was rarely good, so they'd had bad news to communicate to each other before.

This time it felt so different.

'Tam's not strong enough for that sort of surgery yet,' Keelan answered.

The tiny boy struggled visibly for life. He had a urinary catheter in place now, and his body was still swollen with fluid, although he'd been started on a medication to help his kidney function. His muscle tone was floppy and his stats on the monitor should have been a lot better.

'No, he's not,' Daniel Nguyen agreed.

'So what's left?'

'We treat the symptoms of his heart condition more aggressively, we combat the yeast infection, we continue intravenous feeding and increase support for his breathing.'

'A stronger diuretic for his kidneys, something to lower his blood pressure, a couple of heart stimulants, antifungal agents, antibiotics, oxygen settings turned up higher...' Keelan trailed off, extrapolating all of this into multiple problems down the track.

Broncho-pulmonary dysplasia, if Tam remained on a ventilator for too long. Eye problems for the same reason, especially if he continued to need these high oxygen settings. A brain bleed, due to side-effects from the blood pressure and heart drugs. With or without the antibiotics, bowel problems remained a possibility. And antifungal medications were nasty at the best of times.

All of this, and more, even if everything they did to help the heart was sufficient to hold it up until Tam was big enough and strong enough for the surgery he would need.

Daniel watched Keelan in silence for a moment, then said quietly, 'I've seen babies in worse shape than this one come through in perfect health, no developmental delay, happy personalities, only the most minimal long-term problems with their eyesight or their size.'

'But you've seen babies in this kind of shape who didn't make it at all.'

'Yes, I have. Which is why I called you in.'

'To say goodbye?'

'To OK the aggressive treatment. Is this what you want, Keelan?'

'Yes!' He said it without hesitation, and felt a wash of anger towards Brooke that he knew wasn't entirely fair. There was no guarantee, even with perfect prenatal care, that she would have carried the twins for longer than she had.

The thing that angered him, though, was that she hadn't tried. She'd coasted along, taking for granted that her path would be strewn with rose petals, the way she always had, the way Louise had always encouraged her to, despite everything Louise had said about 'not being able to manage her'.

Even if Brooke had still been around, Keelan doubted she'd have known what to do in a situation like this, where to find the courage and the commitment.

Tam needed someone to fight for him.

No, that wasn't quite right. Even at this tiny size, the fight had to be Tam's. Keelan had heard nurses talk as if this was how it happened. 'She decided to live.' 'He found the strength for one more fight, and then he didn't look back.' 'She just didn't want to do it any more, and so she let go. We couldn't bring her back this time.'

Tam had to decide to fight, and he had to know that someone—Keelan himself—applauded him for it, loved him for it.

'Keep doing everything you can, Daniel,' he told his colleague. 'I'm going to sit with him for a while.'

'You're going to watch those monitor figures?'

'No, I'm going to watch him. Touch him. I—I really want him to know I'm here tonight, if that's possible.'

Dr Nguyen yawned. 'Not much night left.'

He stepped towards Andrea, Tam's nurse, and gave her some low-voiced instructions, and they both fiddled with ventilator settings and IV flow rates for a while. Tam's chart rustled as they added several more lines of scrawled, cryptic notation.

Keelan watched them at work, then vaguely realised that if he wanted to put his arm inside Tam's incubator, he should wash his hands again. When he came back, Andrea was ready for him and he sat amongst all the machinery that surrounded the baby, and cupped his hand around the tiny head, capped in thick, pale blue knit cotton.

He lost all track of time, all awareness of the other activity in this section of the unit. And he didn't watch the monitors.

Just live, OK?

Fight, Tam.

Choose life.

Tavie's thin, high-pitched crying awoke Jessie at just after five.

On her way to the baby's room, she saw Keelan's open door and his empty bed. The covers had been flung to one side in a heap, as if he'd projected himself out of them at speed.

She put up a new feed and changed the baby's nappy. Tavie's skin in that area no longer looked such an angry red, thank goodness, and there were no raised areas and no sections of broken skin. In her judgement, it wasn't thrush, or any other cause for concern.

Next, she went downstairs, but Keelan wasn't there either, and his car had gone from the garage.

To the hospital?

Where else?

The callout could have been for one of his own patients, or it could have been because of Tam, and Jessie couldn't put her mind at rest when she didn't know. She thought of phoning the hospital…actually picked up the telephone from the hall table to dial…but didn't feel it was her right. If they'd lost Tam in the night, Keelan would deal with the formalities and with the grief, and her own responsibility lay in caring for the twin that was left.

After all, Tavie remained frail, too.

Waiting for news, Jessie made a pot of coffee in the chilly kitchen, then carried her mug up to the much warmer nursery, setting it down carefully where there was no chance it could spill even a drop on the baby. She found Tavie awake, alert and quiet, with her feed still running easily through the tube that passed through her nose and throat, down to her stomach. No alarms went off, and her colour was perfect.

Seizing this ideal opportunity, she checked the baby's weight gain—ten grams, which deserved a cooing congratulation. 'You good, beautiful girl!' She gave Tavie a sponge bath, with tiny gauze pads and cotton buds dipped in clean, warm water, and went through the tiny girl's mouth care routine.

'Still awake, sweetheart, even after all that?' she cooed again. 'Can you see how tense I am? I'm really trying to hide it, little girl. Look, I'm smiling at you, giving you a big, important smiling lesson, and you don't know how thumpy my heart is. Wouldn't your dad phone us if something was going on with your brother? Or does he actually think you've let me sleep?'

Thinking she heard a noise, she paused for a moment but, no, that wasn't the automatic garage door opening. The house stayed silent. Jessie considered trying Tavie on a bottle feed, but the baby had to be tiring by now. Yes, her semi-translucent lids looked heavy… She was drifting off…she was asleep. The bottle feed could come later.

Jessie grabbed a quick shower, but the clammy feeling wouldn't wash from her skin. If Keelan hadn't called by seven, she'd phone the unit. She had a bad feeling about the way those bundled covers lay like a discarded crash test dummy on his king-size bed.

'Hey, Baby Hunter, did you pee?' Keelan heard Tam's nurse say, breaking his reverie. She glanced at the new fluid that had appeared. 'Hey, you did! Good boy!'

Keelan looked up, eyebrows raised, and she nodded. 'That's what we want.' She weighed the nappy and announced, 'Twelve mils. Wonder Boy!'

Outside, dawn had broken, and the humming sound of morning traffic had begun to build. A clock on the wall read six-fifteen. Keelan uncupped his hand slowly from Tam's head, feeling a spot begin to burn in the top of his spine.

'He looks better,' he observed out loud, sliding his wrist back from the warm, moist incubator. 'His colour is definitely better.'

Less mottled, more even and pinker.

'Stats have improved, too,' Andrea said. 'Sats are up, blood pressure's down. Prettier pattern on the heart graph.'

Keelan looked at the monitors. The figures hadn't changed all that much in an hour, but at least they'd changed in the right direction.

Tam had decided to keep fighting.

For the time being.

A wave of limp-muscled fatigue washed over him, and the rest of his life rushed back into his awareness like a flood tide. He had paediatric unit rounds at eight, the toughest of two tough case conferences at eight-thirty...

Did he have time to get home first? Sleep was out of the question, but he could manage breakfast at least, a look at Tavie and a chance to report to Jessie on what had happened with Tam.

'I'll be back later,' he promised Andrea Stanton vaguely, although Stephanie Vincent would be covering Tam's care by then.

In the car, he drove on autopilot, scarcely aware of streets still blessedly quiet at this hour.

At home, at just after six-thirty, Jessie must have heard the garage door. She met Keelan in the front hallway, already dressed in neat stretch jeans and a figure-hugging blue top. In any other state he would have struggled not to appreciate the way the outfit casually emphasised her ripe, healthy body, and the way she seemed at ease within it. Today, though, the male stirring in his loins was a brief irritant and nothing more.

The ends of her bright hair were damp, as if she'd

just showered, he noted, and her eyes were wide and concerned.

'When I woke up at five and realised you weren't here…' Her voice sounded shaky, reflecting his own emotion. 'Was it Tam?'

Keelan nodded. 'I left you a note,' he said, in a voice made of cardboard. 'You didn't see…?' He looked past her. 'Oh, there it is, on the floor under the sideboard.'

The window on the upstairs landing was open, and he remembered the draught streaming down from it two and a half hours ago, chilling his neck. It had blown the piece of paper off the table.

The lost note didn't seem important right now, but all the same he promised vaguely, 'Next time, I'll…' He stopped, wondering what kind of a next time there might be. The very idea made his stomach liquefy.

Jessie just stood there, waiting for him to say more, to say something that mattered. He could see that she was too scared to ask, and that something in his face had made her think the worst. Or maybe she'd been thinking the worst ever since she'd woken up to find him gone.

And she was too close to the truth.

He didn't know how to reassure her, and rasped out finally, 'He's still alive.'

'But he's not…'

'Not great, no. I need…' He trailed off, trying to work out what he did need, which way he should move, what he should do first. 'Coffee. Breakfast.' No, not yet, even though he didn't have a lot of time. 'How's Tavie?'

Switching his trajectory to head up the stairs, he almost barged into Jessie, still standing close with those wide blue eyes fixed on him, and she grabbed his arm to fend him off.

Looking up into his face from just inches away and gripping a fistful of his sweater sleeve, she said, 'Tavie's fine, putting on weight, had a bath… Um, Keelan, you feel as if you're shaking, and I—Tell me what happened with Tam. You're making me scared. How bad is he? What does his doctor say?'

He closed his eyes for a moment, then opened them to find her still there. And against all good sense, he wanted her to be. Exactly this close. Exactly this needful. He wanted *someone* to share in this. It touched him to the depths that she'd spent the past hour and a half worrying, sweating, imagining dire things, just as he had.

Her care and concern linked them.

'Heart's failing further,' he said, 'And he's battling infection. He's on all the drugs now, all the support they can give him. They can't do anything more, short of surgery, and he's not well enough or strong enough for that. It's up to him.'

'And you don't think he's going to do it?'

'I'm not sure how to bear the wait, or my own helplessness, even if he does.'

They looked at each other again, finding nothing to say. Jessie reached blindly around to the back of his neck and tucked in the escaping label of his sweater with tender fingers. She seemed to realise how tightly she'd scrunched his sleeve, and smoothed that out, too, then ran her hand up to his shoulder and rested it there, as if she didn't know what else to do with it.

Neither of them said a word.

Keelan knew he should push her away, regain control, go and get coffee or see Tavie or something—anything other than standing here letting Jessie touch him, console him, share in all this—but he couldn't do it.

He cupped his hand beneath her elbow, then moved to splay his fingers across her back. He felt warmth, and the even, regularly spaced knobs of her spine marching up between her shoulder blades. His gaze lost itself on her lips, which were pale and make-up free but looked so soft and full, parted in wordless concern.

He touched his other hand to her hip, felt the hint of bone beneath a firm curve of muscle and skin, and let himself settle deeper into the contact. She watched him, her eyes beginning to narrow and soften, and he could see the moment when she reached a decision—the same moment that he did.

Her palm came to lie against his jaw, and she lined up their kiss with the precision of a potter shaping the pouring lip on a jug. There was plenty of time for him to turn away, but he didn't do it. The responsibility was as much his as hers. *More* his. She was only acting on his wordless invitation and need. He knew the signals he'd been giving out.

The first touch of her mouth brought the blood rushing through him in male response. Those lips felt every bit as good as they looked, every bit as right, moving against his. The balance of initiative shifted between them at once, from her to him, and he tightened his arms around her, nudged her lips apart with his mouth and deepened the kiss until they were both gasping for breath.

Keelan stroked her shoulders, her back, the curve

of her rear, the tops of her thighs, claiming and exploring each part. He felt the generous press of her breasts against him, and a slow, sinuous rocking of her hips that she might not even have been aware of. Her hair smelled sweet and fragrant, its tumbling strands silky on the skin of his cheeks and temples.

She felt so warm and giving and real, and so utterly responsive. Beneath the snug blue knit of her top, he could feel her pebbled nipples thrusting against him as she arched her spine. He knew she'd be as moist as he was hard, and that they would be very, very good to each other if they took this further.

He forgot his reasons for not wanting it.

He even forgot the babies.

He simply drowned himself and this new, sweet-smelling woman in the sensual magic of touch and taste and discovery. He didn't want to take this anywhere, he just wanted to be in it now, the one pleasurable refuge, the one piece of selfishness he'd allowed himself since hearing the news about Brooke.

Jessie was the first to come to her senses, minutes later, but even so she couldn't push Keelan away and end their kiss without a painful struggle inside.

He felt and tasted so good, like cold water for a dry thirst, like home after too long away. His body was hard and strong, every bit as male as she'd known it would be, yet he moved tenderly against her, his mouth and hands searching and sensitive, not demanding or rough.

She had to remind herself in the harshest terms that something like this could feel right, even when it wasn't.

Hadn't she been through a beginning like this once before? Hadn't it felt necessary then, too? John Bishop was a very different kind of man to Keelan Hunter, but both men had called forth her empathy and her care.

She didn't stop to analyse any deeper similarities, or to look for any deeper differences, she just found the strength, finally, to twist her head and push her hands against Keelan's chest and say, 'Stop!'

He didn't. Not right away.

He didn't seem to hear her. His mouth landed on her jaw and her neck, sending thrills of perfect sensation coiling and chasing each other down across her peaked breasts, her tingling skin, into her swollen inner heat. He made a sound low in his throat, like a man protesting against being wakened from a dream.

'You don't want this,' she told him. She locked her arms straight, with her hands hard on his shoulders. 'I know you don't. I know why it's happening, too. We're sharing something, all this fear about Tam, as if we were both his parents, but we're not, and we don't want this…this baggage, this complication, either of us. I am really not in the market for something like this with a temporary employer! It's not part of the professional package on offer!'

A pair of brown eyes as hard as polished stones met hers, Keelan's fatigue and stress etched in tiny lines that fanned out from their corners and criss-crossed beneath his lids. His mouth looked almost numb.

'If you're so clear on that, why let it happen at all?' he demanded. 'Why start it? Didn't you start it?'

Her confidence faltered. 'Yes… In a way. But I

was...' She shook her head impatiently. 'Does that matter?'

He let a beat of silence hang in the air, then admitted, 'No. You're right. I'm looking for excuses.' His arms slid from her body and he pressed his palms to the sides of his head, as if he could push out the craziness of what had just happened. 'I won't do that. That's wrong. I'm sorry,' he said.

'So am I. I should have known better.'

'No. It was my responsibility not to let something like this...' He paused. 'Travel any further. Totally mine. And it won't happen again.'

'No. OK. No arguments there.' Her voice sounded thin, even to her own ears. She firmed it. 'I'll stay well out of your way.'

'Yes.'

Nothing like this had happened with John, Jessie realised vaguely in the back of her mind. There'd been no attempt to undo the initial mistake, by either of them. John had taken everything she'd offered at once, without looking back, and she'd offered it without question.

Then in the end, months later, when she'd realised what a self-destructive limbo she'd become locked in and had found the courage to leave, he'd told her that the whole thing had been her own fault—the fact that it had happened in the first place, and the fact that she was unable to follow it through.

The really hard part was that she still believed him.

Less than three years ago. She'd been old enough to know better.

'I'm making coffee,' Keelan growled, and turned towards the kitchen.

'None for me, thanks.'

Her employer paused before he reached the kitchen door.

'I'm due back at the hospital at eight,' he said.

'Yes, and I know you have a full day.'

Just go, for both our sakes.

'Mrs Sagovic should get here at around nine. She's caring, and she's pretty bright. If you think it's possible to train her in how Tavie's alarms and monitors work over the next week or so, please start. I can't help feeling… I really got the feeling during the night that Tam gained some strength from having me there. That might be—' He broke off and swore under his breath. 'You know, I really understand what the parents of my patients do to themselves now. The wishful thinking. The mind games and the bargains with God. The placebo effect, in full, living colour.'

'It's not wishful thinking, Keelan,' Jessie told him, believing it. 'It *is* important that Tam knows we're there.'

He shrugged, distancing himself yet again. 'We'll act on that assumption. We'll do this right. We'll make sure at least one of us spends some good time with Tam every day, which means that Mrs Sagovic needs to know how to take care of Tavie.'

'She's already looking stronger, and she's gained weight since Barb weighed her at the hospital yesterday. If all goes well, she'll be off her alarms soon. A few weeks.'

'Time seems to run on a different scale for Tam. I'm not thinking beyond a few days.'

'No.' Jessie controlled a sigh. 'I suppose not.'

* * *

Over the following two weeks, Tavie continued to grow and strengthen, while Tam continued to hold on, with the help of aggressive treatment and a barrage of drugs. Keelan brought home the first set of photos he'd taken, and there was already a marked difference between Tavie as a newborn and Tavie now. The contrast in Tam's appearance wasn't so encouraging.

On most days Jessie saw more of Keelan's fifty-six-year-old housekeeper than she did of Keelan himself—not surprising, since she deliberately kept out of his way and knew he was doing the same. Sometimes she could laugh about it—an edgy, cynical kind of laugh like a two-edged sword.

He left notes for her in the kitchen now, pinned safely beneath the tea canister on the granite benchtop.

'I'm going to stay right through and sit with Tam tonight. Probably until around ten. Can you get something delivered for dinner, whenever you want to eat, and leave enough for me? Thai or Vietnamese, for preference. Pizza's OK, too. Suit yourself.'

'Mrs S. is coming in all day today. If Tavie looks good, can you plan to spend the afternoon in the unit with Tam?'

'On hospital call tonight, so I won't be home. Plenty of pizza left. I'll phone some time for a report, so switch off the ringer if you're sleeping. Tam a touch feverish in the night, but fine now—6 a.m. Dr N. trying naso-gastric feed today, if all well.'

When they did see each other, they were polite and careful, like new colleagues in a hospital unit who didn't want to tread on each other's toes. What a pity they couldn't have fallen into this pattern from the beginning!

When Tavie had been home from the hospital for three weeks, Dawson Hunter came to visit his tiny granddaughter. He must have arranged to meet his son here at a specific time, as the two of them came in together.

When she heard their voices, Jessie was upstairs, sitting in the rocker with the baby in her lap, attempting a bottle feed. Tavie's suck had strengthened, but she still tired quickly, and her nasogastric tube remained in place. Without it, she wouldn't have received all the nourishment she needed. Fortunately, unlike many preemies, and especially the formula-fed ones, she had a strong stomach valve for her size and kept most of her feeds down.

She had celebrated her one month birthday last week, but her gestational age had not yet reached thirty-four weeks. She no longer forgot to breathe when she got startled or stressed, but it still happened sometimes when she fell into a deep sleep.

Mrs Sagovic—getting more and more clucky over Tavie every day, and shocked at the photos of Tam, who remained so fragile in contrast—had become adept at tickling the little girl's feet or stroking her forehead to rouse her when the breathing alarm went off, and Jessie had begun snatching an increasingly precious hour at the hospital with Tam every morning, and occasionally in the afternoon as well.

Little fighter.

He clung to life, and he'd put on a tiny amount of

weight—real growth, not retained fluid—but no one wanted to relax yet.

'I'm not!' said a man's voice downstairs, mid-conversation. Jessie knew it must be Keelan's father, but they didn't sound alike. Dawson Hunter, QC, had a voice like cement rattling in a mixer, exacerbated at the moment by an emotion she could detect but couldn't name. 'This will be easier. With the other, there's no point.'

Two sets of footsteps echoed on the hardwood stairs.

'He's doing better than he was,' Keelan said.

'That, I can't imagine! But it's your area.'

'I'm speaking as a parent, not as a doctor.'

'Yes, well…a parent… Dear God! How did we get to this?'

'Jessie?' Keelan called from the landing, lowering his voice.

'Yes, we're here,' she called back. 'She's feeding. Falling asleep, naughty girl.'

She looked up as the two men appeared in the doorway, Keelan's father first. Not quite as tall as Keelan, but close, he had to be in his mid-sixties, with a commanding head of grey hair, a prominent nose and weathered skin. His mouth was pressed tightly shut and he bristled with tension and reluctance.

'Dad, this is Tavie's nurse, Jessie.'

'Hi,' Jessie said. 'It's good to meet you, Mr Hunter.' She tapped Tavie's cheek gently, hoping she'd stay awake long enough to meet her grandfather properly.

Dawson raised his eyebrows slightly in greeting and gave a short nod, then unglued his white-lipped mouth to say in apparent disbelief, 'And this is the big one! The strong one! I can't even imagine…'

'She's growing as hard as she knows how,' Jessie answered with a smile, even though he'd probably been talking to his son, not to her. The two men seemed like magnets with their poles positioned to push each other away.

Keelan hadn't fully explained why his father had been unable to put in an appearance before this. 'He couldn't,' he'd said a couple of days ago, during a brief conversation on the subject.

That hadn't told Jessie much. There were many different kinds of 'couldn't'. Now that she was face to face with the man, she suspected the emotional kind, and her heart went out to him, despite his brusque, instinctively arrogant manner…or perhaps because of it. He found this whole thing agonising, and he'd just lost a daughter.

Understanding clicked inside Jessie like a camera coming into focus—something she already knew at heart but had been in danger of forgetting. Beyond the trappings of wealth and success, the members of this family struggled with the same complex, difficult emotions as anyone else.

You didn't have to let someone's different background create barriers. If you tried, you could break those barriers down.

'I'm sorry,' she said, and began loosening the blanket away from Tavie's little face with her finger. 'It's hard for you to get a good look at her like this, and this chair's too low.'

'No, I can see.' The older man hesitated, then stepped closer and bent lower. 'I can see,' he repeated, in a softer tone.

He crouched and his knees cracked. Jessie tapped Tavie's cheek again, and the baby opened her dark blue eyes, crinkled up one side of her nose and pursed her lips, with their tiny, translucent pink sucking blisters. She seemed nicely alert, interested in what she could hear and see, even if the sights were blurry.

Keelan's father rocked forward on his haunches, and put his hand on the rocking chair's wooden arm. 'She's beautiful…and she looks so much like Brooke,' he said in his gruff voice, and then his shoulders began to shake.

He stood up blindly and turned away from Jessie and the baby. Keelan put an angular arm around his shoulders and squeezed. 'Dad?' he said, sounding at first confused, then comprehending. 'Dad…'

They were the tears of a man who hadn't cried in half a century, rusty and painful and deep. Jessie caught one glimpse of Keelan's face, appalled and concerned, then the two men left the room together without speaking, their arms still locked together. Once more, Jessie heard their footsteps on the stairs.

Tavie didn't understand what all the fuss was about. She just thought that the light patterns she could see in the window were very interesting and pretty. And she had no idea how precious and important she was, and what a good, difficult thing she'd just done, unlocking her grandfather's pent-up grief.

'There's still a long way to go, darling girl,' Jessie told the baby. 'But your grandad's going to be OK, with you around. The two of you are going to think each other are pretty special, I think.'

She felt a wash of tenderness, and when Tavie drifted off to sleep, she kept the baby snuggled on her lap for a long time.

Chapter 5

When Dawson had left, after indulging in a stiff whisky out in the garden, Keelan stood in the front hallway for some seconds, debating with himself what to do next.

He still felt very emotional, pained by the amount of grief his father had displayed and yet hopeful in a way he hadn't been before that some unexpected blessings might come from Tavie's birth and his own involvement in her life. His complex, angry grief over his half-sister's death had eased a little.

By becoming the twins' father, he realised, he might enable Dad to find comfort and satisfaction in his new role as a grandfather.

'I should have come before this,' Dad had said, as they'd stood together in the driveway beside Dawson's latest luxury car. 'I'm sorry. I'll come again soon. And I'll stay longer. Hold her, or something. Give her a bottle. I just didn't want to…in front of that…you know, the girl, Tavie's nurse.'

'I understand, Dad.'

'Do you?' He'd collected his feelings again with difficulty, and had asked in a much more matter-of-fact tone, 'Is she good, the nurse? Do you have faith in her? Because I can't help thinking, such a fragile little girl in the wrong person's care…'

'No, Jessie is very good,' Keelan had answered at once. 'No doubts on that score.'

Except for his growing doubt as to how he and the twins would manage when she eventually left. This was just a job for her after all, not a lifetime commitment. As far as lifetime commitments went, he had no evidence that she'd ever made any of those, with all those years knocking about from London to Adelaide to Liberia to Saudi Arabia.

They hadn't talked much over the past couple of weeks, of course. He hadn't learned much more about her than he'd read in her résumé or discovered during her first three days under his roof. You could view the fact that they hadn't talked in one of two ways. First possibility—that they'd sensibly decided to keep an appropriate professional distance after one unfortunate lapse of judgement. Second possibility—that they were running scared.

The second possibility was ridiculous even to consider, Keelan revised immediately as he headed up the stairs. What power could one kiss have to scare him? He'd kissed women before.

OK, so 'scared' was the wrong word. He didn't want to scare *her*, more to the point—ruin any possibility of a healthy working relationship, so that she'd leave and he'd have to start again with someone new. He sensed she might bolt, just decamp, if things went too sour between them. Her career history suggested she might have done so in the past, and he just didn't want that. Tavie was thriving. Tam was…still here.

Stephanie Vincent had said to Keelan the other day, 'His oxygen sats are definitely better when you or Jessie are touching him. I love that!'

And it was true. He'd noted those levels himself. You couldn't fake the tenderness that Jessie showed, or the attention to detail. The charts she still kept to record Tavie's progress were meticulous, yet frequently softened and personalised with little notes to the baby, accompanied by forests of exclamation points.

'Wow, Tavie!!!' or 'Bad girl!!! How come you don't like breathing at 3 a.m.!!!'—as if she expected that the baby's charts would be kept down the years as mementoes, to show to Tavie herself when she was old enough to understand.

In the baby's nursery, he found Jessie relaxed and dozing, with Tavie snuggled in her arms. The baby stayed asleep, but the nurse opened her eyes as soon as she heard Keelan in the doorway.

'Dad's left,' he said.

'It was great that he came,' she answered.

'Yes, it was.' He added after a moment, 'To be honest, I didn't expect him to break down like that. I hope it didn't make you—'

'No! Oh, no! Uncomfortable? Of course not. It

seemed as if he really needed it, Keelan. That Tavie might really help.'

Unconsciously, she tightened her arms around the tiny, blanketed bundle, and something shifted inside Keelan as he took in the tender picture—Jessie's shoulders protectively curved, the baby's dark little head, the light from the window making the fine hairs on Jessie's arms gleam like white gold.

'I thought maybe you might have gone out together to eat or something,' she finished.

'No, he had a business dinner.'

'And did he see Tam?'

'No. He didn't feel ready for that yet.'

'Mmm. Sometimes people can't make a commitment to the baby until they know if the baby's committed to life,' Jessie said.

'One way of putting it. Accurate, probably.'

Keelan shifted his weight, oddly unsure of his next move. The unsure feeling irritated him. In seventeen years of successful adult life, it remained a rare experience, but it had become much more familiar since his sister's death.

Striding across the room, he pulled a second chair out from the wall and sat down. 'My turn to hold her? Can you pass her across without waking her?'

Jessie smiled. 'I think she's out for the count. She had a good feed.' She rose carefully, mindful of the nasogastric tube and the wiring for the alarms.

When Tavie was settled in Keelan's arms and still safely asleep, he asked, 'How many times did her breathing alarm go off last night? Really go off, I mean, rather than a false one.'

Those could happen often if the baby shifted position too much. It had to be tiring for Jessie, getting up several times a night to reset the device after a false trigger, in addition to running Tavie's tube feeds, checking her vitals and responding to her cries.

'Just once,' Jessie said, her face brightening, because this was an achievement for Tavie.

Jessie did look tired, although Mrs Sagovic had told Keelan that the nurse tried to find time for a nap each day. The nap must be adequate compensation for the disrupted nights, in Jessie's own view at least, because she never complained. And the fatigue around those dazzling sunlight-on-water eyes suited her, in an odd way.

'Is that a personal best for her?' Keelan suggested, smiling back.

He watched Jessie as she sat down again in the rocking chair. She kicked off her sandals and lifted her feet to the seat, hugging her arms around her knees.

Pretty feet, he noticed. Neat, soft heels and tapering toes, painted in clear polish. She used the motion of her body to rock the chair gently back and forth. Didn't look as if she was thinking about it, probably because she instinctively did the same thing whenever she held Tavie there.

'Yep,' she answered Keelan. 'She's getting stronger every day. How long do you want to keep the alarm in place once the genuine triggers taper off to zero?'

'You're asking me how nervous I am, right?'

'Seeing if your nerve level matches mine. To be honest, Keelan, I—I won't sleep any better without the alarm's false triggers, if I'm even the slightest bit afraid we've taken her off it too soon.'

'No.' He felt a frown crease his forehead. 'And I want you to know how much I appreciate your level of care.'

'Oh, of course. Thanks. As if I'd give anything less, though, when it's so important.'

She was a study in contrasts, he decided. Sitting there with her legs curled up and her feet bare, her hair scraped back in a ponytail that needed brushing, she looked as if she took life pretty casually. Yet she'd had the commitment not only to work in the highly specialised and emotionally demanding area of neonatal care, but to take on two separate stints for Médecins Sans Frontières in between. Had those simply been passports to travel for someone who wanted to see the world?

On an impulse, wanting to understand her better, he said, 'Tell me about Liberia and Sierra Leone. What was the hardest part about working in that sort of situation?'

'Um, the infrequency of hot showers?' Her smile was impish this time.

'No, seriously.'

'Seriously?' She sighed. 'In some ways, the hardest part was stepping back, afterwards, into a world where people take hot showers for granted. And good medical care. And water. And food. The sheer *plenty* jars more when you return to it than the scarcity jars when you first encounter it.'

'And then you worked in London for a year.'

'It's what Australian nurses are supposed to do—use their qualifications as passports to travel.'

Just as he'd thought. She'd even used the same expression.

'Storing up life experience?' he suggested.

'Definitely!' Her expression was complicated, and he guessed that not all of the experiences had been good ones. Would have asked more, except that it would have seemed like prying, given the clouded look that still lingered in her eyes.

'But not putting down roots,' he said instead.

'I thought I might have done, for a while, but that turned out to be wrong.' Again, her tone and her expression suggested he shouldn't go any further in that direction—which, of course, made him want to do just that. She thought for a moment, then added, 'I don't have high expectations regarding roots, I guess.'

'No, I think I'd got that impression already,' he drawled.

She gave him a sharp look. 'That's not a problem for you, is it? As a philosophy of living, it's not something that impinges on the way I do my job. In some ways, it probably helps. I couldn't be so committed to these babies if I had a lot of competing demands in my personal life.'

'True.'

And he'd met nurses like that before. Doctors, too, for that matter. They seemed to live for their work, and you'd swear someone simply took their batteries out and stored them in a box whenever they weren't haunting their particular domain, obsessing about patients or protocols or professional politics. They could be scary people.

Jessica Russell didn't quite seem to fit that profile somehow, but Keelan couldn't put his finger on the difference. It shouldn't matter to him, in any case.

Tavie snuffled in her sleep. She was turning into a noisy baby. On the nights when Keelan was scheduled to get up for her and therefore had the monitor in his room, she sounded like a piglet or a kitten. It disturbed his sleep, but he forgave her for it because, in fragile contrast, Tam usually lay so still and quiet.

With all the noise in the NICU, the sound of crying babies was eerily absent. They had tubes between their vocal cords, they were too heavily medicated, or they just didn't have the strength.

'Is she waking up?' Jessie asked.

'No, just pigletting.'

She laughed. 'Pigletting. I like that. It fits.' She stretched her legs down to the floor again, and slipped her sandals back on. 'Want to put her in her cot?'

'I should. I have a couple of calls to make. And I'm getting hungry. Any preferences?'

She made a face. 'I was going to…' She stopped, as if rethinking her quick response, and took a breath. 'Actually,' she continued slowly, 'I was going to hide in my room until you'd eaten, then sneak downstairs and cook myself scrambled eggs on toast. I'm ready for a break from container food. Would you mind?'

'You don't need to sneak, do you? Or ask about using our eggs?'

'No, but you know what I mean. I'm poking fun at the way we've been avoiding each other. Maybe I shouldn't.'

'Avoid me?'

'Poke fun at it.'

'I guess it has had its comical elements at times,' Keelan conceded. 'But, no, I don't think we should avoid each other. That was a difficult day, the night Daniel Nguyen called me up to the hospital to talk about Tam. What happened was…' he searched for the right phrase '…out of character for both of us, I imagine. We're scarcely candidates for a successful affair.'

'No. Poles apart. Backgrounds, for one thing. Life-styles. Priorities.'

'I'm glad you agree.'

Their eyes locked, and they both understood that there was one area in which they weren't poles apart and hadn't acted out of character three weeks ago. The chemical attraction between them remained, volatile and intriguing, even while it was unwanted and un-comfortable.

'So,' he went on. 'Scrambled eggs. Want to make some for me?'

'Bacon on the side? Grilled tomatoes and mush-rooms? Toast triangles?'

'Sounds great.'

'You go and make your phone calls, then, Keelan.'

'I'll open some wine, and we can eat outside. It's early, and it's warm.'

She'd had evenings like this with John many times, Jessie remembered half an hour later as she and Kee-lan sat on the stone-paved rear terrace, with steaming plates and chilled white wine in front of them.

Deceptively beautiful evenings, those London ones had seemed—innocent and romantic and poignant.

But in the cold light of day they hadn't been any of those things.

She'd taken on a private nursing assignment while

looking around for something in the hospital system, and she hadn't minded that it had been very different work to what she'd done in the past. She'd ended up staying with them quite a bit longer than originally planned.

During that summer, she would spend long days nursing John's wife Audrey at home while John was at work, running his successful management consultancy. By eight or nine in the evening, Audrey would be lying in a restless, medicated sleep upstairs. Jessie would have spent the previous hour fussing around in the kitchen, eagerly planning to spoil John with a delicious, private meal. More often than not, he would get home late, just as she was beginning to abandon hope.

'Business drinks. Mind-numbing. Sorry, my darling. And you've cooked? Audrey's asleep?'

Having been stricken with multiple sclerosis sixteen years earlier, Audrey had endured her worst exacerbation phase during the four months Jessie had nursed her. From her first days in the Bishops' employ, Jessie's heart had gone out to both of them. To Audrey because of what she suffered with so little complaint, and to John because he was heroically, stoically committed to a marriage which, he'd made clear, could no longer provide him with companionship or stimulation…or sex.

And he'd milked and manipulated Jessie's empathy from the first.

Why had she taken so long to see it?

He was good at manipulation, but she blamed her own naïvety and idealism and woolly principles more.

'Not as hungry as you thought?' Keelan's question

cut across her thoughts, and she realised she'd been too deeply locked in memories to eat properly.

'Just as hungry as I thought,' she answered, obediently heaping bacon and tomato onto her fork. 'Just savouring the evening, taking my time, because it's so nice.'

Too nice.

Like London.

They had Tavie's monitor on the wrought-iron table in front of them, but she was quiet at the moment. Keelan was quiet, too, apparently in the same sort of thoughtful mood as Jessie was. The way he sat opposite her, and so close, it was hard not to be aware of him. He half filled her field of vision every time she looked up.

Physically, he'd become so familiar to her now. The shape of his head, as smooth and regular as a classical sculpture, with its straight Grecian nose. The colour of his skin, a light, even-toned olive. The muscular mass of his torso, not over-developed but impressive all the same, because he sailed and swam. The way the dark hairs softened the contours of his forearm.

It would be very easy just to keep looking, to remember the way he'd felt against her body, to imagine how it might feel to be in his arms again, skin to skin, to crave his woody, living, masculine scent in her nostrils.

Music drifted to their ears from the compact disc Keelan had put on inside the house. Some folky, Celtic thing. Jessie didn't know what it was, but she liked it. The Sydney spring evening felt like a summer evening in suburban London, warm and green and filled with birdsong.

The Bishops had had a beautiful home, and with

no children in their lives it had always looked perfect, filled with antiques and works of art and surrounded by a manicured garden perfumed by flowers. Jessie had assumed at first that John's consultancy must be very successful indeed, but she'd later learned that the real money had been Audrey's, inherited just after she and John had married.

Jessie had also come to understand that John's affair with herself hadn't been his first, and hadn't been the momentous, miraculous bonding she'd believed it to be, but only the latest in a long string, with some strands in that string running parallel.

Many women fell for the vibes John put out, and for his subtle allusions to the fact that his marriage was an empty shell, that Audrey's life would not be long and her death a merciful release. Tragically, he would someday be free to marry again. In the meantime…

'You can't know how much this means to me,' he told Jessie, more than once. 'To have you here, to know how much you care. God knows, I'd never do anything to hurt Audrey. She must never know about us, and I can't make you any promises. Not yet. It's a poor bargain for you. For me, it's everything.'

Hmm.

What an idiot I was.

She hadn't come to her senses, or rediscovered her principles, until she'd found the evidence of another love interest in John's life—convenient to act upon, thanks to the many business trips he'd taken. She'd played the wronged, cheated woman in a horrible emotional scene, and he'd been derisive in response to her naked hurt.

Wake up and smell the gravy, Jessie.

Surely Audrey was the only woman who had any right to complain about his fidelity? he pointed out, his urbane, civilised logic as slippery as eel skin. Wasn't there a teeny-weeny double standard going on here?

Although Jessie didn't buy that argument, she knew she was in no position to take the moral high ground. How could she have suffered such a disastrous loss of perspective?

She left a week later, racked with guilt when Audrey told her, in her effortful, indistinct speech, 'I'll miss you. You've been the best.'

Never, never, never again.

Never fall for a man because his troubles make him seem like a hero. Never take him at his own valuation. Keep your ideals and your empathy for your work.

John had risked nothing, and had lost nothing. Like Keelan, he was too well set up in life to be cast adrift when an ill-advised relationship failed. For someone in her own situation, Jessie understood now, the risks were much greater. She hadn't had a lot to begin with. Not much money. Not much security. Not many close emotional ties. At the end of the wrong affair, she could lose even the little that she had.

'Is there any season of the year when Sydney isn't beautiful?' she asked Keelan quickly, struggling to pick up a conversational thread. She didn't want to dwell on the past.

'When it's raining,' he answered. 'Which can happen in any season, so I haven't really answered your question.'

'When it's raining,' she echoed.

It had rained a lot in London.

She finished her meal quickly after this, and although she accepted his offer of decaf coffee, she took it up to her sitting room and drank it while reading a book—one of those he'd commented on—from her suitcase. She'd unpacked them and arranged them on the bookshelves in her bedroom, but that had probably been a mistake. She should have left them in storage, to emphasise the transience of her life here.

Two weeks after Dawson's first visit to Tavie, he came again, in the middle of the day. Keelan was held back at the hospital, and Mica Sagovic had gone grocery shopping, so it fell to Jessie to usher him in and play hostess.

For a man of his position, he seemed awkward and lacking in confidence, and Jessie understood that she was probably seeing a side to him that few others had ever seen, and that the man himself might not have known he possessed until recently.

'Tea or coffee?' she offered at once, then after a sideways glance she added, 'Or something stronger?'

While looking distinctly tempted by the 'something stronger', he settled for coffee, and she suggested, 'Why don't I take you upstairs so you can see Tavie, and I'll bring the coffee up to you in a few minutes when it's ready?'

'Oh. Yes. Is she awake?'

'Not right now.'

'I thought you might bring her down.'

'We tend not to do that. It's still awkward to move her, although we're hoping she'll come off tube feeds and oxygen next week, and then it'll be easier.'

'Right.'

Jessie led the way upstairs, aware of Mr Hunter following her. Her neck prickled, and she felt unexpectedly emotional—the safe, generous yet distant form of tenderness that she should have felt for John Bishop, and should feel now for Keelan. She really wanted this second meeting between grandfather and granddaughter to go well.

When they reached the baby's room, Tavie was awake and beginning to fuss, and Keelan's father said, 'Oh. What does that mean? Is she hungry?'

'I expect so. And bored. She's starting to want a bit of entertainment now.'

Jessie thought for a moment. Tavie had begun to be weaned off the supplemental oxygen for set periods each day. She took half her feeds by mouth. It would be possible...

'Since she's awake,' she added, 'would you like to help me with a milestone for her? Her first trip outside? We could take her into the back garden.'

'Would that be safe? If you haven't done it before...' He looked around the room as if it was a fortress that only just managed to keep hidden dangers at bay.

Two weeks ago, he'd only submitted to a three-minute visit before fleeing. This time Jessie was determined to keep him longer, and to make the interlude more rewarding for both the man and the baby.

'I think I've been waiting for the right moment.' She touched his arm briefly. 'It would be a celebration, don't you think?'

'I'm in your hands,' he answered gravely. 'If you know what to do with all this equipment.'

'We can leave most of it behind for a short period,' she assured him.

He stood back and watched while Jessie detached the lengths of tube and wire. She thought of giving him Tavie to carry downstairs but guessed the idea would terrify him. Tavie had her new, unused pram sitting in the little storage room beneath the stairs. If Dawson could bring that outside for her, they could put Tavie in it and park her under a shady tree, safely bundled in blankets. She'd love it.

'This much effort,' Keelan's father murmured at one point, when Jessie had had to send him back upstairs for a lambskin to pad the pram with. 'Is it worth it?'

'It'll be lovely,' she answered confidently.

And it was.

Jessie settled Tavie in the pram and left her in her grandfather's care while she made the coffee and found some biscuits to go with it. Waiting for the liquid to drip through the filter, she tiptoed to the back door to see how they were getting on, and saw that he'd positioned his chair right beside the pram.

He had his eyes fixed on the tiny girl, who gazed up at the moving patterns of the green leaves, waving her little hands around excitedly, as if she thought she might catch one.

Way too much to read into a seven-week-old preemie's random arm movements and blurry gaze, but Jessie knew she wasn't reading too much into the body language that Dawson Hunter displayed. He found his granddaughter fascinating, and she'd brought him to a level of contemplation and stillness that he would rarely achieve in the rest of his busy, high-profile life.

When Jessie appeared with the coffee and biscuits, Dawson shifted his chair several inches away from the baby's pram, as if he'd been caught out in some sinful display, sitting so close, watching so intently. She didn't comment, just handed him the cup and saucer with a smile and offered the biscuits a short while later.

'Tam's getting a little stronger,' she told him.

'Keelan says his heart may yet give out before he's strong enough for the surgery.'

'His doctors are walking a knife edge with the timing,' Jessie agreed. 'It's been a battle to get his infections under control. Tam needs us to be hopeful, I always think.'

'New Age mumbo-jumbo,' the older man growled. 'It would have been better to let him go. To spare all of us this nightmare.'

He passed the back of his hand across his forehead, as if brushing away a fly. Jessie pretended not to notice. Tavie started fussing. 'She's ready for her bottle. I'll go and warm it up.'

'What about the tube?' The business end of it was still taped to Tavie's face and threaded up through her nose and down into her stomach, although Jessie had detached and capped the other end.

'She likes the bottle better now. Doesn't like the tube one bit. We're holding our breath because a couple of times she's looked as if she was trying to pull it out.'

'She couldn't do that!'

'Some NICU people say that if a baby is strong enough to pull out the tube, she's strong enough to do without it. Would you like to give her the bottle?'

'I could give it a try. I was never much of a hands-on parent.'

'Second chance, then,' Jessie suggested lightly, then realised that her comment had far more meaning than her tone had conveyed, in the light of his daughter's recent death. She winced inwardly.

I'm usually more tactful than that!

But Keelan's father seemed to take her words differently. 'Yes, I've been extraordinarily lucky,' he said soberly. 'I'm only just beginning to understand that.'

Jessie left him alone with Tavie again while she mixed and warmed the forty mils of special preemie formula that the baby could now manage at one feeding session. She brought some pillows to help Mr Hunter and his granddaughter get comfortable together in the outdoor chair.

Keelan appeared on the terrace while she was still helping his father and Tavie get their positioning right. 'Starting to wonder where everyone had got to,' he said. 'Dad, I'm glad you got here. Sorry I was held up.'

'We've been managing pretty well,' his father said. 'Haven't we, Jessie?'

'Very well. Her first trip into the open air, Keelan, and she loves it. I knew she would.'

She saw him take in the fact that his father had the baby on his lap, bottle included, and couldn't help deliberately seeking eye contact to telegraph her satisfaction. She raised her eyebrows at Keelan and gave a tiny nod that said, Isn't he doing well?

Keelan nodded back, and mouthed, 'Thanks.' And just that one, tiny, secret communication between them, that warm, short connection with his dark eyes, was enough to shatter any illusion on her part that she'd kept her attraction to him under control over the past few weeks.

She hadn't. It had only grown.

Any further along this path, and she'd be a mess.

No, thank you. I'm not going there again.

She flashed her gaze down to the baby instead, and watched the tiny, singing stream of bubbles rising against the bottle's clear plastic sides.

Chapter 6

'Yes, of course I'd like you to come and see Tam, Dad, but I'm not going to push,' Keelan told his father.

'No, well, once he's home, all right? I don't like hospitals.'

'He won't be home for a while yet. Christmas if he's lucky.'

'We'll see.'

Not for the first time, they seemed to be having the most important conversation of the day while standing next to Dawson's car in the driveway, driver's side door hanging open, when they'd supposedly already said goodbye.

This didn't score as a coincidence, Keelan was sure. Unconsciously, Dad did it on purpose. At the last moment, he got up half the necessary courage—enough to ask the hard question, while still hoping he could run away from the answer by jumping behind the wheel and gunning the engine up the street.

Simple honesty was the best response to this strategy, Keelan had decided. He wondered, sometimes, if successful men of his own generation were as startling a mix of strength and weakness as were successful men of his father's age. He thought perhaps they weren't, that there had been some progress, some balance achieved. He hoped so.

Another car approached down the quiet street. Looking up, he recognised his mother's blue Volvo and the silhouette of her neatly coiffed head. His heart lurched sideways, and he almost elbowed his father out of the way so he himself could take the vehicular escape route Dad had been looking for. So much for emotional progress...

My lord!

His parents—his bitterly divorced parents—were about to encounter each other, out of the blue, for the first time since their very precisely choreographed and ultra-polite meeting at his own wedding to Tanya nine years ago. He'd had no idea that Mum was coming down today.

He froze.

Dad hadn't seen Mum yet. She parked under a tree on the opposite side of the street, a little further up the hill, and started across towards them, waving cheerfully. Apparently she hadn't recognised Dad's car, and he'd slid into the driver's seat now, masked from her view by the glare of the sun on his windscreen.

'Surprise!' she trilled, smiling, still some metres

away. 'Love, I didn't want to tell you that I was coming. Just in case. Because there's been this kerfuffle over—' She broke off suddenly, her eyes fixed on the red Mercedes, and added in a very different tone, 'Dawson!'

'Susan,' he growled back, and slid awkwardly from the car into a standing position again.

Neither of them said anything further, and neither of them took their eyes from each other's face. Keelan seriously contemplated pushing past his father, sliding into the driver's seat of the Mercedes, turning the key that was still in the ignition and getting the hell out of the situation.

He restrained himself and broke the ice with the scintillating word, 'Well…'

As the wronged partner in the long-ended marriage, Mum had the right to her son's loyalty and the right to snub her ex-husband to an extent limited only by her imagination. Typically, though, she didn't. Instead, after a yawning pause, she reached out a rather shaky pair of hands, gripped the man's shirtsleeves and hugged him.

'Oh, Dawson, I'm so sorry.' Her voice shook, too. 'I can only imagine how these past weeks have been for you. For Louise, too.'

'Hasn't been easy,' he said, that gravelly gruffness filling his tone. 'I haven't spoken much to Louise.'

'No…'

'I think Phillip has been very good. And his girls.' Louise had two stepdaughters, since her recent remarriage, aged in their mid-twenties.

'I'm glad.'

Keelan's parents let each other go, slowly.

His mother went on, 'Are you coming or going, Dawson?'

'Going. She's absolutely beautiful, Susie. It's good of you to take an interest.'

'Take an interest?' Her eyes blazed. If she'd been a cat, you could have seen her fur standing on end. 'Dawson Hunter, she's…my… granddaughter!'

Keelan's scalp tingled at the implacable rebuke in those five words.

His father looked unutterably shocked. 'But—'

'My son has adopted her. That makes her his daughter. My granddaughter. Yours, too, of course. And Louise's. But mine just as much. Never, ever think otherwise, Dawson.'

'My God, Susan, of course, if that's the way you see it, and the way you feel…'

'It is. Keelan, can we go inside? Let's not keep your father standing here when he wants to get on his way. I'm sure we'll see more of each other now, Dawson. I… uh… That'll be…interesting, won't it?'

Keelan's father could manage only the briefest of nods. Keelan ushered his mother inside, but when he looked back, before closing the front door, he saw that Dawson still sat motionless behind the wheel, as if he didn't have the co-ordination skills to start the engine.

'She'll be asleep, and tired out. It's a pity. You just missed her first experience of the big, wide world.'

Laying Tavie back in her cot, Jessie heard Keelan's voice in the front hallway and wondered who he had with him now.

'I'm staying for several days,' said a female voice.

'Here?'

'If you'll have me, dear. I wanted to let you get settled before I came down, to give you time to, well, start feeling like a parent, but now I'm feeling selfish and I couldn't wait any longer to see her properly. So will you have me?'

'Of course I'll have you, but you might prefer better accommodation than I can offer. There's no spare room any more. Tavie has her nursery, and I've given Jessie a bedroom and a sitting room.' Keelan's voice got closer as he spoke.

Keeping her curiosity down to a simmer, Jessie set up the alarms again and clipped the pulse oximeter to Tavie's foot. Ninety-eight per cent, the monitor indicated, which was great after the baby had been breathing regular air for a whole hour with no respiratory support.

'You are so good and strong, little girl,' she told the baby, even though she'd fallen asleep.

'Jessie, my mother's here,' Keelan said, from the doorway. 'She had some strange idea that it would be more "convenient" if she didn't tell us she was coming. Convenient for whom, I'm not sure, but anyhow here she is.'

'With a very warm, thoughtful introduction from my son,' said a trim-figured woman of about sixty. She had Keelan's dark eyes, and they twinkled, framed by beautifully tinted light brown hair. 'It's good to meet you. I've heard all the right things.'

'Um, tell me what those are, and I'll be flattered, shall I?' Jessie murmured, softening the cheeky response with her tone. Keelan had set up this mood, and his mother had followed through, but Jessie wasn't sure if she was allowed to join in.

'Keelan, have a look out the front and tell me if your father has left yet,' Susan Hunter murmured. 'He acted as if I'd kneecapped him with the granddaughter thing. I don't know why he thought I'd feel differently.'

'Some women would have.'

'And deprived themselves of a grandchild?' She caught sight of the baby, still dwarfed by the expanse of the cot mattress, and bundled in a white cotton blanket. 'Oh, and she's gorgeous! Oh, she is! So much bigger and stronger than the first time I saw her! I don't want to hold her, she's asleep, but, oh, I wish I could!'

Keelan stepped back into the corridor and went to the landing, where the window looked out onto the street. Coming back a few seconds later, he reported, 'Dad's still there.'

'Well, he's not my responsibility,' Keelan's mother said, sounding very firm about it.

Jessie got the impression, however, that at some level Susan felt he still was. Possibly, she even wanted him to be.

'Well, she *was* screaming, Dr Hunter,' the A & E nurse said in an apologetic tone, 'until two minutes before you got here.'

Her gesture presented a tranquil tableau of mother and toddler looking at each other as if not at all sure what to do next. No one was crying. No one appeared to be in pain, although the little girl did look rather pale and wrung out.

Keelan approached the bed in the paediatric section

of the emergency department, and got an apology from
the mother as well. She was in her early forties, rather
tired-looking, but with a pretty face and Snow White
colouring that her little daughter also shared.

'I'm sorry, she seems fine now.' The mother smiled
and spread her hands. 'I do tend to panic with her a bit,
because of her having Down's. She started screaming
at home, and then she stopped, and then she screamed
again and I brought her straight in. We're not far. She's
hard to interpret sometimes, and she only has a couple
of words. She'll be two next month. I guess she just got
herself into a state, or ate too fast, or—But she really
did seem to be in such a lot of pain!'

'Hang on, we won't let her off the hook just yet, now
that I'm here,' Keelan said.

The child had shown some other symptoms, according to a report from the resident who'd examined
her—rigid, tender abdomen, low blood pressure, flac-
cid body; pale, septic and very sick appearance, as well
as the strong evidence of serious pain that her mother
had mentioned.

He examined the little girl. She had several classic
Down's traits—a flattened head, a slight heart murmur which her parents had been told was minor—and
seemed like a lovable and loving child. Loved, too.

'She's our only one,' the mother said, still apologetic. 'I do panic.'

With reason this time. Without warning, little Laura
stiffened and began to scream again, in severe and unmistakable pain. Tears streamed down her cheeks and
her mother could do nothing to console her.

'Let's have another look at her BP,' Keelan murmured, and sure enough it had dipped again. 'I think she probably has an intussusception,' he said. 'A sort of telescoped segment of the intestine. It'll pouch into the adjacent intestine, and while it's happening it's very painful. Then it'll push out again and everything seems fine. You'd swear they've forgotten all about it, and nothing's wrong.'

'So you're saying...' The mother frowned, waiting for the other shoe to drop, hugging her child and soothing her. Experience with a Down's baby had taught her never to take good news for granted.

'It does mean surgery,' he had to tell her. 'Straight away, so that she doesn't have to go through many more bouts of this. That vulnerable segment of the intestine will have to be taken out. But it's not a complex operation, and you should have no ongoing problems. It's very rare to find this condition in a child over two.'

'So it's not related to the Down's, or—or indicative of any other problem, or something we'll have to watch for...'

'She should be absolutely fine, Mrs Carter. I'll arrange a bed for her upstairs and talk to the surgeon straight away.'

The surgery didn't take long to set up, and there were no more children in the emergency department that Keelan needed to see. He looked at his watch. If he could get out of here before someone else collared him, he could manage a side trip to the NICU on the way back to his own unit. Jessie would probably be there at this time of day.

He tried not to think of this as an added inducement, but knew he was kidding himself.

He could give himself a mental pep talk about it.

He should!

Having given himself numerous such talks over the past few weeks, he had the lines down by heart and could play them in his head like a tape. He could also choose to visit Tam this afternoon, instead of right now, by which time Jessie would be home again with Tavie. That way, she wouldn't be a distraction.

Or he could just forget the avoidance strategies and enjoy the pleasure of her company.

Why didn't the two of them launch into a hot affair, in fact?

They were both single, sensible adults, and they were living under the same roof, with all the privacy they needed, and a king-size bed. The attraction existed on both sides. His senses told him this, not any particular arrogance about his male magnetism. And yet he was pretty convinced that if he tried to get her into bed, she'd turn him down. A large part of her wouldn't want to, but she'd do it anyway.

Because…?

She had more self-control. She had a clearer perception of their differences, and of all the ways in which a relationship between the wrong people could turn sour. She'd been bitten before, and she'd be twice as shy this time around.

Pick one answer. Pick all of them.

She was probably right.

He sighed through the corner of his mouth and hit the lift button for the seventh floor. Saw her as soon as he got halfway into the unit, and all the tension and awareness and intuition between them flooded back into the air again.

'Hi,' she said. She smiled, then looked away too quickly, the turn of her head a little giddy and the angles of her body self-conscious.

'How's he looking today?' Keelan asked her, wondering if he betrayed as much as she did with his body.

What did Jessie pick up? What did other people see? It shouldn't hit them this hard when they saw so much of each other. Familiarity should have rubbed off some of the heady, unsettling glow after nearly three months.

But it hadn't. The glow only got worse.

Stephanie had Tam's chart resting on top of the respirator while she added some notes, but glanced at all three of them when she heard Keelan's question. She made a little sound with her tongue and her teeth that he didn't like.

'He's hanging in there,' Jessie answered. 'Struggling a bit. I don't want to say that. Do I, Tam, sweetheart? But he is. The weight's not going on the way we want. Slowed to a standstill this week—you looked at his numbers yesterday, didn't you?'

Keelan nodded. Today was Thursday, and he'd had a busy week. He'd barely managed to see the baby and he felt out of touch, remorseful and newly anguished about Tam's slight but definite downturn over the past few days, as if his necessary preoccupation with his own patients was to blame.

In contrast, Tavie's health had gone from strength to strength. After Keelan's mother's visit, Jessie had steadily weaned the little girl onto longer and longer intervals of breathing room air, and bigger and bigger mouth feeds. Tavie had conformed to the unwritten preemie rule about readiness for oral feeds, and had finally pulled out her nasogastric tube one day.

During the three days that followed, Keelan and Jessie had debated whether they might need to put it back in. If she fell asleep during too many of her bottle feeds and couldn't finish them… If her weight gain slowed or stalled…

No, thanks, Tavie had told them very clearly, via her stats and her observations and her behaviour. I hate the tube. And I can handle this. See, I'm staying awake because this sucking stuff feels very nice, and I'm still growing. Probably a good idea if you keep me on the breathing alarm at night for a bit longer, though.

Keelan's mother had been absolutely captivated and had stayed for four nights. She and Jessie had got on well. They'd kept certain boundaries in place, but the boundaries were friendly ones.

'Come for a visit with Tavie as soon as she's strong enough,' Susan had begged Keelan, on the morning of her departure, a month ago now. 'And bring Jessie to share the load. She'll need a change of scene soon. You couldn't have asked for a better carer for the baby.'

The invitation still hovered in the back of Keelan's mind, but he hadn't planned a time to take his mother up on it yet.

'And he's retaining fluids again,' Jessie finished. Her hand rested lightly and protectively on top of Tam's incubator. 'Dr Nguyen increased the diuretic this morning.'

'Is he around?'

'Parent conference,' Stephanie put in, using a tone

that conveyed too much. Shut away in the privacy of the unit's tiny conference room, some baby's parents were getting bad news.

Meanwhile, the flurry of nervous yet happy activity at the far end of the unit told Keelan that a different set of parents would be leaving with their baby in a few minutes. Home. Healthy. Safe.

A wave of sick envy poured down on him, tightening up his throat, making blood beat in his head, and for the hundredth time he thought, And every day there are parents feeling like this, getting torn apart like this. It's horrible. And there's nothing to do but suf- fer it…

'Yikes, Ethan!' another nurse suddenly exclaimed behind him. 'Are you just trying to scare me, or—? No, you're for real! You're not supposed to do this! And not this fast! *Yikes!*'

Keelan whipped around, his whole body yanked like a marionette by the urgency in her tone. Stephanie asked with the same urgency, 'Get a doctor?'

'Who's around?'

Keelan zapped his focus across the unit, seeking to answer this question for himself. He already knew that Daniel was in conference with those poor parents. Dr Cathy Richler should be here… Yes, but fully involved in a procedure on another very ill baby. Residents? Busy or absent. Even doctors needed bathroom breaks and occasional nourishment.

'What's going on?' he asked the other nurse. Carol something. He didn't waste time checking her badge. Should know her last name, but it had flown from his head. Hardly heard her answer, because he could ob- serve the evidence for himself.

The baby boy had paled to parchment white, his skin textured like paper. On the monitor, his heart numbers had fallen, and they kept falling, while his blood pressure had climbed to dangerous heights. This had to be the aftermath of an IVH—an intraventricular haemorrhage. A brain bleed, if you wanted to be totally blunt about it. Sometimes you didn't, because it sounded too scary, but the baby's parents weren't here right now, so there was no need to pretend.

The real problem was that the evidence only showed up, as now, after the event. You could treat the symptoms, but you couldn't prevent damage to the brain that might already have happened.

'So fast!' Carol said. 'He was at risk. They're always at risk, these ones—he's a twenty-eight-weeker, four days old—but he'd been looking so good and stable. Now...'

'I'm not calling Nguyen out of that conference,' Stephanie said.

Keelan cold-shouldered the technicality that this wasn't his domain.

'He needs something to boost his heart rate,' he said. 'And look at those sats.' He dredged his mind and found the weight-to-dosage figures he'd known by heart during his times in the NICU in the past, scaled down from the figures he usually needed upstairs but not so very different in principle.

He announced the result out loud, then added, 'That right, Stephanie? Carol?' They'd both nursed in this unit for years. They'd know if he'd somehow got it wrong, although he was sure he hadn't. Double-checking in his head, he saw both nurses nod.

Jessie also agreed. 'Yes, that's right.' Then she added, 'But let me tell Dr Richler what's going on.'

'You should,' Keelan said. 'I'm not waiting for her, though.'

This could have been Tam.

In the few seconds it had taken Keelan to react Carol had already begun to prepare the minuscule doses of medication while Stephanie had grabbed the equipment they'd need to bag oxygen into the baby boy in order to get those saturation figures on the monitor back up. Keelan snatched the bagging equipment from her and began to work on the baby. If he responded quickly to the treatment, they could cross their fingers that the bleed had been mild, no long-term effects, a small piece of bad luck instead of a terrible tragedy.

Because this could so easily have been Tam during his first days of life.

Jessie disappeared from Keelan's field of vision, her walk calm and steady and graceful as always. He forgot about her in the urgency of getting this baby right again, absolutely determined that one set of parents, at least, would be spared his own anguish today.

Lord, this blue-white, papery little face was so tiny and crumpled! He'd forgotten just how much delicacy of movement you needed. He held the bag in place, squeezed, counted, squeezed.

Come on, baby! Do this for me. For us. For your mum and dad. For *my* boy, Tam.

'Yep,' Carol said a few minutes later. 'Look. Sats are climbing. Colour's getting better.'

Ethan's blood pressure had fallen to a safer level, too, and his heart rate had improved. Another ten minutes and he had fully stabilised. You never would have known the bleed had happened, looking at his stats. They couldn't know for certain about the long-term consequences, but the outlook was promising, the way he'd bounced back so quickly.

Stepping back, letting go, Keelan found Cathy Richler standing there, the corner of her mouth quirked.

'Branching out?' she drawled.

'Call it a refresher course.' The closest he planned to get to an apology. 'I did consider this specialty, you know. And I have graduates of yours—' infant graduates, he meant '—in my care.'

'OK, I won't tell anyone,' she said. She and Keelan had always respected each other. 'Particularly since you got the right result. How bad did it look?'

Carol answered for him, reeling off the rock-bottom figures Ethan had reached seconds before they'd begun treatment.

'Hmm,' Cathy said, then leaned close to the incubator and addressed the baby, face-to-face. 'Drama king! What are we going to tell Mum and Dad, hey? They've gone out to lunch together, and I was the one who made them do it. They're going to think it was all their fault for not being here, little guy, you know that, don't you?'

Yeah, Keelan knew how that felt!

He decided to stay on until Daniel had a moment for him. Jessie sat in the one chair beside Tam, but when she saw the way he hovered, she stood up and said quietly, 'Can I get you something, Keelan? Coffee and a sandwich?'

'Mmm, please. That'd be nice,' he answered, feeling the usual wash of tenderness and magnetism that flowed between them.

That was what made it so hard. Magnetism…physical, chemical attraction…was one thing. You could box that up, keep it in its place, act cynical and call it raging animal libido. But when it came pre-blended with an equal mix of tenderness, the whole thing got a lot harder. Blame the babies, who made both him and Jessie feel like parents.

'Ham and salad?'

'Whatever comes.' His stomach felt hollow, but the hunger seemed distant and unimportant. He honestly didn't care. Cared far more about the look in her blue eyes, the little frown, the soft, concerned mouth. 'Just whatever,' he finished, the words like a reluctant hand pushing her away.

Daniel showed up before Jessie got back, and obviously knew from Keelan's face what he wanted to talk about. 'You want to take another look at the issue of surgery?'

'This isn't working, Daniel. It was for a while, when we were getting him over the infections, but now it's just the heart and we're going—he's going—one step forward and another step back. I'm not seeing what we're going to achieve here. He's so tired. He needs more help. Even with the risk.'

'Have you seen Keith? Said any of this to him?'

Keith Bedford was the paediatric heart surgeon who, with a junior surgeon assisting, would perform the operation to close the holes in Tam's tiny heart. Keelan knew him well, because he had paediatric heart patients of his own upstairs.

'No,' he answered. 'I wouldn't skirt your involvement on that. Let's present a united front. He's not going to be very keen.'

'Would you be?'

'I'd rather—I couldn't stand just watching him slide and slide, a little each day.'

'So is this about you? What you can stand?'

'No, it's about what Tam can stand. And I think he'd stand an aggressive boost, even with the risks, better than he's standing this wait-and-see, growing and feeding routine. It isn't working. I want to conclude that now, not wait to conclude it when it's definitively too late to act. And the harder the heart has to work, the more I'm concerned about the ticking time bomb of that thinned aorta wall. He needs the surgery.'

'Let's schedule a meeting with Keith. You want to be there?'

'Yes. Make it today, if we can. I can rejig most of my schedule, make the time. If we agree on this, Keith can operate Monday. I'm getting the worst feeling about waiting longer. And that's as a doctor, not a parent.' He stopped and frowned, heard the uncertainty vibrating in his own voice. 'Lord, I *think* that's as a doctor. Who the hell knows any more?'

He felt a soft touch on his sleeve. Jessie. With his sandwich and his coffee. She'd obviously heard enough of what he and Daniel had said to be able to put together the whole conversation. She looked very worried.

About him or about Tam?

Suddenly, he wanted her at the meeting with Keith and Daniel as well. For support. Input, even.

But then he braked hard on his emotions and got

his perspective back. She had to get back to Tavie. She wasn't Tam's mother, or even officially—yet—his nurse. She didn't need to be there, and it wouldn't be fair to give her any responsibility for the decision.

He took the sandwich in its white paper bag and the coffee in its lidded styrofoam cup, and said, 'Thanks. Do you want to head off now?'

'Will you tell me when something's been decided? As soon as you can get to a phone?' She added quickly, 'Sorry, that's not fair of me, but I'm going to be thinking about it all afternoon.'

'It's fine. Of course I'll phone. It depends on Keith. I'm not sure of his schedule, when we'll be able to meet. And I'll try and get home for dinner, too.' It sounded like a promise from a busy husband to a neglected wife, but he didn't care.

She nodded, said goodbye to the nurses and Tam, and left. He watched her go, and if Daniel and Stephanie and Carol were watching him watching her, and wondering why he couldn't drag his eyes away, he didn't care about that either.

At five-thirty, Jessie heard the rumble of the garage door when she'd just tiptoed into the baby's room to check that Tavie was still sleeping nicely. She'd been wakeful and fretful in the early afternoon, then she'd had a good feed and had settled down at around two. She would probably wake up again within the next half-hour.

At the familiar sound of Keelan's arrival home, Jessie felt a spurt of unreasonable anger—the channelling of a tension she'd been suffering under all afternoon.

Keelan had promised her that he'd phone as soon as he had any news, but she'd heard nothing, and she'd been on tenterhooks, wondering if the meeting had taken place. She couldn't imagine that Keelan would be home this early if he hadn't yet cornered Keith Bedford. He'd have waited at the hospital.

Entering the house, he saw her poised at the top of the stairs and said at once, 'I'm sorry, I know I told you I'd phone, but Keith and Daniel and I have only just finished our meeting. I didn't have anything else urgent, so it seemed best to come straight home and tell you in person.'

'Tell me…what?'

'He's willing to operate. He agrees that the real danger now is in waiting too long. Barring any unforeseen developments over the weekend, they'll do the surgery on Monday morning.'

'Whew!'

'You think that's the right decision?'

'Why are you asking me that, Keelan?' Jessie started down the stairs, as Keelan started up. 'I don't—'

'Because you said "Whew", as if you were relieved. As if you'd been waiting for this, and wanted it.'

'I—No, I mean, if you're relieved, then I'm relieved for you. I'm just…overwhelmed a bit. That's why the "Whew". It's—'

'Hey.' They reached each other in the middle of the stairs and stopped awkwardly. The treads were wide ones, but there wasn't a lot of room all the same. He brushed a strand of vibrant hair from her face. 'I'm treating it as good news. Don't fall apart on me.'

Jessie laughed, and it came out breathy and awkward. 'Sorry, is that not in my job description?'

'Most of this is not in your job description. None of this.'

The air vibrated, and Keelan put his hand on her arm to steady them both.

To keep that treacherous air in place.

Or something.

Jessie knew she ought not to look at his face. It wasn't safe. She couldn't help it, though. She wanted to—to drink in the painful pleasure of seeing him this close, feeling herself enveloped in his unique aura, sharing so much with him, watching his mouth when she was close enough to kiss it and his eyes when she could feel his gaze on her skin like radiant heat.

Every nerve ending in her body trembled and sang, and hot liquid seemed to pool inside her. The strength drained out of her legs like water from an open pipe. She really felt as if she couldn't stand and sank to the carpeted stairs, her fingers circled around his hard forearm, clinging to him for support.

She thought he'd follow her, sit beside her and consummate the touch of mouth to mouth that she could already taste, but he didn't, which left him towering over her, leaning a little because she still held onto his arm.

'You're just exhausted, aren't you?' he said.

'No. Yes. Of course.'

'Why didn't I see it?'

'Because you're exhausted, too.' She propped her elbow on her thigh and pillowed her cheek on the heel of her hand, waiting for something definitive to happen.

The kiss. Or the deliberate creation of distance.

Neither event did. Keelan and Jessie both simply stayed where they were on the stairs, clinging awkwardly to each other's arms. If he was looking at her the way she'd looked at him just now, she didn't know, because she'd at least managed to focus her eyes on the stair rails instead of his face.

'Listen, Mum wants us to bring Tavie up to see her,' he said finally. 'She told me when she was here that we'd both need a break within a few weeks, and she was right. We do.'

'But Tam's going into surgery on Monday.'

'Which means this weekend is our last chance until… Well, our last chance for a while.' He stopped, clearly fighting the spectre of possibilities that he didn't want to put into words, and that Jessie didn't even want to think about. If Tam didn't survive the surgery, they'd have plenty of chances to get away for a weekend in future.

'My schedule's pretty clear,' he went on after a moment. 'Tavie's strong enough to travel, if we're careful. Tam's in good care. Let's do it. I don't like the way you look today. Pale and wrung out and totally on edge. This weekend will be tough otherwise, hanging around waiting for the surgery on Monday. I don't think it'll do Tam any good at this stage to have us there, and these next weeks are going to be…'

Again, he stopped and didn't finish. They could only hope that the weeks ahead would be tiring, too, with all the time they'd be spending at the hospital, because if they weren't spending time at the hospital, it could only mean that the surgery on fragile Tam had failed.

'We could head up to Mum's late tomorrow afternoon,' Keelan continued. 'Take some snacks in the car and have a late meal when we get there. It's a great place, right on the beach, plenty of space and air. Bring a book and a swimsuit.'

Jessie laughed, somewhat shakily. 'You can stop, Keelan. I'm sold, OK? I'm packing. I'm digging out the swimsuit.'

He let her go at last and stepped carefully back down the stairs. 'It'll be good for both of us. I can work my schedule tomorrow so we can leave at four, if you can have Tavie ready.'

'If she co-operates.' Jessie hugged her arm against her chest, still feeling the sensation his touch had left on her skin. 'She was a bit fussy this afternoon, for a while. I didn't get much done until she finally fell asleep.'

'What would you like for dinner?' He stepped down another three treads, sliding his broad shoulders against the pale lemon-cream wall. 'Shall we eat late, take Tavie out for a stroll first, if she wakes up? It's a warm evening, and I think she's ready for another milestone.'

'A stroll would be great. Mica made a batch of pasta sauce yesterday. How does that sound?'

'Nice. With salad?'

He'd retreated all the way to the bottom of the stairs, and since both of them had just been gabbling at each other, with a tenth of their brains engaged, about the minutiae of their plans for the next two hours, the whole atmosphere felt safer now. Lighter. The air had stopped vibrating, and contained only the faint echo of all that awareness, like the echo that followed the dying sound of cathedral bells.

Jessie could breathe.

Chapter 7

Tavie took the journey to her grandmother's in stride like a veteran traveller…until the last twenty minutes of driving, when she suddenly decided that enough was enough and cried loudly for it to be over.

'She can't be hungry. Her nappy is fine. She's not sick.' Keelan ticked off the options for the fifth time.

'She's just frazzled,' Jessie said, also for the fifth time.

'And so are we.'

'Do you want to stop?' she asked.

They'd had a seductively pleasant drive until now. Hard to maintain any sort of distance when cocooned together in a moving car on a highway. It hadn't seemed particularly dangerous. They'd simply talked, or listened to music and news, or stayed silent.

But Jessie had no illusions. It wouldn't take much.
The right touch or the right look at the wrong time, and
the air would sing as if criss-crossed with firing bul-
lets. Her heart would sing, too, no matter how much
she tried not to hear it.

There had been an unspoken agreement that they
weren't going to talk about Tam. Jessie had spent some
time with him that morning, and they would see him
again late Sunday afternoon when they returned to Sydney. Meanwhile, they knew he was in good hands, and
they wanted this weekend to be about enjoying Tavie
and getting a break.

By this time Jessie had grown used to the feeling of
knowing where every bit of Keelan's body was positioned in relation to her own, of catching movements or
gestures or voice tones from him that made her insides
melt with wanting. She thought she could probably en-
dure it, if she was careful, until it went away.

Which it would.

Surely.

It had with John Bishop, quite suddenly, after that
telling argument about fidelity. She'd been left with regret and shame, but no longing or pain.

'What, you think we should set up camp by the side
of the road?' Keelan said, in answer to her question
about stopping, above the sound of Tavie's piercing
cries. 'No, we have to get there, just get her peaceful
and settled.'

They spilled noisily into Susan Hunter's spacious
beach-front house some minutes later, bringing an atmosphere of chaos that Keelan's mother took cheerfully
in her stride. 'And here's your Aunt Lynette, Keelan.'

Another woman, clearly Susan's sister, hovered in the background. 'She's here to give me grandmother lessons, and I'm obviously going to need them.'

'I'm sorry, Mum. We think she's just stressed from the drive. She slept most of the way, until just this last… month, it feels like. Year.'

'Twenty minutes,' Jessie corrected, squeezing out a smile. 'We fed her halfway, and had a snack ourselves. I think we should try a bottle, Keelan, just to soothe her, even if she's not very hungry. Can I sit somewhere quiet with her?'

'Let me show you where I've put you all,' Susan said. 'There's an armchair in the baby's room.'

'I can make up her bottle,' Keelan's aunt offered.

'Here's her bag,' he said and tossed it to her like a rugby ball, without even looking to see if it had found its mark. His eyes were on crying Tavie again. 'The formula's in the tin, should be near the top. Don't overheat it.'

'If I could have a couple of pillows in the chair…' Jessie suggested.

'Four adults, one baby, and it still feels like we don't have enough pairs of hands,' Susan said.

But it broke the ice, and by the time Tavie finally settled, stopped crying and went to sleep, Jessie had forgotten that she didn't quite know how she fitted in here in Susan Hunter's lovely home, and whether she was viewed as a friend or an employee…or some other option she hadn't even considered, because she didn't dare to.

The house was gorgeous, with views, through its huge windows, over the dunes to the beach. On a wide wooden deck that looked silver in the moonlight, there

was an awning for daytime shade, an outdoor table
and chairs, and a big gas barbecue. Inside, the floors
were tiled in cool ceramic or glowing polished cork,
and the decor had a relaxed, summery feel, with lots
of blue and white.

You could hear the ocean in the background, eter-
nally washing and crashing onto the sand.

As well as Keelan's mother and aunt, Lynette's husband Alan was also there for the weekend. A keen fish-
erman, he warned everyone not to expect much in the
way of baby-care from him, but possibly they'd get
something nice and fresh from the ocean for breakfast. He'd be rising before dawn to try his luck on the
rocky tidal shelf just to the south.

Keelan didn't attempt to persuade him to take more
of an interest in his little adoptive great-niece. Tavie's
immune system would still be fragile, so it didn't make
sense to have too many people closely involved in her
care.

Keelan and Jessie hadn't eaten yet, even though it
was now after nine, but the delectable aroma issuing
from the kitchen suggested that dinner had been saved
for them—a chicken and white wine casserole with
mushrooms, sour cream, herbs and vegetables, served
on a bed of fluffy rice.

After the delicious meal, Keelan's mother and aunt
both pushed Jessie in the direction of an enormous bath-
tub in a palatial bathroom. Susan even lit candles and an
aromatherapy oil burner, then produced a huge, fluffy
blue towel and told her, 'Don't you dare fight this, because you're here for a break. I'm not having my granddaughter's primary carer collapse in an exhausted heap.'

She finished in a different tone, over the sound of hot water plunging into the porcelain tub, 'And Tam's going to need your strength and energy over the next few weeks. Keelan, too.' Another pause. 'Keelan, most of all.'

Tavie only woke up once during the night, and they'd already agreed that Keelan would go to her, so Jessie didn't even hear about it until breakfast. She'd slept wonderfully, and felt as cosseted as a pedigreed cat.

Keelan's aunt brought her a late breakfast of coffee, pink grapefruit, croissants and grilled tailor-fish that had still been swimming a couple of hours ago, with fresh bread, butter and lemon, and she ate it out on the deck. She couldn't remember ever being spoiled like this in her life.

'We have the day all planned out,' Lynette Schaeffer said. 'Morning here on the sun deck with the weekend newspapers, while Sue and I take the baby for a stroll. A simple lunch. Tavie has a big nap in the afternoon, after all the fresh air, and you and Keelan head for the beach. Tonight, we'll babysit, while he takes you to a wonderful Italian restaurant in Handley Head, over-looking the water.'

'Has Keelan signed off on this?' Jessie had to ask. 'Where is he?'

'He's in the shower. And he will sign off on it. His mother can be very persuasive! And when I tell her you've agreed…'

'But I haven't. Have I?'

'Your face is speaking for you. Don't fight it, dear.'

On the strength of this cryptic comment, Jessie wondered, with a fluttery stomach, just how much Susan had seen and guessed during her Sydney visit, and how much conspiring she and her sister had done.

I *am* fighting it, though, she thought. I have to…

But then, just a little while later, Tavie stepped in and joined the conspiracy, and at that point Jessie couldn't pretend to herself any longer about anything.

They had the baby girl all ready to go for her morning walk, as per the plan, lying on her sheepskin in the pram, swaddled in blankets, shaded by the canopy, protected with netting and recently fed. She still seemed tiny to her great-aunt Lynette, who was used to her own very robust grandchildren, but the way she kicked and looked so alert, no one could doubt that she was getting stronger every day.

And the two older women, Keelan and Jessie were all grouped around the pram, down on the path that ran in front of the house, when Tavie reached a milestone they'd all been talking about and waiting for, but hadn't yet seen.

She smiled.

'At me!' Jessie said, emotion flooding her in a painful rush. 'Oh, you're smiling at me!'

Tavie didn't just smile with her mouth and her eyes when she saw that familiar human shape bending over her. She seemed to smile with every muscle in her body. Her little hands stretched like pink starfish, her breathing went fast and excited, and her whole face lit up.

'Oh, let's see!' Susan said. 'Keep doing it for Grandma, darling. Grandma wants to see, too.'

Tavie obliged. Her dad got one, and even her great-aunt. But the best and longest smile came when she looked at Jessie.

How can I ever let this go? Jessie wondered, her stomach rolling at the thought of what she'd lose when Keelan didn't need her any more, just a couple of months from now. She'd lose far more than she could put into words, far more than she even dared to think about. The baby, the man, a home that was warmer and better than anything she'd ever imagined.

She wouldn't think about it. She couldn't afford to…

The realisation came anyway, despite the desperate fire wall she'd tried to construct inside her head.

She'd fallen in love with Keelan, and all her barriers lay in ruins.

When? How?

She could try to map it all out, pinpoint each subtle or sudden change in her perceptions, but even if she succeeded, it wouldn't change the basic fact, she knew. Love didn't operate that way.

Suddenly one day it was just there, as much a part of you as, say, your taste for spicy food or your aversion to the smell of mint toothpaste. And it could feel as frightening inside you as a newly diagnosed disease or an unexpected stab of pain.

Beside her, standing close, Keelan laughed. 'Wow! Oh, wow!'

He sounded choky and tight in the throat, as if he couldn't risk more words without breaking down. Jessie wanted to reach out for him, hug him and hold him and lean on him while they watched the baby together, but this wasn't her right, or her role, and that felt more frightening than ever, now that she understood what had happened inside her.

How can I let any of this go? she thought. It's going to tear out my heart.

A minute later, Susan and Lynette set off with the pram, leaving Keelan and Jessie free.

And alone.

Neither of them was used to it. In Sydney, they always had something or someone to hide behind. Keelan's work. Mica Sagovic's cheerful, slightly bossy presence. Tavie. Now they both stepped back from each other instinctively, as if they needed greater distance now that their three chaperones were gone. Keelan's uncle had also gone out—to the local bait shop to discuss tides and other fishing-related topics.

'We're supposed to read the paper now, I think,' Jessie murmured. She still felt shaky inside, dizzy and sick and hugely off-balance, as if she'd been tumbled over and over through the water by a rogue wave.

'On the deck,' Keelan agreed. 'Sipping cool drinks when the sun gets hotter.'

She manufactured a laugh. 'Oh, you got the bulletin, too?'

'I did.' He shrugged, and gave that delicious smile of his, suggesting its usual shared secret.

They turned and began to walk back towards the house, still keeping carefully apart.

'I wonder,' Jessie said, speaking too fast, 'if you could ask your mother and your aunt to stop treating me like family.'

And you and me like a couple.

'Is that what they're doing?' Keelan opened the door for her, and let her precede him up the stairs that opened beyond the entranceway. Passing him, her skin tingled and she couldn't breathe. 'They claim they're only treating you like a friend who needs a break.'

'But you don't buy that either, do you?' Still a little breathless, she flung the question over her shoulder on her way up the stairs.

'Not entirely.'

'So you've talked to them about it already.'

He shrugged, skirted around her and picked the weekend newspapers off the coffee-table. 'I had a word or two.'

'When?'

'Last night.'

'Well, then, it hasn't done any good, because they're still doing it this morning.'

And I like it too much. I'm greedy for everything I want it to mean.

'We can ride it out,' he said calmly, as if it didn't matter much. 'It's only until tomorrow. Here, have the *Herald*.' He handed her the thick fold of newsprint, but their fingers didn't touch. 'I'll take the *Australian*. We can ignore each other all morning, if you want.'

'I don't want—I'm not avoiding you. I just don't want—'

'Them thinking what they're thinking?' His voice dropped. 'About us?'

He'd come right out and said it.

'Yes,' Jessie answered. 'That.'

She hugged the paper to her chest like a shield, and they stared at each other, all pretence dropping away. An electric charge filled the air, softening every bone in her body. Keelan put the second newspaper back on the coffee-table in an untidy heap and stepped towards her. He was close enough to touch her, but he didn't. The possibility that he soon would seemed like both a promise and a threat.

'What exactly is it that's stopping us from acting on this, Jessie?' he said. 'Remind me. Because I'm not sure that I know the reason any more. I did know, but it's been swamped by…other things. Left behind in Sydney, or something. I kept thinking this would go away, that we could push it away by avoiding each other, but it hasn't gone at all.'

'Yet,' she insisted, hugging the newspaper tighter against her body.

'So you still think it will?'

'Oh, yes!'

For him, if not for her.

'You're quite a cynic, aren't you?' His eyes dropped to her mouth, as if to suggest that she told sweet lies from time to time as well.

Was she a cynic? she wondered.

In regard to John, yes, but only because of how badly he'd hurt her, how unscathed he'd been at the end of it in contrast, and how much she regretted her own decisions. In too many other areas of her life she wasn't nearly cynical enough. She only pretended.

Her heart was a puppy asleep in front of a tractor wheel, completely vulnerable unless it woke up in time.

One whole, huge, naïve part of her desperately didn't want this feeling for Keelan to *ever* go away. It felt too good and too important—nourishing her, making her dizzy, giving her hope and home, and terrifying her, all at the same time.

The rest of her winced and shuddered, waiting to

get crushed, and she didn't want him to know anything about how she really felt.

The depth of it. The strength of it.

'I suppose I am…somewhat cynical in some areas,' she answered him coolly, because this answer seemed safest.

'So tell me why we shouldn't just go with it, give in to it, enjoy it,' Keelan said.

His brown eyes raked over her again, touching on her lips, which she scraped nervously with her teeth, and her wrists, bent across the newspaper.

'Cynicism is an asset in a situation like this, isn't it?' he went on, and his voice had the texture of raw silk. 'Plenty of people launch into relationships they know have zero likelihood of lasting, and surely that's part of the appeal.'

'Zero likelihood…' She gave a cautious little laugh. 'Yes. My track record isn't good, is it? Personally or professionally. If it was, I wouldn't be here in the first place. I'd still be…somewhere else.'

Adelaide. She'd had a relationship there that hadn't lasted. London. Or somewhere in the developing world with the doctor who'd been her lover in Sierra Leone and who was still, judging from the occasional post-card, totally wedded to his work. She couldn't even re-member, now, how she'd felt about him.

Nothing like this.

Nothing anywhere near as dangerous and turbulent as this.

'Plenty of people see that as a plus,' Keelan was say-ing. 'The fact that it has to be short term. And it seems as if you're one of them, so present your case.'

'I have no case to present. I'm not sure what you're saying, Keelan, or what you want.'

'Oh, you know what I want.' He moved closer, his open hands hovering lightly near her elbows, which were angled outwards because of the wad of newsprint she still clutched against her chest.

'Sex,' she suggested bluntly, because the word was practically written across his face in big block capitals.

'For starters,' he agreed, just as bluntly. 'To be honest, you've got me so close to the brink I'm not going to be able to think straight until we get that out of the way. If we do.'

Their eyes met once again, and she knew that he could have left off those last three words. They weren't necessary. They didn't apply. There was no 'if' any more. Sometime between driving up from Sydney last night and standing here with Keelan right now, 'if' had evaporated completely. Now there was only 'when'.

'Let's talk about it,' he suggested, his voice dropping to a growl. 'You've sampled different professional environments on several continents. Big, richly endowed hospitals, tiny, primitive clinics, attractive private homes. I'm not going to assume that you've sampled relationships in the same way, but…have you?'

'A couple of times.' What did she want him to think? What would protect her best? 'Yes, several times.'

'With no intention of looking for something that might last? You have no desire for that?'

'Sometimes things do last,' she said. 'But I'm a realist. Haven't we talked about this? I'm sure you'd only get serious about a woman who has a lot more to offer than I do.'

'Hell, do you doubt yourself that much?'

'I don't doubt myself.' She lifted her chin instinctively. 'But I do have a healthy awareness of our differences. You're not going to risk messing up your life with a relationship that doesn't fit the mould. You're not going to risk squandering your assets.'

'My assets?'

'Your family, your background, your reputation, your rock-solid position in every area of your life.' She spoke as dispassionately as she could, wondering if he would argue. 'The assets you want for the twins, too. You'll want a capital gain when you marry, an advantageous alliance, someone you're sure of on paper, as well as someone you love.'

'I've been married before, you know.'

'Yes, you've mentioned it. Tanya.' She said the name with a deliberate sourness, even though she felt no genuine hostility towards Keelan's ex-wife. 'And wasn't she a doctor? From a very well-established New Zealand family?'

'Yes, she was. And it didn't last. I've been thinking about that lately.'

'And you've concluded that this time around you're looking for a serious commitment with a lower middleclass, footloose nurse, with a fractured, uncaring family and a dubious sexual history on three continents? I don't think so!'

He pivoted on his heel and made a sound deep in his throat that she couldn't interpret. 'Don't put yourself down! Don't you think you're insulting both of us with that statement?'

No, I'm just putting some essential protection in

place before I give in, trying to find out where you stand. Being realistic.

'If we're going to do this, let's shatter the illusions before, not after, Keelan,' she said coolly, burning up inside.

'Right. Go ahead. Shatter away. Because we're definitely doing this.' He stepped close again, and laced his arms loosely around her. She felt the power of her body's response, like water dragging on a rudderless boat in a strong current. 'And soon.'

'It's an affair,' she said, giving him what he wanted. 'It's not going to last.' Time for greater honesty now. 'It's going to hurt at the end...'

'Yeah?'

'I already know that. And it's...nothing to do with you in a way. Part of it. It's because of the way Tavie smiled at me just now. I—I couldn't care *for* her without caring *about* her, and she's not mine, so—'

'No reason you can't stay in her life, is there, even if you don't meaningfully stay in mine? Get a hospital job in Sydney, and visit her whenever you want. Tam, too. Be their Auntie Jessie.'

Jessie closed her eyes and shook her head. 'I'm not staying in Sydney.' She looked into his face again. 'I'll take another assignment with Médecins Sans Frontières probably.'

Again, she said it in as cool and practical a tone as she could, making it sound like a positive plan instead of a blind escape and a desperate bid to get her priorities back. She couldn't stay in Sydney purely in order to fill a peripheral role in another family's life, once

Keelan's inappropriate, inconvenient attraction to her had flared and burned out.

Now, feeling as she did, she knew there had to be more. If she gave herself to this, was she opening a tiny chink of hope that one day there might be, or was she sabotaging that hope forever?

'What about hurting me?' Keelan asked lightly. 'Any predictions on that?'

'Men can get hurt, too. Of course. I think there'll be some regret. Of course,' she repeated ineptly. Her voice didn't come out nearly as cool as she wanted it to. 'Endings are often messy, and while some men don't mind mess in their living space, most run a mile from it in their emotional lives. They want everything clean and uncluttered. My prediction? You'll be thoroughly glad if I get on a plane and fly far, far away. Like Tanya did.'

'You don't think you'll break my heart?'

'No. I don't. You're too sensible for that. Too much else on your plate. And too much in control.'

He had to be in control, because she certainly wasn't.

They stared at each other again.

'OK,' he said, after a moment. 'You've shattered the illusions. Now I'll set out the ground rules.'

'I guess there would have to be a few of those.'

'This ends when you leave—and when you leave is a decision either of us can make. But while it's happening, it's not half-hearted. It's exclusive. Nothing on the side. It's intense. Sexually, and in every other way. It's not something we hide, and it's not something we flaunt. It just is.'

'Those aren't quite the rules I expected.'

'No?'

She shrugged, aware that she'd flushed a little. She felt the slide of his hands across her skin.

'I thought there might be more about boundaries,' she said. 'No waking up in the same bed or something. And discretion. Not letting anyone get the wrong idea. Never getting seen at certain restaurants.'

'Nope, there's none of that. Are you ever going to put down that newspaper? I think it's safe now.'

Jessie laughed, and blurted out the most honest statement she'd made in minutes. 'There's nothing safe about this.'

'No,' he said slowly. He pried her arms loose and took the newspaper. Looking down, she saw that the ink had left black smears on her pale blue top, darkest where the print had pressed against her breasts. 'That's one thing we might both agree on without further negotiation. Seems like part of the attraction. That we're heading into the danger of the unknown.'

Right now.

Right at the moment when his mouth touched hers.

The newspaper rustled as it dropped onto the table, and Jessie didn't give it another thought. The first time Keelan had kissed her, it had been blind, rather desperate, full of an uncertainty that had come from both of them. This time it was intensely sensual—no, *sexual*, why beat around the bush?—and both of them knew that they weren't willingly turning back.

Keelan held Jessie's shoulders and printed her lips with the heat of his mouth, like some potent, fiery liquor. Her whole being seemed to arrow into this one seamless, endless point of contact. Every sense channelled into it, like a high tide funnelling into a deep, narrow strait. And every emotion channelled into it, too—the love she'd discovered, the passionate need to stay in his life, to mother his babies and to belong. All of this, in one kiss.

Gradually, however, their bodies shifted closer, fitting together like a hand sliding into a glove. Her breasts against his chest, her hips against his groin, two pairs of thighs like jointed woodwork.

His arms wrapped around her, cradling most of her weight. She felt as boneless as a piece of fabric, her body held together only by the beating of the blood through her veins.

'Keelan…' His name made a sigh in her mouth.

She sounded as if she was begging for the next step, and this was the meaning he took from that one breathless word. 'Yes,' he said. 'We'll go to my room.'

She didn't argue, didn't even want to.

They moved as far as the corridor, pulling on each other's arms, but then he groaned and stopped, pressed her shoulder blades up against the wall and pulled her hips roughly towards him with both hands. She arched her back, gasped and swallowed and kissed him fiercely again, wanting him to feel the way her nipples jutted, and to understand the pleasure she felt when she kneaded the muscles of his back with her fingers.

Impatient and clumsy, she dragged his sage-green polo shirt up to his armpits, until he completed the action for her, reaching around to pull it forward over his head. He tossed it through the open doorway of his room, and then she ran the palms of her hands down his chest, exulting in the hard, hair-roughened planes she'd known she would find.

In this moment, those planes of skin and muscle belonged only to her, and she explored them in naked appreciation of her new right of possession.

'Take your top off, too,' he told her.

His words were rough and careless, and he didn't try to disguise the way he kept his eyes on her body, waiting for what he'd see next. His open need aroused her even further, made her pulse and crumble inside.

Every inch of skin on fire, she complied with what he'd asked, crossing her arms, taking the fabric in her grip and pulling it upward. She heard rather than saw the moment when he caught sight of her breasts, cupped in a dark blue lace bra. His breath hissed across his teeth and shuddered into his lungs.

Above her head, the top tangled around her wrists, handcuffing her arms back against the wall and jutting her upper body forward.

Keelan took full advantage of her temporary imprisonment. He splayed his hands over her stretched ribs and buried his face in the valley between her breasts. Her torso twisted with pleasure and he slid his hands higher, cupping the lace and thumbing the edge of the fabric down to release her nipple into his waiting mouth.

She writhed and flapped ineffectually at the twisted top, didn't much care if she had to stay like this a bit longer. Be honest, she could have freed herself if she'd wanted to. She wondered if she'd ever want to, but couldn't imagine it right now.

Keelan slid his hands inside the back waistband of her jeans and traced the taut contours of her cheeks beyond the high-cut edge of her underwear, and the sensitive crease where thighs and bottom joined. He kissed her mouth and her neck, then came back to her breasts and ravaged them, making them swell and ache.

'I'm stuck in this top,' she breathed. 'Let me get free, because I want to—'

Women's voices sounded outside, and Keelan suddenly stilled at the same moment that Jessie's unfinished sentence cut out. They both listened, and recognised his mother and his aunt, locked in chatty, sisterly talk, as well as something about Tavie's nappy-change bag.

They hadn't brought it with them, but should have done. They didn't want to disrupt Keelan's and Jessie's tranquil morning, but it couldn't be helped.

The doorknob downstairs rattled a little as it opened.

Keelan didn't say a word at first. Eyes fixed on Jessie's face, he nudged his thigh between her legs to press into the swollen heat that pulsed against the centre seam of her jeans. Then he gave her one last, searing kiss, eased back and lifted his arm to lower her hands and twisted sleeves down in front of her.

'Later,' he finally muttered. 'I guess this has to happen later.'

'Yes,' she agreed, not knowing how either of them would stand the wait.

Chapter 8

The cold salt water felt fabulous on Jessie's over-heated body. She wore a navy and white tank-style swimsuit that seemed to cling far too closely and reveal far too much today, although by any Australian standard it wasn't a provocative garment.

There were only a few other swimmers on the beach, since the water in November still contained the chill of winter. Beside her Keelan body-surfed, launching himself forward in the curve of each wave just before it broke and powering towards the shore amidst the tumbling white foam.

Lunch had seemed like one long ache of awareness between the two of them. A couple of times Jessie could have sworn she'd seen a significant, satisfied look pass between Susan and her sister. But then she had come to her senses and realised that they'd just been smiling at Tavie, fast asleep in her canopied pram between the two older women, knocked out by the fresh sea air just as Keelan's aunt had predicted she would be.

There had been no earth-shattering understanding passing between the two sisters in regard to what had happened between Keelan and herself. Jessie was the only person in Tavie's life whose world had completely shifted on its axis today.

'Off to the beach, you two,' Lynette ordered, a little later. 'It's getting quite hot. We'll feed her if she wakes up.'

'The bottle is—'

'I know all about bottles, Jessie, don't worry.'

So here they were, herself and Keelan, pretending that all they could think about was the water, the sun and the salt, when really…

Oh, dear heaven, Keelan's body was gorgeous!

Jessie had taken this in from day one as a simple fact. His whole frame was so strong and so confident and so beautifully built. Any woman with breath in her body would have to see it. Now her awareness of him was very different, however. So much more personal, so much more detailed, and filled with a hunger and a need that she didn't know how she'd ever assuage, no matter how heated and intense their affair became.

They had claimed ownership of each other this morning, and that had seemed so right and inevitable and necessary, but now she felt a little frightened again, wondering if it might be possible to put on the brakes, wondering if she should want to.

There was a term for it in the area of commerce, she

thought—the cooling-off period. Some kind of contractual window during which the buyer could change his or her mind and not make the purchase after all.

Tavie's urgent need for a nappy change this morning had given Jessie and Keelan a cooling-off period. They needn't go through with this after all. They could cool their heated libidos and renege on the entire agreement.

But, no, she didn't want to renege, or to cool anything.

She wanted Keelan more than ever, her senses pushed to the brink by what had happened between them this morning, and by what had happened so powerfully in her heart. The sea might be cooling her skin, but it couldn't cool her feelings. Every time he looked at her, she got that helpless, boneless, light-headed feeling again, and it both exulted and terrified her.

So this was what love felt like.

'Had enough?' he asked finally, as they stood in the shallows with the foam still churning around their legs. Water glistened and streamed on his chest and arms, and down his thighs below the baggy black board-shorts he wore. 'Your lips are going blue, and my ears are aching.'

'It's great,' she answered breathlessly. 'But, yes, I've had enough.'

'Next on the agenda, we're supposed to go for a walk.'

'Right.'

'But we can stage a revolution, if you want, and refuse to submit to this dictatorial conspiracy.'

'I'm OK with a walk,' she drawled, through closed lips.

'Beach to the north is pretty deserted, especially once you get to the headland.'

'So are you saying you want to head south?'

'No. I'm not.' His eyes were fixed on her face, and filled with a light that Jessie couldn't misinterpret or ignore. 'I'm voting for north.'

She couldn't find words or breath to answer.

They left the water, found their towels and buffed the salt water from their bodies. Keelan put on his polo shirt and Jessie slipped into her strappy lemon yellow sundress, still without speaking. At first they walked just where the highest-reaching waves sank their frilly edges into the sand, but Jessie had had enough of the cold water and soon moved to where the sand was dry.

'Still chilly?' Keelan asked her, and her nod gave him the cue they'd both been looking for.

He put his arm around her and pulled her close against her side. She laid her head on his shoulder, and felt his mouth press her temple and her hair, both places sticky with drying salt.

'You're very quiet,' he said after a moment.

She laughed, knowing he wouldn't understand her odd, upside-down source of amusement. 'Nothing to say.'

Everything to say.

That would have been more truthful, and that was why she had laughed.

She simply didn't dare to open her mouth, for fear of what might spill out—foolish words of love that she knew he would never say in return, feverish demands for a reassurance that he would never give.

Perhaps he'd been right earlier.

She did doubt herself.

Or she doubted her place in the universe. Why should *she* be blessed with something miraculous and right and lasting, when so many people got it wrong, and when she'd got it so disastrously wrong herself, with John Bishop, in similar circumstances? Whatever the magic ingredient was that allowed someone to find that kind of love, she wasn't at all convinced that she had it, or knew it.

'Silence is nice,' Keelan said.

'Mmm.'

Because I can put all my energy into remembering to breathe, she added inwardly.

'I won't ask what you're thinking, but I'll tell you what I'm thinking,' he offered.

'Yes?'

'Wondering just how secluded it is…in the lee of that headland. If there's no one there, and if there's a sheltered patch of grass…'

'It's not that secluded!'

He laughed this time. 'Putting me and my male needs firmly in place?'

She took a steadying breath and confessed, 'And mine. My needs are just as—But I'm being…practical.'

Cool-headed.

As far as that was possible.

'I guess sand is not an ingredient we really want this time around,' he conceded. He brushed some grains of the stuff from her forearm as he spoke.

'Other times, though?' She smiled, turned to him and did the same, where some adhered to his jaw. 'Have to admit, it hasn't ever entered my fantasies.'

'Next time we'll bring our towels. And you can tell me a bit more about those fantasies of yours. Show me a couple.'

Her fantasies? There was really only one, at this moment—the fantasy that, strong as it was, this shared desire for each other was just one part of a complete package.

Jessie closed her mouth firmly again and pressed her lips tightly against her teeth, to make sure she didn't say it.

They kissed, of course, in the secluded lee of the headland Keelan had talked about. Waiting for it, she could have thrown herself against his chest and begged, but managed to retain enough control to spare them both such an embarrassing degree of emotion.

Instead, he was the one who took the initiative.

'The breeze has dropped here,' he said. 'We're protected by the cliff. You feel much warmer now.' He ran his hand lightly down her arm. 'Delicious. Radiating heat.'

'So do you,' she managed to answer, as he turned her in his arms.

His skin had been buffed by the wind and the waves, and felt as smooth as polished stone baked in the sun. She slid her hands up inside his shirt at once, splaying her fingers across his back.

'Your mouth has turned pink again.' He touched it lightly with his lips, just a soft brushstroke of sensation. 'And you taste… warm, salty.'

'So do you,' she repeated.

She closed her eyes as he tasted her again, his mouth still soft and light on hers. She had to fight to hold herself back to his lazy, leisurely pace, and it made her ache in impossible places. He wasn't planning to rush this, to go too deep, too soon, yet she was already trembling.

A sound of need escaped from her throat like a bubble rising in water, and she would have whimpered if she hadn't dammed the feeling back. Was this really as easy for him as it seemed?

No, perhaps it wasn't.

His control suddenly seemed to break, and their kiss deepened the way a flowing stream could suddenly deepen into a dark, spinning pool. His arms tightened around her, the bruising press of his mouth parted her lips and drew her tongue into a sinuous dance. She lifted her hand to the back of his head and ran her fingers up through his hair, loving the shape and the texture and the scents of sea water and shampoo that she released into the air.

'You're fabulous…beautiful,' he said raggedly. 'I want you right now, and the only way, let me tell you, that I'm going to stand the wait is by promising both of us that it will be even better that way. If we've held back just a little. If we've had to dam this inside us. It will be…better…even better than what we have now.'

'Yes. Oh, yes.'

Sliding her dress up her thighs, he cupped her bottom through the still-damp fabric of her swimsuit, and Jessie felt the weight and heat of his arousal hard and insistent against her.

Yes. She had this, at least. This proof of need and connection.

With a shock, she realised she'd never wanted a man quite this nakedly, this physically. Giving herself to

John, she'd surrounded herself with a misty glow of romance and sacrifice. Only in hindsight had she acknowledged that their love-making had often been a disappointment to her on a sensual level. A few years earlier, when she had assuaged the fatigue and stress of work in an African clinic with Gary, they had both been looking for time out and release more than a truly passionate connection.

This felt different.

This felt like something she should run a hundred miles to avoid because it might so easily shatter her into pieces, only she didn't have the will or the strength to run anywhere. Instead, she shored her weakened limbs more firmly against Keelan and gave him everything she had with her kiss.

By the time they stopped, both were breathless and dishevelled. Jessie's dress and swimsuit straps had slipped down her arms until the tops of her breasts threatened to spill into Keelan's demanding hands, or his even more demanding mouth. Her hair, already tangled by the sea, whipped across her face in salty strands so that he had to push it aside with impatient fingers to keep his delectable contact with her lips.

When his hold on her finally eased, she felt the shuddering breath he drew and heard the edge in his laugh.

'I'm starting to repeat blatant lies to myself about sand,' he said, mocking himself. 'And beachcombers. Wouldn't be so bad, would it? If our skin got chafed? If someone wandered past? With a camera? And no one's going to, are they?'

'Keelan—'

'Don't worry. Not serious here. Very serious, but not about here. Later. We're going to dinner, and—'

'Yes, dinner's in the plan. But there's nothing mentioned about after dinner.' Jessie didn't know if she was teasing him or what. Looking into his brown eyes, she saw the suffering, and the amusement, and wondered what her own expression said back to him. More of the same, she guessed.

'Dinner's an ambiguous word,' he answered, 'and it fills an open-ended slot. I could feast on you. Cover you in whipped cream and lick it off. Or put a chocolate-coated strawberry between our lips and—'

'Mmm!' She closed her eyes, almost tasting the sweet red juice of the fruit, mingled with the taste of him.

'That would be dinner,' he claimed. 'Dessert. Definitely in the plan.'

Weakly, she leaned her forehead into his shoulder and told him, 'I'm not going to argue this with you on the basis of what the word "dinner" means.'

'But you're going to argue?'

'Maybe. I don't think so. I don't know.'

'Have to warn you, I'm going to take that as a challenge. By the end of the evening, you'll know.'

'Hello?' Keelan murmured, as they came along the path between the dunes half an hour later and arrived within sight of the house. 'There's another car out the—' He stopped and swore. 'That's Dad!'

Jessie sensed his immediate wariness, although they weren't touching. She could almost hear the questions jangling inside his head as well. After a moment of strained silence, he began to speak them out loud, answering most of them himself in the same breath.

'What's he doing here? Did Mum know he was coming, I wonder? Can't imagine she did. What's the time? Must be well after four. I should have worn my watch. He's not planning to stay, surely?'

Jessie listened to the litany until this last question, then cut in with one of her own. 'He knew we were coming up?'

'Yes, I mentioned it to him Thursday evening when he phoned.'

Since Dawson Hunter's first two visits to Tavie, he'd begun to drop in a couple of times a week to spend time with his granddaughter, and he expected regular reports from his son by phone as well.

Keelan didn't say anything more, and they reached the house a minute later. Upstairs on the sun deck, they realised that Dawson must have only just arrived.

The atmosphere seemed strained, though he looked relieved to see his son, as if counting on him as an ally. Alan offered his ex-brother-in-law a beer, but apparently no one heard. Dawson himself said in a tone of mingled defensiveness and belligerence, 'I knew this would be a big weekend for her, and I wanted to see for myself how she was doing. I dropped in. Is that wrong, Susan?'

'Dropped in? It's a four-hour drive.'

'Hmm. I can do it in three and a half, if the traffic co-operates,' he muttered. 'Send me straight back, if you feel so strongly about it.'

'I—I don't.' Susan spread her hands. 'Not really. I just wish you'd—'

'Warned you?'

'Yes, if I'm honest!'

'So you could, what?'

'Make up a bed for you in the laundry alcove downstairs, because that's about all the room we've got left.'

'And that's where you'd put a visiting dog.'

'Dawson…'

'Dad,' Keelan said, stepping into the fray. 'Specialist in knocking us all for a loop.' He clapped his father on the back. 'Tavie's doing really well, if you were worried.'

'Of course I was. She's so small for a long car journey.'

'She got a bit frazzled by the end, but she settled down as soon as we got her into a quiet environment and gave her a feed. She's been great today, hasn't she, Mum?'

'She had a bottle at three, but now she's back asleep, like a little lamb,' his mother confirmed.

'Beer, Dawson?' Alan repeated, and this time he got a grateful nod.

Lynette and Susan exchanged significant looks, and this time Jessie knew her imagination wasn't playing tricks when she read their meaning.

Lynette's look said, Why don't you just kick him out right now?

Susan's answered, Because I have a horrible feeling I don't want to, even though I probably should.

Next, after a strained pause, Lynette announced aloud, 'Alan and I were thinking of going to the club for dinner tonight, by the way, Susan, as long as you're feeling comfortable with Tavie.'

'Club?' Alan queried, not quick enough on the up-take to please his wife. 'What club?'

'Any club, Alan, for heaven's sake! The RSL, the Surf Lifesavers, the golf club. Wherever we like.'

'I thought we were—Oh. Yes. Give other people a quiet night, if they want one.' He telegraphed a hunted look towards Susan and Dawson that told everyone he'd got the point now. Leave the two of them alone to sort something out, whether they wanted to or not. 'Of course. That was the plan, wasn't it? You're going out, too, aren't you, Keelan? Jessie?'

'Yes, but they're not going to the club,' Lynette answered for them, in a tone decisive enough to sharpen a blunt axe. 'They're going to that lovely Italian place, just the two of them. Early. So they can start with a re-laxed drink at the bar. And that's what we're doing, too. And since it's almost five, those of us who are shower-ing had better start.'

'That's me,' Keelan said.

'And me,' Jessie added. There were two bathrooms.

'We don't need to, do we, Alan?' Lynette decided. 'I'll change—it'll take thirty seconds—and then we can head off. Phone me on my mobile, Sue, if you need me home again.'

'I…uh…' Keelan's mother trailed off, looking help-lessly at her ex-husband, her pushy sister, her unhelpful son. 'I imagine Dawson and I will be able to manage between us.'

'Her two grandparents,' Dawson said, then turned to his ex-wife. 'Susie? Will you give it a try?'

It was so painfully apparent that he was asking about far more than just a single evening of shared babysitting that every molecule of air in the room suddenly seemed as fragile as spun glass. Jessie held her breath, unbearably moved by the naked, vulnerable appeal in such a large, arrogant and successful man, and by the emotion and uncertainty that Susan showed.

She couldn't answer her ex-husband at first. Her hands worked and twisted in front of her, and her mouth fell open, though no sound came out.

'I need…a lot of time,' she finally said in a strangled voice. 'I need…a lot more than this.'

'But it's a start, Susie,' came Dawson's hoarse voice. Jessie had already begun her retreat into the house, with Keelan, Lynette and Alan close behind her. 'Just tell me it might be a start.'

If Susan answered, it wasn't audible from this distance.

'How would you feel about it, Keelan, if they did get back together?' Jessie asked, two hours later.

He thought about her question for a moment, his fingers laced in hers across the restaurant table. He'd brought the subject of his parents up on his own, without prompting, just as they'd finished their main course, and Jessie had to fight not to read too much into such a personal topic. He needed someone to listen, that was all, and she was the person he happened to be with.

They shouldn't be touching like this, caressing each other's hands, yet she couldn't bring herself to ease hers away. All they'd done since they'd arrived at this beautiful waterfront restaurant had been talk and touch. As for eating and drinking, she'd hardly noticed any of that! But all of it felt impossibly intense, as if the talking was laying a foundation for the body magic that they could hardly wait for, and much more.

'Protective, I think,' he answered her finally. His finger stilled in hers. 'Towards both of them. Mum, in particular. If Dad hurt her again…'

'Is that what's holding her back, do you think? The risk of getting hurt?' Jessie couldn't help leaning towards him, couldn't take her eyes from his face.

'I don't know. I imagine it's more complicated than that. Their history together is so complicated after all.' He looked down, putting his eyes into shadow and making the thick crescents of his lashes look darker. 'She's a very sensible woman, my mother, but she has the capacity for strong feelings as well, and that's a difficult combination sometimes. She'll look very carefully before she leaps, because she has such a keen eye for the consequences, and such good memory for all the good and bad there was in their marriage. It's a hard ask, on his part.'

'Do you think he's aware of that?' Jessie sipped some wine absently.

Keelan looked up, and she watched his mouth—the way it pouted for a moment into a kiss shape on certain words, the way his tongue rested for a moment against his lower lip. 'Not fully. Not yet. But Mum will make damned sure that he is before she makes him any promises.'

'You sound as if you're still on her side.' She squeezed his hand, and ran the ball of her thumb lightly across his knuckles.

Again, he thought for a good while before he answered. 'I've tried not to make that too apparent to Dad, since his divorce from Louise, because that was such an admission on his part that he'd made a huge mistake. Actually, I'm just trying to be fair, and to look at the whole thing with my eyes open.'

The way he'd said his mother would. Jessie suspected they were alike in many ways, although superficially he resembled his father more. Talking with Keelan about his family on this level held a dangerous satisfaction for her. It created the illusion that she belonged.

She recognised the feeling. She'd had it before.

Last time she hadn't even tried to fight it. This time she kept up the struggle, even though she knew she'd already lost. And suddenly she found herself spilling everything to him about John, in the context of questions she and Keelan both had about marital infidelity and forgiveness, comparing what had happened between Keelan's parents with what *hadn't* happened between Audrey and John.

'And, of course, I played Louise's part.' Her hand rested on the table now, a willing prisoner beneath his.

'Not really,' he said. 'I don't think that's true, from what you've just told me.'

'The other woman? The woman who was prepared to betray someone I respected and cared about for the sake of what I thought was love?'

'Louise never respected or cared about Mum. She was terrified of her. But that's irrelevant. What I'm interested in is the fact that you still blame yourself to such an extent.'

'Shouldn't I? I was terribly in the wrong.'

'At first, I guess, but—' He switched tack suddenly. 'Did you see it coming?'

'See…?'

'What you felt. And his response.'

'No, I didn't.' She stared down at her empty plate, hardly noticing when the waiter took it away, while she was speaking. 'It blind-sided me completely. I was still calling it empathy and admiration, when suddenly he and I were alone in the kitchen one day and he took me in his arms and I discovered just how much I'd been kidding myself.'

'You might have managed to put up some barriers if you'd had more warning,' Keelan suggested.

'Maybe.'

'And you were the one who ended it.'

'For the wrong reasons.'

'No. The right ones.' He stroked a strand of unco-operative hair back from her face. 'Without Audrey herself ever knowing, and that was right, because in her situation knowing wouldn't have helped. I might concede that your wake-up call came from the wrong direction—that other woman—but when it did come, you got everything into perspective very quickly, from the sound of it.'

'Why are you working so hard to let me off the hook, Keelan?' She frowned and shook her head, unsettled by the intent way he still watched her. 'Telling you all this was supposed to be about giving you some insights into what's happening with your parents.'

'Yes?' He tilted his face, sceptical and almost teasing.

She flushed. 'Yes, I—I think so.'

'Nope.' He sounded very decisive now. 'We're not doing that at all. We're doing something else. Clearing our emotional in-trays, I think. So that there's plenty of room.'

'Room?'

'For so much else, Jessie. For holding each other, skin to skin, without any baggage getting in the way. It's my turn now—to tell you about my divorce.'

'Keelan, I don't want to weasel out anything from you that—'

'Shh… Let's just talk.' He took her hand again, and leaned across the table. 'Let's do this. Let me tell you about Tanya, and what broke us apart. I've only glossed over it to you before.'

Deep down, she wanted to hear everything and anything he wanted to tell her, so she didn't argue. He wasn't long-winded about it. A couple of years into their marriage, an old crush of Tanya's had come back into her life. Not someone she'd ever been involved with, but someone she'd wanted.

'And they had an affair?' Jessie said, when Keelan paused.

'No, they didn't. But she must have been getting signals from him. It would have been against her principles to leap into bed with him while she was still married to me, but it wasn't against her principles to sabotage our marriage in every other way she could think of. I was…totally bewildered for a long time, didn't understand that she was deliberately driving me away to leave her own slate clean.'

'Driving you away?'

What woman in her right mind could possibly do that?

Me, came an insidious little voice inside her.

Isn't that what I'm trying to do, a part of me, because I'm so sceptical and scared?

'Suddenly, everything I did was wrong,' Keelan said. 'Ranging from petty things like not buying her flowers often enough to major issues like "you don't communicate, you close yourself off," which I couldn't see the...' He stopped, then continued, 'Maybe it's a guy thing. These vague accusations, the suggestion that I was clueless because I couldn't even get a bead on the accusations, let alone address them.'

He shook his head and went on. 'I really thought, for months, that they were genuine grievances I should work on, or we should work on together. But when I tried, she upped the ante. 'Now you're just bringing me flowers because I complained. Don't you get it?' Well, no. I didn't. But it worked in the end. When we split, I thought it was a mutual decision. Amicable separation. Irreconcilable differences. You know the drill. I really thought we'd both tried. Until she flew back to New Zealand to move in with Rick just a few weeks later. He owns a big construction company there. Doing very well. They have two little girls, and I wish them well. At the time, I felt...' He shrugged.

'Conned,' Jessie suggested, because she knew about feeling conned.

Something they had in common that she would never have suspected without all the talking they'd done tonight.

'Most definitely conned,' he answered. 'Wondering why I hadn't seen what was happening while I was in the middle of it.'

'Because people don't. So often, people don't. It takes hindsight. Don't blame yourself for that, Keelan.'

'And I'm going to tell you the same thing. Don't keep racking yourself over Audrey and John. Don't see all that as a pattern you're bound to repeat.'

He said their names as if they were people he knew, and Jessie understood what a lot of ground they'd covered tonight. It felt good, but deeply dangerous as usual.

'Our waiter is hovering,' he said a moment or two later. 'Do you want dessert?'

'Real dessert?' she blurted out at once, remembering what he'd said on the beach about chocolate-dipped strawberries and whipped cream. 'Or…?'

He sat back and laughed, then leaned close again and said in a low voice, 'Believe it or not, yes, I was actually talking about real dessert. But if you're too impatient for the other kind…'

She blushed at once. 'No! I mean…' She trailed off, then took her courage in her hands, fixed her eyes on him steadily and said, 'I'm up for both.'

The house was very quiet when they got back at almost eleven. The sky had clouded over, the air had cooled and freshened, and there was no moon. Jessie thought she could smell rain in the air. She hoped everyone would sleep well tonight…

Inside, the bedrooms were dark, with doors ajar. Tavie 'pigletted' in her sleep, the sound coming through louder on the monitor in Susan's room than it did from the baby herself. In the big, open-plan living room, they discovered Dawson asleep on the couch, which had been made up with sheets, a quilt and pillows.

Their arrival had woken him, unfortunately. He stirred, sat up and said croakily, 'Back safe? That's good. She had a fussy period, but Susie got her settled.'

'Sorry to wake you, Dad.' Understatement on Keelan's part. His tone sounded a little strained.

'I should have gone for the alcove outside the laundry, but I thought your mother might need help with the baby if she woke up again before you got back, and I might not hear down there. Changed her nappy tonight,' he added, trying but failing to sound offhand about the feat. 'She kicks beautifully, doesn't she?'

'Dawson, you're not giving them a blow-by-blow description, I hope!' Lynette said, appearing in a robe from the bedroom she and Alan were using. 'Keelan and Jessie are supposed to be...' She stopped. 'Well, getting a break.'

'Hardly preventing that with a bit of a report, am I?'

But he was, of course.

Jessie felt as self-conscious as if they'd both been caught naked. Her whole body, which had been swimming with anticipation and nerves and aching, terrifying need, now felt bathed in floodlights. She hugged her arms around herself as if touching Keelan was the furthest thing from her mind.

'You're fine, Dad,' Keelan assured him, his throat rasping. 'No problem. Goodnight, now.'

Along the corridor, a minute later, he muttered darkly to Jessie, 'Are you getting a sense of *déjà vu* here?'

He brushed his knuckles from her ear to her neck to her collar-bone, painting her with a hot trail of awareness and desire. Leaving the restaurant half an hour ago, they'd paused for a long time beside the car to kiss.

Here in the driveway, they'd reached for each other at once, every touch containing impatience and promise.

'I will get a very strong sense of *déjà vu* if you tell me "Later", like you did this morning,' she admitted. 'And you're going to, aren't you?'

'Is there a choice? The layout of this house does not facilitate privacy.' He pinned her against her bedroom door and traced the contours of her lips with the tip of one finger, his imposing body almost menacing her with the strength of his desire, and hers. 'Pity they didn't put one of us in the end room. I wasn't planning for this to have to be quiet and stealthy. Not at all. I want it to be anything but.' He brushed his mouth against her ear and whispered, 'Have to tell you, Jessie, I've been wondering all day if I could get you to make a lot of noise…'

'Keelan…' she breathed, throbbing deep inside.

'Thought Dad would be downstairs, and the others asleep with their doors closed.'

'There's tomorrow,' she said. 'When we get home.'

It seemed too far away, both physically and emotionally.

'There'd better be tomorrow,' he answered.

'Or there's the beach.'

Her words were punctuated by the sound of rain beginning to spatter onto the roof, and all they could do was sigh and shrug and laugh.

Chapter 9

Keelan and Jessie pulled into the hospital parking area at five the following afternoon, after an easier journey than Friday's northbound one had been and a relatively relaxing morning. They'd talked a lot, looked at each other a lot and said an impossible amount to each other with their eyes.

'She didn't wake up,' Keelan said.

'She's starting to.'

'Her first visit to her brother. Maybe she's getting excited about it.'

'The nurses will love seeing her. I want to see them deeply impressed at how much she's grown and how strong she looks.'

Impressing the nurses wouldn't be hard when they had Tam for comparison.

Back in the familiar environment of the hospital, the reality of Tam's impending surgery came crashing down on both of them again, and the fact that they didn't talk about it was more significant than if they had. Jessie knew that Keelan's thoughts would be running along the same tired, difficult track as hers.

They'd had their weekend away, and Susan and her sister, and even Keelan's father, had been unflagging in their efforts to make it easy and pleasant for the two of them and for Tavie, but this was the world they really inhabited. Jessie felt the first tinge of inner questioning about the depth and meaning of what had flared so powerfully between herself and Keelan.

Would it hold up *at all* here in the city?

Or would it all vanish, no more than a brief illusion?

Keelan had phoned the NICU late yesterday afternoon and again this morning, to receive cautiously positive reports about his little boy. Tam was hanging in there. His surgeons were confident that the planned procedure would take place. They didn't talk about the percentage chance of success, and Keelan told Jessie that he hadn't asked.

Percentages weren't relevant when there was no choice.

Nurse Barb McDaniel, who'd been one of Tavie's main carers during her stay, was rostered to look after Tam on this shift, and she was delighted to see Tam's sister again, after the two adults had been through the necessary hand-washing routine in the big sinks just beyond the unit's swing doors.

'Oh, she's amazing!' Barb said. 'Well, they always are, but this one! No, I'd love to hold her, but I won't.

Keep her in her car capsule. What does she weigh now? And she's not on any oxygen or supplemental feeds any more? That's fantastic! See what your sister's given you to live up to, little man? All we need is that heart ticking over nicely, and you'll be powering along, threatening to catch up and overtake her.'

Tavie delivered a fabulous smile. She'd get hungry soon. Jessie wondered how long Keelan would want to stay. She could prepare the baby's bottle down in the car, if necessary, feed her and wait for Keelan there.

'Has he had a good weekend?' Keelan asked, standing beside the transparent humidicrib.

'Hanging in there.'

Jessie felt Keelan stiffen, wanted to run her hand down his arm in a gesture of support, but didn't dare. He swore.

'You don't know how I hate that expression now! I'm sorry, I'm not blaming you for using it, Barb. I just wish we could hear something different for a change. His colour's not very good today, is it?'

'No, he's fighting to keep those lips looking pink, and his hands are a bit too mottled for my liking. He's put on a few grams.'

'Which he could shed just as easily.'

'Did you sign the consent forms on Friday, Dr Hunter?'

'Yes, all of that.'

'And Dr Bedford outlined how he's planning to proceed?'

'In more detail than I wanted, to be honest.' Like any doctor, he knew too much, and he'd seen failure as well as miracles.

As was often done with preemies, the surgeons would perform the surgery here in the unit, tucked away in a tiny annexe room, rather than tiring Tam with a long trip down to the basement-level operating suites. It would be a lengthy process—several hours—and the apparent size and position of the largest hole, as well as its complex arrangement of entry and exit points, would dictate open heart surgery through the side of the organ.

Jessie could only imagine, but she could imagine far too vividly. She'd been in NICU units during surgery on a baby and, even though she hadn't been directly involved, she knew what it would be like.

There would be two surgeons, two nurses and an anaesthetist, all jostling for space around the tiny child. He would need minuscule doses of the required drugs—a sedative to put him to sleep, an agent to numb the surgical site itself and a narcotic for pain. As with any surgery, he'd be draped, taped and painted with a sterilising solution, and the planned line of the incision would be marked. It would no doubt look like a huge swathe of territory on his tiny torso.

When his skin had been pulled back, and the armature of muscles that stretched over his tiny ribs had been cut and folded, he would be at the mercy of surgical instruments hardly bigger than sewing pins, in the hands of a grown man's fingers that could, despite their size, move with the delicacy of a bee dancing.

The blood vessels in a baby this young and this small were not much stronger than sodden paper. Even a tiny tear in one of the really important ones could be fatal—a death dive via sudden, irreparable blood loss. The holes would be patched with a special synthetic fabric, as would the thinned section of Tam's tiny aorta. Dr Bedford would be soaked in sweat by the time he finished, even if everything went perfectly to plan.

Jessie knew how long those hours would seem for both herself and Keelan tomorrow. She'd be at home with Tavie. Keelan had commitments with his own patients. Knowing that there was nothing he could do for Tam, he hadn't tried to postpone those. They'd provide a more productive focus for his thoughts. Doubtless he would be called down to the A & E department more than once as well to give his verdict on a potential admission.

'Going to be a long day,' Barb McDaniel said, summarising, in just six short words, the track Jessie's thoughts had taken.

'Keith is starting at eight, he told me,' Keelan said. 'I'll be in here during my lunch-break—if I get one. He's hoping the surgery will be done by then.'

Tavie started to fuss a little.

'I'll take her down to the car,' Jessie said. 'Stay as long as you want, Keelan. She'll take her feed on my lap in the passenger seat. It's in the shade, nice and peaceful. Take an hour, if you want.'

'I'd like to spend some time with him,' Keelan said. 'But I'd like you to as well.'

'We'll fit that in this evening, if we can. If Tavie co-operates.'

He nodded, reached out, squeezed her hand, and like so many times before, it felt as if they were parents, sharing all of this completely, only the sensation was so much stronger today, so much more physical, buried deep inside Jessie and radiating out to her fingertips and to the sun-bleached ends of her hair.

She wanted to kiss Keelan, hold him, tell him, It's going to be all right. And she wanted to cry with him, bury her face in his shoulder and feel their bodies shaking together with inextricably mingled emotion.

Instead, all she could say in a husky voice was, 'See you in a while. Just when you're ready. Don't hurry.'

Down in the car, she cuddled little Tavie and sang to her, gave her the bottle she'd prepared earlier—which Tavie was generous enough to take colder than usual—and even played peek-a-boo.

'This is probably a little too advanced for you, sweetheart, but it's keeping *me* entertained, and I need that right now!'

Tavie was fast asleep again by the time Keelan appeared. He looked very strained, and didn't say much in the car. Jessie didn't need to ask why. Tavie had one of her fussy periods in the evening, which turned a simple dinner of ham and cheese omelettes into a lengthy process during which the two adults never got to sit down at the same time.

'Let me take care of her now,' Jessie said at eight o'clock.

'No, I really want you to go back up to the hospital.'

And she knew that in the back of Keelan's mind, although he'd never say it out loud, was the fear that if she didn't go and see Tam tonight, she'd miss out on her last chance to say goodbye.

Keelan was shameless in his need to anaesthetise himself after Jessie had gone to the hospital. He got

Tavie ready for bed and tried rocking her in the chair in her room, but she remained fussy so he gave up and went back downstairs, found himself a beer and the junkiest television on offer.

Maybe the baby had been sensing his tension. Now that he sat sprawled on the couch, absorbed in the nth repeat of a paint-by-numbers, G-rated action movie, Tavie seemed ready to sleep more peacefully. She lay in a warm little bundle with her body on his chest and her head on his shoulder, and he could feel the tiny puffs of her warm, milky breath on his neck. The pictures on the television screen provided the only light, and her little face lay in shadow.

He didn't want to have another try at putting her in her cot. Just didn't want to move. So they both stayed put.

What a weekend!

Two major undercurrents of unresolved feeling still twisted together inside him even now. Tam was having life-or-death surgery tomorrow, and he and Jessie were desperate to sleep together, with the entire universe apparently conspiring to prevent it.

He'd learned a lot more about her over the weekend—her doubts, her vulnerabilities and her strengths. He knew, now, how much of that footloose attitude of hers was just a protection. And he also knew that she was nothing like his father's second wife.

Which left him with very few barriers in place in his feelings about Tam and his feelings about Jessica Russell.

Pretty tough to live through.

He still wondered about his parents, too, and whether

they'd really have a second attempt at their marriage. It looked distinctly possible, after what he'd seen yesterday and today.

Meanwhile, by one definition, he and Jessie were already up to the third attempt at theirs.

Tonight? When she got back from the hospital?

No. Hardly seemed possible that she'd want to. He wasn't crass enough to toss Tavie into her cot like a football so that he had his hands free for ripping off the nurse's clothes.

He ached.

Focus on the movie, Hunter. Pretend you don't already know exactly what's going to happen in every scene.

His eyelids began to feel heavy and his limbs relaxed. Tavie had the right idea. Jessie would be back soon. She'd wake him up if necessary. Sleep was a refuge that had eluded him for most of last night, and he knew he'd wake early in the morning. If he could flick off the television with the remote control and snatch some now…

The first he knew of Jessie's return was the feel of her hands as she gently lifted the sleeping baby from his chest. He dragged his eyes open, but she told him in a whisper, 'Don't move. I'll take her upstairs. Just stay right there.'

Tavie stirred a little but remained asleep, and Jessie wasn't gone long. When she returned, Keelan was still groggily attempting to wake up enough to move. Within two seconds he was as awake as he'd ever been in his life, and one part of him, at least, was moving just as nature intended.

Jessie's lush, firm rear end had planted itself squarely and confidently on his thighs, and two soft arms had wound around his neck. 'I'm sorry I was at the hospital so long. It was—Tam was…hard to leave. But I'm…'

She stopped, must have sensed the initial tensing of his muscles in sheer surprise. Her voice faltered. 'Keelan? Isn't this…?'

'Yes.' He swore. 'Yes! It's what I wanted, and want. Painfully. But after a long day—after *this* day—I thought that you might have changed your mind, lost your—'

'No,' she said, without hesitation. 'No.'

Keelan's whole body surged, charged with electricity, burst into flames. He stole the initiative from her openly at once, slipping one hand between her thighs and curving the other around her neck to pull her against his mouth. Her lips were warm and sweet and hungry.

He kissed her until they were both breathless and dizzy and half-drunk with the taste of each other, and he kept on kissing her because it felt so fabulous to get utterly lost in her like this.

Eventually, with eyes closed and fingers gripping his shoulders for support, she pivoted to straddle him. He loved her impatience, and the way it was so obvious how much more she wanted, how much closer she wanted their contact to be. Her knees pressed into the back of the couch, and her breasts felt heavy and powerfully erotic against his chest. He cupped his hands around her hips and wondered how they'd get upstairs, then just a few seconds later, *if* they'd get upstairs.

When she eased herself back from his touch, crossed her arms across her front and pulled off that same thin, figure-hugging blue sweater she'd worn yesterday morning and got herself tangled in against the corridor wall of his mother's house, Keelan abandoned any more thought of moving anywhere.

This was going to happen right here and now. Only...

'We have no protection,' he managed to say.

'Yes, we do...' She pulled something from her pocket, pressed it into his hand, then blushed and looked touchingly uncertain. 'I thought of it. Is that...?'

Shameful? Was that the word she couldn't quite say?

'It's enough reason for my lifelong gratitude, Jessie,' he told her seriously.

Her breasts were fabulous, and swollen dramatically with passion, their nipples hard through her skin-toned bra. Deftly, she unclipped it and he pulled it down, loving the way the cups fell from her body to release her weight into his hands.

She closed her eyes again, hair spilling over her face like a drift of autumn leaves caught by a breeze. Her body shuddered at every touch he made, and her breath went in an out like that of an athlete after a race.

Her responsiveness made the electric charge in his own body even stronger.

Somehow they moved until they lay horizontal on the long couch, again with Jessie poised over him, hair hiding her face, rock-hard, darkened nipples pushing on him, sending their message of pleasure and need.

'How much patience do you have?' he growled at her.

'None.' The word hardly counted as speech, it had so much breath in it.

'Good.'

He snapped open the fastening on her jeans and

began to drag them down. She helped him, shimmying her hips in a way that had his own dark trousers stretched painfully tight across the front. Her body could rock like a belly dancer, and he wanted to rock with her. After a little clumsiness, a little laughter and a lot of distracted, desperate caresses, they had nothing getting in the way any more, except that small piece of latex she'd been so unsure about, and he strained against the soft heat of her lower stomach which pressed on top of him, making him crazy every time he let himself slip.

'You're so perfect,' he told her. 'Your skin, your shape, the way you move.'

'So are you. Don't wait. Let me feel you.'

They rolled and she held up her arms, shaped herself for him and made his entry effortless. He shuddered and she held him, her breath coming in time to his own rhythm, her warmth enfolding him in an ecstasy that clawed higher and higher. It seemed impossible that the peak they surged towards could be any steeper, any further, yet the climb continued and every second of it felt better than the last.

He felt the exact moment when her world spun out of control, felt the dig of her nails in his back, moved in unison with the whip of her hips and spine, and heard the cries from her that vibrated like the soundbox of a cello. Then his own cries overtook hers, the last remnant of his control shattered into a million pieces, and his senses blurred and merged into one dark, headlong current.

They lay tangled together afterwards for a long time, too overwhelmed to speak. And, anyway, hadn't their bodies already said everything about how perfect and earth-shattering their love-making had been?

Keelan kissed Jessie's hair, her temple, her shoulder, deeply savouring his right of possession, the way he could hold her and touch her wherever he wanted, without any fear of protest or of overstepping her boundaries.

There was something so generous about her. Courageous, too. To have given herself like this, to the babies and to him, without the promise of anything in return. Keelan knew he'd short-changed her in suggesting a cool-headed affair. Tavie was at least giving smiles in payment now, but Tam hadn't yet even promised to live.

A sour jet of fear surged inside him as he thought this, giving his mouth an unpleasant taste, and he shut his eyes blindly to any consideration of the future. He could make no promises right now. Not to Jessie, and not to himself. Maybe everything they both felt had far more to do with Tam than either of them had realised.

In all honesty, he couldn't discount this possibility, because he knew it happened to people all the time. In war, in grief, in crisis. When your gut was churning with fear about the future, about the prospect of gut-wrenching loss, you didn't know what you would feel about each other this time next year, or next month, or even next week.

Kissing her one last time, in the soft curve of her neck, he murmured, 'It's late, Jessie.'

Her eyes looked soft and sleepy and full of questions. She wanted more.

Women usually did, and in the past he'd always been happy to give it, and say it. 'I'll phone you tomorrow evening,' or 'That was amazing,' or 'Can't wait till I can see you again.' After he and Tanya had slept together for the first time, he'd said, 'I love you,' without hesitation.

Tonight, however, he couldn't think of anything that would be safe or fair. He knew he didn't want to hurt Jessie. Or himself.

In the end, all he said was, 'Sleep well,' hearing the inadequacy of the line but knowing he had nothing better.

She nodded and gave a tentative smile. 'You, too.'

Then she disappeared up the stairs on soft feet, her bundled clothing gathered in her arms and her bare, pale body vulnerable in a way it hadn't been as they'd made love.

Keelan listened in the darkness and heard the movements she made as she prepared for bed. Water ran through the pipes, and a couple of floorboards creaked. A faint light came from her room and reflected against the wall that flanked the stairs, but then it ebbed away as she closed her bedroom door.

He waited another few seconds until no more sounds filtered down, and only then did he make a move himself.

Jessie had known that the following morning would be endless, and it was.

The night hadn't exactly passed in the blink of an eye either. Having dozed and dreamed for long, delicious minutes in Keelan's arms on the couch, she had lain awake as restless and jittery as a caffeine addict once she'd reached her own bed.

She'd wanted Keelan beside her so badly, but he hadn't come.

Why?

Regret, already, about what they'd just done?

Or was it only women who felt that kind of remorse? Maybe he'd simply felt a replete and very male sense of release which had launched him into an excellent night's sleep.

Oh, and he probably needed it!

She couldn't be selfish enough to wish her own restlessness on him when he must be so worried, as she was, about Tam. And she couldn't expect that the way they'd made love had tilted his whole universe, the way it had tilted hers.

At six in the morning, Tavie announced loudly that she was awake and hungry and ready to play. Jessie went to her and tried to gain a sense of peace and contentment from the feel of that warm, delicious little body, and the huge smile that came in the middle of Tavie's feed so that milk pooled in the baby's pink mouth and ran out at the corners.

'Angel sweetheart,' she whispered to the little girl. 'Precious darling. Gosh, I love you!'

Tavie thought that was fine.

Tavie didn't know what her brother had to go through today.

Jessie still had the baby on her lap when she heard Keelan in his room, and then the faint, rhythmic thrum of water piping into his shower. He appeared a few minutes later. 'I'm heading straight to the hospital,' he said. 'I'll grab breakfast there later.'

'And you'll phone me as soon as—'

'Of course. I can't promise when you'll get to see him, though.'

'That's all right.'

'You should be there. This is so…' He stopped, opened his hands. 'Backwards somehow. Wrong.' He scraped his fingers across his newly shaven jaw, and they almost looked as if they were shaking. 'But I don't know what to do about that.'

'It's OK.' She had to tell him so, because the last thing he needed was a litany of all the reasons why it wasn't OK at all.

'I'll be home when I can. If Mica is free this afternoon, get her to stay on. Leave Tavie with her and come up. See you some time.'

'Yes. See you.' She couldn't manage more than this, and he didn't wait.

She heard him leave the house just a few minutes later.

Mrs Sagovic arrived at eight-thirty. She hadn't been here on Friday, so she didn't yet know that Tam was scheduled for surgery today. When Jessie told her, she threw up her hands then clasped them together, her eyes bright with tears. 'That tiny boy!' She'd seen how fragile he was in the photos that Keelan and Jessie had both taken. 'I can't believe it!'

'There was no choice, Mica. It's the last throw of the dice.'

'And you're not there?'

Jessie shrugged. 'I'm here. With Tavie. I couldn't have stood in on the surgery, and I wouldn't have wanted to. And what's the use of just pacing the corridors outside? If it goes badly…' She didn't even want to say it.

The housekeeper hugged her, and murmured something in her mother tongue.

'Keelan did wonder if you could stay this afternoon so I can go up there then,' Jessie said.

'And where is he?'

'With patients.'

'Of course I can stay. Whether I can push myself together to clean Dr Hunter's house is another story!' She threw up her work hardened hands again and cried, 'That little boy…'

'Keelan is going to phone when there's some news. He doesn't think it'll be before lunch.'

'Then that's when you should go to the hospital. At lunch. That man needs someone with him.'

'His mother wanted to come down, but he wouldn't let her, in case—in case the surgery went—'

'What does "let" mean?' Mrs Sagovic cut in. 'She should have come anyway!'

The housekeeper's manner suggested that these Australians of northern European origin didn't have the slightest idea when it came to family relationships, compared to people who shared her own Mediterranean heritage. She probably wouldn't have been impressed with Jessie's parents, or with Brooke Hunter's mother, Louise.

But she'd underestimated Keelan's mother, as it turned out.

Susan arrived at just before noon. 'I couldn't wait for a phone call.' She hugged Jessie, seeming warm and a little shaky—tired, too, after the drive.

Dawson had driven back to Sydney yesterday afternoon, and Jessie took a moment to wonder whether the two of them would see each other while Susan was down.

'I can't wait for a phone call either,' Jessie answered frankly. 'But no one's taking any notice of that. He hasn't phoned.'

'Which can only mean the baby's still in surgery. Can't believe it can take that long and still have any chance of success.'

'Can I drive you up, Susan? Mica's ready to push me out of the house. She'll think we're incurably wrong-headed if we don't go.'

'Yes, can you drive me? Please? We *are* incurably wrong-headed if we don't go, but I'm not sure that I could get back behind the wheel. I would have gone straight there, only... I'm terrified. I'm so scared.'

'Mmm.' Jessie nodded, her throat tight.

'Let me bring in my bags...'

Jessie helped, and then the two of them took Keelan's second car, ushered there by approving nods and pats from Mrs Sagovic. 'Yes, I know the baby is waking up. I can take care of her. You must go.'

The unit seemed quiet when they arrived, and the door to the annexe was still firmly closed. 'The team's still in there?' Jessie asked Stephanie.

'Yes, they are.'

'I thought surely...'

The other nurse shrugged and smiled, then said, 'Dr Hunter was called down from Paediatrics about ten minutes ago. He'll be here soon.'

'So we wait,' Susan murmured.

'We wait,' Jessie confirmed.

The wait wasn't long. Only about six hundred heart-beats, every one of which Jessie felt like a painful blow in her chest. Keelan arrived, and didn't seem all that surprised to see his mother. He managed a pale smile and a few token words of greeting, and he hardly seemed to look at Jessie at all.

Which in the greater scheme of things didn't matter right now, but…

Then suddenly Keith Bedford appeared, surgical mask still in his hand and clothing darkened with moisture. He put his hand on Keelan's arm. 'We had some problems, I'm afraid,' he said.

Chapter 10

'What problems?' Keelan's white lips hardly moved.

Having beat so painfully for ten minutes, Jessie's heart now didn't seem to be beating at all, and that was worse. She couldn't speak, but heard the stricken sound that came from Susan's throat, beside her.

'Well, the surgery itself went better than expected in many ways,' Dr Bedford said. 'One of the holes was small enough to leave alone. It'll close over on its own. The biggest, yes, was very tricky but we made a successful repair, as we did with the other two moderate-size holes and the thinned section of aorta. Unfortunately, right in the middle of it all, Tam developed a third-degree AV block.'

Susan cast a terrified, questioning look at Jessie, but she could only shake her head. She knew what Dr

Bedford was talking about. The electrical impulses in the baby's heart had been slowed or blocked somehow, and had ceased to take their normal path through the heart's conduction system, resulting in compromised or, in the most extreme scenario, non-existent electrical communication between the heart's upper and lower chambers—the atria and the ventricles.

Sometimes the lower heart chambers generated electrical impulses on their own, but these weren't enough to keep the heart muscle at full function. There was a serious risk of full cardiac arrest. Had this happened to Tam?

But she couldn't explain something so complex and technical to Susan now, not while the heart surgeon was still speaking, not while she didn't yet know what the outcome had been.

'We've put in an external pacemaker wire,' the surgeon said.

'And he's survived? He's...' Keelan slowed and shaped his mouth carefully around the phrase Jessie knew he hated. 'Hanging in there?'

'Yes. He's doing well. But you know the consequences of this, Keelan. If his heart doesn't resume its natural pacing on its own, he'll need further surgery to implant a permanent pacemaker.'

'OK.' Keelan gave a brief, jerky nod. 'How long will you give him before a decision on that is made?'

'If it hasn't happened within a few days, then it's not going to. After that has become evident, if it becomes evident, we'll wait until he's recovered from today's surgery and then go in again. Obviously, it's a much more minor procedure.'

Jessie heard Susan give a cautious, shaky sigh of relief at this final piece of comparative good news.

'Can we see him?' Keelan asked.

Dr Bedford narrowed his eyes. 'Not all three of you. Not yet. Two of you. And I want you in masks, caps, gowns and shoe covers. I'm keeping him in the annexe until someone else needs the space, basically. At least twenty-four hours, I hope, and preferably longer. This has been touch and go for him the whole way. And it still is.'

'Two of us,' Keelan muttered.

'For a couple of minutes. Bevan's still monitoring the reversal of the anaesthesia. Page me if you have any questions. I'll be in again to look at him later this afternoon. But you know what to look for yourself, what to expect.'

Keelan only nodded. His eyes flicked to Jessie, and then to his mother.

'You see him, Susan,' Jessie said quickly. Her throat felt as if there was a bone lodged in it, sideways.

'No, Jessie. I want you to go.'

Jessie closed her eyes. Susan was being incredibly generous, but a grandmother took precedence over an employee, and officially that was all she was. 'No,' she said. She had to fight so hard to keep her voice firm that it sounded almost angry. 'I'm not. You must. With Keelan.'

This time nobody argued.

Nervously, Susan accepted Keelan's guidance in putting on the sterile garments Dr Bedford had required. The bright royal blue of the stiff disposable fabric cap seemed to suck the colour away from her face. She wasn't a large or imposing woman, but Jessie hadn't really registered her slightness of build until now. Normally she carried with her such a strong sense of life, but at this moment she looked shrunken in trepidation.

And, of course, she was the right person to go.

Keelan touched the heel of his hand lightly to his mother's back, propelling her in the direction of the annexe where Tam still lay, and within a half minute they had disappeared, leaving Jessie alone.

She felt empty, frozen, grief-stricken. Keith Bedford's casual decree that Tam couldn't yet be crowded with more than two visitors had only emphasised the uncertainty that coloured everything she felt.

It surely wouldn't have eased her fears over Tam if she had known exactly where she fitted into Keelan's life—his present and his future. And yet, perversely, she felt that nothing could be harder than the way she felt now.

She was so scared for Tam, and yet she didn't remotely know if she had the right to take comfort in the love for Tavie that grew stronger inside her every day, let alone the love for Keelan that felt like something she'd known since she'd entered this world, and would know, just as painfully as this, until she left it again.

All of that might end in a matter of weeks, when Keelan decided he didn't need her any more.

Keelan and Susan weren't with the baby for long. He had his hand on her shoulder when they came out, and Jessie could see that Susan had found it very emotional, and very hard, to see the way her little grandson must look—motionless enough to seem frozen, lost in wires, his chest seemingly weighed down and lopsided with a dressing that would be huge and terrifying on such a tiny body.

'The monitors say he's alive. That was the only way I knew,' Susan said.

'His colour looked good,' Keelan said. 'He looked good.'

Jessie nodded. Colour was important. You clung to things like a baby's colour at a time like this.

'Can I take these things off now, love?' Susan asked.

'Yes, Mum, that's fine. There's a bin just outside.' He pressed his fingertips to the bridge of his nose. 'Then, do you need me to…? What do you need me to do?'

'Tell me where the cafeteria is, because I need some tea.'

'Something to eat, too. You look pale.'

'A sandwich. Just show me where it is.' She hung on his arm, apparently in need of the support.

Not knowing what was expected of her, Jessie went down with them in the lift. She let them get out first, then peeled off quietly in the direction of a visitors' bathroom. She didn't think they'd noticed.

Later, she would find Susan in the cafeteria, because the older woman would probably want to be taken home. Meanwhile, not the slightest bit hungry, Jessie decided she would go outside for a bit and find some fresh air and some sun for her face, out by the little piece of garden that flanked the hospital's original colonial-era building.

It must have been ten or fifteen minutes before Keelan found her, and one look at him striding across the grass towards her told her how angry he was. Tight lines etched his face, and his shoulders had tensed and lifted as if padded like an American football player's.

'Where the hell did you get to?' he demanded. 'I looked around and you'd disappeared. Not a word. When? Why?'

'I wasn't hungry.'

He swore. 'Is that an answer?' His hands closed hard around her upper arms. 'You came down with us in the lift, and then you disappeared.'

In a shaky voice, she tried to make light of it. 'I'm here now, aren't I? Didn't vanish forever.'

'Made me realise, once and for all, how I'd feel if you did,' he growled, so low that she wasn't convinced she'd heard him right.

'How you'd feel if I…?'

'Vanished forever.'

'Abducted by space aliens?'

'Stop!' He bent and pressed his forehead against hers. 'Jessie, last night…last night…'

'Was pretty good, I thought,' she murmured.

He had his arms around her now, chafing her softly, squeezing her as if he couldn't hold her tightly enough and never wanted to let her go. It was the best feeling she'd had all day, and it gave her just a little bit of courage—enough to let him know just a little bit about how she felt. She looked up into his face, and saw the light and the determination there.

'It was more than good,' he said. 'It was amazing. Fabulous. Unique. Perfect. And I didn't say that.'

'No, you didn't.'

'Because I didn't want to send the wrong message. What might be the wrong message,' he corrected himself quickly. 'I couldn't think straight, didn't trust anything about how I felt—last night, the whole weekend, weeks ago. And I'm still not sure if—'

'I understand, Keelan,' she cut in. 'I understand how impossible it is for you to be sure about anything right now.'

'No.' He pressed a finger to her lips. 'Now I'm sure about quite a few things. I'm not sure, though, if I was right to hold back last night. How much did that hurt, Jessie? How much did that leave you in the lurch?'

'Well, it did,' she admitted. 'Both those things.'

'Will it undo the hurt if I don't leave you in the lurch any longer?' He didn't wait for her to answer. 'I love you. That's the only way any of this fits together. I couldn't see it, couldn't feel it properly before, for so many reasons. And when I did feel it, I didn't trust it. But now... I was burning to say it as soon as we'd seen Tam, wanted to point out the cafeteria sign to Mum and tell her, "Follow that." But then I turned to check on you, and you'd just gone.'

'Only to the bathroom. You didn't notice.'

'No, I damn well didn't! But that doesn't mean— When I had to choose between you and Mum coming in to see Tam just now, and you jumped in and chose for me, and you chose Mum, it was so wrong.'

'No. Tam's grandmother...'

He ignored her. 'Totally my fault. I could see that. It stuck in my throat, too late to do anything about it then, until I could get you alone, as soon as I'd got Mum to the damned cafeteria. I hung back last night, doubting the best love-making of my life, and in doing that I denied you the right to see the baby you should be able to call yours, and I didn't want to wait a moment longer to give you that right.'

He stopped, as if suddenly unsure.

'If you want it,' he continued. 'If you want to call him yours. Do you, Jessie? Will you be my wife? Can we make a family together, so that Tam and Tavie can be yours for the rest of their lives?'

'Ours,' she whispered, holding him more tightly and pillowing her head against his chest. 'That's what I want. For them to be ours.'

'Ours. Yes. Ours.' He pressed his face into her neck and hair, and time seemed to stop in the hospital garden, even though the shadow on the old sundial crept several degrees around the tarnished bronze face.

'It's not an easy way to start,' Keelan told Jessie finally.

'I've never looked for things that were easy.'

He pulled back a little and looked at her, his face set and serious. 'No. I know. But you've made everything so much easier for me from the moment you walked off that plane nearly three months ago. Can't imagine how I'd ever do without it.'

'Neither can I. Keelan, I've come home…'

'Just where I want you. Can't believe I'm this lucky. Can't help hoping it's part of a pattern, and that Tam's going to be this lucky, too.'

'Oh, yes.' She pressed her cheek against his, then instinctively they both turned so that their mouths met in the kiss of two people in love, sharing their hope and their fear, knowing this was only the beginning. 'He has to be this lucky. He's fought so hard.'

At almost the same time, high up in the hospital

building, a little boy's heart remembered how it was supposed to beat. The pacemaker wire came out that same afternoon. After that day, Tam never looked back, never took a backward step, and neither did his parents.

Three months later, Tam and Tavie both attended a Sydney garden wedding that made everybody in the Hunter clan very happy. The bride looked radiant. The groom looked as if he'd discovered the secret to eternal youth…

And the bride and groom's thirty-five-year-old son stood with his fiancée at his side and a healthy baby girl in his arms, and had a hard time keeping his feelings in check.

'Are you taking notes?' Keelan whispered to his future bride as he watched his parents saying their vows. 'We have our own wedding coming up pretty soon, and you keep telling me I haven't got long to decide on the wording of the ceremony.'

'Thirty-five days. Not that I'm counting,' Jessie whispered back.

'I'm counting. Can't wait.'

'We haven't waited for very much, as far as I can work out,' she teased him. 'We're living under the same roof. We're already parents.'

'Can't wait for the honeymoon.'

'Oh, that. Oh, yes, that! We do have to wait a bit longer for that.'

Jessie blushed and laughed and closed her eyes to receive Keelan's kiss, while baby Tam cooed in her arms and closed his little fist against her heart.

* * * * *

**IF YOU ENJOYED THIS BOOK
WE THINK YOU WILL ALSO LOVE**

**HARLEQUIN
SPECIAL
EDITION**

Believe in love. Overcome obstacles. Find happiness.

Relate to finding comfort and strength in the
support of loved ones and enjoy the journey
no matter what life throws your way.

6 NEW BOOKS AVAILABLE EVERY MONTH!

Mariella Jacob was one of the world's premier bridal designers. One viral PR disaster later, she's trying to get her torpedoed career back on track in small-town Magnolia, North Carolina. With a second-hand store and a new business venture helping her friends turn the Wildflower Inn into a wedding venue, Mariella is finally putting at least one mistake behind her. Until that mistake—in the glowering, handsome form of Alex Ralsten—moves to Magnolia too…

Read on for a sneak preview of
Wedding Season,
the next book in USA TODAY bestselling author Michelle Major's Carolina Girls series!

"You still don't belong here." Mariella crossed her arms over her chest, and Alex commanded himself not to notice her body, perfect as it was.

"That makes two of us, and yet here we are."

"I was here first," she muttered. He'd heard the argument before, but it didn't sway him.

"You're not running me off, Mariella. I needed a fresh start, and this is the place I've picked for my home."

"My plan was to leave the past behind me. You are a physical reminder of so many mistakes I've made."

"I can't say that upsets me too much," he lied. It didn't make sense, but he hated that he made her so uncomfortable. Hated even more that sometimes he'd purposely drive by her shop to get a glimpse of her through the picture window. Talk about a glutton for punishment.

She let out a low growl. "You are an infuriating man. Stubborn and callous. I don't even know if you have a heart."

"Funny." He kept his voice steady even as memories flooded him, making his head pound. "That's the rationale Amber gave me for why she cheated with your fiancé. My lack of emotions pushed her into his arms. What was his excuse?"

She looked out at the street for nearly a minute, and Alex wondered if she was even going to answer. He followed her gaze to the park across the street, situated in the center of the town. There were kids at the playground and several families walking dogs on the path that circled the perimeter. Magnolia was the perfect place to raise a family.

If a person had the heart to be that kind of a man—the type who married the woman he loved and set out to be a good husband and father. Alex wasn't cut out for a family, but he liked it in the small coastal town just the same.

"I was too committed to my job," she said suddenly and so quietly he almost missed it.

"Ironic since it was your job that introduced him to Amber."

"Yeah." She made a face. "This is what I'm talking about, Alex. A past I don't want to revisit."

"Then stay away from me, Mariella," he advised. "Because I'm not going anywhere."

"Then maybe I will," she said and walked away.

Don't miss
Wedding Season by Michelle Major,
available May 2022 wherever
HQN books and ebooks are sold.

HQNBooks.com

Love Harlequin romance?

DISCOVER.

Be the first to find out about promotions,
news and exclusive content!

f Facebook.com/HarlequinBooks

Twitter.com/HarlequinBooks

Instagram.com/HarlequinBooks

Pinterest.com/HarlequinBooks

You Tube YouTube.com/HarlequinBooks

ReaderService.com

EXPLORE.

Sign up for the Harlequin e-newsletter and
download a free book from any series at
TryHarlequin.com

CONNECT.

Join our Harlequin community to
share your thoughts and connect
with other romance readers!
Facebook.com/groups/HarlequinConnection

HSOCIAL2021